D0335201

BANISHMENT

Also by by Dinah Lampitt

Sutton Place
The Silver Swan
Fortune's Soldier
To Sleep No More
Pour the Dark Wine
The King's Women
As Shadows Haunting

BANISHMENT

Dinah Lampitt

Hodder & Stoughton
LONDON SYDNEY AUCKLAND

First published in 1994 by Hodder and Stoughton Ltd
A division of Hodder Headline PLC

10 9 8 7 6 5 4 3 2 1

British Library Cataloguing in Publication Data

Lampitt, Dinah
Banishment
I. Title
823.914 [F]

ISBN 0-450-58784-3

Typeset by Keyboard Services, Luton

Printed and bound in Great Britain by
Mackays of Chatham PLC, Chatham, Kent

Published by Hodder and Stoughton Ltd
A Division of Hodder Headline PLC
338 Euston Road
London NW1 3BH

For Amanda, Brett and Sally-Anne Lampitt –
with my love.
An author who speaks about his own books
Is almost as bad as a mother
Who talks about her own children!

Acknowledgments

My thanks are due to several people who helped me with the preparation of this book. First of all I would like to express my appreciation to Sofia Nazar, Promotions Manager of Newark Town Council, who kindly invited me to watch the Sealed Knot recreate the Siege of Newark during the 350th Anniversary of the Civil War in the summer of 1992. Thanks to the Sealed Knot, too, for one of the most exciting spectacles I have ever witnessed. I would also like to thank the National Trust for allowing me to see Greys Court during its closed season and Peter Harries, custodian of that great house, for sparing me his valuable time. Special gratitude is due to Bob (the Bank) Nicholls and to Dr Sharon Pegram Heron. Bob introduced me to Oxford and with him I spent a glorious day on the trail of King Charles I and his Queen. I have never enjoyed a research trip so much. Dr Pegram Heron was kind enough to consider Nichola's case and explain to me exactly what would have happened to her after she went into a coma. Thanks, too, to Sharon and Keith Washington who found the private door through which the King so discreetly visited Henrietta Maria, and who took such excellent photographs of it. As always, appreciation of my courageous agent, Shirley Russell, goes without saying. Grateful thanks also to Rohini Patel who sacrificed a whole summer to get this manuscript out on time, and my excellent new secretary, Tina Eastwood, who kept me sane. Finally, I would like to pay tribute to the late Basil Sugden of Libra Bookshop, Mayfield, Sussex. His untimely death in September, 1993, will leave a gap in many lives and it saddens me enormously to think that this will be the first of my books not to be launched under his auspices. Thank you for all you did to promote me, old friend.

To roam
Giddily, and be everywhere but at home
Such freedom doth a banishment become

JOHN DONNE

PROLOGUE

That night, after she had gone quietly to bed, the dream came, clearer and more sharply defined than ever before. Even though she had believed she would never again experience its strange and disturbing imagery, still it had come out of the darkness to haunt her once more. It began, as it sometimes did, in a hospital corridor down which she felt compelled to go, carried along like a leaf on a brook, unable to control her actions. As always, this eddying flow ceased before a room, the door of which swung open to receive her.

The body lay inside the room, the body that over the passing years she had seen so many times before. Yet on this occasion it was different, in its natural state, all the tubes that had been attached to it, in order to help it live, removed. It lay like the Sleeping Beauty, waiting for the kiss that would awake it, the kiss that now would never come.

There were people in the room, parents, friends, and she saw to her surprise that some of them were weeping. Two doctors were present, one of whom turned down the dials on the ventilator.

"Will she go peacefully?" said a woman's voice, breaking with emotion.

"Oh yes," the doctor answered quietly. "Now she'll just drift away."

And then he raised his hand and switched off the life-saving machine.

The dreamer shuddered as, for a second more, she hovered by the shell of what had once been a human being, then she turned and ran, on and on down the never ending corridor, on and on and into darkness. Then she sat bolt upright in bed, breathing deeply to calm herself, slowly realising that she was finally safe and that none of it could ever harm her again.

Yet tonight there seemed a special need to think about everything that had taken place, to remember each and every occasion on which she had experienced the dream and been terrified by its sinister message. For though she truly wanted to banish the past, a compulsion was upon her to relive each moment before memory blurred and slid away and was gone for ever.

So it was that she slowly got out of bed and went downstairs to a room where a fire still burned low in the grate. And there, sitting in the shadows, gazing into the flames, completely and utterly alone, Nichola Hall thought back to the beginning.

Chapter One

It had started with an ending, a theatrical last night to be precise. The West End theatre had been packed, as much with teenage girls coming to see the leading man as anything else, and the electric current passing between actors and audience had held all of them in its grip. So much so that Lewis Devine, talented and beautiful, the darling of the National Theatre, well loved by Hollywood, had broken down and wept on his final exit, reducing several of the cast, to say nothing of the onlookers, to the same state. It had been the stuff of which theatrical legend is made, the power of the play, Arthur Miller's *The Crucible*, transcending all.

After the final words of the piece had been spoken there had been a second of stunned silence before the tumultuous applause had rung out. Nichola Hall, who had played Abigail Williams so strongly that one night she had caused a woman in the stalls to faint, had been cheered, as had Glynda Howard, taking the part of Elizabeth Proctor. But Lewis had received a standing ovation, which he had accepted with studied humility, head bent, arms wide, dark hair shadowing his face. Eventually, though, he had walked off the stage while the audience were still clapping and the house lights had come back on. His final exit had been as memorable as the rest of his performance.

Backstage, Nichola recalled, everyone had been buzzing, high on adrenalin, those who loathed one another embracing most enthusiastically of all. It had given her a sweet sly thrill to see her fellow actresses flocking round Lewis, hanging on his every word, smiling predatory smiles. For she had not really liked any one of them, a feeling they totally reciprocated, and she delighted in having an intrigue that no other female guessed at – at least none that she knew.

Simply put, Nichola's secret was that she and the celebrated actor were having an affair, were engaged in a highly charged and illicit relationship, the clandestine nature of which had been made necessary by the fact that Lewis was heavily married. Where Richard Burton had had his Sybil whom no mistress was allowed to displace, that is until the advent of Elizabeth Taylor, so Lewis Devine had his Marjorie, the faithful girl he had met and wed when he had been unknown and struggling.

Nichola had never been quite certain whether Lewis's wife exhibited supreme self confidence or was merely too insensitive to see what was going on. Because, for inexplicable reasons of her own, Marjorie preferred to bring up her family of three in the Cotswolds, far from London's various pollutions, thus leaving the actor open to attack from the street wise marauders with whom he came in daily contact. The third alternative, that his wife might long ago have ceased to care what he did, simply had not occurred to Lewis's mistress.

Nor did it as Marjorie had come in through the stage door that night – she always attended first and last performances – and smiled vaguely in Nichola's direction, aware that everybody knew who she was even though she was a little uncertain about their various identities. Feeling irrationally irritated, Nichola had gone into the dressing room, shared with two of the other leading ladies, and had started to remove her make-up.

Thinking back, she remembered how strangely silent the room had become when she had walked in. And then how the other two had burst into conversation about Marjorie. For no apparent reason, it seemed that they both thought Lewis's wife was a wonderful woman. Just to annoy them, Nichola had put on a skin-tight cat suit and flaunted her sensational figure about the place, before applying fresh make-up and brushing her costly hair cut. Then she had lit a cigarette, inhaled deeply and blown smoke into the atmosphere.

There was to be a last night party, of course. And to make it special it was to be hosted by Lewis Devine at his flat in Putney overlooking the river. Nichola, who had spent so many stolen nights there, had listened to her fellow actors as they had discussed Lewis's home and what it would be like, with barely concealed amusement. For since his triumph in Hollywood when he had been nominated for, though not awarded, the Oscar, Lewis had achieved star status even amongst his peers. And he had picked Nichola, above all of them, with whom to fall in love. Smiling to herself, she had stood up, said, "See you at the party", and left in an aura of expensive perfume. As she had been closing the dressing room door Nichola had heard one of them say, "Slut" just loudly enough for her to overhear.

That drive to Putney had been an extraordinary one, she recalled. For from the very second she had got into her car she had been filled with a sense of destiny, a presentiment that in some way or another her life was coming to a crossroads which would move her irrevocably in a new direction. And this had fired her with a desire to remember all the things that had brought her to this point. Nichola had felt a need to review her life as a whole, to see what had made her the glamorous Nichola Hall, actress and men's woman, whose love of the stage was only equalled by her love of lovers.

She had been born in April, 1967, a Taurus, one of the most undeniably sensuous signs of the Zodiac, child of a latter day debutante and the Deb's Delight Nichola's mother had married, subsequent to the season she had been given by her parents in which to secure a husband. Naturally, a union based on such flimsy foundations had rapidly fallen apart at the seams and Nichola's mother, Frances, had run off – or bolted as was the fashionable phrase – with the Honourable Johnnie Carstairs, stockbroker and polo player. Much to everyone's surprise, particularly her father's, Nichola had suddenly found herself being brought up by him.

Faced with this unexpected dilemma, Piers Hall had decided against employing nannies and au pairs, preferring to ship his eight-year-old daughter off to boarding school, then dump her on various relatives during the holidays. Eventually though, in a flurry of desperation, he had married his secretary, who thereafter had treated her stepdaughter with a kind of gushing disdain. Nichola, manipulating the situation, had consequently enjoyed an expensive lifestyle and a place at drama school, all paid for by Piers, now suffering from guilt as his second wife had produced several puny children who claimed his attention to the detriment of his first born.

Nichola had supposed, as she drove towards Putney listening to the radio and smoking yet another cigarette, that she was a psychologist's dream, that her adult behaviour would have been laid entirely at the door of her lack of childhood affection. But in reality it wasn't like that at all. The reason why, from the age of seventeen onwards, she had collected men like others do stamps, was because she enjoyed the company of males and relished the carnal act as much as they did. She had once heard herself described as a nymphomaniac and though she had turned furiously on her accuser she recognised a grain of truth in the statement. Nichola was, though there was no female equivalent in the English language, an out-and-out unrepentant rake. She had even gone so far, in truly masculine fashion, as to write down the names of every man she had slept with in a notebook under the heading of The Collection.

Now, driving along to Lewis's party, aware that his wife was considered to be firmly ensconced, gamely devoted to supporting her man as he scaled the high peaks of success, Nichola knew that she was of necessity in the midst of metamorphosis. She wanted Lewis, not only because she loved him but also because he was a household name, known to the non theatre-going public for his unforgettable appearances on screen, from which his dark hair and piercing blue eyes blazed forth magnetically. And if she was to be successful in coaxing him out of the cosy web that Marjorie had spun for him there must be no question of Nichola's fidelity. Good time girl she might once have been, but now she must change all that, yet retain her allure. The path she must tread would have to be that of her Taylor to his Burton, the siren who lures him on to the rocks of divorce then glitters so dazzlingly that he remains permanently besotted.

It had all seemed a rather daunting prospect and as she had parked the car and walked carefully towards Lewis's front door, aware of the distant sound of Marjorie's laughter, Nichola had girded herself mentally for battle. Subtle sensuality must be the keynote from now on, she thought.

For security reasons Lewis had not left the front door open, despite the fact that it was a hot sultry night with a hint of thunder in the air. Not quite certain who might answer, Nichola had stood braced, ready to smile the sort of smile that a mistress gives her lover's wife, equally prepared to walk past Lewis aloofly, yet with a certain brilliance in her eye that would immediately remind him of their liaison. It had been something of a shock, therefore, when it had been flung open by Delia Hope, a thrusting young actress with Northern origins who had played the part of Mary Warren and had only been prevented from stealing the show by the force of Glynda Howard's and Nichola Hall's performances.

"Oh hello," Delia had said, and had given Nichola a replica of the smile she had been planning to bestow on Marjorie.

Momentarily, she had been caught off balance. Delia's dislike of her was profound and only just disguised by the thinnest veneer of cordiality. Why then, Nichola had thought, was she smiling like that? Somewhat warily, she had gone up the stairs to Lewis's flat.

It was a gorgeous apartment, matching him perfectly. Occupying the whole of the first floor in a spacious Victorian house, it had a balcony embellished by wrought iron lacework overlooking the river. To crown this Lewis had had the interior created by a chi-chi out-of-town designer who had practically rendered the place impotent by his dazzling display of good taste. Colours, fabric and lighting blended in self-conscious harmony, even down to the fresh flowers that were banked everywhere.

"Lovely place, isn't it," breathed Delia. "Have you been here before?"

"Many times," Nichola had answered.

"So have I," the other girl had informed her sweetly, before drifting away.

Nichola had stood still for a moment, wondering what she was meant to presume from this remark, in fact exactly what it might be Delia was trying to convey to her. Yet a swift glance in Lewis's direction had done little to reassure her. He was earnestly engaged in conversation with Bill Cosby, their stage manager, and had not even looked up when she had come into the room. Undaunted Nichola had collected herself and sailed into action.

"How do you do," she had said, going straight up to Marjorie and holding out her hand. "I don't believe we've met. I'm Nichola Hall who played Abigail Williams."

The eyes which looked into hers, dull shade of grey though they might be, were tougher than she would have expected, belonging to a woman who lived in the country as they did. To Nichola, urban dweller, anyone who resided further out than Bromley was a bucolic, a hick, and it was surprising to see that Marjorie might be intelligent despite all that. And then Nichola remembered that Lewis's wife had been an actress before she had given up her own career to run her talented husband's household for him. Just for a moment it occurred to Nichola that her rival, the woman she wanted to see off, was a sight shrewder than she had imagined.

"You were very good," Marjorie had said. "Particularly in the possession scene. I loved the way you and the other girls all collapsed on the floor like a pack of cards."

"I am so glad you enjoyed it, Mrs Devine," Nichola had answered over-pleasantly.

"Well, it's a wonderful play of course," Lewis's wife had continued, "but so hard to do. They say it always brings out the worst in people."

Nichola had gazed at her in surprise. This was a gambit she had not expected. "Do you mean as actors or individuals?"

"Oh not as performers, tonight proved that. No, I've heard it said that the play itself causes unrest. Just as the reality must have brought all the beastliness and brutality in people to the surface so does its mirror image."

Nichola had been astounded that the woman could hold a conversation on this level. But then, she considered, Lewis would not have stayed with a bore, however good a homemaker. It would appear that his wife might not be so easily disposed of after all.

"But do let me get you a drink," Marjorie was continuing. "What would you like?"

"Oh, don't worry, I'll help myself. Is the bar in the kitchen?"

"Yes." Marjorie had smiled, looking amazingly ordinary and unglamorous. "Hope to speak to you later, Nichola."

"Right."

It had all been a great shock to her, Nichola recollected, and she had been glad to leave the spacious living room and make her way to the superbly appointed kitchen where two girls from a catering company were labouring over the last of the buffet.

"Wine?" said one.

"Yes, please. Dry white."

"Here you are."

And a glass had been poured, none too graciously Nichola thought. Just then both of them had visibly brightened, suddenly all sultry pouts and simpers. Without turning her head, Nichola knew that Lewis had come into the room and a second later she felt his arm slide round her.

"All right?"

She had tensed so that the touch of her perfect body – supposedly one of the most beautiful around – was tight against him. "Fine. And you?"

"Wishing we were alone."

"Really?"

Lewis had smiled. "I saw you in deep conversation with Marjorie. What was all that about?"

"She was telling me how horrible it is to wash your socks."

Lewis had ruffled her hair with a lazy hand, causing the two catering girls to quiver. "I don't believe a word you say."

Nichola had turned to look at him, sure of herself, aware that she was ten times more attractive than Marjorie could ever be. "That, my darling, is entirely up to you. Now I must go and circulate."

And with that she had made her way back to the living room and looked round for someone to talk to. Her immediate instinct to join a group of men had been tempered by her new resolve not only to be faithful but to be seen doing so. Smiling, she had approached Glynda Howard, knowing that the leading lady at least tolerated her.

The antithesis of a glamour girl, for all that Glynda had a certain quality of being ugly-beautiful. Articulate, clever, she was one of the great ladies of the theatre, easing her way towards a damehood without striving. In many ways Nichola envied the older woman's style which affected not to care about clothes, to eat plenty of red meat and carbohydrates and smoke and drink prodigiously. Yet despite this, Glynda retained a lean, almost rawboned, figure and looked marvellous in anything she put on her back. Nichola also admired the leading lady's makeup which consisted of mounds of mascara, a slash of lipstick and nothing else. At forty, the actress was her own woman, quite content to let the younger ones challenge her, well aware that nobody could usurp her unique position.

"You were supreme tonight," Nichola had said, and meant every word.

Glynda had nodded. "You weren't so bad yourself." She had lit a black cigarette. "So what's next?"

"I'm to be screen tested for a Merchant Ivory production."

"Well, that can't be bad. You'd probably fit in there. You're the type."

"Do you think so?"

"Oh yes, they like 'em young and lively."

"And what about you, Glynda? What's your next project?"

The leading lady had flicked up one thin, expressive shoulder. "I'm going on holiday for two weeks then into rehearsal for Lady Bracknell at the Aldwych. I intend to say handbag as if it's a four letter word."

Vaguely aware that Lewis had come into the room and been buttonholed by Delia, Nichola had pealed with laughter. "I must come and see that."

"I'll get you some comps." Glynda had downed the contents of her glass and held it out. "Get me another one, there's a good girl." She was the type of woman who was able to do this and cause no offence.

"What is it?" Nichola had asked.

"Vodka and tonic, darling. I can't stand all that wine stuff. Gives me acidity. It's a double, by the way. Saves going to and fro the bar."

Pleased to be seen in the role of helper to the great lady, Nichola had returned to the kitchen.

". . . my God, the energy," one of the catering girls was saying. "A wife and two screw bags . . ."

"At least!"

"Yes, but I'd join the queue, wouldn't you?"

They had stopped guiltily as Nichola walked in and she knew by their very expressions, let alone the glaringly obvious remark, that they had been talking about Lewis. The unpleasant words 'screw bags', in the plural, repeated themselves in her brain and just for a moment Nichola had stood still, absorbing their meaning, before she got a vodka for Glynda and an even larger one for herself.

There were two directions in which her thoughts could have gone. The first, that the girls, who knew nothing of Lewis and were merely watching avidly, were presuming that he slept with all and sundry. The second, that they had actually witnessed something from their observation post in the kitchen. Did the self-satisfied expression on Delia's face, her strange remark about having seen Lewis's flat before, have the unpleasant connotation which Nichola now suspected? Feeling strangely cold, she had returned to the living room, full of apprehension.

Lewis and Delia were both in there, but not together. Nichola's lover was standing with his wife, paying pointed attention to every word uttered by the woman who preferred staying at home and taking walks in the Gloucestershire countryside to being a theatrical consort. Nichola thought it sickening. Similarly, the girl from the North, who even her enemies had to admit was a superb actress, was holding her own court in the midst of a laughing group. Unlike Nichola, Delia had somehow managed to remain popular with her own sex, and this was now obviously paying off. Realising that she was temporarily out on a limb, Nichola handed Glynda her glass and looked round for somebody to talk to.

The chi-chi designer had installed a small white piano in a recess near the balcony and sitting at it, idly strumming an Ivor Novello number, was James Milligan, the oldest member of the cast, a well-loved character actor who had taken the part of Giles Corey.

"Heavens, Jim," said Nichola, going over to him, "that dates you."

He looked up at her and winked. "Ah, dear Ivor. Would it surprise you to learn that I appeared in the chorus of *King's Rhapsody*?"

"It would astound me. You can't be *that* old." James was the sort of man to whom one could make this kind of remark, knowing it would be taken in good part.

"My dear girl, I am as old as God – well, his younger brother at least." He had patted the piano stool and Nichola had sat down beside him. "Ah, to have your youth and my experience, to have seen it all and yet be young in body."

"That sounds very Faustian to me."

"Perhaps, perhaps. Though I wouldn't change, really. I'm at an exciting age, peering death in the face while still keeping a foot in this world."

"Doesn't that frighten you?"

"What?"

"The thought that your time is running out?" Nichola had not meant to put it quite that tactlessly but James remained unperturbed.

"Not in the least. I merely await my next incarnation."

He had said this so straightforwardly that Nichola had gazed at him, surprised. "Do you believe in all that?"

"Oh yes, you see—"

He was cut short by one of the catering girls calling from the doorway, "The buffet is about to be served. All right, Mrs Devine?"

Marjorie had visibly taken charge, a fact which, Nichola remembered, had annoyed her, because it should have been she who stood there being charming, ushering the guests into the dining room where heaps of plates and cutlery wrapped in paper napkins stood waiting.

Nichola must have unwittingly made some little move of irritation because, glancing up suddenly, she had seen that Delia had noticed and was smirking at her.

". . . think we'd better eat now," Marjorie was saying, "because Lee Lovage is coming straight from the Inn on the Park to play dance music and should be here at about half past one."

"What time is this party going to end?" someone had asked.

"After breakfast," Lewis had answered cheerfully. "It's Sunday tomorrow, remember."

"Well, I won't stay up till then," Marjorie had said, not rudely but just as a plain statement of fact. "I'm not much of a night hawk. But as far as I'm concerned you can all come to Sunday lunch. I'll cook."

There had been a cheer and Nichola had thought: *This* is her hold on him, her general affability. And yet she's the wife who helped him rise, watched him climb the ladder, so by all the laws of show business it's high time she was ditched.

Yet, in her way, Marjorie was just as much her own person as Glynda. For during one of the quieter numbers played by Lee Lovage, who turned out to be an energetic black woman, she had disappeared towards the bedroom in which Nichola and Lewis had enjoyed so many delectable hours of lust, and had not come back.

"A determined lady, that one."

"What do you mean?" Nichola had asked nervously, looking up to see Glynda, observing all.

"Nothing to look at, frankly boring, but by God she's got Lewis where she wants him."

Nichola had died inside. "Do you think so?"

"Of course I do. He'll put it about until he drops but he'll always go back to her."

"But why, for God's sake?"

"Because she's his safety net. She presents no challenge. She'll always be there not asking too many questions. She keeps the home fires burning and joins in when she has to. Honestly ducky, can you see a girl like you putting up with that kind of life?"

"But Lewis can't be that chauvinistic!"

"A lot of actors are, haven't you noticed?"

"*What* are a lot of actors?" Delia had asked, joining them. She had obviously had her fair share of alcohol and was hell bent on needling.

"Selfish, sweetie," Glynda answered. The mouth with its gash of lipstick had twisted into a grin. "Anyway, I'm not getting involved in that kind of discussion. I need another drink. I'll leave you two to your girlish chatter." And she was off in a swirl of mahogany hair.

Nichola came straight to the point. "All the evening I've had the feeling you're trying to tell me something. Well, now's your chance. What is it you want to say?"

Delia lowered her eyes. "I don't think this is quite the place to discuss it."

"Very well, I'll do it for you. Ever since I got here you've been hinting that you and Lewis are having a fling. Right?"

Delia's voice had dropped to a whisper and a poisonous gleam had appeared in her eyes. "It's no hint. We *are* sleeping together. So just get out of my way before I tell him all about you."

"And what precisely do you mean by that?"

"That you, my dear, are a tramp and not good enough for Lewis Devine. One of my closest friends was at drama school with you. She knew about your famous Collection—"

Her words seemed to ring out and Lee Lovage had suddenly begun to play very loudly. Nichola realised that the party had thinned out and there were only about six people left in the room.

"Shut up," she muttered. "You're making a scene."

"*Me* make a scene? I like that!" Delia had answered. "Darling, you're famous in our profession, did you know that?"

"For what?" Nichola had asked, daring her.

"For flaunting it around, just like Vivien Leigh used to. In fact you remind me of her quite a lot. I think you must be her reincarnation."

There was a silence which even the pianist couldn't fill and then Glynda, appearing with a refilled glass, had stepped into the fray. Nichola noticed that she had a look about her reminiscent of Miss Jean Brodie.

"Now that is a fascinating subject," she had said commandingly. "In fact, having read a great deal about reincarnation, I became so interested in the whole topic that I went for hypnotic regression."

"My dear," James had added, coming to join them, "I believe in it firmly. As a boy my parents took me to Greece. I had the most extraordinary experience of *déjà-vu* at Delphi. It quite unnerved me. I knew damn well, even though I was only twelve years old, that I had been to that place before."

Lewis stepped up, his face so expressionless that Nichola knew he was furious and hoped it was not with her. "What happened during your regression?" he said to Glynda abruptly.

"It was really quite extraordinary. I was a gamekeeper in the 1800s, living somewhere on the Yorkshire Moors. I was shot dead by a poacher."

"Your name wasn't Oliver Mellors by any chance?" asked Bill Cosby, the stage manager.

"No," Glynda had answered with a quelling glance, "it was Joseph Fairbrother. I can remember that distinctly."

Lee had stopped playing, listening to the conversation, and Lewis had spoken into the sudden quiet. "I can hypnotise people, you know."

Nichola had looked at him in astonishment, thinking that this was an aspect of her lover she didn't even know.

"It's obvious you do that to audiences, darling," Delia had said, slipping her arm through his.

Lewis had disengaged himself. "I didn't mean that. I'm talking about real hypnosis. When I was in rep I played Svengali in a stage version of *Trilby*. The name part was taken by some obscure, noisy little creature who has since sunk into total oblivion. Anyway, during one rehearsal, loud though this girl was, she suddenly became strangely quiet and when I looked at her more closely I saw she had gone into a genuine trance. I had inadvertently put her under. It was a great temptation to leave her as she was, I can tell you."

"What happened?"

"Oh, I counted her out of it in true textbook style, then I began to dabble in the art. Very interesting it is too."

"Have you ever done a hypnotic regression?" asked Glynda, slurring very slightly.

"No, but I'm willing to try."

Nichola did not know, even now looking back, why she had said, "I'll volunteer as your subject. Delia says I'm the reincarnation of Vivien Leigh, so let's find out."

Lewis had hesitated. "I don't want to take part in some private joke."

"It's not a joke," Nichola had insisted. "I'm genuinely interested."

"Go on, Mr Devine," Lee had said from the piano. "This is fascinating."

"Very well." And instantly, or so it had seemed to Nichola, Lewis's voice had assumed a magnetic, compulsive timbre. "Lie down on the sofa."

She had done so, staring up at him as he went to the switches and dimmed the lights, aware that by candlelight her chic, elegant face looked especially beautiful.

He had picked one candle up and drawn a chair close to the

couch. "Now, Nichola," he had said, "I want you to look at this flame. Look at it hard until your eyes grow heavy, so heavy that it is no longer possible for you to keep them open. At the same time your limbs will become so relaxed you will feel them sinking down and down into the sofa."

He was an actor giving a performance and his audience was spellbound. There was no sound in the room except for the occasional raising of a glass. Nichola, thinking back, remembered just how heavy her eyes had grown and how tired she had suddenly felt.

"Is she faking?" someone had whispered.

"No," Lewis had answered quietly. "Look at her breathing."

It was an extraordinary phenomenon, Nichola thought. For though she had been able to hear everything that was going on, she no longer felt part of it. She recollected being certain that without Lewis's specific instruction she would have been unable to save herself if there had suddenly been a fire.

"Can you hear me?" her lover's voice had asked her.

"Yes."

"Are you quite comfortable?"

"Yes."

She had heard Delia audibly murmur, "She's putting it on."

"Shut up," Lewis had answered in his ordinary voice. Then the soothing tone he used to Nichola had returned. "Now I want you to imagine that you are entering a tunnel. Is that right?" he had added, obviously asking Glynda.

"Absolutely."

"The tunnel is quite narrow, like the ones the old canal barges used to go through. But this tunnel will take you back in time. Do you understand?"

"Yes," Nichola had answered.

"Good. Now keep going down the tunnel until you see something."

Even now, Nichola remembered that first faint glimmer. "There's a light – at the end."

"Probably a train coming the other way," Delia had said, and Glynda had answered in her Miss Brodie voice, "Don't make yourself look foolish."

Lewis's voice had risen over theirs. "What's happening now?"

"The light's getting nearer. It's very bright. I don't like it actually."

"Keep going towards it," Lewis had said.

"I don't want to. I want to turn back. It's too bright. It's hurting my eyes."

And Nichola had been aware that her body had started to twitch, while her eyelids had fluttered wildly.

"Are you all right?" Lewis had asked, a note of concern clearly audible in his voice.

"No. The light is going to blind me. I want to stop now. Please stop me, Lewis."

She had heard him speak to Glynda. "What shall I do?"

"Make her go on. She's passing through the time barrier."

His soothing tone had come again. "You must go through the light, Nichola. Only by doing so can you discover what lies beyond."

But she had been in an agony of distress. "No, don't make me," she had screamed. "I'm afraid. Oh help me!"

And then Nichola had suddenly gone still.

Lewis had stared about him in consternation. "Glynda, for Christ's sake, is she okay? Did this happen to you?"

"I honestly can't remember, but she's obviously gone back. Ask her some questions."

"What?"

"Well, who she is or something."

Before he could utter a word there had been a movement from the sofa and Nichola had let out a low moan, a sound almost animal-like in its obvious distress.

"I don't like this," murmured the girl who had come with the lighting director.

"I think it's a bloody good performance," said Delia scathingly, but her voice was drowned by a terrible cry.

"Dear God!" exclaimed Glynda involuntarily.

For on the sofa Nichola was writhing about so violently that she seemed in danger of falling to the floor.

"She's in agony," shouted Bill Cosby. "For God's sake Lewis, bring her out of it."

The actor had by now recovered from his initial shock and was once more in full Svengalian flight. "Tell me who you are." he demanded resonantly. "Tell me your name."

There was no reply other than for another terrifying scream as Nichola gripped her body low down.

"She's in labour," shrieked Lee Lovage. "Look at that! She's having a baby."

"This is incredible," Lewis cried exultantly. "I've actually done it!" He downed a glass of wine. "Who are you?" he repeated, but the only answer Nichola gave was one long continuous wail.

Bill jumped to his feet. "Lewis, for God's sake put an end to this. It can't be doing her any good."

Delia, unrepentant, said, "I think she deserves the Oscar."

Lewis turned questioningly to Glynda, who drained her vodka with a gulp. "Best get her back, darling. It is getting rather grim."

"Nichola, I'm going to count from ten to one," Lewis stated, with just the first hint of panic in his voice. "When I reach one you will wake refreshed and well. You will remember nothing of what has taken place. I shall start counting now and soon you will be wide awake."

He did so, very rapidly. Yet for some reason Nichola did not respond to his words. Instead, the ghastly screams continued, chilling the blood and sending a frisson of sheer terror through the entire room.

"Ten, nine, eight, seven, six, five, four, three, two, one. You will awake refreshed and well," Lewis repeated frantically.

But Nichola seemed no longer able to hear him, lying on the sofa, her eyes closed, very still and very limp and suddenly rather white.

"What's up with her?" Glynda asked harshly.

"She won't come round," answered Lewis, and now he was visibly panicking. "My God, she won't come round."

Bill took over. "Nichola," he said, taking one of her hands and slapping it gently, "it's me, Bill. Can you hear me?"

There was no reaction at all.

He leant forward, peering at her intently. "My God, her breathing's failed!" With shaking hands he grabbed the unconscious girl's wrists. "Her pulse is gone. Ring an ambulance, for

Christ's sake. Something's gone horribly wrong. Nichola," he called again, "Nichola, can you hear me?"

"Ten, nine, eight—" Lewis started desperately but was drowned by the fearful cry that came from Lee Lovage. "She's died in another time and it's killed her in this one. Oh my God, my God!"

But nobody took any notice of her as with calm desperation Bill began to give Nichola Hall the kiss of life.

Passing through the light had been like walking into the sun. She had been bathed with such a glow, such a radiance, that she had thought she would be blinded by it. Then, suddenly, all the brightness had vanished and there had been nothing but darkness beyond, darkness and a well of pain into which Nichola had fallen, plunging downwards into agony. As searing contraction after searing contraction had ripped through her body, she had screamed aloud. Then all the terrible sensations had focused and she had been overwhelmed by an urge to rid herself of the thing that was causing her so much pain. Gripping her legs tightly, Nichola had started to bear down. And then everything had blurred and gone out of focus, and there had been nothing but a numbness and a chill beyond anything she had ever experienced.

"She's dying," said a female voice close at hand.

"Oh no," came the answer. "She mustn't! She mustn't do that! Not my Arabella."

Far, far away it seemed that somebody was breathing into Nichola's mouth. Then there was nothing but grey mist which came swirling towards her in a dense cloud and hid her away from all the hands that were reaching out to touch her.

Chapter Two

There was mist everywhere, long swirling fingers of it inside her head, little pools on her eyelids like pennies for the newly dead. It was in her nostrils, choking her, wisping round her body, making it clammier and colder than it had ever felt before, as Nichola slowly and with some difficulty started to return to consciousness.

She would have liked to have opened her eyes, then, and seen the reassuring sight of her lover's face, to have rejoined the party, laughing casually, telling everyone she could remember very little about it. She was longing for a drink, a cigarette, needing to draw the smoke deep into her lungs, but because of the mist she could neither move nor speak. Paralysed, Nichola could only lie inert as her faculties slowly restored themselves to life.

The first thing to come back was her sense of smell. There was a sharp odour, like blood, quite close to her, together with a scent of herbs. There was also wood smoke in the atmosphere, oppressively so, as if the wind had gusted down a chimney and blown back its acrid contents. Then, as she breathed in this pungent concoction, sensation suddenly returned to her limbs and Nichola cried out loud.

She had never known anything quite like it. Behind her back was the excruciating hardness of unyielding wood but this was nothing compared with the feeling in the lower half of her body. It was as though she had been kicked, savagely and repeatedly, her legs heavy with pain, her vulva seared with agony.

"Oh God!" she moaned, and wondered from what depths of her brain this nightmare had been conjured to haunt her.

And then she remembered the indescribable pain she had

endured during the regression and shuddered from head to foot.

Hearing returned, for close at hand a baby mewled its newborn cry, a high persistent unhappy wail.

"There, there, poor mite," a women comforted, and there came the sound of footsteps on a wooden floor.

Panic overwhelmed her, sheer blind fear that any illusion created by hypnosis could seem so real, even down to the torment Nichola was experiencing in the lower half of her body. Gasping and fighting for breath, the actress slowly opened her eyes.

She was in a long room panelled throughout in sombre oak, its atmosphere dark and heavy, only the fire that burned in the large stone hearth at one end giving any comfort or cheer. Lewis's chic Putney flat, his smart London residence, had vanished completely. Nichola Hall knew then for certain that she was suffering an hallucination. Yet the apparent reality of it – the harsh smell, the thin cries of the infant, her own pain – was terrifyingly genuine.

"Lewis, bring me back," Nichola called frantically, and opened her mouth to shout out her terror.

A hand shot into her line of vision, a roughened hand with a smear of blood on it. "She's shedding the afterbirth," said a female voice, and with that the woman pressed on Nichola's body so hard tears involuntarily filled her eyes. Something slithered out between her legs, something that she could not bring herself to look at, something that the owner of the rough hands took away instantly. Unable to help herself, Nichola started to cry.

"Here, this will ease you," put in a gentler voice, and with that a solution of warm water and herbs was poured over her suffering extremities. Forcing herself, Nichola looked up.

A young female leaned over her, a female in a floor-length brown dress, its starkness relieved only by a white collar and cuffs. It was a costume so reminiscent of her own in *The Crucible* that Nichola almost felt a sense of relief. She was obviously dreaming about the play, the subconscious not letting go of the thoughts and ideas that had been uppermost in her mind for the last few months.

"Now, let me help you from the birthing chair, Mistress Arabella," the girl continued, holding out both hands.

"Abigail," Nichola answered, certain now of what was happening. "There isn't an Arabella in the script."

"The pain's crazed her," said someone else, and the woman whose workworn hands had pushed so hard on Nichola's abdomen, came into view.

The actress thought she had never seen anyone quite so harsh, the features beneath their white cap stark and unattractive in the cold grey light that came in through the leaded windows. Yet as the younger girl pulled Nichola to her feet she was glad of the creature's strong arms which half carried her towards a huge curtained four-poster bed that stood against the far wall.

Suddenly, Nichola could bear no more. "I hate this regression, dream, whatever it is," she called out. "Lewis, wake me up. For God's sake wake me up."

"Shush," said the younger woman. "Don't upset yourself." In a softer voice she said to the other, "Has the birth truly unhinged her?"

"Obviously. But still we're lucky to have her with us. I thought we'd lost her."

"So did I."

There was silence while they heaved Nichola into the enormous bed and tucked her into its spaciousness. Then the grim-faced woman turned to the girl.

"Why did you breathe into her mouth like that?" she asked curiously.

"I just wanted to get air into her, that's all. Her breathing was so shallow and she seemed too tired to do it for herself."

"Well, I reckon you saved her life with it, for better or worse."

"You shouldn't say such things, Hannah. A life is always worth saving."

"That's as may be," the woman replied abruptly, and turned

to the wooden cradle which stood on its rockers beside the bed. Out of it she lifted a tightly swaddled bundle, a bundle which opened a sad small mouth and let out a cry.

"Here," she said, holding it in Nichola's direction. "Here's your daughter. Don't you at least want to see her?"

The dream had turned into total nightmare and Nichola lost control. Putting her head back, she started to scream, hearing the sound reverberate through the dimness of that oppressive room.

"Help me," she yelled. "Oh Lewis, please wake me up. I hate this regression. I'm afraid."

But there was no answer from that quarter. Her lover either could not or would not come to her assistance. Despite her reasoning power, which told her all that she was seeing and hearing was illusion, a trick of her mind, Nichola had never been more terrified. Turning her head into the pillow, she sobbed without restraint.

The older woman made a sound of contempt. "It wasn't that hard a labour to make her so witless. I've delivered mothers far worse, I can assure you."

"Make up your mind," the girl retorted angrily. "Why, you said yourself she nearly died."

"It might have been better if she had, if she's going to reject that poor babe of hers."

"She won't do so, I've known her all my life. She's a good heart, has Mistress Arabella. It's just that she's exhausted. If we let her sleep her senses will be restored when she wakens, you see."

"I hope you're right for everyone's sake. Anyway, I'll be off. There's nothing more I can do here. I'll come back when it's time for her to feed the hapless mite."

"What shall I do if she cries out?"

"Give her a draught of this sleeping potion."

The voices grew more distant and, through her sobs, Nichola heard the opening and closing of a heavy door. Then the silence grew immense, the only noise the distant tick of a clock, the spit and crackle of the fire's flames, the minute sounds of the newborn child.

If I lose consciousness, the actress thought frantically, I might wake to find that it's all over, that Lewis has said the right words and I'm back.

"Here, give me some of that medicine," she called out.

There was no answer and, sitting up, Nichola saw she was alone in that gloomy room, through the windows of which now came the cold grey light cast by falling snow.

"Oh God!" she said aloud. "Won't this misery ever end?"

For answer the room's heavy atmosphere rushed to consume her, dark with shadow. "Damn you, Lewis," she shouted, her fear now tinged with anger. "Damn you for doing this to me. Get me back, you bastard."

It was at that moment the baby cried, obviously awoken by Nichola's protests. "Shut up, you beastly little phantom," she yelled at it furiously. But the more she remonstrated the more it mewled, and in the end she was forced to put down an angry hand and rock the cradle hard. Immediately the cries became muffled, indeed almost inaudible, and the actress had no choice but to lean over and peer into the depths of the crib. Beneath its curved wooden head she could see that the infant now lay on its face, its minute nose pressed into the bottom coverlet.

"Oh for God's sake," she exclaimed, and with enormous reluctance leaned over further and picked the helpless creature up. It stopped wailing and, opening its eyes, looked at her with the strange perceptiveness of the newlyborn.

What dream can this be, Nichola thought wildly, that is so real I can smell the skin of this child?

The baby sneezed pathetically, frightened itself and cried again, then nuzzled against Nichola's breast. To her intense horror she realised that the front of her shift was open and that it had taken her nipple.

"Oh no!" she shouted in disgust and would have thrust the child straight back into its cot had she not felt an incredible sensation. There was a flow between her and the thing sucking at her, the hypnotic regression had entered the realms of pure fantasy. She whose only accidental flirtation with motherhood had ended in the blessed relief of abortion, having stupidly slipped up with a member of The Collection, was breast feeding a baby. And yet, in the midst of all the turmoil, all the fear and anguish, there was something intensely peaceful about what was happening. The sensation of the infant sucking contentedly, one tiny hand holding on, was unbelievably soothing. With a deep sigh, Nichola let her head fall back against the pillow, leaving the baby where it was.

She must have closed her eyes for a second for when she opened them again the girl was back in the room, lighting candles, drawing curtains against the freezing twilight, throwing more logs upon the fire. She looked up, startled, as Nichola sighed, then hurried over to the bed.

"I thought you were asleep." She stared in disbelief. "But you're feeding the little one. The midwife said to wait till she returned."

The utter impossibility of the situation bore in on the actress once more. "Oh God, let me wake up soon," she said on a wail of despair.

The girl came close and put her hand on Nichola's forehead. "Don't fret yourself, Mistress. I'm here to help you."

The actress seized her wrist. "Are you? Can you? Do you know how to get me out of this wretched trance?"

"Sleep," the other woman answered firmly. "That is what you need. When you wake up everything will be different."

"Will it really? Do you promise me?"

"I do, Mistress, I do."

"Then take the child away and give me that draught. The sooner this torture is over the better I shall be."

She was too exhausted to cry. Indeed, swallowing a cup of the dark juice the girl brought her was almost a relief and Nichola prayed she would lose consciousness straight away.

In fact she must have done so for almost immediately a dream came. She saw a body being wheeled into an ambulance on a stretcher trolley, recognised Bill and Glynis standing on the steps of the Putney house, supporting a white-faced Lewis between them. Passing inside the ambulance, unseen by its attendants, Nichola realised that the body was being given oxygen and was on a drip. Staring at it, she thought the face seemed somehow familiar but did not know who it was. With a shriek of its siren the ambulance took off into the night and the last thing Nichola was aware of was the flash of its blue light reflected on the empty pavements of the sleeping city as it hurtled urgently through the darkness.

It was the wail of the baby that woke Nichola Hall once more, the continuing cries penetrating her deepest consciousness and striking the chill of fear into her heart even while she drifted up through layers of sleep towards wakefulness.

"Oh no," she said, terrified to open her eyes, "oh please God, no."

Yet the same heavy smell was in the air, smoke and herbs and dark, dark wood.

This is impossible, the actress thought wretchedly. No regression, no trance, could last this long.

And somewhere deep in her brain, and for the very first time, came a warning signal, the dawning of an idea that the experiment in hypnotic regression had somehow gone terribly wrong.

Nichola sat bolt upright and looked round, seeing to her acute distress the drawn curtains of the canopied four-poster, beyond them the glow thrown by the fire. Instantly, despair gave way to hysteria and opening her mouth wide she screamed at the top of her voice. There was the sound of running feet and the drapes were pulled back hastily to reveal the girl's anxious face.

"Oh, Mistress Arabella, what is it? You gave me such a start."

Nichola could not answer, rigid with terror as the first intimations of truth now dawned. It seemed to her, though her rational mind could scarcely credit it, that the dabbling with hypnosis had had unspeakably sinister results. It would appear that the impossible had happened, that Lewis had sent her back to another century and she had become marooned there.

"Oh God!" she yelled. "What have you done to me?"

For it was growing more obvious with every passing second that everything she was seeing and feeling was real. And yet Nichola could not relinquish the hope that this *was* the hypnotic regression, that she was currently living in another existence and might still return to her own time when the experience was over.

"Where am I?" she said weakly to the girl, who still hung over her, eyes wide with concern.

"You're at home, of course. Oh, don't talk so wild, Arabella. It'll do you no good."

"But where is home?" Nichola persisted.

"You know full well. It's Haseley Court."

"Haseley Court where?"

The girl sighed deeply. "Oh Mistress, it breaks my heart to hear you like this. I'd best give you another draught."

"No, no," Nichola answered hastily as the servant produced the cup and bottle from behind her back. "Let me feed the baby first, then I'll take whatever you want me to."

It had been a ploy to buy time, yet it was surprisingly pleasant to hold the tightly swaddled bundle in her arms and see it stop crying instantly. In a frenzy of contrary emotions, Nichola put it to her breast where it began to suckle contentedly.

"Listen to me," she went on urgently. "Something unbelievable has happened. I'm not Arabella. There's been a muddle up. It's all to do with an experiment that's gone terribly wrong. I'm actually Nichola Hall but somehow I've got into Arabella's life. Do you understand me?"

She could have been speaking a foreign language for the girl stared at her uncomprehendingly before saying, "This babbling can do nothing but harm, Mistress. Try to stop it before Sir Denzil comes, I beg you."

Out of utter desperation a kind of cunning was born. Nichola attempted a look of contrition. "I'm sorry, but I can't help myself. You see, the truth is I lost my memory during labour. I don't know who I am or even who you are. Please don't be angry with me."

The girl appeared even more amazed but eventually her expression softened. "I suppose for one as near to death as you have been it is a miracle you are even able to speak, let alone remember."

And she sat down beside Nichola on the bed and put her arm round her shoulders.

"What happened to me exactly?" the actress asked cautiously.

"The waters of your womb broke yesterday and I called for Hannah the midwife. You laboured twenty-four hours and then the pushing of the babe seemed too much for you. You went so still and so white that I feared you'd gone."

"What did you do?"

"I breathed into your mouth while Hannah soaped her arm and got the child away."

Nichola froze. "The kiss of life. Do you know, I can remember it vaguely. I thought it was Bill that did it."

The servant shook her head. "There was none here but Hannah and me. Because of the circumstances Sir Denzil wouldn't let anyone else attend you."

Unbelievably, panic was giving way to curiosity. "What circumstances?"

"Well . . . you know."

"No, I don't. I've told you, I can remember nothing."

"Well, you not being married, Mistress, that's what."

"So this is a bastard?" said Nichola, looking down at the baby which had fallen asleep at her breast.

"It's Michael Morellon's child."

"And who is he?"

"He was your betrothed until your fathers went on opposing sides."

It was all too much. "I think I've heard enough," Nichola said, feeling a sudden surge of hopelessness which left her drained of strength. "Just tell me who I am, who you are, and where this house is situated."

"You're Arabella Loxley, daughter of Sir Denzil Loxley of Haseley Court, Oxfordshire. And I am Emmet Fenemore who has been in your service since I was twelve years old."

Nichola decided on one last attempt to reason with her. "Really, none of those things are true. I'm not your mistress but Nichola Hall, an actress. All I want is to go to sleep again in the hope that when I wake up everything will have sorted itself out. Now take the baby and let me get some rest. But if by any chance I am still here tomorrow I want you to promise to help me."

"God knows I'll try," the servant answered, and Nichola saw that Emmet was weeping as she poured some more of the dark juice into a cup and gave it to her to drink.

Almost at once the dream came. Nichola stood outside a hospital and watched as an ambulance pulled up. The body she had seen earlier was wheeled out and received by two nurses and a doctor who hurried it through the doors of Casualty. Running alongside them, Nichola saw that they were following signs to Intensive Care. Then the dream faded and she slept peacefully for a while before a great sense of the unfamiliar woke her once more.

This time she was prepared to be in the oak room but still her heart sank and she felt fear run like ice through her blood. Sniffing the air, recognising that distinctive smell, Nichola knew that her misgivings were confirmed. She was still trapped on her extraordinary journey. Terrified but wanting to look round in more detail, the actress crawled silently to the foot of the great bed and peered through the crack in the drawn curtains.

Stark daylight flooded the room, giving it a chilly and forbidding look despite the fire that consumed logs as big as branches in the massive hearth. Lit like this, Nichola could see the detailed carving of the heavy wood panelling and thought that for all its sombre quality it still had a rigid kind of beauty, vividly reminding her of some of the National Trust properties she had traipsed round in the past. Once again the authentic smell of woodsmoke, the feel of the bed's heavy drapery beneath her fingers, the warm glow of the fire, endorsed her belief that her mind, her psyche – she did not dare to think of it as her soul – had become entrapped in another century.

Thoughts of her mind led to those of her body and it struck her forcibly, and for the first time, that not only did the bruising and soreness she felt correspond with having recently given birth to the baby at present sleeping quietly in its crib, but that somehow she had even been able to feed it. The very concept was almost too daunting to consider and Nichola sank down in a heap, leaning against one of the bedposts, wondering if something even more ghastly than she had at first imagined might have taken place. Frantically, she snatched off the white shift in which she was dressed and stared downwards.

The body at which she gazed was not her own. Gone was the beautiful figure, the lean lithe frame, of which she had been so proud, in its place the outline of someone much shorter, and someone who had indeed recently borne a child. There was spare flesh round the stomach, the breasts were enlarged and blue veined, and when she drew to one side the strange nappy-like garment she was wearing, Nichola could glimpse bruising.

"Oh my God!" she whispered, sickened by what she was seeing.

Trembling violently, she braced herself for what must inevitably come next. At the far end of the room, standing beneath the windows, was a table covered with a heavy cloth, the various pots and jars that stood on it indicating that it was used for the purpose of applying cosmetics. Above it, hanging on the wall, was a mirror set in a carved wooden frame. With grim determination, clinging to various bits of furniture for support as she moved, Nichola made painful progress towards it then, holding tightly to the table's edge, peeped into the glass.

Clouds of darkness came, though whether caused by the effort of moving or by the sight she beheld, Nichola did not know. All she was aware of at that moment was that another face was looking back at her, that her own svelte beauty, her 1990s chic, had vanished. In its place was something so far removed from her own style that she could only gaze at it in horror. And then Nichola saw the sky blue eyes of her reflection roll upwards and as a black spiral caught her in its coils, she fell down to the floor and into oblivion.

Chapter Three

Piercing through the darkness like a shout came a vision of the body. It lay in a room on its own, various machines attached to it, monitors bleeping the beats of its heart, the patterns of its brain. Beside it, in awful stillness, sat two people whom Nichola recognised as her father and stepmother, and she was horrified to observe that her father, who in his day had been a man about town, a dashing escort to young ladies of high society, had been reduced to tears.

"Daddy," Nichola called out, but he did not hear her and the mirage began to fade. And then she was shivering and shaking as she wakened to a freezing consciousness, her teeth chattering in her head, her body shrinking beneath currents of cold air. Slowly opening her eyes, the actress could see from where she lay on the floor that two of the panes in the lead-lighted casements of the bedroom in Haseley Court had been broken and, even as she watched, a hand appeared through the gap and pulled the catch down. She was too weak to scream, too weak to do anything except watch as the window opened and a man, holding the spars of a wooden ladder to support himself, climbed nimbly through.

"My God!" he exclaimed as he almost fell over her, "Arabella, are you all right?" And with that he picked her up and carried her back to the bed.

Nichola's certainty that everything she was experiencing was real, was yet again endorsed by the tactile presence of the man holding her. He was as human as she, even down to the smell of the buff coloured coat he wore, the faint stink of horseflesh about him.

"God be praised, you've had the child," he said, laying her gently back on the bed. "Was the pain great"?

"What I can remember of it was terrible," Nichola answered.

The newcomer looked contrite. "I shrink that I should have inflicted such a thing on you and then was not here at your hour of need."

Nichola stared at him curiously. "So you must be Michael Morellon."

The visitor appeared thoroughly startled. "Of course I'm Michael," he answered abruptly, then his eyes narrowed and he stared at her closely. "You're mazed, aren't you? Childbed has wreaked its terrible confusion."

Nichola stared back at him, wondering whether to attempt an explanation then, even as she considered it, realising how hopeless it would be. The regression must have been so successful that clearly her mind had become lodged in the body of another. The body of a girl called Arabella Loxley who had apparently died in childbirth and must have become host to Nichola's psyche. So how, in the face of such an extraordinary occurrence, could she ever convince any of these people of the terrible facts? And yet some perverse instinct forced her to try.

"Listen, Michael," she said urgently, "the truth is that I'm not confused, indeed I know exactly what has happened. You see, I'm not Arabella. My real name is Nichola Hall and I am an actress from the twentieth century. I arrived in Arabella's body as the result of an experiment in hypnotic regression. I don't expect you to understand any of this but I sincerely hope you're going to believe it."

Almost as a reflex, Michael made the sign of the cross. "What babble's this?" he asked, his face tight with fear.

"No babble at all, it's what happened."

His expression became stricken. "Oh poor soul, poor soul. That the birth of our child should have brought you to this."

At that moment, right on cue, or so Nichola thought with a certain wry amusement, the baby let out a whimper and Michael, distracted, turned to the cradle. "Do I have a son?" he asked softly.

Suddenly, Nichola lost her temper with him, irritated beyond belief that no one she had encountered so far in this benighted century – surely the seventeenth if her knowledge of period costume was to be trusted – believed a word she said.

"It's a girl," she answered bitterly, "which will no doubt be a terrible disappointment to you."

Michael's eyebrows drew together and his attractive face darkened. "A daughter pleases me as much as a boy," he said angrily. "You of all people should know that. That remark was not worthy of you, by God." Instantly he was all contrition. "Forgive me. How could I raise my voice to the woman I love so much? The woman who has borne me the most beautiful child?"

"Oh God," replied Nichola miserably, "if only you understood! Listen, I'm not your baby's mother. I'm someone entirely different."

For answer Michael drew her into his arms, stroking her hair and uttering little words of comfort which, despite everything, Nichola found quite soothing. Close to him like this she could see his features distinctly and suddenly found herself studying the man intently. She was looking at a handsome face, indeed one which would have attracted her had all things been equal. Bearing more than a passing resemblance to the actor Michael York, this Michael wore his hair longer, to his shoulders, while his eyes were a different shade of blue, almost mauve. But the broad mouth, the slightly flattened nose, the strong jaw and muscular build were uncannily similar.

"I once acted in a film with your lookalike," she thought, then realised she had said the words aloud.

"Hush now," Michael answered, "this is but a passing phase. Soon you will be restored to normal, I feel certain of it."

"If only I could be," Nichola said on the breath of a sob. "If only there were somebody to help me get back."

"But I will help you," he protested roundly. "I will never let you down. Indeed if it weren't for the worsening crisis I would have married you and all would have been well, the child born beneath my roof and you not forced to suffer these fierce delusions."

Once again came a thrust of curiosity. Nichola wiped her eyes on the sleeve of her shift and looked at the man who was holding her so tightly. "What crisis?"

A look of disbelief crossed Michael's features. "How can you ask? Is your memory gone?"

Suddenly it was easier to lie, to play along, just as she had done with Emmet. "Yes, it has. The servant even had to tell me my name. So please help me. What was it that stopped you marrying—" She hesitated over the word then finally came out with, "me."

"Your family and mine have divided loyalties," Michael stated simply. "Your father supports the King while mine is sympathetic to Parliament. Our betrothal was broken off because of it."

It was a relief to hear the baby cry and watch Michael pick it up, his back to her, for just at that moment she could not have endured his close scrutiny. The truth was that she had never been more shocked. Just as she had suspected, the hypnotic regression had succeeded brilliantly. She had gone back to the time of the English Civil War and there, or so it would appear, was now entrapped.

The impossibility of the situation washed over Nichola like a rough sea. Nobody from the century in which Lewis's experiment had placed her could possibly grasp what had happened. The art of hypnotism was yet to be discovered by Dr Mesmer, so even the basic premise would be beyond their comprehension, let alone the dire result. It occurred to her then that there was no further point in trying to convince Michael, Emmet or anyone else. It would be better to preserve her strength until something happened, either that she woke to find herself back in her own time, or discovered some way of going into a trance and returning by that means.

She realised that Michael was speaking to her, the baby in his arms, his expression sweet as he gazed at his daughter. "What have you named the child?"

"Nothing as yet."

"Then would you countenance Adelina after my mother?"

For the first time since she had awoken in Haseley Court, Nichola laughed, and the sound startled her. "No, I'm afraid I wouldn't. How about a Shakespearean name? You *have* heard of Shakespeare, I take it?"

"Of course," Michael replied with a certain indignation. "I have visited both The Fortune and The Hope and there seen the works of Shakespeare and Jonson, to say nothing of John Webster. You should know that."

It was easier to reply, "Michael, please accept that I have no memory," than to argue.

He looked guilty again. "My poor girl, I pray God you will recover soon. But now, what of our daughter? It would please me to think of her as something when I am far away."

"Miranda," said Nichola, casting about and coming up with the first Shakespearean heroine she could think of.

Michael frowned. "An unusual choice."

Nichola became bored. "Well, whatever you like then."

"Miranda, it is." He was suddenly still, listening. "There's somebody coming. I must go. The King is heading for York and I'm due to join the forces of the Earl of Essex. So heaven forbid I get captured now."

"Hurry up then," said Nichola, strangely anxious.

Michael bent over and the touch of his lips was warm on hers. "Goodbye, darling. Take care of yourself and the little one." And with that he put the baby back in its crib, stroked it with a quiet hand, and was out through the window in a flash. His head was just disappearing as the door opened and Emmet appeared. Glimpsing him, she rushed to look out.

"God be praised but that were Master Michael! He risked his hide coming here, for sure."

"What would have happened if he'd been caught?"

"I reckon Sir Denzil would have taken a whip to him."

Nichola shuddered. "How savage."

The girl nodded, "Aye, but these are savage times, Arabella. Families are splitting up and brother is turning on brother. Heaven alone knows where it will all end. And heaven knows where *you'll* end if you don't eat soon. You've had hardly a thing since the baby was born."

"I'm not very hungry."

"But you must consume food to rebuild your strength. You're suckling a child and need to take nourishment."

Yet again it was easier to comply. "Very well, if you bring me something I promise to eat it."

The girl smiled and went to the door where she turned and lingered for a moment. "Is Master Michael well?" she asked, her voice a shade too casual.

She's got a thing about him, Nichola thought with some amusement. "Very," she answered, then added, "he's delighted with his baby, of course. But he looks very young for fatherhood to me. Randy little devil. When did he start screwing Arabella?"

The servant stared at her blankly. "I beg your pardon?"

"When did he and Arabella first do it?"

"I don't know what you mean."

"Oh to hell with everything," Nichola answered crossly. "I suppose I'd better play the part even if it's only to shut you up. What I want to know is when Michael and Arab . . . I . . . first went to bed together."

Emmet looked profoundly annoyed. "I've a mind not to answer one question more until you stop talking about Arabella as if she wasn't yourself."

"Well, when did they . . . we?" Nichola responded carelessly.

"You bedded together when you were betrothed two years ago and you know it. It was agreed by both your families that relations could begin. Though your father was not best pleased by the unfortunate result."

Nichola was astonished. "Really? Is it customary for people to sleep together before marriage?"

"It is often done, yes."

"But how old were we?"

"You were fifteen, Master Michael three years more."

"Good God!" exclaimed Nichola, startled by the realisation. "Is Arabella still only seventeen?"

Emmet looked reproving. "Now don't start that nonsense again, I beg you." And she left the room briskly, her heels banging angrily on the wooden floor.

Sighing, Nichola leaned back against the pillows, her mind teaming with thoughts. It was becoming glaringly obvious with each passing hour that the only way to survive this ordeal was by pretending she was Arabella and to continue doing so until the day she met someone capable of understanding her plight. It would seem an advantage in these circumstances, Nichola considered drily, that she was an actress by profession, capable of taking on the role of a seventeen-year-old ingenue who, by reason of betrothal customs, had become a mother before her wedding and now was caught up in the toils of civil war.

"By the sword divided," quoted Nichola, remembering the television series she had watched as a schoolgirl. And through the terror and fear and sense of disbelief which still consumed her, she felt the first thrill of excitement.

If I can only look on it as a part, she thought. If I can just hang on to that I should be all right.

Yet doing and thinking were two very different things, and as shadows darkened the room once more, Nichola could only contemplate the future with trepidation and a growing sense of alarm.

Having eaten quite heartily and drunk two goblets of red wine she slept soundly, to be awoken by the baby which cried to be fed during the early hours of the morning. Wondering at her own ability, the actress picked it up with a certain amount of skill and then, having very little option as the child was extremely wet, set about the task of changing it. This involved getting out of bed and going to the table above which hung the mirror. With the baby held firmly in her arms Nichola crossed the room and put the little creature down on the flat surface, removing the linen square which was obviously the seventeenth-century version of a nappy.

Free of restrictions, the infant kicked its legs and Nichola found her natural dislike of children tinged with interest. She had never seen anything quite so newborn, quite so small and delicate, and it both repelled and fascinated her. Very gingerly she set about washing the child, pouring cold water from a ewer into a basin and dabbing at its minute bottom. It cried a little with the chill but was quiet enough as Nichola tied on a clean linen square. And it was then that she caught a glimpse of her moving reflection in the mirror and, bracing herself, took a good look at Arabella Loxley.

Though the girl did not have the kind of appearance that Nichola personally admired, she was nonetheless stunning judged by the standards of any century. Heavy coils of golden hair, stringy now because of her recent labour but only needing a wash to spring back into life, fell beside a softly rounded face. Staring at it in amazement, Nichola saw a small chin, full lips and clear sea blue eyes surrounded by a thick fringe of dark lashes. There was nothing chic or svelte about this creature, instead she possessed a classic loveliness which made Nichola quite breathless.

"But you're still not my scene, ducky," she said out loud and then felt cheapened, shabby, that she had had the temerity to criticise someone no longer able to answer back.

Yet the contrast could not be more pronounced between the boyish model-girl looks the actress loved so well and this timeless beauty who gazed at Nichola intently from the mirror's reflecting glass.

"Rotten figure though," said Nichola, prodding, but again felt degraded. Arabella had just given birth to a child and could hardly be expected to match up to Nichola's highly-toned, worked-out, carefully-dieted physique. Nevertheless the thought that she was now trapped in another woman's frame began to frighten her once more and the actress hurried back to bed, realising that she had started to shake. It was at this point that the baby, dumped back in its cot, let out a cry, reminding her that it was still waiting to be fed.

"Oh do shut up," said Nichola miserably, "I really can't cope with you as well."

But the high wails continued until she was forced to lift the child out of its crib again. It yelled all the more as she shook it hard. "You're not even mine," she muttered at it through clenched teeth. "I wasn't the one who gave birth to you."

Though the fact remained that she had experienced pain once she had passed beyond the light. Indeed she could dimly remember the sensation of wanting to bear down. So perhaps, in a way, she was partially responsible for the little thing. Suddenly sorry for it, Nichola put the infant to her breast and heard its crying subside as it began to suckle.

"This is so unreal," she said aloud. "Do you realise I never even wanted children and now I've got you. And not only that, I've actually given you a name. You're Miranda, do you hear? Miranda Morellon." It occurred to her, then, what a wonderful stage title that would make. "And tonight," she continued, "the part of Hedda Gabler will be played by that rising young star, Miranda Morellon."

And then she stopped in fright. Her door was opening very slowly and Nichola realised that someone had probably been standing in the darkness listening to every word she said. Not knowing what to do she took the coward's way out and dived beneath the bedclothes, complete with Miranda, but not before she had glimpsed a thin face with dark eyes staring at her fixedly from the now gaping doorway.

She was woken by frosty sunlight and the sound of whistling, and Nichola struggled from her coverings to find that Emmet was in the room, already tending to the infant.

"Gracious Arabella, you were sleeping deep. Your father came back from a visit during the night. Did you not hear the hullabaloo?" she said, looking over her shoulder.

So that was the gaunt creature who had come to stare at her in the small hours. Nichola shivered. "I heard nothing. I fed Miranda, then I slept the rest of the time."

"Miranda? Is that what you're calling her?"

"Michael and I agreed upon it yesterday."

Emmet put her finger to her lips. "Don't mention that name. Sir Denzil won't countenance to have it spoken. For it is said the King has reached York and that the country is now rapidly slipping down the hill towards war."

"Is this 1642?" asked Nichola, remembering that in 1992 the 350th anniversary of the outbreak of the Civil War had been celebrated.

"Of course it is. I wish you would try to collect yourself."

"I think I'm coping admirably," the actress answered sharply. "Anyone else would probably be in non-stop screaming hysterics."

"I don't know what you mean and I'm not listening any more," the servant replied, equally crossly, once again reminding Nichola of the impossibility of her position. For how could a set of people entirely taken up with the grim prospect of a war in which brother would fight brother be expected to listen to what, to them, was nothing more than the lunatic ramblings of a girl crazed by childbirth?

"Oh my God!" said Nichola, and Emmet looked at her with concern.

"Are you all right? Sir Denzil's coming to visit you this morning."

"Is he? Then I'm getting up."

"But you can't. Women must lie in two weeks after being delivered."

"I can't help that. I'm perfectly capable of sitting in a chair by the fire. Now, help me out of bed then get some hot water. I'm going to have a bath."

Had she realised the effort involved in such an exercise, Nichola thought afterwards, she might well have contented herself with a thorough wash. Yet having made the decision she was determined to stick by it. With a great deal of exaggerated effort two maids bore a great wooden tub into the bedroom, and were shortly followed by a line of complaining servants, each one bearing a bucket to fill the thing. Eventually Nichola stepped into the lukewarm water only to discover that there was no soap and she was expected to rub her body with oils. However, she managed to get Arabella's skin clean and then washed her hair as best she could.

Drying it before the fire, Emmet said, "What to do? I've never known you so particular, Mistress."

"It's my new resolution. You're going to see plenty of this."

"Oh dear," the servant answered, genuinely alarmed.

The robing which followed was, in many ways, enjoyable. It had always been Nichola's delight to dress up in period theatrical costume and now she was experiencing the real thing at first hand. Arabella had certainly changed shape since her pregnancy and the laces which fastened the skirt were left loose while the long boned bodice, with its lace edged neckline and beautiful lace cuffed sleeves, was kept similarly slack.

"I've no time to curl your hair," Emmet said frantically, "I'll just have to brush it through."

And Nichola experienced the odd sensation of bristles plunging through a mass of shoulder length waves. It was unnerving, preparing a body that was not hers to meet a father who, or so Nichola guessed, was angry and unhappy at his daughter's fall from grace. And when his booted feet finally stamped up the stairs, then stopped in the doorway of her room, just as they had done the night before, she knew why a note of nervousness entered Emmet's voice whenever she mentioned Sir Denzil Loxley by name.

He was tall and spare, in fact thin to the point of being cadaverous, though the skull-like face Nichola had glimpsed the previous night was not quite so sinister by daylight. For all that, the sunken eyes and hollow cheeks of this dark shadow of a man were alarming enough, and Nichola, wondering how he could have sired such a beautiful offspring, felt herself shrink away as he came into the room and sat down opposite her.

"You're delivered then?" he said, his eyes raking her body.

Nasty old creep, she thought and aloud answered, "Yes, as you can see. I gave birth to a daughter some days ago."

"Is she well?"

"Perfectly, thank you."

He glared at her. "And where are your manners? Was it not your habit to call me Sir?'

"It was, but now that I am a mother it is no longer," Nichola answered calmly and watched him go white. Good, she thought, having taken an instant dislike to the man.

"Mind yourself, Arabella," came the answer, not shouted but hissed, which was altogether more alarming. "While you're under my roof I'll have obedience, d'you hear?"

She could have retorted contemptuously, Nichola knew that, but she sensed danger in Denzil Loxley and a warning bell sounded in her brain. For her own sake and that of the baby it might be better if she acted meekly; yet to be completely cowed went against the very nature of her spirit, so she compromised.

"I'll do as you wish as long as I'm here," she said.

"And what do you mean by that?"

"That one day I hope to leave this place."

Surprisingly, Sir Denzil answered, "It is an outcome for which I pray daily."

Nichola stared at him. "You want me to go?"

"I want you to make another match. I want you to have your own household. That is a matter of utmost concern to me."

"Oh, I see." The actress was wildly curious. "And is it the custom that I should go looking for a husband myself or do you do that for me?"

An expression of pure astonishment crossed the skull-like face. "You know perfectly well what the custom is. Only the extremely wealthy select their children's partners. We come from the minor gentry and you were free to choose Michael Morellon, provided his father and I gave our consent. But now that you have a child, now that the country is dividing, things will be different I can assure you."

"What will happen?"

"You'll have to content yourself with what is left over."

"My God," Nichola exclaimed without stopping to think, "I'm glad this isn't real."

There was a profound silence broken by Sir Denzil saying, "Will you explain that last remark," and the lips in the bony face compressed into a harsh line, making it quite clear that his words were an order not a request.

Emmet cleared her throat, breaking the intensity of the atmosphere. "Mistress Arabella's been fair mazed since her confinement, Sir. Sometimes she don't talk at all sensible."

"Obviously not. Arabella?"

She couldn't resist it. "It's true enough. You could say that the birth turned me into a different person."

Even though she hadn't looked up, Nichola could feel Emmet's eyes on her and knew that the girl was gazing at her in a sharp, questioning way.

Sir Denzil stroked his lean chin. "Well, there's little room for strangeness in anyone's life these days. I suggest you try and put yourself to rights, and quickly, too."

Miserable old bastard, Nichola thought. Suppose his daughter had really gone mad. I wonder what he'd have done. Put her in solitary confinement most likely.

Out loud she said, "Would you like to see the baby?"

He started, obviously aware of his breach of good conduct.

"Certainly. I take it you have named her Constance."

"No, I haven't. She's to be called Miranda. Why?"

The skull face went white. "You know perfectly well why. That was your mother's name and your daughter should follow suit in her honour."

"I'm afraid it's too late. Miranda has been decided upon," Nichola answered, then wondering if she had gone too far, added, "Perhaps she could use Constance as her second name."

There was a momentary hush during which Sir Denzil went even paler, then he snarled, "You will not cross me like this, Arabella. I am master in my own house and as long as you are beneath my roof you will comply. The child is to be baptised tonight and shall be named as I wish."

Nichola stood staring at him, wondering how any girl could have survived in his clutches, then she reasoned that he was probably not representative of the age in which he lived, merely a singularly unpleasant man.

Eventually she said, "Do what you like. You cannot stop me thinking of her by any name I choose."

Without another word, Sir Denzil swept from the room, not even bothering to take a look at his grandchild, leaving Nichola gazing after him feeling more distressed than she would have believed.

"What a pig of a man!" she exclaimed as soon as he was out of earshot. "Poor Arabella, oh poor little thing."

"Look," said Emmet, speaking quietly but with a nervous intensity, "you mustn't go on like this, Mistress. I'm beginning to believe now that something *did* happen to you during the birth, that somehow you *are* different even though you look the same. But if that's true I beg you to hide it. Sir Denzil's always been an iron man and he won't put up with it. He was hard with your mother, though it fair broke him up when she died, and he'll make your life hell too if you resist him. The best thing you can do is agree with what he says until your strength has returned and you're feeling more your old self."

"But Emmet darling," said Nichola, taking the girl's hand between hers, "it's my *old self* that is rebelling. Believe me or believe me not, I am used to a different kind of father, one whom I could push around. Having to give in to this old bugger will be sheer hell for me."

Emmet looked at her seriously from a pair of eyes of which, Nichola noticed for the first time, one was hazel and the other blue. "I don't understand what has happened to you, Arabella. You know I don't. So all I ask is that you stop making things difficult for yourself – and for me."

Nichola nodded. "Okay. I hear what you're saying. I'll toe the line until I can find a way to escape." She paused, then added, "I think perhaps I would like to see a physician or someone like that. Who knows, they *might* be able to help. Can you arrange it?"

A look of relief crossed the girl's features and Nichola felt desperately sorry for her. "I'd do anything to see you restored. I'll send word to Dr Rich of Oxford this very day," she answered earnestly. "And now I think you should go back to bed. It's unheard of for a woman to be up so soon after delivery."

"One moment more," said Nichola firmly and, hurrying over to the windows, threw open one and leaned out, determined to see something of the place to which her mind had been so abruptly sent.

The gardens of Haseley Court had obviously been designed in an earlier century, for Nichola found herself gazing down on a paved and-cobbled courtyard bordered by crisp box and elegant yew trees. To the right of this lay a topiary garden, full of fantastic beasts and birds. Craning her neck she could see the distant glint of frozen water and guessed the house might well have been moated at some time. Yet in all this abundance there was no colour anywhere for the land lay under snow, a fact which immediately made Nichola wonder what time of year it was.

"What month is this?" she called to Emmet, who was busily straightening the bedclothes.

"March, the nineteenth to be precise."

"The weather's very severe for spring."

"Aye, it has been for days. It seems a terrible thing with all those men on the move."

Nichola turned to look at her. "What *is* happening exactly?"

"Well, I only know what we pick up in the servants' hall but the rumour is that the King left London in January and it was a great mistake, and he'll never get back in. They say he's been wandering about the southern counties with only a few supporters and now has gone to York."

"And what's happening elsewhere?"

"Parliament is in contention with him about the constitution, whatever that is. Your father's said publicly he's with His Majesty but Sir David Morellon is for Parliament. He believes the King is under the sway of evil councillors and doesn't know his mind."

"And the whole country is beginning to split over the issue?"

"That seems to be the long and short of it."

"What a time to be regressed to," Nichola said, meaning it as a protest, a complaint, but feeling instead that same inexplicable thrill of excitement she had experienced earlier. "What an incredible time!"

"You're smiling like you used to," Emmet called out.

And Nichola, putting her hands to her face, discovered that she was.

Chapter Four

After the doctor had gone, Nichola sat alone, staring out of the window but seeing nothing. He had come from Oxford on horseback, a boy carrying his box of remedies and instruments strapped to his saddle, riding close behind. But even as he had entered the room hope had died. Dr Roland Rich, large and honest looking, with bluff features and huge silly blue eyes, Nichola could see instantly, would have not the faintest idea what she was talking about if she were to tell him the truth. Yet once again, some basic instinct for survival had forced the actress to the sticking point.

"I hear you suffered much in childbirth, Mistress," Rich had said by way of opening the conversation. "Ah, tis women's curse I fear. But there, there, both you and the infant have survived and that is something for which we must give thanks."

Heaven help me! Nichola had thought, barely concealing her impatience. Forcing a smile, she had answered, "It is not really my body that suffered, Dr Rich, but rather my mind. Do you deal with cases of mental illness in your practice?"

The silly eyes had narrowed. "Insanity caused by birth is not unknown, of course, though rare, rare. However, Mistress, if I may make so bold a remark, you do not look deranged to me."

Nichola had weighed her next words carefully. "I am not mad, Dr Rich. It is an experiment involving the mind that I want to talk to you about."

He had motioned the boy to put down the box and leave the room. "Experiment?" the physician had repeated.

"Yes. There is a part of the brain that takes over when one is asleep. Would you agree with that?"

Dr Rich had cleared his throat and shifted a little in his chair. "The dreamer's mind, yes."

"Well, it is possible to send that mind on journeys, you know."

"Oh yes?" He had put the tips of his fingers together and regarded her with an unreadable expression.

"Journeys which can take it to other times and places."

Dr Rich had suddenly become very still. "Are you talking magical practices, Madam?"

"No I'm not," Nichola had replied swiftly. "I'm talking about an experiment in hypnotic regression."

She might as well have spoken to him in a foreign language for all he understood. The doctor had stared at her, blinking rapidly. "To regress means to go backwards, does it not? Are you trying to tell me that you have been sent somewhere, Mistress? Have you then been bewitched?"

A warning note had sounded in Nichola's brain and a sudden realisation of the deep waters into which she might be straying had come to her, cold as a chill. The terrible events in Salem, Massachusetts, upon which the play *The Crucible* had been based, had taken place in 1692, fifty years exactly after the year in which she now found herself. A belief in witchcraft was obviously very much alive and common to all classes, and that would include priests and doctors. Sensing danger, Nichola had drawn in breath, wondering how to extricate herself.

"If someone has done this to you," Rich had continued into the fraught silence, "you must tell me their name. Is there anybody in this house that you suspect?"

"Of course not," Nichola had replied, choosing each word with care, "it's just my own foolishness, Dr Rich. The birth gave me strange ideas. I don't know what I'm talking about half the time."

As if he had sensed her deliberate change of tack, Rich's eyes had narrowed even further, a look of cunning flaring in their depths.

"Does your father know about this condition?"

Nichola had suffered the first symptoms of panic. If Denzil Loxley were to be informed that his daughter was bewitched the consequences would be dire.

"Oh yes," she had said casually. "Sir Denzil knows that I have been mazed by childbirth." She had deliberately used a phrase she had heard on the lips of both Michael and Emmet. "That's why he wanted me to see a physician. He felt certain that a man of your skill could soon bring me back to normal."

Rich was obviously not as silly as he looked. "I think I'd best check with Sir Denzil before I proceed," he had said.

"He's not here," Nichola had answered truthfully. "As you know there's talk of war everywhere and he has much to do organising his neighbours."

"Then I must come back. Meanwhile I will leave some medicine for you. If it fails I shall order that you be bled." He had gone to his box and produced a bottle of vivid acid-yellow liquid. "Drink this three times a day after meals."

"What is it?"

"The urine of a hare, an old-fashioned but excellent remedy for dissolving humours affecting the brain. I must also advise you, Mistress, to avoid crowds and overeating and to ensure bowel regularity."

It said much for the low state of her sense of humour that Nichola had not laughed in his face. But she had experienced too close a brush with the superstition of another age to do anything more than meekly take the bottle and promise Dr Rich to try to curb her flights of fancy. Nevertheless he had obviously not been reassured for he had turned in the doorway.

"I shall come tomorrow to see how you progress, Mistress Loxley. And in the intervening hours I want you to think carefully whether anyone has uttered any form of words that could be taken as a source of maleficium." He had paused, obviously considering something else. "Is your child quite well?"

"Very," Nichola had answered hastily. "Healthy and strong I assure you."

"Ah." And with that he was gone.

As the door closed behind him, Nichola had sunk into a chair and wept, as much from relief as anything else. Then she had gone to the table and poured herself a cup of wine and sat with it, gazing blindly out at the grey afternoon, wondering what she should do.

She had to make a decision, that much was obvious. Either she could go on actively seeking ways to return to her old life, probably meeting with superstition and fear at every turn, or she could wait for a chance occurrence, a dream perhaps, or meditation which might induce a trance in which she could think herself back. Yet while she waited how was she to cope? It would appear, Nichola thought gloomily, that she had little option but to take on Arabella's identity completely.

Considering it sensibly, it seemed the only thing to do. She knew she was capable of acting the part, now she must hesitate no longer. Nichola drained her wine glass and suffered a moment of sheer despair before her courage returned and that inexplicable prickle of excitement which she had experienced twice before, laid itself along her icy spine.

From that time on a most extraordinary life had begun. Every day, just as she awoke, Nichola felt a plummeting of her heart, a constriction of her stomach that she was still in Haseley Court, that a miracle had not happened during the night, while her subconscious mind was dominant, sending her back to her own time. Then, after that first shock was over, she was always pleased to get out of bed and spend the rest of the day in a state of wonder, like a child, her disappointment dispersed by everything she was discovering.

Nichola had always been obsessed with her looks and body, like many of her contemporaries, and now she decided that if she was to inhabit Arabella's shell she should set about improving it. In spite of the difficulties posed by seventeenth-century eating habits, she went on a diet and started an exercise routine, a fact which thoroughly startled poor Emmet, who had come upon her mistress, wearing only her small clothes, bending and kicking as she worked out.

"Gracious, Arabella, what devil's play is this? Where's your modesty, pray?"

"Gone when I had the child. Now leave me alone, there's a good girl. I need to get back into shape."

The servant had left the room with the resigned expression she constantly wore these days, convinced that something strange had happened to the girl she had known most of her life, but not at all certain what it could possibly be. She was puzzled, too, by

Arabella's sudden interest in cosmetics, an entirely new departure. Whereas before Mistress Loxley had rarely applied them, now face painting was a daily occurrence. Her lips were rouged to a delicious shade of pink, her cheeks bloomed, her eyelashes seemed strangely darker. In fact it was known to all the servants that Arabella had been visiting the store room where the herbs and compounds were kept and mixing things for herself.

It had been in a moment of impatience, succumbing to a sudden longing to have those sharp chic looks again, that Nichola had almost cut Arabella's thick coils of gleaming hair. Afterwards she realised what a mistake it would have been, and was glad that Emmet had come through the door and angrily asked what she was doing and whether she was trying to ape a boy.

"But I love short styles."

"Then you must learn not to," Emmet had retorted fiercely and the actress, after glaring, not liking in the least to be crossed by another woman, had suddenly burst out laughing. She was growing quite fond of Emmet who reminded her of a robin, all black hair and vivid cheeks, with a dark rose of a mouth, her whole physique tiny to the point of appearing deceptively frail.

The servant had been a tower of strength in fending off the persistent Dr Rich, resembling a bloodhound now that the scent of witchcraft had been trailed before him. Having told him how well her mistress had responded to his treatment Emmett had asked Rich to examine her foot, complaining that she feared arthritis might be setting in. The physician had solemnly informed her that as it was habitual sexual excess which weakened the joints, thus causing the complaint, it was highly unlikely she had more than a sprain. Nevertheless, such delaying tactics had worked, and by the time the doctor was ready to interview Sir Denzil Loxley, Arabella's father had again gone out. Realising that, for the moment at least, she was out of danger, Nichola had addressed herself even more carefully to the role she was now determined to play to the full.

She had continued to feed the baby, despite the fact that it was something of a tie when she longed to be out and about, looking at the house and garden or exploring the countryside. Her dislike of children had by now been tempered to a state of indifference. She could not truthfully say she was fond of Miranda, yet there was still that strangely peaceful quality about the times when she suckled the child. There was also a certain academic interest in watching her grow, something that Nichola had never experienced at quite such close quarters before.

But the aspect of Arabella's life which appealed to the modern woman most was, astonishingly, the beauty of the surroundings in which the girl had lived. Careful questioning revealed that a house had stood at Haseley since the time of William the Conqueror, that much of the present building had been erected in the reign of Henry VIII, that what had once been a moat had now been converted into a small lake full of fish. With the snows gone and birds singing in the gardens of Haseley Court, April came and brought with it the start of a late but flower-filled spring.

One great advantage of spending so much time out of doors was that Nichola rarely came across Sir Denzil, in fact she had by now perfected the art of seeing as little of him as possible. At dinner time though, a meal of many courses served sharp at noon, came their daily meeting. She would sit at one end of the oak table, Arabella's father at the other, and they would converse down its length. As this involved shouting there were often long silences during which Denzil Loxley either stared at his food or at Nichola, a habit which made her increasingly uncomfortable.

It occurred to her, covertly watching him, that Arabella's father, apparently a widower for fourteen years, might harbour unnatural feelings towards his beautiful offspring, who was looking even lovelier since Nichola had added her modern touches. If so, the actress thought, her position might well become untenable and she would have no option but to leave and try to make her own way, though that prospect was so daunting it hardly bore thinking about. However, on this particular day, when the last thing she wanted was to be sitting down for a huge meal with him, Nichola, against her better judgement, finally spoke out.

"Sir, what is it about me that you find so interesting? You have been staring at me for the last ten minutes and I'd be obliged if you'd tell me why."

He quivered, aware that servants were in the room, but had the good grace to look embarrassed. "I'm sorry, I had not realised I was doing so. My thoughts were many miles away."

"With the King?"

"Yes," he said, distractedly.

"And how is the situation?"

Sir Denzil looked at her in genuine astonishment. "You've never been interested in politics. Why do you ask?"

"Because the situation is quite fascinating. There is going to be civil war and I would like to find out everything I can about it."

Sir Denzil attempted to look bland, an expression which did not sit easily on his skeletal features. "Oh, there's going to be war is there? How do you know that, my dear?"

"Because it is fairly obvious," she answered, stepping neatly out of the trap. "The situation is deteriorating daily, I believe."

"Who told you so?"

"I hear you discussing it, particularly with Sir Giles Hoyton."

Sir Denzil smiled, his skin stretching tightly across his bones. "Eavesdropping is not to be commended but if you are eager to learn—"

"Oh, I am." Nichola felt a sense of revulsion that she should have to pander to this terrible man.

"Of course, your mother was too young to take much interest in the day's affairs," he was going on, "though had she lived I dare say she would have done so. She was not without a lively mind but was taken too early for it to develop as it should."

"How old was she when she died?"

"Nineteen. Did you not know?"

"I wasn't absolutely certain."

"As you are aware, she went in labour, giving birth to my son, who also did not live. The loss of that boy grieved me to the heart."

"I wonder you did not remarry and have more children," Nichola answered with the slightest edge to her voice. Women were obviously expendable but the death of a son was an entirely different matter.

"I had no wish to," Arabella's father replied coldly. "Twice was quite enough for me. At least so I thought then."

She almost exclaimed, "Twice!" but stopped herself in time. That he was a widower when he married Arabella's mother was something the girl no doubt would have known. Instead, Nichola answered, "I see," and busied herself with her food.

"I don't believe you do," answered Sir Denzil quietly.

She looked up, startled, and saw that he had motioned to the two footmen to withdraw.

"I think that now you're of an age to understand," he went on, gazing at her reflectively.

A tremendous need for caution overcame the actress. "Understand what?" she asked tentatively.

"That I have always been betrayed by women, Arabella. My first wife disgraced me, my second did not love me. I had no wish – then – to risk unhappiness a third time."

"What exactly are you saying?"

"That the first Lady Loxley committed the ultimate sin. She practiced adultery with one of the footmen, then ran off with him and disappeared into the crowds of London."

"Wow!" exclaimed Nichola, without thinking.

"After a sufficient number of years had passed I was able to have her presumed dead and so was free to remarry."

"Arabe . . . my mother?"

"She came to me pregnant," Sir Denzil stated flatly. "She had had relations with some ne'er-do-well who vanished from the county when he learned of her condition. Her father was in despair and offered her to me."

"Did she have any say in the matter?"

"She was relieved to find a home and a man to give her child a name. She gave her consent willingly enough. So you see, my dear," and Sir Denzil raised his wine glass to her, "I am, after all, only your stepfather. We are not blood related in any way."

Nichola longed to say, And now you fancy me, don't you, you dirty old man? You brought Arabella up, watched her grow beautiful, and then got all the usual itches and urges. I wonder if she was aware of it.

Aloud she said, "How strange that history repeated itself and I had a bastard, too. But Michael and I would have been married had it not been for the situation, so he hardly deserted me."

"I don't want his name mentioned here," Sir Denzil answered angrily. "His father is not only for Parliament but actually one of its members. Indeed he is in London at this very moment helping to organise the Parliamentary forces, as a member of which body his son has offered himself."

"And why are you so violently opposed to them?"

"Because I am a King's man by tradition. The monarchy stands for continuation, for maintaining the status quo. I have never been a lover of change." He paused and drained his wine cup. "And so, Arabella, your betrothal is broken and you are free to marry whom you wish." His dark eyes glowed as he refilled his glass and looked at her over the brim.

In a strangely distant kind of way, Nichola felt sorry for him. It was obvious that he had had a fixation about his stepdaughter for quite some years and had very probably jumped at the chance of ending her association with Michael Morellon. However, Arabella had presumably found him as unattractive as she did, and there had been no hope of any future there.

"I know," she said coolly.

"And would you go unwillingly as a bride?"

The actress answered him with her own ideas, temporarily forgetting Arabella. "I don't think marriage is the be all and end all, if that's what you mean. In fact I think it is probably only important for the protection of children. I'm old-fashioned enough to believe that. However, as children don't really interest me it wouldn't particularly worry me if I stayed single."

Sir Denzil looked thoroughly shocked. "But you have a daughter! How can you say such things?"

"Because I believe them. And now, Sir, if I may, I would like to finish my meal."

And with that Nichola, even though dieting, picked more heartily at her food than she had for some considerable time and refused to speak further.

She carried Miranda, in a basket, out of doors that afternoon despite Emmet's vigorous protests.

"You'll kill the child with too much air."

"Oh rubbish. The poor little thing is getting positively pale. It's not cold out."

Ignoring her, the servant swaddled the hapless infant in a cocoon of clothes before allowing Nichola to carry it outdoors for the first time in its life.

Turning right beyond the cobbled courtyard, the actress walked past the fantastic topiary then made her way down a sloping path to the walled garden. Once there, she proceeded to the centre and sat down upon a stone seat by the sundial, placing the basket beside her and propping the baby up a little so that it could see. Even though this place was mainly used for the propagation of vegetables and herbs there was still a profusion of spring flowers and Nichola, feeling the skittish sunshine of an April day on her face, closed her eyes.

It occurred to her as she sat basking how strange and uncharacteristic it was that she, who adored life in town and used to swear that a blade of grass made her feel faint, was enjoying the beauty of Haseley Court and its rural surroundings so much. For though there was much about life in the seventeenth century that she found appalling – the difficulty of taking a bath, the lack of medical knowledge and, worst of all, the hideous close stools instead of lavatories – its quiet, unpolluted, traffic-free calm was something she could both enjoy and admire. The beautiful clothes, beginning to fit snugly again now that she had worked on Arabella's figure, were another constant source of delight. Nichola was even revelling in a way of life devoid of telephones and television, though how soon it would be before she got bored by this was anybody's guess.

A cloud went over the sun at that moment and the actress opened her eyes as a very rapid shower sent her running for cover, the baby in its basket bumping along beside her. There was a hut just beyond the wall where the gardeners kept their tools and Nichola rushed inside, putting the basket on the floor. Looking down she saw that the child had slipped sideways and was now lying in a most uncomfortable position. A vague sense of pity had her bending over and turning the poor thing, and it was at that moment that Miranda suddenly smiled up at her.

"Good heavens!" Nichola exclaimed, unaware that babies communicated at quite so early an age and, as if to prove that it wasn't an attack of wind, Miranda did it again.

"Well, well," Nichola went on, picking her up and, doing something of which she wouldn't have believed herself capable, tickling and grinning and making silly noises – just to get Miranda to give another toothless, guileless, smile.

The baby, encouraged by its supposed mother's sudden attention, behaved enthusiastically, and had actually got Nichola to laugh when a sudden movement in the doorway had her staring up in alarm. A man stood silhouetted against the fickle sun and for a moment the actress did not recognise him as he stepped into the hut's shadowy confines. Then she saw who it was.

"Michael! What are you doing here? Sir Denzil said you were in London."

"I'm on my way there. There is to be a mass parade of the capital's Trained Bands on 10 May. I shall march with them. But I don't want to talk about that, I came to see how you are, how Miranda is."

"We're well. Look," and Nichola held his daughter up.

In a second he had taken both of them in his arms and pulled them close. Nichola, forgetting all about being Arabella, thought back to her carefree days of easy-going sex and decided that Michael would most certainly have been an asset to The Collection. "You're rather gorgeous," she whispered, at which he looked at her most oddly.

His train of thought was obvious. "And what of you? Has your health restored itself? Have your strange delusions gone?"

"Oh, yes. I'm feeling much better."

"Yet you have altered," he said, staring at her narrowly, "there's something different about your face."

"I've started to use paint."

"So I noticed. But I don't mean that. Something has changed about your eyes, the look in them, the very essence of you."

"Motherhood," Nichola answered simply. "Perhaps I've grown up."

"Whatever it is," Michael replied, kissing the baby, who obligingly smiled, then placing her back in her basket, "it has made you even more beautiful, even more desirable. Oh Arabella, how hard it is to be separated from you like this."

There was raw attraction flowing like a current between them and Michael muttered, his iris-coloured eyes darkening, "Next time we meet it must be for a few hours."

Nichola understood exactly what he meant. "How can you let me know?"

"I'll write to you."

"But if Denzil Loxley were to find out he'd hit the roof."

"What a curious phrase. Listen, somehow I'll get a communication through to Emmet. Will that be satisfactory?"

"It will be nice to hear from you however the message arrives," Nichola answered softly, moving closer to him and smiling.

He swept her up as if she were a doll, and it gave Nichola a start to realise that Arabella was so much shorter than herself, almost childlike in comparison. Held tightly against Michael Morellon, the actress relished his proximity. He might well be a twenty-year-old from another century but she certainly found him as exciting, was as aroused by him, as any of her modern-day lovers. And his kiss left her in little doubt about his sensuality. It was neither hard nor soft, but seemed to draw her mouth against his in a way that Nichola would have thought of as practised, had she not realised by now that Michael was without artifice, that he spoke and behaved in an entirely natural way.

"Do you still love me? Despite all you've been through?" he whispered against her ear.

Nichola answered for Arabella. "You know I do. I shall miss you greatly."

"And I you. But now I must go. I fear Sir Denzil lurking under every bush."

"A very suitable place for him indeed!"

They grinned simultaneously then Michael kissed her again, this time swiftly. "Take care, sweetheart, and of Miranda. I will return as soon as I can."

"Are you going to remain in London?"

"It depends."

"On the Earl of Essex?"

"In the main."

"He can't be the same Essex that Queen Elizabeth fancied."

"It's his son." Michael looked over his shoulder. "I daren't stay talking. I'll get a message through soon." And with that he hurried from the hut, leaving behind him an impression of strength and determination.

"A very pleasant young stud," Nichola remarked to Michael's daughter, laughing to herself at the idea that she could make as many outrageous statements as she wished in private. Then, picking up the basket in which the child was now sleeping, she continued her walk through the gardens, desperately trying to recall everything she could about the outbreak of the Civil War and how long it had lasted. The outcome she knew. Charles I was doomed to go down, Oliver Cromwell to take charge of the country, closing the theatres for good measure.

"Miserable old sod," Nichola said to herself, then realised with the strangest sensation that she had, for the moment at least, been utterly lost in thoughts about England's past rather than her own.

But I must never lose sight of that, she reflected, otherwise I might not get back.

And this made her frown as she wended her way back to the confines of Haseley Court.

Chapter Five

Even though she was dreaming and aware of the fact, Nichola for all that felt afraid. She was alone in a room, its only other occupant the body. She heard with horror the regular sound of a ventilator, the noise it made reminding her of a despairing sigh, and realised for the first time that the body was on a life support system. She strained to look at its face but, as always, found it impossible to do so. And yet she had this inexplicable empathy for the woman – for she could see it was a female who lay there – and longed for her to recover, to be well. Weeping inconsolably, Nichola woke to find the tears still wet on her cheeks.

She had long since relinquished the hope of a miracle, or that sleep would somehow transport her back to the party at Lewis's flat. Now she expected to see the oak bedroom at Haseley Court, the cradle containing Miranda standing close to the great bed, the hangings closed to ensure her privacy. To make matters worse, a kind of bored despondency had taken the place of her initial excitement. Now endless days stretched before her in which she did little except oversee the running of the house, a task which Nichola found totally dull and had as little to do with as possible. And that, other than for talking to Emmet and, less frequently, to Sir Denzil, seemed to be that. She had once visited Joyce Mildmay, the daughter of a near neighbour who nonetheless still lived ten miles away, but conversation with a vapid girl from another century had proved so difficult that Nichola had not bothered to repeat the experiment. Her only interest seemed to be in watching Miranda grow.

But if I'd wanted domesticity and child rearing I'd have gone for it in my own century, for God's sake, the actress thought, and screamed with frustration.

A need for physical love was also partially causing her depressed state, for this spell of enforced celibacy did not appeal to Nichola at all. Thus she found her thoughts turning more and more frequently to Michael, wishing she might hear from him. But there had been no word and she guessed that he was still in London, heavily involved with Parliament's intransigence towards the King.

The actress did not enjoy questioning Sir Denzil – who continued to lust after her while hypocritically attempting to act as a stepfather should – but it was the only way to glean information about what was going on. He seemed a fount of knowledge for a minor Oxfordshire knight and Nichola sometimes wondered if he was some kind of Royalist agent. Yet, if so, it was a secret he guarded well.

From what she was told it appeared that the mass parade of the London Trained Bands of militia, held at Finsbury Fields on 10 May, had gone well. The population of the city had turned out as if for a public holiday, to watch the Earls of Essex, Warwick and Holland take the salute.

"Curse Holland for the popinjay he is," Arabella's stepfather had hissed on hearing the reports. "He was once the Queen's favourite and now he has turned coat. As for that villain Essex, he has refused to join the King at York and has resigned his post as Lord Chamberlain."

A very different viewpoint from Michael's, Nichola had thought, considering for the first time that all life was made up of viewpoints, all valid, all opposing, and that this was the basic cause of mankind's troubles. In Lewis's perception she had been attractive, sexy and a talented actress. In the eyes of her female contemporaries, she had been a ruthless scheming bitch who slept her way to the top.

"Yet it was still *me*," Nichola had said to herself, then had shivered as she realised that she had used the past tense.

As far as the beleaguered King, ousted from his capital, was concerned, the news did not appear to be good. At York, where he had set himself up, only 200 gentry and one regiment had arrived to support him. In fact Charles had been so desperate that on 3 June he had called a mass meeting of the county freeholders, then been surprised when 40,000 people turned up and the gathering had grown entirely out of hand.

"A mêlée," Sir Denzil had described it.

But there had been worse things in store for the benighted monarch. Parliament, daily becoming more confident, had issued Nineteen Propositions, requiring the King to cede his right to appoint his ministers, to give up all claims to the military, even to relinquish the care and control of his children. Not believing for a moment that Charles would so much as consider such a thing, Parliament had put out a further proclamation on 6 June in which it claimed sovereign power owing to the King's incapacity to rule.

Poor little bugger, Nichola had thought, remembering from her history books that Charles I had been of very small stature, a tiny doll of a man, under five feet tall.

Yet, according to Denzil Loxley, then had come the backlash, though he had not used that word. It was obvious to all the uncommitted, who viewed the situation fairly, that Charles could never agree to what virtually amounted to terms of surrender, and there had been a groundswell of sympathy in his favour. On 13 June, the King had issued a counter proclamation in which he denied aggressive intent. And he had followed this by another statement, answering the Nineteen Propositions and warning the nation of the dire consequences, the chaos and upheaval, of an uprising of the people against the monarchy.

"For all that, they haven't listened," Sir Denzil said gloomily, turning from the supper table to stare out at the late June sunshine. "There are miserable little riots throughout the land, with the common people attacking what they believe to be papist houses. And it will get worse this summer, mark my words."

"Are they really afraid of papists or is it just an excuse to get their hands on some loot?" Nichola asked.

Sir Denzil's glowing brown eyes looked at her sharply. "How acute of you to ask, for in my opinion mere spoil and plunder is their aim."

"Typical," said Nichola, "nothing changes. Give a few louts half a chance and there'll be an affray."

"A strange remark from one so young," he answered, using that soft voice which always unnerved her. "What have you seen of life to know that things remain the same whatever the conflict? And what, my sweetheart, is a lout?"

"I meant to say louse," she answered eventually, "it was a slip of the tongue."

"Ah," said Sir Denzil, steepling his fingers consideringly.

There was a silence into which broke the sound of an evening thrush singing a song of sunset. The severe winter and the capricious spring had finally given way. In the gardens of Haseley Court a haze, drenched with the scent of flowers and heady roses, hung daily in the air to be sniffed and relished by the occupants of the great house. Waterfowl dipped on what remained of the moat, then preened the drops of crystal water from their iridescent rainbow feathers. Beyond Haseley land the great elms basked in patches of dappled sunshine, while the cornfields were flecked with drops of blood where the poppies thrust their languorous heads. For Nichola it was a summer without traffic, without exhaust fumes, without tailbacks of angry sweating motorists and, as such, had done much to raise her flagging spirits. Yet the thought that the country was descending to civil war hung constantly over the inhabitants of Haseley Court, including herself.

"Royalist sheriffs are starting to enlist men across the country," Sir Denzil remarked, refilling his wine glass. He was drinking more than usual, Nichola noticed, and wondered whether it was his way of coping with his feelings for her.

"Will you go?"

"How can I? I dare not leave the management of my estate in the hands of a seventeen-year-old girl."

It was difficult to answer, impossible to say that her mind was ten years older and that, had she any liking for such things, she could have coped perfectly well. Nichola remained silent.

"Even though that girl be the most charming, the most lovely in the county," he went on, his skull face animated. "It is a miracle, Arabella, how much the birth of your child has matured you. Before you were a pretty chit, now you are a thoughtful beauty."

The actress stood up. "Thank you for the compliment, Father. I'm afraid that I have suddenly grown tired. Good-night." And she walked from the room without a backward glance. Through the closed door she heard Denzil Loxley mutter an oath and refill his glass. She knew then that the situation was getting dangerous, that one of these days he would have one bottle of wine too many and make some sort of sexual approach.

Great God, Nichola thought, trust me! I had my work cut out dodging randy old men in my own time. Now I'm in another and end up doing exactly the same thing.

Yet much as she longed to get away from Arabella's step-father and seek the safety of the oak room, turning its key in the heavy lock, the essence of the evening was so appealing that Nichola made her way outdoors, passing Emmet still at work as she went.

"What are you doing?" she asked, surprised to see the girl sweeping the kitchen hearth, a job she normally would have considered beneath her.

"Getting the house ready for Midsummer Eve."

"What do you mean?"

"Oh Arabella, you know full well. You used to do this with me not two years since. If you sweep the hearth clean then place a dish of bread and milk by the side it will please the fairies."

Nichola stared at her in pure astonishment. "Fairies?"

Emmet glanced over her shoulder. "Don't say it like that. They are in all places, listening. Look you, Arabella, you may have changed since Miranda was born but you must not mock what you do not see or hear."

It could have been Glynis talking about ghosts. "I don't," Nichola answered automatically.

"Then come sweep with me and we'll leave our shoes by the fire so that the fairies will reward us with a threepence."

"They'll never believe this at home," the actress answered and, shaking her head at her own folly, picked up a broom and started to sweep, leaving her shoes, with their elaborate ribbon roses, neatly side by side at the hearth. Then in her stockinged feet she stepped out into the grounds.

A nightingale was singing in the far woods and the lawns were drenched with the glow of sunset, while the air was heavy with the scent of a night not yet quite come upon the land. Breathing deeply, as if she were drinking wine, Nichola wandered down through the wild garden towards the moat, seeing the enfilade of tall trees, the green waters, turned to crimson by the sinking sun.

"If there's a fairy about," she said cynically, "I hope it will grant my wish and get me out of here pretty bloody fast."

Afterwards she could never explain it, never knew what it was to her dying day, but something moved down at the far end of the moat, something white and flimsy that was gone as Nichola swung round to get a proper look at it.

"This is too much," she gasped, laughing at herself. "I'm starting to share their fantasies now."

And yet something *had* been there, she could have sworn it. Shivering slightly, Nichola realised that her feet were wet and that with the dying of the sun the evening had suddenly grown cold.

The message from Michael arrived on Midsummer Eve while Arabella was out with Emmet preparing the Midsummer fire, to be lit at the moment the sun went down to protect the house from evil spirits. The servant had been up before dawn, gathering herbs while the dew was still upon them, for these were to be cast into the flames to add to the strength of the enchantment.

"All this superstition," said Nichola, though smiling, as she breakfasted on a slice of bread and Marmulate of Cherries made to the master cook's own recipe.

The girl flushed, looking more like a rose than ever. "Did you not sweep the hearth with me, Mistress? And did you not find a coin in your shoe?"

"Yes, but—"

"And who do you think put it there?"

"My stepfather," Nichola answered promptly.

"Not he. 'Twas the fairies and you know it."

And Nichola, remembering the gossamer thing that had fluttered by the waters found herself unable to laugh. Indeed that night, as if there truly were enchantment abroad, as she assisted in the pagan ritual of building a fire, one of the gardening boys who had been heaping twigs beside her slyly put a crumpled piece of paper into her hand.

"Mistress, my Mam said I were to give you this."

"Thank you." His hand remained outstretched and she put a coin into it. "Say nothing to anyone."

She dared not read the note for Sir Denzil had come out on to the terrace to watch, an extraordinary expression on his face as his eyes followed Nichola stacking the bonfire.

He's mentally undressing me, she thought. And suddenly she longed for this vile regression, this foreign age in which she found herself, to come to an end. She wanted to go home to all the bitchery, violence and despair, of the late twentieth century.

"The world was awful and getting worse but it was what I was used to," she muttered, and found that she was sobbing, a raw harsh sound that came from her heart.

"Don't fret," said the gardening lad, entirely misunderstanding. "May my tongue turn black if I betray you."

"Is it that you're missing Master Michael?" whispered Emmet, standing so that her body was between Nichola and Sir Denzil's glittering stare.

"Yes, yes," answered the actress, and it wasn't altogether a lie.

"Well, he'll be with you soon, I reckon."

"Why do you say that?" asked Nichola, convinced that the girl had not seen the note changing hands.

"Because I wished it from the fairies."

And now a different emotion was making her cry, an emotion so strange it was hard for Nichola to come to terms with it. For suddenly she, who had never been highly regarded by her own sex, to say the least, found herself so well liked by another female that the simple soul had made a Midsummer wish for her mistress, rather than herself.

"Come here," Nichola muttered through her tears and pulled Emmet into an affectionate hug.

"I'd die for thee," the girl whispered, "so don't distress thyself more."

"Tell me one thing," Nichola asked in reply, "have you felt that about me recently, since the child was born?"

"More," the servant answered, "because now I know you're vulnerable."

And with that extraordinary remark Nichola had to be content.

She read the letter later that night, by candlelight, behind the drawn curtains of the four-poster bed.

"My darling," it began, "I write from London but will soon be on the move. I shall be in Oxford by the time this reaches you. I will wait for you in Lambs Wood beneath our tree on Midsummer Day between early dusk and sundown. If you do not appear I shall understand but I will be there come what may. With affection, your Husband in all but name, Michael."

Nichola smiled at the way Arabella's lover had signed himself and thought how difficult it was to be cynical with these people from the past, whose sincerity was so patent. Remembering Emmet's gesture of affection, she was once more touched to the heart. Getting out of bed, she went to the window and stared at the bonfire on to which the girl had thrown her herbs to ward off the spirits of the air, whatever they might be. It still glowed brightly and even at this late hour one or two of the servants, forming a circle, were dancing round it.

Thinking hard, Nichola recalled that not only had Cromwell

closed down all public places of amusement but he had also forbidden the celebration of Christmas as a holiday, banned the use of spices because they supposedly excited the passions, to say nothing of vandalising the great and beautiful houses belonging to those who opposed him. But what was concerning her at this moment was the fact that superstitious rites had been much frowned upon by the Puritans, and that the Civil War had seen the end of the harmless type of ritual at which she was now gazing. Trying to think impartially and taking into consideration every folly and foolishness of the King, it was still hard, brilliant man though he might have been, not to perceive Oliver Cromwell as anything but an old killjoy.

Surely I'm not taking sides, thought Nichola as she slowly got back into bed. Oh God, don't let me get caught up in all this. Just help me get back. Please.

For a fear was upon her, a fear that she ruthlessly thrust to one side yet which continued to grow, a fear that she would never get back to the 1990s, that she was cast away in the seventeenth century and would not see her own time again.

It had not been difficult to discover which of the many clumps of woodland near Haseley Court was known as Lambs Wood, though 'our tree' had posed something more of a problem. Yet, undeterred, Nichola had slipped out of the house during the late afternoon, her morale raised by the thought of seeing Michael. The promiscuity which was so very much part of her make-up rejoiced in the idea that he was probably going to make love to her, even though this provoked strange thoughts of two people from different centuries enjoying sex.

Just as the day grew dusky, Nichola finally entered the shadow of the trees, hoping that she was not taking an undue risk by doing so. Then she realised that there was nobody about, that the entire population of England comprised five million people at the most, that going into the woods alone was not the foolhardy venture of the late twentieth century. Even so, her heart was beating fast as she peered through the greenish gloom, calling Michael's name.

"Here," she heard him answer and, following the sound,

found him sitting on the grass beneath a graceful beech, his buff coat rolled behind his head, a blanket already spread upon the ground.

The mocking part of Nichola thought, he obviously came prepared, but she thrust such irreverent ideas aside as he sprang to his feet, such a look of happiness on his squarish features that he put himself beyond criticism.

"Arabella, you're here."

"Yes."

"Thank God for it," and he drew her down on the rug beside him.

Rather to Nichola's astonishment he started to make love to her straight away, kissing her mouth, fondling her breasts, and certainly wasting no time on conversation. And then she realised that to him she was his lover of old, someone who would understand that in a war situation speed was of the essence, that he must return to his command, she to her home. And this urgency, this sense of compulsion, stopped Nichola from her usual habit of stepping outside herself and mentally awarding her lover points. Instead she found herself caught up in the rush of his ardour and was wildly excited, girlishly so, when he entered her. She could not remember when she had enjoyed sex so much as she arched her body into his and returned every move. And then, like a bursting fountain, she reached her climax only to feel Michael Morellon shudder a minute later.

"Oh my love," he said, "I had forgotten what it was like."

"So there has been nobody else?" asked Nichola, out of curiosity.

"No one."

He sank down beside her, taking her into his arms and holding her close to his chest, then with his eyes closed, said, "The birth of the child has changed you."

"In what way?"

"It has freed you of your inhibitions. I have never known you so unrestrained. I could almost believe that silly story you told me of becoming somebody else."

"But you don't?"

His eyes opened again. "How could I? I have only to look at you to know who you are."

Nichola was silent, weighing up whether or not to try and convince him. But the drowsiness of the bird-filled evening, the heaviness of her limbs, the wonderfully peaceful atmosphere, persuaded her otherwise. It simply wasn't worth the effort.

"Have it your way," she answered, and promptly fell asleep in Michael's arms.

It was night when she returned to Haseley Court, a night full of moonshine and stars. Looking up, Nichola thought that she had never seen so many galaxies nor, indeed, such a sweep of dark unclouded sky. It seemed that her own century, with its high-rise buildings, its aerials and industrial stacks, had killed the art of gazing heavenwards and so, laughing a little, she walked back staring upwards, tripping over things and not caring, feeling almost light hearted.

That's what a good roll in the hay does for you, she thought, wishing that Michael had not had to go on to Oxford, that he could have stayed with her for a few days at least. But he had set off on horseback, looking very unprotected for all his youth and strength, and she had waved him goodbye with a catch of the breath, wondering if she would ever see him again, if perhaps she might find her way back to her own time before he returned. And though this was what she wanted more than anything else, Nichola could not help but experience a certain sadness at the idea.

Still staring skywards, she made her way into the house by way of the door leading off the cobbled courtyard. Yet as soon as her foot was over the threshold the tune she was humming died on her lips. Something was wrong, she knew it instinctively, and without stopping to think why, Nichola rushed up the back staircase towards her bedroom. Even before she got there the sound of Miranda crying could be heard quite distinctly and Nichola, guiltily wondering if the baby was on its own, hurried inside.

Emmet was already there, walking up and down with the yelling infant, and turned with a look of relief on her face as the actress came through the door.

"Oh there you are, Mistress. I was praying you'd come back. I think the child's been took sick."

"What's the matter with her?"

"The poor thing's got a nasty cold and it's making her cry."

"Oh, is that all."

"Don't be so hard-hearted. You know that colds can lead to more serious things."

"I'm sure there's no need to worry. Here, give her to me." And, with a certain amount of reluctance despite her earlier panic, Nichola took the screaming red-faced bundle in her arms.

The baby certainly looked terrible, though how much of this was caused by crying and how much by illness it was difficult to tell. All Nichola could think was of how she, who really hated this sort of thing, was going to cope with the situation. And then she remembered Miranda's funny little smiles, her obvious pleasure, as far as a baby could express it, when Nichola had played with her, and felt ashamed of herself.

"Come on now, come on," she said, and rocked the child backwards and forwards soothingly.

"It's your Mamma," said Emmet, "be calm."

Miranda gave a pathetic cough and sneeze but the crying subsided and Nichola, much relieved, went to put her back in her cradle.

"I fear this cold," Emmet remarked suddenly.

"Why?"

"There's something about it I don't trust. I know it looks normal enough but Miranda's chest is tight, I can hear it. And I've heard such a sound before with my brothers and sisters."

"And what happened to them?"

"Two of them got a fever and died."

"Oh, for heaven's sake. Miranda will be fine."

"I'm not so sure. Remember I warned you about taking her outdoors."

"Fresh air never hurt anyone. She's just picked up a cold

from somewhere and will be perfectly all right in a day or two."

But Nichola had to admit that the child's breathing was harsh and laboured and the cold did seem abnormally chesty.

"This illness that your brothers and sisters had, what was it called?"

"Croup. But it's croup with fever that's dangerous."

The actress put her hand on the baby's forehead and it did, indeed, feel abnormally warm. "Then what's the cure?"

"We must stay with her night and day to stop her coughing herself to death."

This can't be real, thought Nichola. Here am I, not even liking children, discussing infant mortality. My God, I don't want to know.

Even so, she cuddled the child close.

"Aren't there any syrups she can have?" she asked.

"I'll go and fetch something. But they're not guaranteed. Only constant care can save her if it's the fevered croup she's got."

And with that daunting warning the servant went out, leaving Nichola alone with the snuffling infant. Not being at all sure what to do the actress attempted to feed her but Miranda seemed too weak to suck and after a few moments gave up and simply lay exhausted in Nichola's arms.

She sat silently, trying to recall everything she knew about croup and realising that it was precious little and of no help to a child from another century who urgently needed a remedy. Wishing that she liked Miranda better, that she had more patience and knew what to do, Nichola sat nursing Arabella's baby, watching the moon as it continued its progress down the sky.

It was like a judgement on her, she supposed, in the few free moments she had over the next three days. Nichola's vow never to have a child, voiced in the twentieth century, had finally caught up with her in the seventeenth. For there could be no doubt that Miranda Morellon, without the aid of antibiotics or any other modern drug, was fighting for her life.

And, equally, there could be no doubt that there was only her surrogate mother, aided by the redoubtable Emmet, on hand to save her.

Nichola had refused to let Dr Rich anywhere near the place, terrified that he might see witchcraft in the case, fearing his terrible remedies of bleeding and purging, to say nothing of the unspeakable composition of his medicines. As for Sir Denzil, other than for putting his head round the sickroom door, he had not come near, making it quite clear that he had very little, if any, feeling for his step grandchild. The only good thing to come out of the illness, Nichola thought wearily, was that she had seen nothing of him, that she had been saved, if only temporarily, from the look in his over-bright eyes. She was sitting on a time bomb with that man and she knew it. Short of eloping with Michael, a plan which was growing ever more attractive, there seemed little hope of escape. It occurred to Nichola like a blow that she no longer dwelled constantly on the chance of getting back to her own time. Yet even this thought was diminished by her inexplicable concern for Miranda.

The baby lay, hot and sweaty, in its cradle, her breathing tight, the croupy cough racking her minute body. She fed little and Nichola was horrified to see that the child was losing weight, in fact she seemed to be shrivelling away. It was the powerlessness of her situation that infuriated the actress, who felt like an impotent idiot.

And then one night, listening to the great clock striking the small hours, a memory suddenly came back. Nichola dimly recalled a time when she had been staying with her grandmother and had been seized with a terrible cough, struggling and heaving to get her breath. And she also remembered being taken to the kitchen in the middle of the night and being held close to a steaming pan, while a makeshift tent was made out of an umbrella – and that this had instantly relieved the symptoms. Her granny had bought a vaporiser the next day, to keep Nichola's bedroom moist, and after that the croup had gone.

The actress sat up in bed and thrust the curtains to one side, to see Emmet dozing by the fire, the baby sleeping fitfully in her arms. Both returned to consciousness abruptly as Nichola rushed over to them shouting, "Steam."

"What do you mean?" asked the servant, rubbing her hand over her eyes.

"We must take Miranda to the kitchens and let her breathe moist air. Come on."

Without waiting for Emmet to understand, Nichola snatched the child up, its wasted form like thistledown in her hands, and carried her down the stairs, holding her close to protect her from the draughts that whistled round the house even in a hot summer.

Something very odd happened at that moment, with Miranda's heart and hers beating almost side by side. For no explicable reason Nichola found herself in tears, tears of a kind she had never experienced before, tears of genuine distress for someone other than herself. She really wanted this baby to get better, she cared, she knew it, and it was a shock that anyone, particularly a child, could evoke such a response in her.

Nichola found herself dropping a kiss on the child's feverish brow, patting its little limbs, and murmuring, "Come on, darling. Mummy will make you well again."

This last emotion frightened her most of all. Up till now she had thought of Miranda as Arabella's baby, despite the pangs of birth she had suffered at the start of the regression. And now here she was referring to herself as Mummy.

"This is sick," she said, but no longer believed it and wept all the more at such craziness until the sheer practicalities of what she had to do forced her to concentrate. Breaking into a run, she descended another flight of stairs.

The kitchens at Haseley Court had been little altered since the time the house was built and as Nichola entered them she was struck yet again by their cavernous size. It was down here that the master cook sweated to prepare the food for the family, assisted by his army of scullions. And if nothing had changed in the design of the kitchens this was echoed in the hierarchy. The cook ruled over all like an emperor, his assistants his subjects, his rewards enough food and drink to feed a dozen as well as a goodly wage.

Yet tonight, with emotions running high, Nichola was relieved to see the man himself snoring in the cellar doorway, no doubt having fought off the combined heat of the kitchens and the summer day with generous helpings of ale. As it transpired, there was no need to wake him for a vast kettle, hanging over the fire, already sang and steamed, and just as Nichola prepared to lift it off its hook Emmet arrived to help her and together they poured the contents into a bowl. Drawing a towel which she had brought with her over Miranda's head, the actress held the baby close to the steaming surface. Then she wept again, this time with relief, as she heard the harsh breathing ease and Miranda's fight for air grow easier.

"It's like a miracle," said Emmet, at her side, "if only I'd known about such things." She looked at Nichola quizzically. "You really love her, don't you? There've been times I must confess when I've not been certain."

It was a question too close to the bone for the actress to answer. Instead she nodded her head dumbly, aware that with her streaming eyes and running nose she was making a bigger fool of herself than she ever had in her life before.

"Oh, Arabella don't," Emmet went on, her own mouth quivering, "I can't bear to see thee like it."

But Nichola was not listening to her, as she concentrated instead on the measured breathing that was coming from beneath the towel. "She's better," she said.

"Aye."

"We must steam the bedroom night and day. Hang damp cloths about the place, keep bowls topped up with hot water. It will cure her, I feel certain of it."

And with that she lifted Miranda from beneath the towel and held her tightly, peering into her face.

"Emmet, I'm going to take her upstairs and feed her. I think she can manage it now. Can you organise the rest?"

"I most certainly can, Ma'am."

"Then hurry up about it. We daren't let her get congested again."

"I would never have thought you had it in you to do this, Mistress. Truly."

"Quite frankly, neither would I," Nichola answered with a cynical smile.

And afterwards as she nursed Miranda in the great bed, a bowl of steaming water placed on an adjacent table, she wondered what was going wrong with her.

"It's your fault," she said to the baby accusingly. "You've wormed your way in, haven't you, you little beast? God, when I think back to what I said – and look at me now! Lewis will never believe it."

But will I ever get the chance to tell him? she wondered grimly. Then, suddenly deflated, Nichola blew out the candle, even though she lay awake until the birds began to sing.

Chapter Six

It had proved to be a strange and disturbing summer, a summer in which Nichola had been compelled to come to terms with a life led as another woman, a summer in which a great historic event had unfolded before her eyes. Yet, most rewardingly, it had also been a summer in which a baby who, unbelievably, she'd saved by herself, had prospered and grown and returned to the smiling creature it had formerly been. And as a result of this miracle the other miracle had been complete – Nichola's passion had become focused on another human being beside herself.

At first, after that dramatic night when she had rushed the child to the kitchens, she had fought against the emotion. But it had been a pitiful contest and she had been finally forced to admit she truly loved the small speechless thing which had been wished upon her. Then, having surrendered herself, Nichola slowly became happy in a strangely empty kind of way, the only cloud on the horizon the gaunt figure of Denzil Loxley, his dark shadow omnipresent about the house and gardens. And yet, much as she disliked the man, she still found it necessary to converse with him in order to gain the latest information about the state of the country.

It seemed that since midsummer the King had enjoyed mixed fortunes. He had been rebuffed by the towns of Hull, Lincoln, Newark and Leicester but the counties of Herefordshire, Worcestershire and Warwickshire had all declared for him. By now localised fighting was breaking out everywhere. In Manchester there had been street rioting and a man had died, the first casualty of the Civil War. So with Yorkshire very cool in its attitude to him, Charles had marched southwards again.

"His Majesty is calling all his supporters to a general rendezvous in Nottingham," Sir Denzil mouthed excitedly, waving a parchment in the air. "By God, this is war. He cannot but challenge them now."

He had sought Nichola out in the orchard where she sat, struggling to read a book, her eyes tortured by the unfamiliar script, Miranda lying beside her on a rug, the sunshine dappling the baby's body, now restored to its earlier substance.

"How is Constance?" he said, reluctantly flicking a glance in the child's direction.

"Much better thank you," Nichola answered, ignoring the fact that he, presumably to make some sort of point, still referred to the baby by her first name whereas the rest of the household did not. She changed the subject. "Will you be going to the King's rally?"

He smiled. "I will go if you will accompany me," he said softly.

With an unerring instinct Nichola knew that this was what he wanted, that he planned to get her out of the house in order to make his play for her.

"I couldn't leave Miranda," she answered quickly. "I am still feeding her."

A slight expression of disgust crossed Sir Denzil's features and Nichola realised that, lecherous though he might be, talk of natural functions repelled him.

"You could bring her in that case."

"Surely a great meeting of soldiers and supporters is hardly the place for a small baby."

"On the contrary," he answered smoothly. "There will probably be many wives present and this will inevitably mean some children as well."

"May I think about it?" Nichola said warily.

He smiled another alarming smile. "Of course you may, my dear." He turned to go but stopped in his tracks and looked at her over his shoulder. "It is my wish that you comply," he added before he went off in the direction of the house.

I'll just bet it is, thought Nichola and wished him at the bottom of a deep pit. For Sir Denzil reminded her of a hammy actor in a horror film playing a character who murders all and sundry before going completely insane.

"If you imagine I'm off and away with you you've got another think coming," she whispered to his departing back, even though there was much in the idea that appealed to her.

She had performed at the Nottingham Playhouse, taking the part of Miss Hardcastle in *She Stoops to Conquer*, and looked back on the city with fondness. And the thought of seeing it as it once had been, of walking streets that had long ago ceased to exist, was wildly tempting. Furthermore, Nichola realised, she had never ventured more than ten miles from Haseley Court, indeed had seen nothing of the leading characters in the Civil War drama. And now here was a chance to observe Charles I and his court at first hand. Schoolgirl memories came flooding back, of Rupert of the Rhine, a kind of cross between Douglas Fairbanks Junior and Errol Flynn, to say nothing of those of a young but randy Charles II.

As long as the old creep doesn't get me alone I should be all right, Nichola thought, remembering that all ladies who travelled took a maid with them. If Emmet were to accompany the party this might well put Sir Denzil off further, she reflected. It seemed to the actress that if she were clever about it, she could have an exciting trip and still keep Arabella's stepfather at arm's length.

She told him of her decision later that evening as they sat in the formidable tapestry room, heavy with panelling and dark wall hangings representing The Chase. Nichola always found the place oppressive and, for some reason, felt more threatened by him in this particular chamber than any other in the house. But nonetheless that is where he was sitting, working at his papers, and she had no choice but to enter. His emaciated face softened and his lips drew back in a grimace as he saw her.

"Come in, my dear."

"I can't stay long."

"Then come for a while."

Nichola smiled thinly, the way in which she always responded to Sir Denzil's words, and took a seat opposite his. "If I decide to go with you to Nottingham I presume I will have Emmet to accompany me?"

He frowned. "You would have a servant, of course. But Emmet is too valuable here. She knows too much of the way this house is run. I could not spare her."

It was on the tip of Nichola's tongue to say, "Then I shall not go", but she thought better of it. Sir Denzil could dig in his heels over certain matters and she knew by the look on his face that this was one of them. "But I would be accompanied?" she persisted.

"Most certainly." He paused. "Do you not think that, after all, it might be better to leave the child behind? She is not yet six months old and it could well be a hazardous journey for so small a creature."

"But you said I could take her with me."

"Of course you can, my dear," Sir Denzil answered smoothly. "I was merely observing that a journey of such magnitude could prove dangerous for any infant, let alone one that has been so recently ill."

Nichola thought furiously, sensing that she was trapped. "I am feeding her, remember."

"Surely you could cease to do so."

"I had not planned on that quite yet."

The usual look of distaste appeared around Sir Denzil's mouth. "That is women's business, not mine. I am merely questioning the advisability of exposing the child to such risks."

He had sensed that she wanted to go and had backed her into a corner, for he was absolutely right. It simply wouldn't be fair to drag the poor little thing half way across the country to a vast military rally.

"I don't know what to say," Nichola replied lamely.

"Then let me speak for you. It would do you good to venture forth, my child. You have been housebound for well over a year now. Besides, it is my wish that you accompany me and I am still master here, albeit an indulgent one."

He smiled in what he imagined to be a playful manner and Nichola, sickened, felt obliged to cut the interview short. She stood up and curtsied, something she rather enjoyed having learnt how to do so correctly at drama school. "I will give your words careful consideration. Good night, Father." She deliberately stressed the last word.

"Good night, Daughter."

As she closed the door behind her Nichola saw his hand reach out to pour himself another glass of wine and knew that he was nervous lest she should refuse.

Emmet was waiting in the bedroom, staring out of the window, her slight back turned, her arms leaning on the sill, and did not move as Nichola came in, obviously absorbed in thoughts of her own. The actress studied the girl in silence, marvelling at the apparent fragility which masked such a tough little individual. For in her rosy way, her strangely coloured eyes only adding to her charm, the servant was arrestingly pretty. Furthermore she was the only female whom Nichola could truly call a friend.

"Hey," the actress called now, lazily, just as if she were back in her own time, talking to a contemporary, "what shall I do? The old creep wants me to go with him to Nottingham to attend the King's rally but I daren't drag Miranda there, dare I?"

Emmet wheeled round, obviously startled. "Creep?" she repeated.

"Sir Denzil Lecher Loxley."

"Oh Arabella, how can you call him that?"

"Because he is. He fancies me rotten. Hadn't you noticed?"

"He has shown a partiality for you these last few years, I must agree."

"Was he a child molester?"

"Now don't start talking strange again. I hate it when you pretend you can't remember. I thought you were over all that."

"I am, I am," Nichola answered, quite unable to upset the girl these days. "It's just that sometimes I need you to remind me."

"Then here's your answer. He never laid a finger upon you, I can swear to that. But his eyes burned holes in your clothes, at least that's what my Mam used to say."

It was such a descriptive phrase that Nichola burst out laughing. "I would like to meet her one day, she sounds good fun."

Emmet's face fell. "But you know her, Arabella. She nursed you through measles."

"So she did," Nichola answered swiftly. "I recall it now. Anyway, what shall I do about Nottingham? He says you are not to accompany me."

"I'd go," Emmet said firmly. "'Twould be a wonderful chance."

"But I don't want to be alone with Sir Denzil."

The servant looked thoughtful. "Can't you strike up a friendship with another woman and stay very thick with her?"

"But that doesn't take care of the nights."

"Lock your door," Emmet said practically.

"And what of Miranda?"

"I'll get a woman from the village to nurse her."

"I don't like the thought of it."

"It's that or staying at home, Arabella. And you've done her proud. Many a gentry lady would not even consider feeding her child."

"When will she finally be weaned?" Nichola asked curiously.

"At any time between one and three years."

"Good heavens, as long as that!"

Emmet gave her a reproving look. "You know it is."

Nichola smiled. "So I do."

They set out for Nottingham on 16 August, travelling across country to Northampton and then taking the road to Leicester and Derby. Despite the evil conditions, the constant bumping and clattering, Nichola could not take her eyes from the window of Denzil Loxley's coach. It was like looking at a foreign landscape as she gazed at a tree-filled countryside which undulated towards blue horizons, where all she had ever known in her own time was the relentless grind of motorways. Huge uncluttered skies hung above them, the lazy summer clouds throwing a pattern of changing light and shadows over both field and forest. From time to time Nichola glimpsed houses set in parkland, neatly arranged flower beds and bowling-greens set about them, their fine timbers and long peaked roofs a breathtaking study in the architecture of another age.

There were cornfields everywhere, some already harvested, and she caught dazzling glimpses of orchards bearing apple and cherry and plum trees. Not far from these would lie a village, its humble cottages clustered round a green. And in a verdant meadow, kneeling beside a stream, Nichola spied barefoot milkmaids washing their pails. She had never seen anything quite so open nor so lovely, yet equally so deserted and so lonely. For the first time the fact that the entire population of the kingdom only comprised five million people truly came home to her.

Yet the road itself was relatively busy. Sir Denzil's coach was not the only one emblazoned with colour and gilt, though his equipage was modest in comparison with some she saw. And as well as these magnificent conveyances there were carts full of people trundling along the grass track.

"Is it usually as crowded as this?" she asked Arabella's stepfather.

"Indeed not. These must be King's men making their way to the rendezvous."

There were solitary riders too, their horses galloping at full pelt.

"How can they go on like that?" Nichola asked. "Don't the animals get exhausted?"

"If they are privately owned their riders would rest them overnight. But those in a hurry would come by post-horse and pick up another beast at the next stage in order to continue their journey."

"So that's how people get about! By a network of hired horses."

"Of course it is," Sir Denzil answered impatiently. "What is the matter with you today?"

Nichola did not answer, too caught up in the bustle and excitement generated by seeing the King's highway crowded with his loyal supporters making their way to Nottingham in answer to the call. Yet highway was really too grand a title for this trail which meandered through fields bordered by woods and streams. Too narrow to allow coaches to pass one another without jostling, it was really little more than a glorified bridle path. Considering this, Nichola realised that its small proportions might well have made the number of people travelling on it appear larger than it was, for she seemed to remember vaguely that the King had been ill-supported for this first vital rally of the Civil War.

"Poor little man," she found herself saying under her breath and was aware that Sir Denzil had patted her hand, asking, "What's that you say?"

His attitude had changed very subtly since they had left home. Much as Nichola had feared, away from the constraints of his own surroundings, he had become more attentive, more lover-like. She was certain that he was on the point of asking his step daughter to marry him, offering, no doubt, security and money and a home for Michael Morellon's love child.

And what, Nichola wondered, would the real Arabella have answered? Would she have told him to get lost or accepted in desperation?

But it was too difficult to imagine the thought processes of a young female from another century, a century in which it was virtually impossible for a woman to make her way alone, particularly with a bastard child to support.

"I said will we be in Leicester soon?" the actress replied quickly.

"By night fall. We'll stay at The Ostrich."

"What a great name."

Arabella's stepfather looked at her curiously. "You use such odd phraseology on occasion."

"Forgive me, a slip of the tongue," Nichola answered.

Yet for all the smoothness of her reply there was an air of decaying menace about the man that she found distinctly unnerving.

"Will others be there too?" she continued, remembering Emmet's advice to make a woman friend, and already disliking the female servant that Sir Denzil had chosen to go with them.

"No doubt. It would seem that the King's call for all subjects who can bear arms northwards of the Trent and southwards for twenty miles to come and serve his cause has been heeded."

"But we live further away than that."

"Those Royalists who are privy to the rendezvous will journey to Nottingham, be it from however far."

"Do you intend to fight for him then? Will you actually join his army when you get there?"

The skull face broke into a grimace. "Alas, my health does not allow that."

"Really? What's the matter with you?" Nichola asked curiously.

"An affliction of the lungs which would not survive the rigours of the battlefield."

"Then why bother to go?"

"Take care of your tone, Mistress, your questions are baldly asked."

Nichola ignored him. "Tell me," she persisted.

"Because I am loyal to my sovereign. I can pledge money, horses and men if not myself."

"Oh I see."

"And there may well be others in the same position. Not all are able to leave their homes in order to take up arms."

But I bet they will, Nichola thought, wondering whether his illness was merely a convenient excuse or if he really suffered from something unpleasant. Judging by his wasted look and general demeanour, he probably was a sick man, she decided, and considered the idea that he could be a victim of tuberculosis.

This notion and the prospect that poor Arabella might have been forced to marry the man occupied her mind until the coach turned into the cobbled courtyard of The Ostrich. And it was only then that Nichola remembered that *she* was Arabella and that the problem was just as much hers as it was the girl's whose body she inhabited.

The inn itself turned out to be splendid, very old and heavily beamed, and it was with a start that she grasped the fact it was actually comparatively modern, obviously having been built in Tudor times. For the rooms were of the kind that twentieth-century people would have travelled miles to stay in, low ceilinged and enchantingly shaped, and Nichola stood looking about her with pleasure as Margaret, her personal maid, unpacked her dresses and shook them out.

"Shall I help you change now, Mistress?"

"Not on your life. I need a drink first."

The woman curtsied, but not graciously, obviously disliking Arabella, perhaps for some slight in the past that Nichola knew nothing about. "Very good."

The actress caught herself thinking that the servant was like a forerunner of Mrs Danvers in *Rebecca*, and hoped that she would manage to stay civil to her for the duration of what was obviously going to be a closely confined journey.

"Do get some refreshment yourself," she said politely over her shoulder as she left the room and started to descend the wooden stairs.

Though no expert in the history of architecture, Nichola felt certain that the inn was indeed Elizabethan for the staircase had an open well and was decorated with carved newels. And it was through this very well that she glanced down as a noise at the door leading from the courtyard attracted her attention and she looked to see who had come in.

A man stood in the entrance, a man dressed in travelling clothes of sombre black highlighted by a slash of scarlet at his belt, the same colour echoed again in the plumes of his sweeping hat. As he moved his hands, withdrawing his gloves, Nichola saw a diamond of great splendour flash in the dimness of the hall. Absolutely fascinated, she watched intently and at that moment, conscious that he was being observed, the man looked up. Gypsy's eyes stared into hers, eyes the colour of harvest, of cognac, of mellow days and autumn fires, eyes that held within their depths the green dark glow of freshwater streams.

Smiling a little, the man swept off his hat and a tumble of black hair fell forward, hair worn as long as Michael's yet very different in its texture and quality. For where Arabella's sweetheart had long straight brown tresses, this fellow had a mop of curls, dark as a rook's and equally shiny.

"Your servant, Ma'am," he said, and bowed.

Nichola had a brain storm and forgot all about Arabella and the time in which she was living. Instead she grinned and answered, "My goodness, I wouldn't mind you in my Christmas stocking."

He looked puzzled. "Christmas? But it's only August."

"I know. I'm sorry. I wasn't thinking." And with that Nichola composed herself and made her way down the stairs to where he waited.

The man bowed again. "Joscelin Attwood, at your service."

"Nich ... Arabella Loxley, how do you do?" And she held out her hand for him to shake. Instead he kissed it. "A pleasure, Mistress."

It was an interesting face she looked into, saved from any hint of femininity – an impression created by the long lashes veiling the brilliant eyes – by his other features. For the stranger had a broad intelligent forehead beneath the curling hair, a long thin aristocratic nose, a wide mouth and an engaging smile. It was ostensibly the face of a rogue, a scamp, yet it was too thoughtful, too clever, and had a certain air of dignity which belied his mischievous looks. His body, too, was that of a man who knew how to conduct himself. Of medium height and build, it combined a certain strength with an innate elegance which Nichola thought could only come from centuries of good breeding.

"You are staying here?" he asked, obviously weighing her up.

Dragging her attention away from her contemplation of such a fascinating man, the actress answered, "Yes, with my father. He is making his way to attend the King's rally at Nottingham."

Then she wondered if she had spoken out of turn and the newcomer might be a Parliamentarian. As if he had read her thoughts, Joscelin said, "I am bound there as well. His Majesty has no choice but to stand firm and he's going to need every loyal man he can get."

"He certainly is," Nichola answered instantly, only to see Attwood shoot her a penetrating glance.

"You have studied the situation?"

"Of course. These are interesting yet disturbing times."

He smiled with amusement. "You seem ahead of your years, Ma'am. For I vow there are not many women of tender age who dabble in politics."

"Then more fool them," Nichola answered tartly. "Anyway I'm twenty-seven."

It was out before she could think and she saw Joscelin's face darken with surprise. "Good God, I would have put you at ten years less. Forgive me, but I have a daughter of almost sixteen and you look her contemporary."

It was an awkward situation heightened by an inexplicable sense of disappointment that he was married. However, her embarrassment was saved by the unmistakable sound of Sir

Denzil Loxley's soft tread on the staircase behind her. Whirling round, for once almost glad to see him, the actress said hastily, "This is my father, Sir. Sir Denzil Loxley of Haseley Court."

"Oxfordshire?" asked Joscelin and, on seeing Arabella's stepfather nod, added, "Perhaps you know my cousins, the Knollys. They have a house near Henley, Greys Court."

"I have heard of them, of course, though we have never actually met. Are you by any chance also connected with the Avons, Sir?"

"My older brother is the Duke."

Sir Denzil bowed. "It is a pleasure to make your acquaintance, my Lord. Our fathers, I believe, met one another on several occasions."

"Indeed? Then it will give me great pleasure if you and your daughter..." his eyes swept over Nichola with that same expression of disbelief, "...would join me for supper. The landlord is setting a table for me in a private room."

In Nichola's terminology, Sir Denzil oozed charm. "We would be delighted to do so. There is nothing that brightens a stay in a country inn more than meeting new companions."

"Then as soon as I have washed off the dust of the journey I shall join you."

But it was dark by the time they all sat down at table, the candles glowing in their silver sticks, presumably the best the house had to offer, the August sky still faintly streaked with fingers of damson. As it so often did, a feeling of unreality crept over Nichola and she imagined herself taking part in a film, half expecting to look out of the window and see a bevy of cameramen and lighting engineers following all she did. This sensation of illusion had been tempered while she had remained at Haseley Court by a certain familiarity with the house, but now that she had been launched into the outside world, was traversing a country as strange and foreign to her as if it had been another shore, the dream-like quality of her life seemed stronger than ever. Without meaning to she sighed, then realised that Joscelin's remarkable eyes had fixed themselves firmly upon her, a question in their depths.

He had not changed his clothes but had obviously shaved and combed his hair, which now hung to his shoulders in slightly more organised curls. Staring at him covertly Nichola wondered how old he was, yet could not imagine that he was much over forty. Hoping for a clue and also thinking of a clever way out of her earlier *faux-pas* she decided to ask him.

"You said that you had a daughter of my age, Sir. If I may remark you scarcely look old enough."

"Arabella, what next!" admonished Sir Denzil, but Joscelin was already speaking.

"I am thirty-eight but I believe my daughter is a great deal younger than you are."

Loxley's thin eyebrows rose but before he could speak Nichola cut in. "I thought you said she was sixteen, Lord Joscelin, in which case I only lead her by a year."

"Really? I could have sworn—" He did not finish the remark, instead raising his wine glass he said, "Then I drink to both you and her." And Joscelin drained the contents, his eyes looking at her steadily over the brim as he did so.

He's not convinced, Nichola thought, and was relieved when the food came in and Joscelin Attwood's attention was drawn elsewhere.

The meal was enormous by her standards though only a simple supper by those of the times. There was a huge tongue which she recognised as a neat's, the ancient word for a member of the cattle family, together with a collar of brawn, a cold game pie, a barrel of scallops, and a stilton, brought to the table with a special spoon for scooping up the maggots. Picking at the food, Nichola found herself drinking more than usual, Joscelin refilling her wine glass whenever it was empty. Well aware that he was watching her, she avoided his bright glance, a glance which she found strangely disturbing. Yet there was nothing frightening or odd about the man, only a feeling that he might well read her mind and would not find it hard to probe every secret she had. With an effort Nichola tried to concentrate on the conversation.

"It's my belief," he was saying, "that the King's position is not strong. His great mistake was to leave London."

Sir Denzil, who was obviously somewhat in awe of his aristocratic companion, said, "Quite so." Then he blurted out, "I receive private intelligence of His Majesty. I am an agent for his cause and will help, if called upon, to rouse the men of Oxfordshire."

"And has this made you privy to certain information?"

"Only that he hopes thousands will now come to support him."

"Parliament has some good men though," Joscelin answered thoughtfully. "Essex and Warwick to name but two. People may well rally to their side."

"They are traitors to their kind," snarled Sir Denzil, drawing his lips back. "What right have members of the nobility to turn against their King?"

"In a circumstance as grave as this," Joscelin said seriously, "I think we will see many strange divisions of loyalty. I fear it will be impossible to count on anyone as an ally."

Sir Denzil's cadaverous features grew even grimmer than they were naturally. "Where will all this end?"

"Who knows? But no good can come out of civil unrest on such a scale." Attwood downed another brimming glass. "But there's one piece of splendid news for all that. The King's nephews, the Princes Rupert and Maurice, are travelling from Bohemia to join him at the rendezvous."

"Rupert of the Rhine?" asked Nichola. "Wasn't he the son of the Winter Queen?"

Both men stared at her. "He is the child of the King's sister, Elizabeth. *Her* nickname is the Queen of Hearts. I have never heard her referred to as anything else." Sir Denzil frowned. "Sometimes, Arabella, you come out with quite extraordinary statements."

She shrugged, refusing to let him annoy her. "I'm sorry, Father. I thought I had heard her called that. Anyway, Rupert will be at Nottingham, will he?"

Joscelin smiled. "He and his party have already landed in Newcastle. As one of the finest swordsmen in Europe he can only be a great asset to his uncle's cause."

A vision of Errol Flynn and Douglas Fairbanks shot into Nichola's mind again and she laughed with pleasure. "I hope I manage to get a look at him."

"If he is in Nottingham at the same time as ourselves I shall see to it that you are presented," Sir Denzil answered pompously.

"I can't wait!" Nichola exclaimed, and she meant it, the feeling of unreality combined with the thought of actually meeting people who had passed into legend, gripping her like a fever.

"I think the Prince will like you," Lord Joscelin answered, his eyes gleaming in the shadows.

"How do you know that?"

"Because, begging your pardon, Mistress, it is said he appreciates beautiful women."

With a sense of shock Nichola realised that this was the first compliment she had received as Arabella, other than for Sir Denzil's pointed comments, and she had a sudden overwhelming urge to look at herself in the mirror. She stood up.

"If you will forgive me, gentlemen, I would like to retire for the night. Today's travelling tired me more than I realised."

How easily, she thought to herself, she aped the speech and mannerisms of the times in excusing herself from the room.

Lord Joscelin made her a bow. "Until tomorrow, Mistress Loxley."

"Indeed," she answered demurely. But once outside the supper room Nichola hurried up the stairs and drew from her luggage the handmirror that had become an essential part of her personal belongings. Staring into it she saw that Arabella was glowing. The corn coloured hair shone like gold in the candlelight, the pretty ringlets moved like ripples as she shook her head. The eyes were brilliant, transformed to a deep sapphire in the shadows, the rose coloured lips were curving.

"Look at you," said Nichola aloud. "A few glasses of wine and you're grinning like a fool. If Lewis could see you now he'd laugh his head off."

But Lewis was a million light years away, as the saying so cruelly went. And Lewis, who liked a sleek svelte girl in his bed, would probably not have laughed at all but found this honeyed beauty from another century completely unappealing and not worth so much as a smile.

Just for a moment Nichola knew a flash of rebellion, a feeling of protectiveness towards the body she had so strangely acquired, then reality returned and with it the despairing thought that she might never see her lover again to ask him what his reaction would, in fact, have been.

Chapter Seven

The bridge at first and distant glance seemed almost too narrow to allow anything more than foot passengers across the fast flowing River Trent. Yet as Sir Denzil Loxley's coach approached its many arched span it became evident that it was in fact wide enough to permit a single conveyance, for a vast queue of carts and carriages had formed on the near bank waiting to go over one by one. Intrigued by the sight of such a jostling throng, all heaving for position, Nichola stared out of the window, her feeling that she was taking part in a vast costume spectacular growing ever stronger.

There were people everywhere, walking, on horseback, in rough hewn carts, in great and important equipages, each one determined to gain access via the Trent Bridge to the town of Nottingham, which lay on the bank beyond. Staring at them, fascinated, Nichola guessed that not all were bound for the King's rally, for swearing pedestrians, much annoyed that their thoroughfare should be so congested, were deliberately placing themselves in the way of the wheeled vehicles, with the result that those coaches lucky enough to have already got on to the bridge were moving at a snail's pace.

Half way across, she could glimpse the gleaming black of Lord Joscelin Attwood's carriage, the Avon coat of arms emblazoned on its side in a great flurry of scarlet and gilt.

Showy! thought Nichola, and smiled as she saw a familiar hat with scarlet plumes, Attwood's head beneath, thrust itself from the coach window, followed by a hand obviously dispersing coins, for people immediately scattered and the carriage moved forward at speed.

"Our new friend is across," she remarked, much amused.

Sir Denzil did not answer and Nichola saw that his eyes were closed, though she doubted whether he was sleeping for his lips were moving as if in prayer. Despite the apparent piety of this action it made her shiver, wondering what thoughts were going through his festering brain and suspecting that they most probably were centred on her.

An hour later, Arabella's stepfather not seeing fit to hand out a *douceur*, they had managed to traverse the bridge's narrow confines and were entering the town from the south. To the left and westwards Nottingham Castle dominated the skyline, perched on a rock rising well over a hundred feet above the meadows of the River Trent, an awe-inspiring sight. When Nichola had appeared at The Playhouse she had visited the ruins and the castle museum and been sorry that virtually nothing remained of the fortress where, according to legend, the wicked Sheriff had once confronted Robin Hood. Now, even though it had a somewhat ruinous air, she was able to absorb something of the castle's power and majesty and could imagine its magnificence at the height of its splendour. To her astonishment Nichola also observed a river flowing beneath the castle's outer walls, a river which had presumably been used as a source for the moats, but which in her century had long since ceased to exist.

The carriage turned in the direction of the mighty building, hugging the fortress's outer walls, then came to a halt before an ancient hostelry nestling between the ramparts and the river, in fact built into the very face of the rock on which the castle stood. As memory after memory came back to haunt her, Nichola read the legend 'The Pilgrim' painted on a swinging board. Time became crazed as she remembered the future, seeing herself having a drink in this very place, then named 'The Trip to Jerusalem'. Her escort had been a fellow actor, destined to be her lover before too many days had elapsed. At the time they had both been enchanted to discover that it was the oldest pub in England. Trembling at the realisation that she had set foot in the inn before in what, more or less, had been another life, Nichola turned to Denzil Loxley as the carriage drew to a halt.

"We're not going to stay here are we?"

"Of course. Why do you ask?"

"It doesn't look very comfortable, crouched in the rock like that."

"The other grander places are bound to be full, besides, I thought this historic building might appeal to you. It once used to be the castle brewhouse and a stopping place for those knights and men called to crusade against the Saracens." He peered closely. "You have gone very white, my dear." And Sir Denzil took her hand between his.

Hurriedly, Nichola answered, "I need some air, that's all." And with that she opened the carriage door and, without waiting for the three steps to be put in place descended, somewhat clumsily, to the ground below.

Before her flowed the gleaming river, a slithering sparkle of serpent grey beneath the strangely sullen skies, the wind, unusually strong and cold for the month of August, whipping up waves and whirlpools on its glittering surface. On the shore stood a windmill, sails whirling in the enthusiastic breeze, while a companion mill could be seen a little further down the bank. This then had been the castle's source of those two essentials, bread and beer, its connection to the fortress through a series of caves, each one barred by a gate, that loomed behind her.

Nichola had never felt more alone than at that moment, the grim building on its outcrop dominating everything, the prospect before her a desolate waterway, flanked only by one or two dwellings, the sole sign of life a fisherman casting his lines from the further bank. Then the knowledge that this river had vanished long since, in fact had totally disappeared, daunted the actress so much that she began to shake even more violently as an extraordinary idea gripped her.

Standing in this spot, looking at a scene unimaginable to modern eyes, it suddenly occurred to Nichola that it was *this* that was real and that her life as she had lived it was becoming the dream, the thing of unreality and little substance.

Alone on the riverbank, her brain trying to cope with the enormity of the concept, Nichola was paralysed by fear, terrified that the past in which she now found herself was about to consume her and take her for its own, that Nichola Hall, as such, had started to disappear and might never come back again.

She excused herself from supper, full of such dreadful notions that the thought of making conversation was quite beyond her. Cramped in her little room, the rock face only a hair's breadth away, Nichola lay on her bed, watching through the tiny window as night fell over the crowded city and the glint of the vanished river slowly disappeared into the dusk.

She must have slept then for the dream came, the first time for quite some while. Once again she was in a hospital room looking at the body attached to its life support machine. Lewis sat beside the bed and Nichola saw that he was crying. As with everything he did, he wept beautifully, almost as if he were being observed by an audience.

"Oh God," he was saying, the memorable voice resonant, "did I do this to you? Did I really do *this*?"

The body lay unresponsive, but for all that he got up and began to quote *The Crucible* to it, reenacting a scene between John Proctor and Abigail Williams. He interspersed every other line with the words, "Can you hear me? Oh please listen and remember." Yet the body remained inert, the only other sound in the room the rise and fall of the ventilator.

In the dream Nichola called out Lewis's name and saw him start and lean towards the body, an extraordinary expression on his face. But after a moment his features once more grew grave and wiping his eyes with his handkerchief, he stood up.

"I'll come back next week," he said to the silent form. "I'll keep trying. Oh, darling, I can't believe that such a thing has happened. I really can't."

The scene started to fade and Nichola felt as if she were falling down a long black tunnel and, in her sleep, she began to call out. And then a repeated sound awoke her and she sat upright in bed, realising that she was in that strange little inn set within the rock and that someone was tapping on her door. Frightened as she was by what she had just experienced, her reactions still worked fast and, convinced that it was Sir Denzil, she called out cautiously, "Who is it?" Nobody answered and then she saw to her horror that the door was slowly opening.

He stood in the entrance clad only in a long white nightshirt, his gaunt body making him look exactly like a walking corpse.

"What do you want?" Nichola whispered angrily. "It's the middle of the night in case you hadn't realised."

"I heard you cry out, my dear, and wondered if any ill had befallen you."

"I'm perfectly all right," she answered tersely. "Please go back to bed."

"I thought you unwell," he persisted.

"Then you thought wrongly, Sir."

Still Sir Denzil hesitated but Nichola was saved any further embarrassment by the unexpected sound of footsteps making their way steadily upstairs from the rooms below. "Somebody's coming," she stated loudly. "Goodnight, Father."

And with that she turned over in bed and closed her eyes. She was taking a risk, she realised, only too aware that he might enter the room and shut the door behind him rather than be observed. But after lingering a moment longer, Sir Denzil obviously decided on discretion and with relief, Nichola heard him walk softly away.

From the moment she woke the next morning, heavy with dreaming and an awareness that she had only just escaped Loxley's attentions, Nichola had a feeling, almost a premonition, that the next twenty-four hours would be momentous. And, indeed, when she set out on foot to go into town, her maid walking a pace behind her, and headed in the direction of the lace market, a craft that had been started in Nottingham as early as the fourteenth century, it seemed that everyone else was aware of it too.

There were people everywhere, finely dressed gentlemen with stately bearing, hard faced men on horseback, and what looked like an entire regiment of foot soldiers, their breast plates and helmets gleaming in the pallid sunshine. Even if the rumour had not been on every lip that this day, 22 August 1642, the King would declare war on Parliament, the atmosphere alone would have been enough to confirm that great things were afoot. The crowd had that awful air of jocularity which always seems to walk hand-in-hand with disaster, there was an almost tangible atmosphere of frenetic excitement abroad, and everyone seemed to be laughing and drinking toasts. In fact it was a typical scene, Nichola thought drily, of a nation standing on the brink of war.

After the events of the previous night she had wanted to spend as much of the day away from Arabella's stepfather as possible and so took her time about her purchases of lace, then strolled slowly back to The Pilgrim only to find Sir Denzil waiting for her, white-lipped with anger.

"Where the devil have you been?" he asked furiously.

"Buying lace. Why?"

"Because I've been looking for you everywhere. They say the King will ride into town this afternoon, his children and nephews with him. I swear to God if I miss anything I'll have you whipped."

"How dare you?" Nichola answered, rounding on him. "You'll behave civilly towards me or I'll leave here at once."

They glared at one another, frozen in hate, and then Nichola saw that hate turn to something else, saw desire make him foolish, craven almost. "I'm sorry, my dear," he said in a placatory tone which the actress found quite sickening, "it is just that I believe this will be such a great day in our history that I do not want to miss a moment."

"Then go ahead without me," she answered, "I'll join you later."

But he would have none of it, bustling her into a cloak against the cold wind which still continued to blow gustily off the river, then walking her briskly to the market square. A light rain had started to fall as they left the inn and, looking up, Nichola saw that the skies had clouded to a shade of polished pewter. The sunshine of the morning had vanished and with it, apparently, the good mood of the citizens. Now everyone seemed morose, dismal indeed, and it was only the King's men, with their beautiful clothes and striking uniforms who added gaiety to a suddenly sombre scene. Sir Denzil, though, appeared to notice nothing of this as he took his place, rubbing shoulders with both loyalists and the curious alike, all waiting for their sovereign to enter the town of Nottingham and set his seal upon their fate.

At some time in the afternoon, Nichola did not know exactly

when, he finally came, his immediate family riding behind him, a great horde of courtiers and peers, of which Lord Joscelin Attwood was one, making up the rest of the train. A body of infantry marched at the rear, all of them Yorkshire born and bred. "The scum of the county, them!" said someone in the crowd, but the remark was ignored because whatever one's standpoint might be and however wretched a day, it was still a stirring sight.

The King's horse was white, a gallant beast, and astride it Charles's diminutive figure seemed larger and somehow more important. Almost flanking him, there was no mistaking the future Charles II and his brother James. Faces that Nichola had seen in history books were suddenly flesh and blood, and she hung her head for a minute, unable to cope with that reality. Then she looked up again as the crowd gave a cheer for a figure she did not know, a figure clad in scarlet richly laid in silver lace, a figure who flashed his dark good looks in the direction of the ladies and kissed a gauntleted hand.

"Who's that?" she whispered to Sir Denzil.

"Prince Rupert," he answered, and there was a certain gruff pride in his voice that almost made him human.

Nichola stared in amazement. One of the Civil War's great heroes, one of history's most dashing characters, was riding within a few feet of her. Her feeling that this was a film, that all these people were actors and extras, returned, and she almost laughed at the sheer improbability of everything she was seeing, hearing and smelling. For the rank odour of the unwashed populace, mixed with horseflesh and leather and the sharp pungent stink of the upper classes, their expensive perfumes concealing the fact that they did not bathe, was both awful and overpowering.

As the cavalcade passed, all those who had stood to watch began to march behind, either in a passion of loyalty or simply because they wanted to see what was going to happen next. And in this way Nichola was swept from the market square down a beaten track towards the castle. Ahead of her she could see the King's party climbing the hill just outside the fortress's Outer

Bailey, the great troop of courtiers, loyal peers and soldiers directly behind it. Behind them, in turn, the people of Nottingham were clambering upwards to get a good view of the great events. Breathlessly, she ascended with them.

The King and his family, still on horseback, had reached the top of the hill and drawn to a halt, waiting in silence for the last of the onlookers to get to the summit. The rain which had drizzled all that afternoon now turned into a downpour, sweeping over the high exposed field in veils, soaking everyone present. Nichola noticed irrelevantly that a drip of water had fallen from the brim of Charles's hat and was running down his long fine nose, and for no reason at all this made her want to weep.

It was at this moment that the herald raised his hand and suddenly there was no sound to be heard except for the wailing cry of a baby. Into this stillness, reading from the paper he held and stumbling over the words as he did so, the King's messenger spoke.

"By this act shall be signified that a loyal army shall be brought forth for the protection of His Majesty's person and his prerogatives," the man proclaimed falteringly. The declaration of war had been made.

Other than for the cry of the baby there was an uneasy quiet, broken only by the champ of horses and the moaning breeze, and there was almost a sense of anticlimax that anything so far-reaching should have so banal a start. Eventually, though, as if reluctantly stirred into action by the herald's words, two trumpeters blared out a fanfare which was instantly swallowed up by the wind and lost.

Only then did the King's Standard finally come into view, heaved up the hill by three burly soldiers who were helped to hoist it into the air by a fourth. Just for a precarious moment, as all eyes turned to it, the flag hung lifeless at the top of its pole before the vicious current seized it and streaked the pennant outwards.

Nichola stared upwards as it whipped over her head, not prepared for the fact that it was so vast or so gorgeous. The flag was fifteen foot if it was an inch and the richness of its fabric confirmed that it was made of silk. In mounting admiration she gazed at the illustrious coat of arms of England, together with a crown surmounting a Tudor rose, a fleur-de-lys with coronet above, and the motto *Give Ceasar His Due*.

"It's done," said Sir Denzil grimly, satisfied at last. "We're at war." And with that he let out a cheer which was echoed and re-echoed by the King's party and the soldiery, though Nichola could not help but notice that many of the townsfolk of Nottingham remained silent. Yet Englishmen being Englishmen their one objective as they traipsed back down the hill was to fill the alehouses and either to drink a toast to royal Charles's long life or his damnation.

Thundering past them as the crowd descended came the troop of horsemen and Nichola saw that the King was tight-lipped and unsmiling whereas the Prince of Wales – the future Charles II – and his brother, to say nothing of Rupert of the Rhine, were obviously spoiling for a fight and went whooping downwards like the young bloods they were. Amongst the peers escorting the royal party she again glimpsed Lord Joscelin, his face expressionless, giving nothing away.

"Where are they off to?" she asked as the riders passed by and took the track leading towards the town.

"Thurland Hall. The King is staying there."

"I suppose there will be a celebration."

"Of sorts." Sir Denzil's eyes swept round the now almost deserted field and fastened on the wind-whipped Standard. "However gloomy the occasion it is nonetheless a mighty one. Therefore it is the duty of every loyal subject to propose His Majesty's health."

Horribly convinced that he would make the call to arms an excuse for getting drunk, Nichola said, "I think I'll return to the inn. I've seen enough for one day."

Instantly his hand was under her elbow. "You must drink to the King, Arabella. If you do not I will think that you are taking the other side in this dispute."

Unbidden, thoughts of Michael came rushing back and Arabella wondered where he was and how soon it would be before the Parliamentarians knew that war had been officially declared. No doubt one of their spies was even now heading out of Nottingham and towards London in order to convey the news. Remembering her hour with him in the woods and how loving he had been towards Miranda, Nichola found herself hoping desperately that he might survive what was destined to be a terrible and bloody conflict.

"Well?" Sir Denzil was saying.

"I'll have one glass with you, Sir, but that is all."

If I can get back ahead of him, she thought, I might somehow wedge my door. Remembering Emmet's advice to find a woman friend, Nichola wondered just how much Margaret would do for a bribe and decided to try her luck.

The servant had accompanied them to the ceremony, walking her usual decorous one pace behind, and now made as if to take her leave as they reached the track.

"Where are you going?" asked Nichola, a note of sharpness in her voice.

"Back to the inn, Mistress. I'll not intrude on Sir Denzil any further." And she shot her master a curious look.

It instantly occurred to Nichola that the creature was in his thrall, that she could expect no help from that direction, not even by appealing to her woman to woman.

"Then I'll go with you," she said determinedly. "I have no wish to linger in the town, neither do I want to walk back unaccompanied."

Arabella's stepfather overcame the situation with surprising smoothness. "The simplest solution will be for us to pledge our support at The Pilgrim. I had hoped to go to The Salutation where the King's recruiting officers are already at work, I believe. But so be it. What matters the location as long as we raise our glasses like loyal subjects?"

Wily old bugger, Nichola thought, but had no option other than to concur.

Even though it was late summer the evening was threatening, dank and dark and very cold, and it was a comfort to crowd into the noisesome inn and rub shoulders with the townsfolk. Already the divisions of civil war were showing themselves, for while some openly toasted His Majesty Charles I, others were murmuring in corners, casting surly looks at all those who supported the King.

Nichola, observing in silence, wondered what had eventually happened in Nottingham, whether it had declared for Charles or against him, and how long it would be before these people were either at each others throats or not daring to publicly voice their allegiances.

Yet a more pressing matter was the need to extricate herself from Sir Denzil, already well in his cups and feasting his eyes on her, not just tonight but on a more permanent basis. Wild ideas of running away, of living like a hermit and practising meditation so devotedly that by a sheer effort of will she might send her brain back – or was it forward? – to her own time, suddenly consumed her. But a glance through the window showed that the evening was evil, the gale lashing the river into violence, the rain falling torrentially out of a near black sky. Any form of escape must take place at another time, though there was still this night to get through. Without saying a word, choosing a moment when Loxley's back was turned, Nichola slipped upstairs to her room and quietly closed the door.

A voice spoke out of the darkness. "You're up early, Mistress. I was just preparing your things."

Holding her candle high, Nichola peered into the shadows. "Margaret! I wasn't expecting to see you."

"Obviously not. I thought you would have been longer with your stepfather."

"He's drinking with some new-found friends. I didn't want to stay."

"Still yearning for Master Michael?" the servant asked softly.

A warning note sounded in Nichola's brain and she answered, "Today's events have put paid to any feelings I might have had for him. From now on he and I are enemies."

"Then in that case you'll be looking elsewhere no doubt."

And this, thought Nichola, is where I find out exactly what she's up to. Aloud she said, "In time I suppose."

"Then let it be hoped you don't have to look too far afield, Mistress."

"And what's that supposed to mean?"

"That you've a fine man, a bonny man, under your very nose."

"Are you referring to Sir Denzil?"

"Yes, Mistress Arabella. I am."

"But he is my stepfather, he was married to my mother. How can you suggest anything so vile?"

"It is not against the laws of God nor of man," Margaret answered defensively, stepping into the ring of light thrown by the candle flame. "It is not a prohibited relationship. You are not kin by blood."

"But I have always looked on him as such," said Nichola, ice in every word. Then added, "How much has he paid you to say all this?"

In the dim light she saw Margaret flush. "Nothing, Mistress. I speak entirely for your own good."

"Like hell you do! You're nothing but a conniving old bitch. Now get out!" And she flung back the door and held it open.

The servant threw her a look of pure malice before reluctantly sidling past but she turned in the doorway for the last word. "I shall tell Sir Denzil what has passed between us. I've been his loyal helper for many a long year and he'll take your insults amiss, mark my words."

"Get lost," Nichola answered succinctly, and slammed the door behind her.

Trouble was truly brewing. She had an extraordinary feeling at the pit of her stomach, a feeling that told her to be on her guard, to be wary. With this thought uppermost, Nichola did not undress but sat on the bed, her back leaning against the wall, and listened to the sounds of the night.

The wind was howling through the building, blowing the smoke back down the chimneys so that the whole atmosphere was acrid, while beyond the window the vanished river swashed like the ocean. From the room below came the sounds of revellery, shouts, laughter and oaths, and Nichola could distinctly hear the sound of a man relieving himself outside.

I suppose this will go on all night, she thought, and with that idea was born the hope that Sir Denzil might fall asleep with his companions and leave her in peace.

At some time round midnight, her eyes grew so heavy that she was forced to close them, and then she must have drifted off to sleep, in spite of her uncomfortable position. She was woken again by the sound she dreaded most. The door of her room, the key to it long gone, was slowly opening. Silently, Nichola slid down to the floor where she crouched, watching.

Briefly lit by the flare of a candle she saw Sir Denzil in the opening, again clad only in his nightshirt. But on this occasion he obviously meant to waste no time on talking for he headed straight for the bed, moaning gently to himself. Nichola made out the words, "I love you . . . cannot endure another moment . . . I must have you or go mad."

She stood up. "Are you talking to me?"

He spun round. "Arabella!"

"What do you want?"

He took a step towards her. "You are a grown woman now, a grown woman with a child. Surely you can grant me that which I desire most in the world."

"Namely?"

"Your body," and with that he began to tear off his nightclothes. Nichola had one hideous glimpse of skinny legs and white flesh, before she ran straight past him, slamming a fist into his pallid guts as they momentarily drew level. Then she was off, speeding down the stairs and out into that most inclement of nights, with no idea where she was going except that she must get away from Sir Denzil Loxley for good.

She should have turned left towards the town, Nichola realised that too late, but instead she had headed off in the wrong direction, running beside the river towards the open countryside. And then suddenly, out of nowhere, a dark shape reared up before her and, unable to stop herself, she crashed headlong and violently into another human being.

"God's mercy, whatever's this?" said a voice.

"Help me," Nichola gasped, "you must help me."

There was a flash of white teeth in the darkness. "That a day such as this should end with a runaway!"

"Be serious," she answered, and peering up into the gloom found herself staring straight into the face of Lord Joscelin Attwood.

Chapter Eight

The sound of the tormented river had caught in the cavern, echoing and re-echoing as if a woman sobbed within its rocky confines. And, indeed, a woman did, for as Nichola climbed the steps, hewn from the cliff face itself, her own pitiful noises were added to the great sorrowful moan that filled her ears. Never in her life had she felt more relieved to be taken charge of by another adult and never had she thought she could feel quite so shocked. And yet this concept was foreign to her, and she could only put her reactions down to the fact that she was living in a harder, crueller age. But could anything be crueller than the 1990s, she reflected in a brief moment of introspection? And her thoughts turned to cardboard city packed to overflowing, to the millions unemployed, to fine old family firms being driven to the wall.

"Doesn't anyone care any more?" she thought, and realised that she had spoken aloud.

Joscelin looked at her in the flickering light of the sconces secured to the rocky walls and said, "Don't talk now. Tell me what happened when we get inside."

"I'm sorry, I don't know where I am or what I'm doing," Nichola answered wretchedly, still thinking of her own time, of the trouble she was in that he would never be able to comprehend.

"Does one ever?" he asked unexpectedly and just for a moment his smile gleamed in the shadows.

They were climbing the most extraordinary staircase, hewn through the centre of the rock on which stood the castle's upper bailey, connecting the fortress's highest point with the banks of the river. Nichola had never seen anything quite like it and in normal circumstances would have taken more notice of such an incredible cavern. Yet now all she wanted to do was put as much distance between herself and Sir Denzil as humanly possible. In spite of that, she still felt a stir of curiosity.

"What is this place?" she asked her companion, at present steadying her climb by a supporting hand.

"It was used to transport ale up from the brewhouse to the castle. It's known as Mortimer's Hole."

"Oh?"

"You've heard of Roger Mortimer, Earl of March?"

"Remind me."

"He was the lover of Queen Isabella who, poor woman, was married to Edward II, the lill-for-loll King murdered in Berkeley Castle."

Despite Nichola's recent panic an historical recollection came back. "Weren't unspeakable things done to him with a red hot poker?"

"Indeed they were." And Joscelin raised a suave brow.

"Is the place named after him, March I mean?"

"It was up these steps that the arresting party came to seize him. The new King, Edward III, thought his mother's lover was becoming too powerful so arranged for him to be snatched in the dead of night. Some say he was taken in bed with the Queen, others that he was respectably in council. Anyway, it was the end of Mortimer and after that Nottingham Castle was secured for the King."

Nichola glanced back over her shoulder. "And can anyone come up here? Might I be followed?"

"Be easy. There's a locked door at the top with a guard on it."

"I thought the castle was uninhabited."

"It is, more or less. But now that the Standard is flying there is a troop here to protect the place and keep order."

"Of which you are one?"

"Arabella," said Joscelin, hauling her up the last few steps, "you ask too many questions. When I've got you settled, then we can talk."

But she had one other thing to say. "Thank you for helping me. I thought most men of your time would have boxed my ears and returned me to Sir Denzil."

She hadn't meant to put it quite like that, and certainly Joscelin gave her an odd look as he knocked on the wooden door that faced them, quietly said his name, then waited as bolts shot back and a heavy key was turned. Nichola stepped through to find herself in the remains of a tower, some precipitous stone steps leading down to what had once been the castle's upper bailey. Looking round, she saw that despite the ruinous state of the buildings surrounding the great courtyard which lay at its centre, candles had been lit in those to her right and it was towards them that Joscelin now led her.

"What is this place?"

"They were once the old royal apartments, very rough now, but at least they will grant us some degree of comfort and privacy while you tell me your story."

"And where are the soldiers?"

"In the middle bailey, seeking what shelter they can."

A fire had been lit in the old stone hearth, obviously a later addition to the original medieval dwelling, and in front of this a form of camp bed had been set up. Beside it was a table, a pitcher of wine, a cup and a platter of cold meats standing on it. Leaning against one wall, strangely out of place against the cold stone, were the voluptuous folds of the King's Standard.

Nichola stared at it in astonishment. "What's that doing here? It was only raised this afternoon."

Joscelin's face transformed, the mischievous scamp vanished, another man, of much thought, suddenly in his place. "It blew down in the gale, God help us, which will be looked upon as an ill omen if ever there was one. Anyway, it nearly did for me as it toppled!"

"Were you on watch?"

"Unofficially. I was on my way to The Salutation and something drew me to look at the Standard again. It represents so much, really. Centuries of tradition now under threat."

"Are you a committed monarchist?" asked Nichola, and again it was a woman of her own times who spoke.

"I do not believe in the social chaos which will be caused by mobilising the people against the crown. The King, if one looks at him critically, has been far from perfect. But then, what man is?" He poured Nichola a glass of wine which she took in silence. "Charles Stuart has many faults, in the early days too easily influenced by Buckingham, now by his wife, but to me he represents order. Does that answer your question?"

"Very fully."

Joscelin turned to look at her, his philosophical mood gone. Now yet another persona dominated his features, this one alert and practical. Nichola found herself thinking that her first impression of him had revealed little of the complete picture.

"So tell me how you came to be running by the river on such a terrible night."

"To put it at its simplest, Sir Denzil tried to get into my bed. I am his stepdaughter, not blood related at all, and since I've got older he has started to desire me as a mistress – or even more."

"A feeling not reciprocated I take it?"

"You must be joking!" Nichola exploded, then winced very slightly at her modern phraseology, but Joscelin seemed not to notice and merely nodded saying, "I see."

"I don't think you do really. Arabella ... I mean I ... was betrothed to Michael Morellon, son of a Member of Parliament. Apparently, our families allowed sexual relations to begin and I have since borne him a child, a daughter. But now we have been parted because, obviously, he and his father have taken up the cause of the Parliamentarians. I'm vulnerable in a way. A single parent and all that."

Joscelin shot her the strangest glance but merely said, "Go on."

"That's it, more or less. When I first had the baby, Sir Denzil said he would try to find me a husband. But in the last few months I truly believe he wants to fill that role himself."

"I can understand that. You are an exquisite being."

It was Nichola's turn to look at him shrewdly but there was no hint of lechery in those magnificent eyes, merely an appraisal of something fine.

"So now I don't know what to do," she went on. "I can't marry Michael because I'm not even sure where he is and we are, to quote a phrase, by the sword divided. And I'm certainly not going back to live with that old bastard."

"Is he a bastard?" asked Joscelin in surprise, and Nichola realised that he had taken her remark literally, merely as a statement of fact.

She coloured very slightly. "No, I don't think so. I meant it rudely."

"Oh, I see."

"I suppose I could get work somewhere. But then there's the problem of Miranda."

"Miranda?"

Nichola took a deep draught of wine and felt herself become very slightly lightheaded. "The baby. I've got so fond of it, you see."

Again that quizzical look. "Most mothers usually do."

The actress collected herself. "Of course. I don't know why I said that. In any case I am in an impossible position. I can hardly leave her while I work. And what sort of jobs are there available anyway?"

He laughed. "You utter the strangest things, Mistress. You know full well that for a woman of your upbringing there is nothing to do but run a house and that in itself is a full time occupation."

Despite everything, Nichola could not help but pull a face. "Is it?"

"Of course."

She looked at him with a sudden expression of hopelessness. "Then what shall I do?"

Joscelin answered her question with another. "How old did

you tell me you were, Arabella?" he asked softly, his eyes very bright.

Was the heady wine making her careless or was it just general fatigue, for once again in his company Nichola had started to say "twenty-seven" before she corrected herself and answered, "Seventeen."

"Then there's nothing to stop you contracting another marriage without your stepfather's agreement."

"Isn't there?" She looked at him owlishly.

"My dear creature, the age of consent is twelve for females and fourteen for us men. You are well within your rights."

With her wits scattering fast, Nichola said, "Please don't think me forgetful, it's just that I've had rather a shock. Believe me, a glimpse of Sir Denzil standing starkers would be enough to make strong men quail."

Joscelin shook his head, smiling broadly. "I love your manner of speech. It is the quaintest I have ever heard. What does starkers mean? I presume naked."

"*Stark* naked actually."

"Ah," he said, and smiled again.

There was a profound silence, a silence in which all other sounds became magnified. Outside, the cruel wind that had torn the King's proud Standard down and turned the river that once-had-been into a frothing sea, beat at the walls of the derelict old castle. Within, the cheerful fire, lit by some unseen servant, rustled and cracked as it devoured the sun-dried logs. Nichola became aware of Joscelin's breathing, the beat of her thudding heart, the noise made by liquid as it was poured from one vessel to another. And then her companion spoke.

"You could always marry me."

As if she were in slow motion, Nichola turned her head to look at him. "What did you say?"

"That you could always marry me."

"Marry you?" she answered unbelievingly. "But I don't even know you!"

Joscelin's face became expressionless. "Does that matter? Could it not be a union of convenience for us both?"

Nichola stared at him blankly. "I don't understand."

"You are in desperate straits. Separated from the man you love by war, pursued by a lecherous stepfather to whom you have delivered an insult he'll find it hard to forgive. Do you have any choice?"

"But Lord Joscelin, we are strangers . . ." she protested.

"Let me finish," he interrupted her. "I, too, need someone. My wife died almost sixteen years ago, the birth of our child proving too much for her frail strength. My unmarried sister, Meraud, now looks after the girl and so, from that point of view, the house will be run, my estate managed, while I am away fighting. But there is a lack in my life. I need a companion, a friend. Someone with whom I can discuss things in which neither my sister nor my daughter are interested. I am not asking you to love me, Arabella. Frankly that would be ridiculous, though I nurture a hope that that emotion might grow. Be that as it may, in return for a safe haven in which you will be much honoured and respected, I am asking you to share my life with me."

Nichola sat aghast, quite unable to equate what she had just heard with her own outlook, her own beliefs. If her contemporaries eventually bothered to marry after living together it was probably because they had views on children being born out of wedlock. In the past, when the very idea of having a child had seemed utterly repellant, she had given marriage no thought. Lewis had changed all that, of course, but Lewis had been the ultimate prize, the catch that any right minded woman would go after and try to land. Yet now, almost like the hateful arranged unions still endured by some in this century, a man she knew nothing about was asking her to marry him.

Despite the sheer outrageousness of the situation, Nichola allowed her mind to dwell momentarily on the alternative. Her only hope of escape from Sir Denzil was to find a way out of these terrible times and back to her own, and that at the moment seemed almost an impossibility.

She heard herself say, "Please give me time to think."

Joscelin visibly relaxed and she found herself wondering why. Had he experienced that extraordinary phenomenon and fallen in love with her at first sight? If so, he had made a pretty cool job of disguising it. Yet remembering the expression that lay at the back of his eyes, perhaps there had been something.

"Sleep on it," he said. "You can have my bed by the fire. I'll take a blanket. But you must let me know in the morning because, by then, we will have to leave Nottingham if we are to be wed."

"But where will we go?" she asked dully, acutely aware that by now even her bones were tired.

"To Greys Court, my cousins' home. The ceremony can be held at the church nearby."

Nichola mustered up a last burst of energy. "Why are you doing this?" she asked. "Why should you suddenly pick me? You've obviously been on your own for years. Did you meet no one you fancied in that time?"

Joscelin's face changed back to the scamp's. "Which question would you like me to answer first? I'm helping you because I want to. I've picked you – as you put it – because your personality is so unusual, different from that of any woman I have ever come across. And in all the time I have been a widower I have not found anyone who intrigues me quite as much as you do. Will that suffice?"

She smiled at him. "Thank God you didn't mention my looks."

"Why? Are you ashamed of them?"

"I used to be," she replied. "But, do you know, I've got to quite like them now."

"You're rambling," he said firmly. "There's your bed. Now go to."

She had meant to lie awake, turning over her problem in the silence of the night and coming to some sensible conclusion. But the events of the previous day, the flight from Arabella's stepfather, had exhausted the body which she now inhabited and Nichola slept deeply. When she woke it was to see the stone chamber full of light and that someone had restoked the fire. Of Joscelin there was no sign at all. Feeling heavy headed and slightly hung over, the actress heaved herself out of the camp bed and went to look about her.

The sanitary arrangements were primitive to say the least, consisting of a portable close stool which Nichola was forced to use, and a basin and ewer of cold water. Somehow she managed to wash, stripped to nothing, and then dressed herself in the clothes she had worn the night before, which were by now somewhat grubby. Her hair she simply couldn't be bothered even to try and curl. Instead Nichola brushed it out, long and thick and barley bright, and tied it back with a piece of ribbon which lay beside a small shaving mirror, obviously used by Joscelin on his travels. All this done, she stepped outside and it wasn't until she saw the Standard flying again and his Lordship walking towards her with a loaf of bread in his hand that she remembered she was supposed to be giving him an answer to his proposal.

"A better day," he called cheerfully, and Nichola thought to herself that nothing changed, that Englishmen in whatever century still talked about the weather.

"Yes. I see the Standard's raised."

"We did it at daybreak before the town stirred but the rumour is still going round that the wind brought it down and that such a thing bodes ill."

"Do *you* believe that?"

The rogue's face was momentarily serious. "I am not a superstitious man, though I accept there is a supernatural force not tangible to us. So let me simply say I would rather it had stayed where it was."

He was smiling again and Nichola found herself wondering just how many layers there were to this man, who could appear an intellectual at one moment, a dashing cavalier the next.

"Is that breakfast?" she said, eyeing the loaf.

"It is. I've also brought you some cheese and beer."

"That was kind."

"Listen," said Joscelin, "eat quickly. While I was round and about I saw Sir Denzil. He's obviously searching the town for you and it won't be too long before he comes up here to enquire."

"What should I do?"

"I suggest we leave as soon as possible. I've already given orders for my coach to be brought to the Gatehouse."

"Might he not see it there?"

"He could well, but why should he think twice about it? There's no reason for him to connect you with me. You might have gone anywhere last night."

"That's true enough." Nichola paused, her brain teeming with ideas. "But when he hears you've left Nottingham abruptly might he not suspect?"

His Lordship looked suddenly serious. "That is why I suggested we marry in haste. If he should realise and come after you it will be too late if you already have my ring on your finger."

"And if I haven't?"

"As your legal guardian he would have a very good case for demanding you back."

"But what about the baby? I know it's ridiculous but now I can't bear the thought of having to give her up."

"We'll send for the child when the ceremony is over."

"Then it seems I have no choice."

Lord Joscelin looked at her sharply. "Is the idea so very abhorrent?"

Nichola shook her head. "It is simply that I don't know you. Suppose that we are not suited, that our relationship founders? After all, we have nothing to build on."

A part of her brain found itself listening clinically to what she was saying and thinking that she sounded like a candidate for Relate. The seventeenth-century laugh on the twentieth-century bitch was about to be had, there was no doubt of that.

Joscelin clearly lost patience, she knew by the sudden hardening of his features. "Arabella, I could suffer just as much in those circumstances. Now, what is it to be? Are you prepared to throw in your lot with mine or would you rather take a chance that Sir Denzil will forgive?"

"I'll go with you," she said and then, thinking how churlish she sounded, added the word, "please."

For really she had no choice. At least Joscelin was physically attractive and, as far as she could tell, with him she would have a reasonable home and time to devote some serious study to getting back. At the hands of Denzil Loxley she might very well end up dead.

"I'll give you ten minutes to prepare yourself for the journey," her future husband said briskly. "Eat what you can and bring the rest with you. As soon as we have covered a reasonable distance we can stop for food."

"What have you told the King?" Nichola asked curiously.

"That I have had to return home to wind up my affairs. That I will rejoin him in Nottingham within two weeks."

"So you intend to fight by his side?"

"Yes, my dear, I most certainly do," Joscelin answered, and with that set about packing up his things.

One hour later they were gone from the town and, having crossed the river Trent, began the journey south. The gale of the previous day had blown itself out and now was nothing more than a cheerful breeze ruffling the surface of the water as they went over the bridge. In comparison with the previous occasion the span was deserted, only a shepherd bringing his flock to market causing any kind of delay. As the coachman slowed his pace to let the animals pass, Nichola craned her neck, staring back out of the window.

"He's not following," said Joscelin, almost with an air of amusement.

"How do you know?"

"Because he won't start looking elsewhere till he's turned every stick of Nottingham over. And when you consider the number of caves he'll have to look in that could take him some time."

"Caves?"

"They call the place the town of cave dwellers, didn't you know? There are many rock formations like Mortimer's Hole and most of them are inhabited. If you had to run away,

Mistress, you couldn't have picked a better place."

"I didn't *have* to run away," Nichola answered, suddenly stung. "I was forced to it."

Now there could be no mistaking the amusement. "Forgive me, I phrased that badly, I must get used to having a wife again." He paused, "Tell me, Arabella, is one of your reservations about our match based on the fact that I am twenty years older than you are?"

"But you're not . . ." she began, then changed it to ". . . old in spirit. In fact you don't seem old to me at all."

Nichola indulged in a moment of wry humour, thinking that Joscelin was exactly the same age as Lewis Devine, and must have grinned over it, for he said, "This makes you smile?"

"Only because I have never considered age to be greatly important, my Lord. I, indeed, am old for my years – and that's the truth! While you seem to have reached just the right level of maturity."

"God's life, you know how to flatter," he answered, but Nichola could see he was pleased for all that.

"And what of me?" she said, probing. "Do I not seem to you a gauche simpleton, only fit to play with your daughter?"

"That is part of your enigma," Joscelin stated thoughtfully. "Had I not the evidence of my eyes I would say that you are an ancient soul, Arabella."

"What do you mean?"

"That you act and speak like a woman several years older than you actually are."

"No, not that. What did you mean when you spoke of ancient souls?"

"In certain eastern religions they believe that after death the spirit enters another body and in this way lives on."

"And do you believe that? Do you think it possible for someone's essence to enter the shell of another?"

Joscelin Attwood turned to look at her, his aristocratic profile trenchant against the light of the coach's window. "Why, do you?"

"Yes," Nichola answered quietly. "I am certain that it could happen."

"I can see," his Lordship answered after a moment's pause, "that we are going to have some very interesting discussions in the months that lie ahead of us."

"I hope that indeed we are," she replied, and on an impulse leant forward to kiss him on the cheek.

Chapter Nine

A golden evening had given way to silver night. Slowly, imperceptibly, the peach coloured hills had faded to the delicate shade of summer fruit, of ripened raspberries and crisp skinned plums. Then, as the sun had gone to sleep behind them, they had transformed to a colour as dark and inspiring as that of the mighty clarets shipped in from France, destined for the cellars of the noble houses of England. The river, surely not the Thames running so sweetly through unpolluted meadows with never a lock or pleasure boat in sight, had blazed crimson then turned to pewter grey as the rays of light had gone out. And then the moon had risen.

She had climbed her way up the sky as she had done since the dawn of time, briefly illuminating the sunset before she drew the folds of night about her and galaxies of stars appeared in the firmament to light her way. The bright bold dash of day had been changed into countless mysteries by her silver face. The hills had grown black and silent, the river a ribbon of silk, the dips and hollows of the land shadowed by pools of indigo. The Queen of Night had come with her train and transformed the world into a fantasy. And it was in this enchanted light, this bewitching dream, that Nichola Hall first set eyes on Greys Court.

There had been a dwelling place on the site since the Middle Ages, for the ruins of an earlier building could be glimpsed in the moonshine, its crumbling walls and towers casting long fingers of shadow over the lawns of the later house. But, as the carriage drew nearer, the new building became etched against the vivid firmament, drawing Nichola's eyes to rearing roofs and the sparkle of elegant mullioned windows. Staring entranced, she was overwhelmed by the power of a house that had stood strong and stern through bitter winters yet in summer was heavy with the scent of the perfumed creepers that clustered upon its stone surface.

In the darkness of the coach, Joscelin spoke. "Do you like it?"

"It's breathtaking," Nichola answered. "A glorious place."

He smiled in the moonlight. "One day soon you shall see Kingswear Hall, my home on the estuary of the beautiful River Dart, but for the moment Greys Court will give us the shelter we need."

"Is it too dangerous then for us to travel to Devon?"

"Too dangerous and too far. If you are to escape Sir Denzil we must be married without delay."

Looking at him closely Nichola saw that Joscelin was pale, his eyes dreamy and unreadable, and knew that her judgement of him as a man of many and varied facets was proving ever more correct. On the surface he seemed little more than a well-born knave, a scampish man of action. But what a false impression this was. All he had done recently evinced that the man was a maze of hidden personalities, and she experienced a fleeting moment of excitement that she would soon be spending enough time in his company to find out who he really was. Then she pulled herself up short, realising that she, a woman of modern times, was about to enter into a marriage with a man she did not know, and the entire situation was truly impossible.

The moonlit dream continued. The stranger whose wife she was soon to be led her into a house softly lit with the glow of candles. She saw richly coloured tapestries and dark wood, intricate carvings and furniture of antique splendour. Then, following close behind Joscelin, Nichola ascended a curving staircase and found herself in a panelled long gallery which ran the length of the house itself.

"I feel like a trespasser," she said, looking around her.

"Why?"

"Because there appears to be nobody else here. I thought our hosts might still be up and awaiting us."

Joscelin shook his head. "I'm afraid not." He smiled a little sadly. "The fact is that except for the servants there is no one in residence. My cousins grew more and more concerned about the state of affairs during this present terrible year and finally, hearing that the King was about to raise the Standard, left for Germany."

Nichola looked at him in astonishment. "Have many people done that?"

"Several of those who could afford such a move. The penniless masses, as always in times of war, have been left to bear the brunt."

"I don't want to be rude about your relatives but I think it's a bit cowardly just to up and do a runner."

Joscelin's face lit up. "That lovely phraseology again!"

"I'm sorry. I keep forgetting myself," Nichola answered truthfully

"There is no need to apologise, my dear. Part of your attraction is your extraordinary speech."

Nichola felt disproportionately pleased.

"Anyway," he went on, "I agree with you. It's not a very admirable thing to admit about one's kin, but the fact is they just didn't want to be involved in any fighting."

"And what about you? Would you physically do battle for the King?"

Joscelin smiled ruefully. "As I said to you once before, Charles Stuart is in many ways a foolish and insensitive man. But his forebears and mine rubbed shoulders, I have eaten his bread and salt. I would not do so base a thing as to desert him in his hour of need. Also there is an active and aggressive radical Puritan who—"

"Gets up your nose?" Nichola put in, unable to resist.

"Precisely. He is the Member of Parliament for Cambridge. Three years ago he was called to God following the death of his son which tragedy, or so he became convinced, was caused by his own sin. After this he became converted, always a dangerous situation. Anyway, I went into the House one morning when he was speaking. He wore the most awful clothes, which is his own choice I suppose, but what churned my stomach was that his linen was not clean and there were specks of blood upon his neck band where he had cut himself shaving. His face became red and swollen when he shouted, and his voice was sharp and untuneable, painful to the ear."

"I take it you are describing Oliver Cromwell?"

"I am indeed. So, my antipathy to him and my loyalty to the man he challenges lead me to defend the King, physically if need be, even though much of what he stands for rankles my conscience."

"I think you are a great person," said Nichola, after a pause.

"That I am not. I'm human flesh and blood like everyone else, as weak and as beset by doubt."

"But, Joscelin, you have stayed behind unlike those cousins of yours. Did you say their name was Knollys by the way?"

"I did. In fact my great aunt was the notorious Lettice."

Nichola stared at him blankly, wracking her brains and hoping that it wasn't too obvious she had simply no idea who he was talking about.

He smiled. "You look bewildered. Lettice Knollys was married to the first Earl of Essex and was the mother of the second Earl, that beautiful dazzling youth with whom Queen Elizabeth fell madly in love in her old age. But that wasn't all. When she was widowed, Lettice secretly married Robert Dudley, Earl of Leicester, with whom Elizabeth was also in love. So my celebrated great aunt was both mother to and wife of two of the Queen's lovers. Not a fact to endear her to the royal heart."

"There was something extremely excessive about Elizabeth, wasn't there?" Nichola said musingly.

"There was something decidedly odd about her if you want my view."

"And didn't the Earl of Leicester push his first wife down the stairs in order to get her out of the way when he and the Queen started their fling?"

"His wife, Amy Robsart, was most certainly murdered but it was never proved who did the deed."

"Exciting," said Nichola.

"Too exciting for this hour. You said you were tired."

"And so I am."

"Then I'll escort you to your chamber and bid you good-night."

He was being very well behaved, Nichola thought as she closed the door of her bedroom having watched him walk away. If that had been one of her contemporaries on the brink of marriage he would have slept with her without giving the matter a second thought. But this enigmatical and interesting man seemed self contained almost to the point of being aloof. For Joscelin, in the time she had known him, had made no sexual overtures to her, in fact had done no more than kiss her hand. And in a way, this challenged her, making her determined to go to bed with him.

Drawing aside the curtains, looking across the walls of what had once been a medieval courtyard to the great crenellated tower opposite, Nichola sighed and, without warning, experienced a sudden sensation of intense panic. It seemed quite obvious at that moment that she would never get back to her own century, that she was caught in this hypnotically induced timewarp for the rest of her days. Terribly afraid and physically shaking she climbed on to the bed as if it were a refuge, only to experience a horrific waking dream.

Briefly, but with amazing clarity, Nichola felt herself to be lying in a hospital bed, could even smell the place's unmistakable aroma, while her ears were filled by the frightening and relentless sound of a ventilator rising and falling. Just for a second it seemed as if she had somehow returned to her own life, yet she was seized by an unaccountable fear as to where she would find herself. Dreading what she might see, Nichola raised her lids.

"Oh God!" screeched a female voice. "She's opening her eyes. Look!"

There were dim shapes huddled round the bed.

"Nichola," said a voice from a million miles away. "Nichola, can you hear me?"

She didn't know who was speaking.

"Go and fetch a doctor, quick," another voice commanded.

A hand took hers and Nichola heard a fourth voice rising

above all the others. "Arabella, what is it? There's nothing to fear, my dear."

The mist cleared and she saw that the shapes had melded into one. Lord Joscelin was leaning over the bed, looking at her with concern and saying, "Have you had a nightmare?"

She felt too vulnerable to lie. "I don't know. A strange thing happened to me, that is all I can tell you."

"Perhaps you dreamt in that state between waking and sleeping where nothing is ever quite clear," Joscelin answered, his eyes far away.

"I must have done."

"What took place? Can you tell me?"

"I felt I was somewhere else with people I once knew. I could hear their voices."

"I see." He stood up. "Would you like me to get one of the servants to sit with you till morning?"

Nichola shook her head. "No, I'll be all right. It was an hallucination, no more."

He nodded. "The mind can conjure many strange illusions. Now rest, for tomorrow we are to be married."

"Are we really? As soon as that?"

"The rector of St Nicholas, Rotherfield Greys, will grant me an immediate licence, I feel sure of it. The church's history and that of Greys Court have been interwoven for centuries. And besides" – Joscelin raised a dark brow – "the right to nominate the rectors of Rotherfield Greys lies in the hands of the Knollys family."

Nichola laughed, then sighed. "How *easy* everything is. No red tape or bureaucracy."

He smiled in the shadows. "And what, my quaint creature, is red tape?"

"I'll explain in the morning," she said.

"I'm quite sure you will," he answered drily. "Now, clear your mind of all thoughts. Dream no more dreams. We have a great deal to do in the next few days."

But after he had left the room, Nichola's mind ran to what she might have to do over the next few *years*, that is if she could not find her way home. And dominating these thoughts came a vision of two unknown and formidable women, Josceline's sister Meraud and his teenage daughter, Sabina.

Out of a great chest of clothes belonging to some female Knollys, now departed, a wedding dress of sorts was found the next day. Heavy with jewels, its farthingale fantastically large and fine, Nichola found herself having to squeeze Arabella's breasts into the gown's stiff, unyielding bodice. But it was a beautiful creation, silver and pearl strewn, the slashings of the sleeves an elegant shade of sapphire blue. Nichola decided that Arabella's hair should be worn long and loose on this occasion and sent the bewildered servants into the gardens to gather a wreath of fresh flowers. Then those who had gone to bed believing their master's house to be empty and had awoken to find a wedding on their hands, watched in astonishment as Lord Joscelin and his bride set off by coach for the church of St Nicholas in the nearby village of Rotherfield Greys.

The rector had been up since dawn, fetched out of his bed by Milord himself, who had ridden over to ask for a licence and a morning ceremony.

"But why the haste, Sir?" the Reverend John Hollin had enquired, wondering to himself if Lord Joscelin had impregnated some fine young lady who was urgently demanding to be made an honest woman.

"This is a time of war," the prospective bridegroom had replied, with one of his usual lazy grins. "I have already attended His Majesty at Nottingham and intend to return there as soon as I have tied the legal knot. We are not living in an age in which it is sensible for a man to drag his feet."

"And the bride? Will she be returning to Nottingham with you?"

Lord Joscelin had performed his extraordinary trick of changing his expression and with it his whole persona. "No, Sir. I believe we face a long and bloody conflict if we are to save the King's crown for him. I would not subject a woman to the rigours of such a war," he had answered seriously.

"Then she will stay at Greys Court?"

"For the time being, yes. There would be other rigours for her to contend with at my Devonshire home." He had once more smiled his scampish smile. "Namely my elder sister who has run the house for me since the death of my wife."

"Just so," the cleric had replied, putting the tips of his fingers together, and thinking to himself that a thorny path might well lie ahead of the future Lady Attwood.

Similarly, he found himself dwelling on much the same thoughts during the ceremony. For the bride was not only exquisite, a glorious little being, but far younger than he had imagined. Yet she carried her lovely head, crowned by its flowing mass of golden hair, inside the high wired collar, now quite out of fashion, with the composure and fearlessness of a far older woman. If the rector had been a man of fanciful notions he would have said that an experienced lady of the world was masquerading inside the body of someone far less mature. And these ideas led him on to the conclusion that Lord Joscelin's sister, or anyone else for that matter, would not find it easy to ride roughshod over Mistress Arabella Loxley, at any moment to become the second Lady Attwood. For it was indeed time for the vows to be said, for the golden wedding ring to be placed on the gorgeous girl's finger. Mr Hollin found his eyes getting moist, swept beneath the spell of Arabella's charm and delicacy.

A farmer and his wife had been summoned from the village to act as witnesses, picked, mainly, because the man could write. First, however, it was the turn of the bride and groom to sign their names. The rector produced the parish register and watched the curve and sweep of Lord Joscelin's hand as he inscribed his signature, then stared in astonishment as the young woman wrote the word *Nichola* before she crossed it out and signed Arabella Loxley.

What a strange thing to do, Mr Hollin thought, and noticed that Lord Joscelin had briefly allowed a puzzled frown to darken his features before he concealed whatever he was feeling behind a wedding day smile.

Nichola cursed herself, realising that the mistake had happened so naturally she had nearly done the unthinkable and signed Hall as well. And then what would the man raising her hand to his lips in salute have done? Quickly she flashed him a guileless smile, wondering whether Joscelin had noticed the error or whether she had been too quick for him, but his eyes were as unreadable as only he could make them.

"And now, my Lady," her husband was saying, "let us repair to Greys Court for the wedding feast."

"Is there going to be one? Have the servants had time?" she asked, in surprise.

"The answers are yes and no. For, perplexed though they might be, they are putting together a banquet of sorts." He handed the farmer a coin. "Thank you for your services today, Buxton. You and your wife have done well."

"I wish a hearty long life to you and Lady Attwood, Sir," and the man threw his hat aloft, partly, Nichola suspected, because of the size of the *douceur*.

"Amen to that," Joscelin answered, and with a wave of his hand to the small crowd which had gathered outside, helped Nichola back into the carriage.

"There, it's done," he said. "You've no further need to worry. Let Sir Denzil do his worst."

Just for once she was lost for words, not knowing quite how to handle the situation. And then she thought how ridiculous everything was and wished that last night's mirage, that waking dream of such cruel intensity, had not ended. For might not that have been the path leading back to her own times? With a frown, the actress turned to stare out of the carriage window, wondering what on earth she was to do next.

The coach swept up the hill to the house and Nichola was slightly aroused from her apathy by the sight before her. The servants, obviously recovered from the shock of her arrival, had lined the driveway and, as the carriage appeared, threw leaves and flowers beneath the wheels.

"That's very kind of them," she said, moving back to Joscelin, aware that a sudden silence had fallen between them.

"They want to please you – as do I," he answered.

A vile feeling of guilt swept her that all she could think of was how to get away from him.

"Thank you," she said chastened.

"Don't thank me too soon, let us first see what they have made of the feast," he replied, yet even though the words were light hearted he spoke in such a quiet voice that Nichola looked at him sharply. However, his face was as composed as usual and his manner just as charming as they came to a halt before the front door and he helped her descend. Yet there was a wariness about him that made her uneasy and in a sudden rush of pity she wondered if her odd behaviour, her writing the name Nichola in the parish register, had upset and disturbed him. For after all, Joscelin had taken on an unknown quantity in her just as much as she had in him. Gathering her reserves, Nichola took his hand, determined to be kind to him during the time she remained in his century.

"How very considerate of you to order all this. I had expected a truly quiet wedding."

He turned to look at her, his face suddenly so serious that her heart gave a lurch. "Ours may only be a marriage of convenience but it is for all that an occasion worthy of celebration."

Yet another feeling of tenderness swept the actress, stronger than anything she had ever experienced in her life. "I promise to do my best to make you happy," she said, and then with modern boldness kissed him on the lips, standing on tiptoe in order to do so.

He was passionate, carnal, she knew by the very touch of his mouth, fleeting though it was. Instantly, Nichola, who had loved so carelessly, so unwisely and so frequently, realised for sure that she desired him. This, then, would be her way of life until she found the way home. She would have a lusty affair with Lord Joscelin Attwood. Almost at once it occurred to her that she could hardly have a liaison with a man she was married to, and the ridiculousness of the situation made her smile.

"You're happy?" her bridegroom asked, offering her his arm as they climbed to the long gallery, from whence could be heard the distant sound of musicians, more enthusiastic than skilled.

"Yes, I am," Nichola answered, and she was as near to it at that moment as anyone in her extraordinary situation could possibly be.

Loops of garlanded flowers had been hung on the panelled walls and a large table, covered with a white cloth, set down the centre of the gallery. This had been laid for several people to sit down to dine.

"But surely we have no guests," Nichola said, astonished.

"The rector is coming and the local physician and his wife, together with a few people I have met through my cousins. That is unless you have any objection."

"How could I?" she answered, turning her most spectacular smile on him. "You have done it all so splendidly."

"Thank you, my dear." And now Joscelin's eyes shone in appreciation of her. Just for a second Nichola felt piqued that it was Arabella's golden looks that were winning all the admiring gazes and then she pushed such thoughts aside. If she was to stay sane for the rest of her time in the seventeenth century she must accept that she and the girl who had died in childbirth had become part and parcel of the same entity.

"You look magnificent in that dress," he went on. "It could have been made for you."

"It's very tight over the boobs," Nichola replied, once more without thinking, then couldn't help but grin at the expression on Joscelin's face.

"Bube?" he repeated, his brows flying.

"No, boob," she answered. "Why? Is bube rude?"

"It is a vulgar word for the greater pox, yes."

"Which means syphilis?"

This time only one smooth brow flickered. "Indeed it does, though such a disease is hardly a suitable topic for a wedding day, would you not agree?"

"You're teasing me," Nichola said accusingly as his shoulders heaved and he burst out laughing.

"Uds life, would I do such a thing?"

"Yes, you most certainly would," she answered and again experienced another moment of feeling ridiculously happy.

The illusion of being in a costume drama returned, Nichola playing the part of eager young bride, the attractive, slightly older actor opposite her taking the role of dashing cavalier husband. The bit part players and extras, dressed as village dignitaries and servants, entering into the spirit of the piece, were toasting the happy couple for all they were worth. In fact so well was the wedding scene going that nobody called 'Cut' and the hidden cameras rolled on and on.

And then came a part of the scenario which Nichola remembered clearly, having taken part in it in a stage adaptation of *The Wicked Lady*. On that occasion she had been one of the wedding guests but now she was in the lead. The day which had passed in drinking and dancing had given way to evening. The hour had arrived for the bedding of the bride and groom.

With a wonderful noise, silken skirts rustling, laughter loud and joyful, the ladies went up the stairs to supervise the undressing of the leading lady, carried along willy-nilly in their midst. Nichola had drunk too much wine by now for any sense of reality to return and went with them as if she were still in a film, turning on the stairs to see Joscelin standing below, watching her. Impulsively she blew him a kiss before she turned back to her female companions.

The great bed, hung with flowers, stood waiting, two maids close by, demurely ready to help the bride out of her clothes. Knowing the scene as she did, the actress stood passively while they unlaced the old-fashioned gown she had worn. Then she emerged naked except for her stockings and garters which she knew must be kept on, as it was traditional to throw these to the guests just before the bed curtains were drawn and the couple left to their own devices. A lawn and lace nightdress, presumably the property of yet another departed Knollys, was now having the lavender shaken out of it and being held high for Nichola to put over her head. And then, her hair swiftly brushed, she was assisted by the ladies into the four-poster to await her bridegroom's arrival.

With a great deal of swaggering the men came into the

bedroom, the noise they were making belying the fact that there were only five male guests. Joscelin, in his nightshirt, was led in by the wrist in a pretence of unwillingness. Then, amidst great guffaws and jocularity – the reverend gentleman having been left downstairs – his Lordship was manhandled in beside his bride. There was a wild scramble for the stockings and garters and then the curtains were firmly pulled shut by the physician's wife.

"Does everyone go home now?" whispered Nichola.

"Not at all," answered Joscelin, "there will be music, feasting, revelling and kissing until the early hours of tomorrow morning."

"For a quiet wedding this has been extremely noisy."

He smiled a trifle quizzically. "People enjoy any excuse for festivity in these straightened times."

"But what of Oliver Cromwell and the Puritans? Don't they approve of such things?"

"Most certainly not. I almost believe that is why some men are joining the Royalist cause."

"Because they don't want to see an end to their fun and games?"

"Exactly."

"And quite right too. Can you imagine London without theatres, people not being able to see a play?"

He looked at her sharply. "Why do you say that?"

Somewhat bewildered by the events of the day, by the wine she had drunk, Nichola answered, "Well surely they're going to be closed. Now that London is in the hands of Parliament."

"I have heard no rumour of it."

"Well, I think they will be."

Joscelin smiled at her. "I believe I have a witch wife." He turned towards her, leaning up on one arm, his chin in his hand.

"Nichola, there is something I have to say to you and I have to say it now. You see, I am well aware that you only married me in order to escape the attentions of Denzil Loxley and I therefore do not flatter myself that you have any feelings for me at all. So I am going to give you the chance to get out of the marriage should you wish it thus."

She stared at him. "What do you mean?"

"Simply this. The ecclesiastical courts have the power to nullify unconsummated marriages. Other than for that, only a private Act of Parliament can secure a divorce proper and this is so rare that it is not even worth considering. You are a very lovely woman who arouses great desire in me but, despite that, I refuse to tie you to a husband you do not love. Because of my convictions I intend to leave you tonight and will continue to do so until either you tell me you are coming to me through love and not necessity, or that you want the marriage to end."

Silly cheap phrases like, "Don't you fancy me then?" ran through Nichola's head but the real words, the proper words, to say to him, would not come.

"You remain silent," Joscelin continued, "and that is as well. For when you consider this tomorrow you will realise that what I am doing is for the best." His tone took on a certain urgency. "If our marriage is to be lasting and joyful you must love me with your heart, not just with your body. As far as I am concerned you are the most enigmatic, the most extraordinary, female who has ever crossed my path. I know you to be a creature of mystery and yet what it is about you that is so different I do not understand. But one day, if we remain together, I shall find the key to your secret, believe me."

Still Nichola could think of nothing to say but simply stared at him, aware that tears were running down her cheeks. Joscelin, seeing them, misunderstood.

"Your vanity has been wounded but do not react like that, I beg you. I am leaving you untouched because I believe there is a chance there might be something very special between us, that we might indeed be soul mates. That is why I cannot possess you until I have won your true affection."

It was too much for her and Nichola sobbed without restraint, dimly aware that he had risen from the marriage bed and returned to his own apartments. And it was only when she had finally quietened down and was lying still, watching the first splinters of dawn pierce the sky, that she realised that Joscelin had addressed her by the name Nichola.

Chapter Ten

The first intimation that Sir Denzil Loxley had discovered where his step daughter had hidden herself came from Mr John Hollin, who had ridden up to Greys Court on his plump old mare, his cheeks the colour of grapes, both man and beast puffing with anxiety. On being shown into the presence of Lord Joscelin and Lady Attwood, who were just about to go in to dine, he had stated the purpose of his visit without delay.

"My Lord, there is a Sir Denzil Loxley arrived in Rotherfield Greys who is putting it abroad that you abducted his daughter and married her against her will. As you may well imagine I sought him out and took him to task. I told him that I had performed the ceremony myself and had never seen a more radiant or happy bride. But when he demanded to see the parish register as proof, he swore that the signature was not that of his daughter but written by some foreign hand and for vindication pointed to my Lady's crossing out and stated that the bride must, in fact, be called Nichola."

"Pray sit down, Mr Hollin, and have a glass of sherry," Joscelin had responded calmly, "then we may at least discuss the matter in comfort. Arabella, would you be kind enough to pour? There is no point in disturbing the servants."

She had smiled and stood up, obscuring the decanter with her back to hide the fact that her hands were shaking. The rector took a large swig while Milord sipped delicately.

"So what exactly *is* he saying?" he asked, "that I married his actual daughter or a woman posing as such?"

"Both really, for the man has changed his tune. First of all it was a case of abduction but now the story seems to be one of substitution. He's on his way here, swearing revenge."

"I rather thought he might be," Joscelin had answered serenely. "Now, shall we go into dine? Do join us Mr Hollin, I beg you."

"But what of Sir Denzil?"

"I never allow anything to get in the way of a good repast. It is a golden rule of mine." And with that Milord had bowed to Nichola as she led the way into the dining room.

Tonight he was very much the courtier, stylish and witty, utterly imperturbable, and the actress, staring at him down the length of the table, felt herself hardly able to equate this image with that of the sensitive creature who would rather risk losing her than for them to have merely a sexual relationship. Yet if this self denial had been a clever ploy to bring her to his bed nothing could have worked better, though in her heart she knew that Joscelin was incapable of this kind of cunning and was humbled by his integrity.

He was speaking to her. "You are not eating heartily, my dear. Is anything wrong?"

"Yes. I hate the thought that my stepfather is about to set foot in this house."

"He already has, in fact. The servants have asked him to wait while we finish."

"Lord Joscelin!" exclaimed the rector admiringly.

Nichola's husband flicked an imaginary speck of dust off his sleeve. "I told you, Mr Hollin, I do not allow anything to spoil an excellent repast. When I have had my port I shall see him."

"Joe Cool," muttered Nichola, and laughed to herself.

The rector shot her an enquiring glance but Joscelin merely raised a brow to signify that he had heard if not understood. In the brief silence that followed a distant but recognisably angry voice became audible.

"Oh dear, oh dear," said John Hollin.

"A fart in a thunderstorm, if you will forgive the phrase, Rector. He will run out of puff before I even start on him."

"Do I have to see him?" Nichola asked, uneasy at hearing those familiar tones.

"But of course. First of all we must prove to him that you *are* Arabella and not some substituted creature smuggled to the altar in a mass of veils. And secondly he must hear for himself that you married me of your own free will and not under duress."

"But I dread the thought of setting eyes on him again."

"An unpleasant duty but one that must be faced, I fear."

"Would you like me to be present?" asked Mr Hollin nervously.

Joscelin put his head on one side, considering. "I think it might be best if we see him alone and then call you in. Provided that is acceptable to you, of course."

"Perfectly."

"Then shall we go? Or would you like another port?"

Catching sight of Nichola's expression, the rector answered hastily, "I think it might be best to get the ordeal over and done."

"By all means," and with that Lord Joscelin rose from the table to lead the other two from the room.

"Where has Sir Denzil been placed?" he asked the footman pulling out his chair.

"In the library, my Lord."

"Then let it be hoped he does not damage the books." Joscelin smiled at the cleric. "If you will forgive us, Mr Hollin, my wife and I would like a word in private before we face her furious father."

"Certainly, certainly," he answered, and hung back in the dining room doorway, his eyes going to the port decanter. With a sudden urgent movement Joscelin took Nichola's arm and hurried her in the direction of his study. Wondering what he was going to say, she gazed up into his face.

He had changed again, the man of action now obviously dominant. "Listen, sweetheart," he whispered, closing the door so that they could not be overheard, "what are you going to say when he asks you about writing the word Nichola in the register?"

She had been half expecting it and was prepared with an

answer. "That it is your nickname for me and I was so excited I wrote it down without thinking."

The mobile brows rose. "Neat, indeed! And what is the true explanation?"

"I'm afraid I can't tell you. Not yet."

He chuckled quietly. "As I thought. Now concentrate, witch girl. Do not so much as hint to Sir Denzil that we are man and wife in name only or *he* might bring a suit to have the marriage annulled. As far as your stepfather is concerned we are wedded and bedded and all is bliss."

Nichola wanted to say, "I wish it were true," but didn't have the nerve.

"Now are you ready?"

"As ready as I'll ever be to face that dirty old man."

"Then let's to it."

And with that Joscelin strode out of the study to the library and flung open the door.

"You devil," shrieked Sir Denzil without preamble, hurling himself in their direction as soon as he saw them. "You vile seducer! How dare you take my daughter from me. How dare you, Sir!"

With surprising swiftness Joscelin produced a pistol from his pocket and pointed it straight at his attacker, stopping him dead in his tracks.

"One move to lay hands on either of us and I'll shoot you through the head," he said by way of opening gambit. "And no questions asked either. Now sit down and calm down or by Christ's Holy Wounds you are a dead man."

Sir Denzil went white to the gills and a trickle of saliva appeared at one corner of his mouth. "You wouldn't dare," he said, none too convincingly.

"Wouldn't I?" snarled Joscelin in reply. "In truth nothing would give me greater pleasure. You tried to rape a woman, taking advantage of her vulnerable position in your household, and for that you are less than contemptible. If I said you were a hog's turd, Sir, it would be an insult to hogs."

"You married Arabella against her will," Sir Denzil hurled back, clenching his fists and standing his ground.

Joscelin, too, lost colour. "I think you'd best ask her that," he hissed, and motioned Nichola forward.

She regarded Sir Denzil with dislike. "I shall never forget the last time I saw you," she said quietly, "though I wish to God I could. Lord Joscelin rescued me from your disgusting advances and I married him not only out of gratitude but also out of love." She felt rather than saw Joscelin's eyes turn in her direction. "He is the most amazing man I have ever met–" And she found that she meant every word. "–and for you to dare to infer that I was forced to be his wife is more than I can stomach."

"And what, Sir, of your allegation that this is not the true Arabella but a substitute called Nichola?" Joscelin put in. "What say you now? How would another woman know that the last time you and Arabella met you were stripped to your gear? Go on, answer that."

Gear! thought Nichola, guessing what it meant but thinking that now it was Joscelin's turn to use a word in a different context.

Sir Denzil went even paler. "You foul mouthed whoreson, I'll kill you for that."

"One move," said Joscelin, cocking the pistol, "and I fire."

"Arabella," and Sir Denzil turned in Nichola's direction, "I demand that you return home."

"You have no right to demand anything of me," she answered furiously. "I am a grown woman and a mother and can marry whoever I choose. And I have chosen Lord Joscelin and there is nothing you can do about it."

"Maybe not," Sir Denzil answered, "but at least I can pay your husband..." he said the word with loathing "...the compliment of telling him the truth about you."

"What do you mean?" And suddenly, for no good reason, Nichola was nervous.

"That you're little better than a whore."

Oh my God! she thought, but held the words back.

"This strumpet had intercourse with Michael Morellon as soon as they were betrothed. She couldn't wait to bed with him, eager bitch that she was. It was his bastard she bore and then, when he was gone, she turned her attentions on me, having gone mad in childbirth and sworn that she was possessed."

"What *are* you talking about?" Nichola exclaimed.

"Oh yes, I know all about your ravings. Dr Rich told me everything. Your wife, Sir, spoke of the mind going on journeys. Of it being sent to other times and places. She is completely insane and her lechery and lasciviousness know no bounds. The truth behind her vile accusations is that she tried to seduce her own father and now is twisting the evidence. God help you, Lord Joscelin. You will have a life of hell."

"In that entire statement there is just one word of truth," Nichola answered, sick with anger, "and that is that only a mad woman would make advances to you. You are beneath contempt and I never want to set eyes on you again."

"Nor shall you," Joscelin said quietly. "You are to leave, Sir. Now! Your presence is not welcome here."

"Then go I will," Sir Denzil replied, gathering up his tattered dignity, "but know this. You will never see your child again, Madam. Constance shall take your place in my household. She will become the daughter that has been taken from me."

"Oh no!" Nichola shrieked, realising that she was becoming hysterical but no longer able to help herself. "I can't leave that poor baby with you to be abused and ill-treated. You are to return her to me at once, do you hear?"

"Never."

"Christ, I'll kill you," she screamed, and flew at him, nails raking his face.

"Enough," ordered Joscelin, stepping between them. "Arabella, enough. You will get your daughter back, never fear."

"Possession is nine-tenths of the law," Sir Denzil stated, and a terrible smile began to play around his lips. "You will have to take her from me by force."

"My dear Sir," Joscelin answered calmly, "from now on watch your back."

"Are you menacing me?"

"Certainly. Now get out of my house before I do the deed

here and save myself the trouble of having to seek you out."

"I'll take this matter further," Sir Denzil retorted, "don't think you can utter threats of that nature and not be punished."

"Out!" said Joscelin and, opening the door, threw Arabella's stepfather into the hallway by the collar of his coat.

"Good gracious!" exclaimed Mr Hollin, waiting outside.

"Begging your pardon, Rector," Milord added politely.

It was too much for Nichola who burst into the uneasy laughter which heralds hysteria.

"Stop it," Joscelin ordered without raising his voice. "Go to my study and sit down. Rogers shall bring you a brandy. I will join you later. Now, if you men would be good enough to see Sir Denzil off the premises, Mr Hollin and I will finish our port."

And that was that. Depleted of energy and emotion, Nichola sat in the candlelight sipping the strong and warming liquid, staring at the flames leaping in the fireplace. She would have liked to have been able to think rationally but it was too distressing to do so. Her brain was turning on a treadmill like the poor donkey that drew the water in the wheelhouse at Greys Court. Confused images of the past, of the recurring dream, of the scene she had just endured, blurred and melded into one. Wanting to shut everything out, Nichola closed her eyes.

She must have slept a while for a clock was striking midnight as Joscelin opened the door and came into the room. Almost reluctantly, Nichola dragged herself back to consciousness.

"Has he gone?" she asked him, where he stood shadowy in the doorway.

"Hours ago. I have been with poor Mr Hollin who is in a regular twit of nerves," he answered quietly.

"And what about you? Are you all right?"

"Yes." He took a few steps towards her. "My main concern is for your welfare."

Nichola stood up so that she could see his face more

distinctly. "There's only one thing worrying me, other than for the fate of poor little Miranda."

"And what is that?"

"That you might have believed the things he said about me. Because, other than for my liaison with Michael Morellon, I swear there's not a word of truth in them."

"I know that. I found you by the river, remember? Nobody could simulate that kind of distress."

"Except, perhaps, a mad woman."

Joscelin put his hands on her shoulders. "My dear, you are strange, you are elusive, but mad you most certainly are not."

"Thank you. Joscelin—"

"Yes?"

"Will you come to my bed tonight, to make love to me?"

He looked at her very seriously, holding her chin with one hand. "Arabella, do not think that my refusal to do so is because I am odd in any way. I am as lusty as the next man. Yet I have the feeling that between us there is an emotion that might well transcend the carnal act, ecstatic though that will be. Tonight you would give yourself out of gratitude, not love, because there is still something that holds you back, though whether it be that you continue to care for Michael Morellon or is an altogether different matter I do not yet know. But for all that, I believe we could have a love beyond bliss if the day ever comes that you give me your heart. I must wait in that hope. Do you understand?"

"No," she answered, weeping and shaking her head, "I am too shallow a person."

"Do not say such a thing. You are a fine woman, wise beyond your years."

"You know nothing about me."

Joscelin smiled. "And that is where you make a mistake. I know more of you than you think."

"But you could never guess the truth."

"Probably not. But then I really have no need because one day you will tell me."

She slept at once, but then started to dream. At first she was back in her old life, watching Lewis in rehearsal, very conscious of how good she looked in her skin tight body suit and of how his eyes continually sought her out. Then the dream changed and Nichola was wandering through a hospital looking for someone, feeling frightened and alone. It seemed that she passed people she knew, people with long faces who spoke in hushed tones. One she recognised as Glynda, but when Nichola went up and spoke to her the older actress wouldn't answer her, in fact didn't even look at her, almost as if Nichola weren't there at all.

She woke to the soft light of a September dawning, the summer birds quiet now, the sky cool, the colour of pearl. Over the ruins of the earlier Greys Court hung a low mist out of which the crenellated tower of the first Lord de Grey, who had fought at Crécy with Edward III, rose like the mast of a ship. Beyond the ruins lay the wild undulations of the parkland, the trees just showing their first hints of yellow and gold. Unable to sleep any longer, still shattered by the events of the previous night, Nichola felt the need to walk, to be outdoors and breathe the clean, sweet air. Rising from her lonely bed, she dressed herself without assistance and went out into the early morning.

Crossing the lawn, still enclosed by the crumbling walls of the medieval house, Nichola was about to make her way to the gardens beyond the great tower when a movement from the stables caught her eye. Joscelin was there, speaking to a young servant, presently leading out one of the geldings, patting the animal on its rump as it wheeled and stamped beside the mounting block. Suddenly afraid that he was leaving the house, Nichola ran forward.

"Are you going somewhere?"

He swept off his hat and removed his foot from the stirrup. "Only to Reading. I thought I would journey early and be back before noon."

"What for?" she said, realising as she did so that she must sound rather abrupt and rude.

"I am taking this letter to the post-house. They are only

situated in larger towns so I am forced to travel beyond Henley."

"Oh." She was dying to ask to whom the correspondence was addressed but could not quite bring herself to do so.

Joscelin's eyes twinkled. "I have written to my sister to tell her the news of our marriage. I have also asked her to send my servant Caradoc to Greys Court. He might well be useful to us."

"I see."

"My sweetheart, you don't in the least. Caradoc not only considers himself my slave – I rescued him from an evil situation when he was ten years old – but is a lion of a fellow. He'll protect you well when I return to the war and, besides, there is a special errand I want him to do for me."

"Which is?"

"To get your child and bring her here. I want to know you are happy before I leave."

"But why can't we go to fetch her? Why send a servant?"

"Because Caradoc has ways of doing things. Despite his size he can vanish into the night like a shadow. If anyone can get past Denzil Loxley and steal an infant, Caradoc is the man."

Nichola smiled. "He sounds fascinating."

"He's that right enough. Quite a character." Joscelin turned back to the mounting block. "Anyway, let me get this letter off. The sooner Meraud receives it the sooner she can despatch him."

Not wanting him to go quite yet, Nichola said, "What a wonderful name your sister has. How is it spelt?"

"Like this."

She stared at the letter's elaborately folded paper, sealed and addressed on the outside.

"To my honourable Sister the Lady Meraud Attwood at her house Kingswear Hall on the estuary of the River Dart, five miles from Dartmouth, in the County of Devonshire."

Laughing, Nichola had looked up at Joscelin and exclaimed, "How quaint!" before she had had time to think.

"It's a perfectly normal style of address," he answered somewhat severely. "I admit that my sister's name care of

Dartmouth would be sufficient, as we send a servant in three times a week to collect the post. It is taken as far as there by a local carrier who plies from Plymouth. Despite that, however, I prefer to put it in full."

"I'm sorry," Nichola said, realising how patronising she must have sounded. "I don't mean to be critical."

He was not placated. "You obviously do not use His Majesty's postal service often or you would know how efficient it is. Though whether it will continue to be so once the fighting starts seriously is anyone's guess. Anyway, I must away in order to catch today's distribution to the carrier." He leant from the saddle and kissed her cheek. "I'll be back in time to dine with you."

"Good," Nichola answered and waved until he had vanished from view.

With his disappearance a certain colour seemed to have gone from the morning and it occurred to Nichola that life would be unbelievably empty when he returned to Nottingham. The thought of dreary days stretching endlessly ahead depressed her and even the idea that she could ask Caradoc somehow to steal Emmet as well as the child failed to lift her spirits. It suddenly seemed to Nichola that her life in the seventeenth century had reached an impasse, and that she should now make a concerted effort to return to her own time before something happened to stop her.

Remembering the waking dream she stopped dead in her tracks. Had she really heard voices call her name or had it all been an illusion? Whatever it was, it had terrified her, but perhaps she must endure fear in order to get back. Sinking down beneath an oak tree, Nichola leant against it and closed her eyes, determined to try to put herself into a trance.

In common with all drama students she had learned relaxation techniques and now she started consciously tensing her muscles then letting them go limp, breathing in deeply through the nose and out of the mouth as she did so. At the same time, Nichola attempted to focus her thoughts on the word 'black', and clear her mind of all other intrusions.

After a while it seemed to her that she could hear music,

that somewhere someone was playing a tape of Stravinsky's *Petrushka*, a particular favourite of hers. She turned her head slightly to listen and the voices started.

"She's responding. I saw her move."

"Are you sure?"

"Certain. Just a little twitch of the head. Nichola, can you hear me? Do you recognise the music?"

She wanted to say, "It's *Petrushka*" but to do so was unbelievably hard. Her lips attempted to form the letter P but no sound would come out.

"She's trying to speak. Look, look!"

"My God, I think you're right. Oh Nichola, Nichola! Please wake up. Say you know what's happening."

A shadow fell over her, blotting out the rich red sun riding high in the autumn sky, a sign that hours had passed by.

"What's the matter?" said Joscelin's voice, its tone brusque and urgent. "Arabella, what's happening? Come on, come back to me." There was a pause and then he said, "Nichola, don't go."

Somewhere a distant voice said, "She's fading. Oh God, God!"

But now two hands had seized her and she was being shaken and roughly pulled to her feet.

"Oh, God," breathed Joscelin's voice close to her ear, and Nichola opened her eyes.

She stared at him stupidly, owlishly, hardly able to focus, unable to speak.

"Oh, thank God," he gasped. "I thought you were dying. You were inert, lifeless, the colour of a corpse. I could not even detect a breath. You must never do that again, Arabella. Do you hear?"

Still incapable of speech, Nichola stood swaying on her feet, and the next second he had swung her into his arms and was carrying her in the direction of Greys Court, for all the world as if she were a thoroughly naughty child that had stolen out and made itself ill by eating too many sweetmeats and must now be taken home.

* * *

As if he had sensed in some way that her cataleptic state had somehow been self induced, Joscelin seemed to watch over her during the next two weeks. Normally, Nichola would have found it intensely irritating, not wanting to be constantly guarded by her partner, not enjoying the fact that he was studying her every move. But this was a different century and Joscelin was a very different man. In fact she enjoyed being in his company, even more than she had enjoyed being in that of Lewis Devine, though she could hardly bear to admit this even to herself.

By now news of the war had begun to trickle through in the form of letters from various friends. According to them, King Charles had left the East Midlands in mid September and marched west through Leicestershire and Derbyshire to Shrewsbury. This ancient town being in a fine position to gain His Majesty access to the Royalist strongholds in Wales, the Marches and Lancashire, it was an obvious choice for a new headquarters. At the same time the elegant Prince Rupert had begun to make his presence felt by taking his cavalry into Northamptonshire and Warwickshire and there making trouble for prominent Parliamentarians.

"He's demanding money off 'em," said Joscelin, chuckling over the latest correspondence.

"That takes some nerve."

"He's got plenty of that."

"So you'll have to travel to Shrewsbury to catch up with them all?"

"Yes, just as soon as Caradoc has arrived and you're settled with your maid and daughter I'll be off."

"I won't like it at Greys Court on my own."

"But you'll wait here for me?"

She knew he was uneasy, unsure of her, and found it a difficult question to answer in view of her circumstances, her overriding wish to return to her own times.

"I see you hesitate," Joscelin went on. "Tell me, are you still in love with Michael Morellon?"

"No, of course not."

"But you don't love me, do you?"

"I want to go to bed with you if that's any indication."

Joscelin hesitated. "Perhaps we should, perhaps that would help the situation. Keep you by my side."

Nichola could not believe it but she actually heard herself say, "Don't sacrifice what you believe in just because of my desires. I can wait till you are ready."

"By God, Arabella," exclaimed Joscelin, jumping from his seat and going to her. "What a wonderful woman you are. I never thought to hear you say that."

And with that he swept her into his arms and they exchanged the first passionate kiss of their relationship. As if he sought honey, wine, all the sweetness in the world, Joscelin's tongue found hers and made love to it. Instantly she melted against him, tempting him with every move, as only Nichola Hall knew how.

"Damn everything. I've got to have you," Joscelin said, his kiss dropping to her bodice which he pulled open.

His lips were on her breast, Arabella's sweet, small nipples were in his mouth.

"My shaft is straining," he said huskily, "are we private enough here?"

"No, let's go to the bedroom. The servants might walk in if we stay."

And just as if Nichola had had a presentiment there was, at that very moment, a knock on the door, which opened immediately. Guiltily, the pair of them jumped apart.

"I'm sorry to have to disturb you, my Lord," said one of the footmen, eyeing Joscelin's dishevelled appearance. "But a man has arrived at the house saying you sent for him. He gives his name as Caradoc Venner. Shall I let him in?"

"Of all the moments to choose," Nichola's husband said to her ruefully. "Yes, bring him inside and tell him I'll be there in a few minutes."

"Must you go?" she said as the door closed again.

"He has travelled all the way from Devon. I feel that I should at least be courteous enough to greet him."

"Oh bloody hell!" exclaimed Nichola angrily, and at that moment disliked Caradoc intensely even though she had not, as yet, so much as cast her eyes on him.

Chapter Eleven

There could be no doubt that the arrival of Caradoc Venner at Greys Court had heralded a period of change, change which, as far as Nichola was concerned, was quite definitely for the worse. It seemed to her that no sooner had the wretched man set his foot over the threshold than Joscelin had become entangled with the affairs of his other family, that group of formidable females who, up till now, had been safely tucked away in Devon.

Still recovering from the fact that Caradoc had interrupted such a passionate moment, Nichola had at last calmed down and gone to bed. But Joscelin had not joined her and as the great clock had struck one, she had got up again, put a shawl over her nightgown, and made her way downstairs, ready to be angry. As she had stood on the bottom stair, the sound of quiet voices could clearly be heard coming from the direction of her husband's study. Without knocking, Nichola had silently opened the door and stood in the entrance.

She supposed afterwards that she had expected Caradoc to be a kind of walking cliché – a gentle giant, a devoted servant, a son of the soil, one of nature's gentlemen. Yet he had been none of those things, neither had he possessed the air of slight stupidity that Nichola often associated with very large men. Nor, indeed, had Caradoc been as big as she had imagined, for though he was tall and muscular the man was slim to the point of thinness and had about him an air almost of delicacy. Sensing someone watching him, Caradoc had turned and looked Nichola full in the face.

She had thought, perhaps, that he would give her a glance of shy deference, or of delight that his master had found another bride. Though another possibility could have been jealousy, anger over the fact that his place in Joscelin's affections had been usurped by a stranger. But Caradoc's gaze contained none of these elements. Instead Nichola had seen a look of interest, of scrutiny, of almost clinical appraisal. Not knowing quite why, she had started to feel uncomfortable as she returned his stare.

The newcomer was in his late twenties and as supple as a bow, his tall spare physique adding to the general impression of speed and grace which he had about him. His hair, though long and curling and similar in texture to Joscelin's, was much lighter, the colour of cinnamon, while Caradoc's eyes, with their clear discerning gaze, were a deep rich blue. Fleetingly, Nichola found herself thinking that he and Joscelin looked alike and wondered if they could be related in any way. But when Caradoc, who had risen unhurriedly to his feet, spoke, she knew at once that that was not the case. For the servant's accent gave everything away. He was a Devonian peasant and could not possibly be connected with a member of the landed gentry.

He bowed and said, "Caradoc Venner, my Lady."

"How do you do," she answered, just a trifle coldly.

"My pardons for arriving at so strange an hour. I have been riding night and day and thought it best not to delay at the last."

"The fact is, Arabella," Joscelin put in abruptly, "my daughter Sabina is ill and I must go to her."

Nichola turned and noticed for the first time that he was dressed for the road. "Not tonight surely?" she asked.

"I'm afraid so."

She had not meant to burst into tears, particularly not in front of Caradoc, but Nichola's frustration and longing for Joscelin suddenly overflowed. "Oh God dammit," she said, wiping her hand over her eyes. "Couldn't you wait an hour or two?"

He knew exactly what she meant. That much was obvious. "Sweetheart, if only I could," he answered quietly. "But I must make a start. The girl is sick and it's a long journey even at the best of times. And now there may well be troops massing which could slow me up even more."

Nichola turned her eyes in the direction of Caradoc. "Would it be possible to have a word with you in private?" she asked her husband in a subdued voice.

"Of course." It was the servant who answered, not Joscelin,

then the door opened and closed again as he went out.

"Listen, my Lord," said Nichola, hovering between anger and despair, "you've kept me waiting so long that the situation has become intolerable. And now, when you finally decide you want me, you can't stop long enough even to take me to bed."

Joscelin pulled her into his arms, just a fraction roughly. "I've wanted you ever since I first saw you in that inn on the journey north, so it's no new thing," he said. "I was drawn to you as I've never been to a woman, right from that moment. And that is the reason why I married you. And that is also why, at the risk of repeating myself, I decided to leave you untouched until I felt sure of you."

"And are you sure of me now?"

Joscelin held her at arm's length. "No, that's the very devil of it, I'm not entirely. I am dogged by the feeling that if Michael Morellon were to re-enter your life you would be off without a backward glance."

"Then why did you nearly take me earlier?"

"Because, you beautiful young enchantress, I could no longer resist. I am a human male, no more."

"Then let's go upstairs," said Nichola urgently, wanting him to the point of recklessness.

Joscelin tightened his grip on her. "I daren't, sweetheart, much as I long to. Supposing the girl should die."

Before she had had time to think, or control herself, or do anything sensible, Nichola suddenly found herself shouting, "Oh bugger the girl!", and flouncing out of the room with a violent crash of the door. Then, as she rushed upstairs, tears streaming, she had noticed Caradoc watching her from the shadows below.

"Don't stare, it's very rude!" she had shouted over her shoulder, before plunging into her room and locking the door.

Shortly afterwards she had heard Joscelin leave Greys Court and had lain in the moonlight thinking that she must be insane. She was a twentieth century woman, modern in every degree, yet here she was weeping over a man who had died at least three hundred years before she had even been born. But because she had gone back to this man's own time, the feelings he aroused in her were intense and real. Half deriding herself, Nichola began to wonder whether she was falling in love with Joscelin Attwood, and in view of that how she would react if she were to return to her own century that very night.

Without him the house seemed empty, devoid of life. She had wandered disconsolately in the long gallery, kept indoors by a wet autumn day, and had found herself repeatedly wishing that she and Joscelin had parted on better terms. Finally, when the rain stopped, in sheer desperation Nichola had sought out Caradoc to see if any message had been left with him, though something about the very act of doing this went against the grain.

She had found him in the stable yard, backing a horse between the shafts of a small cart, and calmly studied him for a second before he realised she was there. The man was attractive, there was no doubt of that, beautiful in his own way.

"Caradoc," Nichola called softly, deciding he would probably make a better friend than enemy.

He turned, watchful as a hare. "Yes?"

"I want to apologise for shouting at you last night. The truth is that Lord Joscelin and I were not in agreement about him setting off there and then. Consequently I lost my temper. Still, it was unforgivable of me to raise my voice to someone who was not involved."

"But I was involved," he answered. "I brought the message that led to your falling out."

"That was hardly your fault."

"Is it not said that the messenger is sometimes killed for the intelligence he imparts?"

Nichola smiled wryly. "I see you have a good knowledge of the world."

Caradoc's rich blue eyes darkened. "I learned my lessons young." His tone changed. "Now in what way may I help your Ladyship?"

"I wondered if my husband had left any word for me."

"None that I know of."

She felt a stab of disappointment but covered it by lightly saying, "I expect he had no time." Seeing his non-committal expression, Nichola deliberately changed the subject. "So where are you off to?"

"I'm going to fetch your child and maid. My master instructed that I do it at once."

Nichola stared at him. "You can't just walk in and demand them. Sir Denzil would probably have you shot."

A flash of humour lit Caradoc's eyes. "It will be done in such a way, my Lady, that your stepfather will not even know I have called. Until it is too late, that is."

"What do you intend to do?"

"Get word to your servant and arrange to meet her, complete with babe. It will be a simple case of abduction as far as the world is concerned."

"But how do you propose to contact her?"

Caradoc looked bland. "There are ways of doing these things."

"Bribes?"

"It is not unknown."

And he would say no more. Instead, he swung lithely on to the driver's seat and brushed the whip over the horse's rump. "Gee up, there," he called, and the cart began to trundle forward.

Nichola laid a restraining hand on the reins. "You must respect Lord Joscelin very much to do such errands for him. Have you always been his servant?"

"Since I was ten," Caradoc answered solemnly, and urged the cart out of the stableyard before Nichola could ask another question.

She supposed that she had expected Joscelin back within a few weeks, Caradoc a few days, but as time passed and neither man appeared Nichola found herself falling into a state of extreme anxiety, hardly able to concentrate on a thing, desperately worried about the fate of her child and her servant – not to mention her husband. Then right in the middle of an acute attack, a thought came to her. Was reality, her past in other words, now becoming more unreal than the fantasy world in which she found herself living? Breathing deeply, Nichola forced herself to concentrate on her former life.

It was all blurred, or rather had the slight haze of dreams about it. Mental pictures of her father, his second wife, their weedy children, of her mother and Johnny Carstairs, of the men in The Collection, even of Lewis Devine with whom she had been so in love, seemed like those in an old album, half remembered and somehow no longer relevant. Shocked by what was happening to her, Nichola sat silently until it grew dark. Then she shook herself, determined not to be frightened by the inexplicable changes taking place in her, for what, after all, was the point when there was nothing she could do to alter the situation? With an effort, Nichola started to turn her thoughts to the progress of the war.

Joscelin had kept her informed of every development and once a week the Reverend Mr Hollin would call to discuss matters over Milord's port, so Nichola believed herself to be as up to date as was possible without any means of instant communication.

It seemed that the King had remained in Shrewsbury throughout September, his army now swelled enormously by the hundreds of men arriving daily to join him. Meanwhile, or so Mr Hollin believed, the Parliamentarian Earl of Essex had left London, preceded by 6,000 foot and 4,000 horse and, in order to block Charles's presumed advance had turned towards Worcester, a Royalist town. And it was there that the first formal military action of the war had taken place. The King had sent Prince Rupert, that dashing young man always clad in scarlet, richly laid with silver lace, with a thousand horse to back him up, to go to the aid of the townsfolk. The Prince had clashed with the Earl's advance guard at Powick Bridge, south of the city, where Rupert's headlong charge, his brother Prince Maurice, Sir John Byron, Lord Digby and Viscount Wilmot's son Henry, at his side, had splintered the enemy. There had been riderless horses and running men everywhere. The result was total chaos, a complete rout.

And then, according to Mr Hollin, for it was now getting on towards late October and first-hand news was travelling more slowly, the King had finally decided to leave Shrewsbury and head off in the general direction of London.

"He no doubt plans to retake the city, my Lady."

"I wonder if Joscelin got caught up in all that. He would have come back through Bristol and there may well have been troop movement round there," Nichola answered him, wanting that to be the truth, not wishing to consider the fact that her husband might have abandoned her and secretly sent for Caradoc to join him.

"No word from him yet? Dear me!" And Mr Hollin had put the tips of his fingers together in a gesture of anxiety. "I have heard it said," he went on somewhat tentatively, "that it is the Earl of Essex's plan to end the war now, almost before it has begun, by wiping out His Majesty's field army. And he therefore intends to pursue the King until they can engage."

"And where are they all situated at present?"

"I believe in the Warwickshire-Oxfordshire area."

A vaguely remembered history lesson came back to Nichola and she stood up. "Mr Hollin, are the armies anywhere near a place called Edge Hill?"

"I have no idea, my Lady. Would you care to consult a map? Sir Francis used to keep them in the library. I know exactly where they are."

The rector had arrived at Greys Court on his weekly visit, something that Nichola looked forward to now that everyone else had gone. She sometimes thought, with a touch of cynicism, that if anybody had told Nichola Hall the actress that she would actually enjoy the company of a middle-aged, delightfully innocent cleric, she would have laughed in his face. In this desperate situation, however, her values seemed to be changing daily.

"I should like to do so very much," she said, and swept before him, her silk skirts rustling on the wooden floors of the great house.

The maps were in a special drawer which could be pulled out, creating a flat surface on which the contents might be examined.

"There," said Mr Hollin, pointing a rather workworn finger as they bent over the chart devoted to southern England and Wales, "that is what my intelligencer told me. Troops are massing in that area."

"Between Stratford-on-Avon and Banbury?"

"Yes."

"Then that's it. The Battle of Edgehill, first battle of the Civil War, 23 October, 1642."

Mr Hollin gaped at her. "But my dear Lady Attwood, how do you know such things? How can you have information about what is yet to come?"

Acutely aware of the superstitious nature of the populace at large, including men of the cloth, Nichola felt compelled to reassure him. "Oh, don't worry, Sir, I'm no fortune-teller. What I said was merely a guess, an idea of what might yet happen."

The rector looked at her suspiciously. "But I thought you said the date."

"That was a guess too. Who knows how things will develop? All I wish is that I had news of Lord Joscelin and of Caradoc too. He went to fetch my child from Haseley Court, Sir Denzil's house, and has been gone for weeks."

"I expect he is awaiting his chance," Mr Hollin answered wisely.

"What do you mean?"

"That to get past your stepfather and secure the infant without causing an affray would be no mean feat. I imagine Lord Joscelin's man, if what I have heard of him is accurate, will steal in, then out again, just like a shadow. I feel certain that this is at the heart of the delay."

"But I am anxious."

"Naturally so. But let me make a prediction to *you*. I think that all three – Caradoc, child and maid – will be safely under your roof by tomorrow night."

"And what makes you say so?"

"One of my parishioners at market in Oxford told me he saw just such a party. He noted them particularly because he thought he had glimpsed the man in the company of Lord Joscelin."

"Then it is them!" said Nichola triumphantly. And, yet again, she experienced a moment of stepping outside herself, and was filled with wonder that she should feel so genuinely pleased about the return of a baby that wasn't even hers. To say nothing of once more being in the company of an ignorant servant girl who could neither read nor write.

An hour later, as Mr Hollin consumed the last of the port before setting forth into the chilly night, there came the sound of wheels on stone. Hurrying to the oriel window on the south front, set above the porch, Nichola looked out. By the light of the torches attached to the outer wall she could see Caradoc helping Emmet out of a cart, a considerably larger Miranda, visible only as a bundle of shawls, in her arms. Overjoyed, Nichola ran back to the rector.

"They're here, Mr Hollin. Your prediction has come about already," and she dropped a kiss on his amiable brow before hurrying downstairs to greet the new arrivals.

"Well, here's a to do, Mistress," said Emmet, stepping through the front door and looking about her. "I could scarce believe what I had heard. I thought at first 'twas a trick to deceive me. But here you are safe and sound and it's all true enough."

"What is all true?"

"That you had married Lord Joscelin Attwood and become mistress of your own establishment."

"Well, not quite my own. Greys Court belongs to the Knollys family who have gone to Germany to escape the war. It's only a temporary refuge." Nichola reached for the bundle. "Here, let me have the child. I haven't seen her for months and I've missed her, I really have."

"There's no need to sound so surprised," Emmet answered, "she is your daughter after all."

But there's every need, thought Nichola. You are speaking to Nichola Hall who never wanted children if you did but know it.

In the endearing way of the very young, the baby awoke at that moment and not only gave Nichola a quick wide smile but held out its arms.

"She recognises me," the actress shrieked. "Did you see that? I thought she would have forgotten who I was."

And she snatched Miranda to her, kissing and hugging and behaving in a way that once would have been quite foreign to her.

"There now," said Emmet sentimentally, and shot a sly glance at Caradoc, only to see that his expression was blank, the mazarine eyes masking whatever thoughts were going on behind them.

"Perhaps you should congratulate our rescuer, Mistress," she added rather pointedly.

Nichola looked up, confused by the fact she had so much love to give, angry that she had been sufficiently discourteous as not to thank Joscelin's servant for all he had done.

"What can I say?" she said, "other than that you have made me very happy. I owe you an enormous debt of gratitude."

Not moving from his place in the doorway, where he seemed almost poised for flight, Caradoc answered, "I merely obeyed Lord Joscelin's instructions."

"But what difficult instructions they were. A lesser man might have bungled the whole thing."

"Indeed," put in Mr Hollin, speaking for the first time. "You have done an admirable job, young man. Tonight I shall pray to God to reward you."

A momentary smile flickered over Caradoc's lips. "I thank you, Sir. No doubt my immortal soul could do with all the prayers it can get. And now, if you will excuse me."

And with that he was gone, giving a quick bow to the assembled company before he melted into the bitter night outside.

"Odd fellow," said the rector. "Is he always so taciturn?"

"He looks the sort to have a secret to me," Emmet added.

Nichola nodded, addressing them both. "He certainly has an air of mystery. I really must try to find out more about his past."

"Tread carefully," Mr Hollin warned, "I feel he is the type of man to resent intrusion. And now, Lady Attwood, if you will forgive me I must return to my own hearth. I cannot tell you how glad I am to see your little one restored to you. Let it be hoped that Lord Joscelin will soon also join the family."

"Pray for him as well," said Nichola impulsively.

"I am already doing so I can assure you," the rector answered simply, and with that made a formal bow before he, too, departed.

It was during the night that Nichola came to a decision. Thinking about the events of that evening, remembering what Mr Hollin had said about Caradoc's ability to stalk, shadow-like, until he achieved his objective, it occurred to her that if anyone could find Joscelin for her it would be his servant. Nichola could not allow herself to believe that her husband was still residing in Devon. For surely, however angry with her he had been, he would have written to inform her of his whereabouts. So it was obvious, if that were the case, that somewhere during his journey, either on the way or returning, he had caught up with the King's army and been called back into service. And there had been a skirmish at Worcester and men had died.

Nichola shuddered at the very idea and for the thousandth time thought that she must have gone mad. For why else should she care so deeply about a man who, if truth be told, could hold no more substance for her than a ghost? Yet the idea of Caradoc finding Joscelin had taken hold. As soon as it was light Nichola rose and dressed by the warmth of the fire that had flickered all night in her bedroom hearth, then went to look for him.

The servant emerged from the stables just as she approached them and it struck her that he had slept there, for Caradoc carried a pail of water and was preparing to wash himself. As soon as he heard Nichola's steps his head shot up like that of a wary animal and she saw the muscles of his stripped back go tense.

"It's only me," she called softly, "there's no need to be alarmed."

The magnificent eyes flashed. "It wasn't that, my Lady. I merely wondered who approached, 'tis all. In times of war a man cannot be too careful."

Ignoring his reply, Nichola sat down on a bale of straw and came straight to the point. "Caradoc, am I correct in thinking that you do not like me too well?"

He flushed angrily. "It is not my place to like or dislike, my Lady. I came into my master's service when I was a child and it is my duty to serve both him and his family. That is all I have to say."

"Very well, I shall not question you further though I do not think you have given me a satisfactory answer. Now, even if I did not say enough last night, let me make it quite clear that I am most grateful for the return of my child. In fact so well did you undertake this mission that I would like you to go on another."

"If you are about to ask me to search for Lord Joscelin I had already made up my mind to do so," Caradoc answered.

"On your own account?"

"I would have asked your permission first, my Lady. The truth is I was deeply shocked not to find him here last night. The rescue of the infant took longer than I had planned and I had not considered the fact that my master might not have returned before me."

"Do you suppose he is still in Devon? Do you think his daughter has died?"

Was it her imagination or did Caradoc start to breathe slightly faster and was there a momentary stir of emotion in those rich blue eyes?

"I do not think that can be, Madam. My Lord would surely have written in those circumstances."

"That is what I keep telling myself. No, I think it is far more likely that he has rejoined the King and communications have broken down. That is why I want you to make your way to a place called Edge Hill which lies between Stratford-on-Avon and Banbury. I have a strange presentiment that that is where the two armies will clash for the first time. If Lord Joscelin has been recalled he's bound to be in the thick of it."

"How far is it from here?"

"I don't know but I guess about twenty-five miles."

"If you give me a strong horse I can be there by nightfall."

Nichola nodded. "Pick any one you choose, I'm sure you're a far better judge of horseflesh than I am."

"Very well." And Caradoc turned away.

"I'll get the servants to pack you some food."

He swung round again to look at her. "I won't wait for that. The sooner I go the sooner I will find him."

Nichola hesitated, then said, "Caradoc, if he is dead, either bring him back here so that he can be with his kin or make sure he's laid to rest decently."

"On the battlefield that promise cannot always be kept."

"Oh damn you," snapped Nichola, suddenly losing her temper, riled by his impassive behaviour. "Do as I say, do you hear? I want news of that man and I want it urgently. You tell me it is your duty to serve Joscelin's family, then get on with it."

And turning her back on him she stalked off towards the parkland to calm herself before the time came to return to the house.

Chapter Twelve

The autumn which had begun so depressingly, clammy, cold, and thoroughly wretched, ended in a flash of fireworks. The sky, faint blue in September, grey and sullen throughout October, in November transformed to a deep cobalt, the colour of stained glass, and the days were so clear that the slopes across the valley looked near enough to lean over and touch. In the home park the trees turned the shade of a great wine cellar; the crisp amber of sweet Muscadine, the deep sensuous red of Malmsey, the high bright flame of Galloway, the pallid yellow of Rochell. Nichola, crunching over the leaves with Miranda in her arms, was reminded of far off times; of Wellington boots, of her mother before Johnny Carstairs came along, of years which now seemed almost as if they had belonged to somebody else.

In the library of Greys Court, for these days she had plenty of time for browsing, Caradoc having gone in search of Joscelin and no word yet from either of them, Nichola had found a wondrous book. Entitled *The English House-Wife*, the work had been written by G. Markham and printed for someone called George Sawbridge, whose address had been given as At the Sign of the Bible on Ludgate Hill. It appeared to be an up-date of an earlier work, for it claimed to be the sixth time that the book had been "Augmented, Purged, and made most profitable and necessary for all men, and the general good of this NATION." The subtitle had caught Nichola's eye. "The inward and outward Vertues which ought to be in a Compleat Woman".

Strangely, it had contained some rather good recipes. "Take a large Trout fair trimm'd and wash it, and put it into a deep pewter dish, then take half a pint of sweet Wine, with a lump of butter, and a little whole Mace, Parsley, Savory, and Thyme, mince them all small, and put them into the Trouts belly, and so let it stew a quarter of an hour, then mince the yelk of a hard Egge, and strew it on the Trout, and laying the herbs about it, and scraping on Sugar, serve it up." Others had been much more exotic. "To make a Gallantine, or sauce for a Swan, Bittern, Hearn, Crane, or any large Fowl, take the blood of the same Fowl, and being stirred well, boyl it on the fire, then when it comes to be thick, put into it Vinegar a good quantity, with a few fine white bread crums, and so boyl it over again."

With the book in her hand, Nichola had taken to wandering into the kitchens to experiment, the child, who could now sit up on her own, perched on the table, licking from a spoon.

"Why, Arabella, I never thought to find you so domestic," Emmet had said, coming across her mistress stirring things in a bowl, and looking faintly surprised.

"Not so much of that. I'll have you know I used to make a very fine Chicken Masala, to say nothing of my Saumon en Croûte."

"And what are they and when was that, pray?"

"I'm joking," Nichola had answered, and fortunately, Emmet had let the remark pass and the mistake had gone unheeded.

The book, as well as the section entitled Skill in Cookery, contained other fascinating sections, Household Physick being a particular gem. Some of the diseases, including venom in the ear, a pimpled or red sawcy face, a stinking breath which cometh from the Stomach, to say nothing of stinking nostrils, and syphilis, euphemistically called the French or Spanish Pox, had cures too terrible to contemplate.

Nichola's favourite was "For Frenzy, or inflammation of the cauls of the brain, you shall cause the juice of Beets to be with a Syringe squirted up into the patient's nostrils, which will purge and cleanse his head exceedingly; and then give him to drink posset-ale, in which Violet leaves and Lettuce have been boyled, and it will suddenly bring him to a very temperate mildness, and make the passion of the Frenzy forsake him".

"I can think of one or two who could have done with that," she had said to Miranda, to whom she had been reading the book out loud. And the child had smiled, and for a moment looked so like both Michael York and Michael Morellon that Nichola had been quite startled.

Her thoughts had turned to Arabella's lover, who had also been hers for one brief hour, and she wondered where Michael was and how he fared, indeed whether he was still alive. A terrible scenario flashed into Nichola's mind in which he and Joscelin killed one another, and she suddenly found herself feeling acutely depressed. The phrase "By the Sword Divided" seemed to be taking on more and more meaning, particularly as news of the war continued to filter in, via both the servants and, more reliably, the rector.

As Nichola had predicted, much discomfiting Mr Hollin, the Battle of Edgehill had been fought in October, ending in the Earl of Essex's retreat and a victory for the King. Reports differed slightly but all seemed to agree that Rupert of the Rhine had contributed greatly to the triumph, opening the fight with a thunderous cavalry charge which had caused the enemy horsemen to panic and flee, taking with them four infantry regiments. However, there had been grievous losses on the Royalist side too. The royal lifeguards, the King's Red Regiment, had been particularly badly hit and for a while the King himself had been under threat, while the Standard Bearer, Sir Edmund Verney, had indeed been brutally killed. Nichola and the rector had discussed in awed tones the report that he had cut down as many as sixteen Parliamentarians and refused the office of quarter before he was put to the sword. In death his hand had held the Standard so fast that only by hacking it off at the wrist could the flag be wrested from him.

"His body was not recovered," Mr Hollin had added, almost in a whisper. "But they say his ring, with a tiny picture of the King set in it, has been found."

"What about the Standard?"

"It was snatched back not long after it was captured by Lucas's troopers, may God be praised."

By nightfall, or so the rector had heard, over one and a half thousand men from either side had perished from the thirty thousand who had engaged that day. Darkness had seen the opposing armies still on the battlefield, Lord Essex receiving reinforcements from two MPs, Colonel John Hampden and Captain Oliver Cromwell. While the following morning had revealed a stalemate – both camps staring at one another over the wasteland but neither in a condition to restart the battle. Eventually, amidst the cheers of the Royalist hordes, Essex had retreated towards Warwick.

"You look very pensive, my Lady," the rector had said, when their conversation had finally died away into silence.

"I am worried half to death about Lord Joscelin."

Mr Hollin had cleared his throat. "Your love for him is written upon your face, if I may make so bold. My heart goes out to you, my Lady."

She had laughed at him, been about to tell him that he was a sentimental old fool, and then Nichola had stopped short. Was this constant fear for Joscelin's safety, her longing to see him again, a symptom of something far greater?

She had looked at her dinner companion a little sadly. "I was not aware that I wore my heart on my sleeve to such an obvious extent. To be honest with you, Rector, I also have a friend amongst the Parliamentarians. I was wondering, too, if he had survived the battle."

"These are surely the most evil times in our history," John Hollin answered sadly. "Brother rending brother in the name of God and righteousness."

"They still do," Nichola murmured to herself.

"What's that you say?"

"Nothing."

"And what of this Parliamentarian? Is he related in any way?"

"I'll be blunt with you, Mr Hollin. He is the father of Ara . . . *my* child. We were betrothed and began a married relationship. But Sir Denzil supported the King and Sir George Morellon, Parliament. So that was the end of that."

"I'm so sorry. It must be a terrible personal dilemma."

Nichola changed the subject. "Did you tell me the King is heading for Oxford?"

"I believe he's expected hourly."

"And what of the Earl of Essex?"

"He is supposedly crossing the Chilterns. It is nothing short of miraculous that he came out of Edgehill with enough honour left to continue his command."

"But surely," said Nichola, frowning, "that leaves the King's route to London wide open. Who's there to stop him?"

"No one. If he presses on now he can regain the capital."

The actress sat in silence, wishing she had studied the Civil Wars in greater depth, aware that something had happened at Turnham Green which had stopped Charles's and Rupert's relentless march towards the city and altered the whole course of the rest of the war.

Seeing her staring into space again, Mr Hollin misunderstood and said, "I feel sure there will be word of Lord Joscelin soon."

"I hope you are right. Tell me, does the fighting stop as the weather gets worse?"

"Those are the usual tactics, yes. So I dare say my Lord will be home with you for Christmas."

"Christmas!" Nichola exclaimed. "Have I really been here almost nine months?"

"No, only three," the rector corrected her gently. "For I did not marry you until after the King had raised the Standard at Nottingham and then there was a few days' delay while you made the journey."

But Nichola was not listening to him, shaking her head in amazement and saying, "It can't be that long, it can't! I simply don't believe it."

As soon as it was spoken of, she remembered the débâcle at Turnham Green. The King's army had marched up river from Putney and then found its way blocked by a force some twenty-four thousand strong, twice as large as the number of Royalist troops. The Parliamentarians had mustered every man they had, including former deserters, all come together to see off the enemy and stop a repeat of the sacking of Brentford, which Prince Rupert had previously stormed and plundered. Throughout the day of Sunday, 13 November 1642, the two armies had stood face to face and then, during the night, the King had withdrawn towards Oxford, his one chance of ending the war quickly, shattered and gone.

"So what happens now?" Nichola had asked Emmet, Mr Hollin being about his pastoral duties when the news came through.

"It's said that the King will not move on this winter and will keep his Christmas at Oxford."

"And what about the other side? What will they do?"

"I expect they'll keep on fighting, being Puritans and not approving of festivities."

"What a dreary bunch they sound."

"They can't all be," Emmet had answered reasonably. "Michael's not like that. He's bound to be at war for a principle."

"More likely his father's principles." Nichola had sat down on a kitchen chair. "I worry for him, believe me. But not half as much as I worry for Joscelin. I am absolutely convinced that both he and Caradoc must be dead."

"Never," Emmet had said certainly. "I tell you, Mistress, that fellow is indestructible, Caradoc I mean. You have never seen anything like the way he got Miranda and me out of Haseley Court. It was all done with signals and messages and was focused on a night when Sir Denzil was away visiting. In the end I just walked out of the place, cool as you please. I swear to God that not even a sword strike could kill him. He'd find some way to duck it."

"But where does that leave my husband?"

Emmet had looked at her narrowly. "You've become a funny one, Arabella."

"Why do you say that?"

"Because I've known you so long and seen the changes in you."

"Tell me."

"Well, when you were young you were such a giddy thing, all eager for Michael and not a brain in your head. Then you had the baby and started to rave that you were somebody else. And then that somebody else actually seemed to appear. You turned into a good mother and now I could swear you've fallen in love. Such a look comes over you when you speak of that man you married that I reckon he must be a right pretty sort of fellow."

Nichola had smiled. "He's that all right. But as to being in love with him – I don't know."

"Well, I do. He's captured your heart, that one. Much more than Michael ever did."

"Much more than Lewis?" Nichola wondered out loud.

But Emmet obviously did not hear her for she continued with her task of making spice cakes, without answering.

The Knollys, when they departed for Germany, had taken the precaution of removing their cook with them, leaving behind a rather inept deputy whose task it was to feed the servants. This fellow, together with the clerk of the kitchen, a rather grand title for the servant who placed the orders with the various purveyors, was all that was left of the kitchen staff, and since the return of Emmet and Miranda, Nichola had taken to going in there with increasing regularity, more to amuse herself than anything else. So now, with Christmas only two weeks off, she supposed she should be making an effort.

"Must I really serve a banquet like this?" she asked, staring at G. Markham's book in horror.

Emmet peered over her shoulder. "Read it to me. You know I can't."

"...then the great Wild-fowl, as Bittern, Hearn, Shoveler, Crane, Bustard and such like. Then the greater Land-fowl, as Peacocks, Phesant, Pulets, Gulls and such like. Then hot bak'd meats, as Marrow-bone pye, Quince pye, Florentine, and Tarts. Then cold bak'd meats, as Red Deer, Hare pye, Gammon of Bacon pye, Wild bore, Roe pye and such like, and these also shall be marshal'd at the Table... My God, I doubt anyone could move after the first course, let alone that lot."

"That is a *great* feast. We should only prepare such a thing if your husband returns in time."

Nichola dragged her attention away from Joscelin and back to the recipes. "So are you saying we should have a simple meal?"

"Yes. And even though it is a time of war you should invite Mr Hollin and some of your wedding guests. It will make a pleasing interlude for them."

"You're right. I'll ask them." Nichola scanned the pages of *The English House-Wife*. "Heavens, the humble feast doesn't sound much better. Listen. First, a shield of Brawn with mustard, Secondly, a boyl'd Capon, Thirdly, a boyl'd piece of Beef, Fourthly, a chine of Beef rosted, Fifthly, a Neats tongue rosted, Sixthly, a Pig rosted, Seventhly, Chewets – what the hell are they? – bak'd, Eighthly, a Goose rosted, Ninthly, a Swan rosted,

Tenthly, a Turkey rosted, the Eleventh, a haunch of Venison rosted, The Twelfth, a Pasty of Venison, the Thirteenth, a Kid with a pudding in the belly, the Fourteenth, an Olive pie, the Fifteenth, a couple of Capons, the Sixteenth, a Custard or Doucets. It's obscene!"

"I can't think why you're sounding so surprised. Sir Denzil used to serve just such a thing when he had company."

"I imagine it's only because people are so physically active that they don't get enormously fat."

"There you go again," said Emmet reprovingly. "And chewets are choughs as you well know."

"Yes," said Nichola, none the wiser.

"Now, I'm off to give Miranda some food before she goes to bed."

"Bring her in here. It'll be more fun if we're all together."

"The Knollys' nursemaid won't approve of that."

"Tough," answered Nichola, and smiled.

It was the second week of December, the evenings growing dark early, so by the time the child had been fed and washed in the warm water that Nichola heated for her in the kettle it was pitch black. The two women walked from the wing where the offices were situated, conveniently near to the Well House, and saw as they came back into the main house that it had started to snow.

"This should put a stop to the fighting," Nichola remarked hopefully.

"Aye, it should. Though word is going from village to village that Sir William Waller, who's besieging Winchester for Parliament, intends to continue throughout the winter if need be."

"I suppose it's admirable to be so tough."

"I suppose so."

They stared out of the oriel window, Nichola holding Miranda tightly beneath her cloak. Even while they watched, the landscape was changing. The first fine flakes had given way to a heavier fall, crisp and beautiful, landing on the branches of the trees of the home park, crystallising the ancient tower of the earlier building, carpeting the lawns with a sweep of swansdown. Safe in the arms of the woman it believed to be its mother, the child observed, all eyes, silent with wonder, as white fell from the skies and transformed everything it recognised as familiar.

"Look at Miranda," said Emmet, smiling. "That be snow, sweetheart."

"Wasn't it snowing when she was born?"

"Aye it was. The day I thought I'd lost you."

A memory of someone blowing into her month came back vividly and Nichola wondered about it yet again. At the time, in a trance though she might have been, she had thought the resuscitator to be Bill Cosby. Was it possible that both Bill and Emmet had given the kiss of life simultaneously in their different centuries? Was that how she had been drawn through the barrier of time?

"It'll freeze tonight," Emmet was saying. "I'll to my bed to keep warm."

"I think I'll read for a while."

"Then get some logs put on the fire. It will be bitter by midnight."

With both her and the child gone, the customary quiet fell over Greys Court, intensified tonight by the silence of the snow. Nichola made her way to the library, having dismissed the servants to their quarters, and picking up a book started to read, her brain getting more and more used to the script in which an S was replaced by an F with, to modern minds, some hilarious results. Eventually, though, she grew tired and it became a struggle to continue. Putting more wood on the fire, she closed her eyes and dozed in the chair.

She woke abruptly, with a start, her ears straining to identify the sound which had disturbed her. The room was almost in total darkness, the atmosphere acrid with the smell of guttered candles, only the waning fire throwing any light. Nichola sat bolt upright, listening. And then she heard it again. Despite the blanketing effect of snow it was nonetheless distinct. With a beat of muffled hooves and a jingle of harness, a troop of horsemen was coming up the drive and towards the house. Moving silently, Nichola went to the window, twitching the curtain slightly in order to look out.

There were about thirty of them, men and beasts etched black against the moonlit snow. Just for a minute her heart jumped, thinking that Joscelin had returned, and then she recognised the buff coats and helmets with triple bar face guards typical of those worn by the Parliamentarians. With a shock she took in the fact that there was a contingent of enemy soldiers right outside her front door.

Nichola hesitated, uncertain what to do, and then the matter was taken out of her hands by a thundering knock on the front door. Snatching Joscelin's pistol from the drawer in the desk, she went to answer it.

Two of the men had dismounted and were standing in the porch beneath the oriel window, their figures enlarged by the stark white background which glittered fiercely beneath the vivid moon.

"What do you want?" said Nichola, hoping her voice did not betray the tact that she was terrified, not only for herself but for the innocent people lying asleep in the silent house.

"Don't be nervous, my girl," answered one of them. "You'll come to no harm provided you behave yourself."

Her mind racing ahead, Nichola snatched the opportunity they had given her. Assuming an accent known in the acting profession as 'stock rural', she said, "My master ain't here, Sir. There be no one but us servants. He be gone visiting and won't be back for a while."

The other man gave a short laugh. "Aye, visiting Germany. We know perfectly well that the place is empty except for you servants. We therefore commandeer Greys Court in the name of Parliament. Now rouse your companions, girl, my men have ridden hard and long and would like some food before they bed down."

There was something about this last speaker which was vaguely familiar and Nichola peered through the shadows of the porch to see him more closely. Then she smiled in the darkness.

"Just you watch your manners, my man," she said succinctly, "or I'll send my mistress to box your ears, so I will."

"What the devil . . ." he began, but she cut in on him. "My mistress – and yours also, I believe!"

"What?" he exclaimed angrily.

"How very unflattering not to be recognised," Nichola went on, dropping a parody of a curtsey.

"By God . . ." he said, and then he, too, laughed.

It was Michael Morellon.

Chapter Thirteen

Greys Court had become a garrison, there could be no doubt of that. Into the main house had moved Captain Morellon and Lieutenant Field, while the men had been quartered in the stables, complete with their farrier and saddler. The horses had remained below but the two floors above had been designated as a messroom and dormitory respectively, and in this way the entire company was disposed in reasonable comfort.

"But why have you come here?" Nichola had asked Michael on the very first occasion they were alone together.

"I might well ask the same of you."

"Let that be for the moment. Just tell me why a troop of Roundhead soldiers have barracked themselves in a remote spot like this."

Michael had raised his brows. "Oxford, my dear girl."

"You mean you're going to attack it?"

"Of course not, we're far too few. No, now that the King has taken up residence in that city the plan is to block all his possible routes out to London. Should he stir in the direction of the capital there are units like ours poised to mobilise and stop him."

"How cruel."

"War is, disgustingly so. I had never before seen anyone die, but at Edgehill all that changed. I witnessed men leaving this world with no one to comfort them, choking to death on their own blood, spewing up their guts. My own cousin lay a-dying just a few feet away from me, and because I held him in my arms until he'd gone I was reprimanded by my commanding officer."

"Because he was fighting for the other side?"

"Yes."

Nichola had stared at Michael in the harsh unyielding light of the winter's day glittering through the library window. "You've changed."

"Yes, by God."

And indeed he had, the angular features of that square attractive face even more pronounced, the line from cheek to jaw, blade sharp. The sky blue youth had gone from Michael Morellon. He was old at twenty-one.

"You are different too," he had said, leaning forward in his chair, where they sat by the fire, face to face at last.

"In what way?"

"Your whole attitude, everything. I know you have had a birthday since last I saw you but that alone could not account for it." He had picked up her hand, touching it with his lips. "I see you wear a wedding ring."

"Yes. I was married to Lord Joscelin Attwood shortly after the King raised his Standard. We met in Nottingham. To put it simply, Michael, my bridegroom rescued me from Sir Denzil."

"What exactly do you mean by that?"

"He had decided, my stepfather that is, that as he and I were not blood related, our relationship should become intimate. He was attempting to thrust himself upon me, quite literally. And when I ran away from him it was Lord Joscelin who found me."

Michael's eyes had changed from iris to the purple of gemstones. "Are you asking me to be grateful to him?"

Nichola had crossed the space between them, kneeling on the floor beside his chair. "Michael, don't look so savage. It does not become you. Don't feel badly towards Joscelin. He saved me, remember."

She had been going on to say that her husband was a good man, a loyal heart, but Michael had abruptly stopped her. Leaning over the arm of his chair, his mouth had found hers in a kiss of such want, such longing, such infinite tenderness and despair that she could have wept. And then he had slid to the floor beside her, burying his head in her breast, his tears running on to the bare flesh of her neck.

"My God," Michael had said chokingly, "this dreadful war! It has taken you from me and now I will never get you back."

"Never is a long time," Nichola had answered unthinkingly

and, perhaps taking that as a sign of encouragement, Michael had kissed her again, fiercely this time, and almost as a reflex, her mouth had opened to his.

It had probably been as well that approaching footsteps had interrupted them at that moment, forcing them to go about their business, attending to the details of turning Greys Court into a military base. Yet as Nichola had gone to the bedroom floor, reluctantly supervising the removal of Joscelin's things from the room he had so recently occupied, she had been tremendously aware of another presence in the house, and had realised that the whole ambience had changed because of its sudden male intrusion.

Her thoughts had turned inwards and the actress had dwelled long and hard on the fact that she had eagerly responsed to Michael, that the Collector in her had undeniably enjoyed kissing him. It had seemed to Nichola, then, that nothing within her had changed despite her extraordinary empathy with Joscelin, and she had felt bleak and desolate and suddenly sick with herself.

"You're day dreaming," Emmet had said, coming in to the room.

"Yes, I was."

The girl looked sly. "Things won't be easy for you, Mistress, with Master Michael under the same roof. After all, you do have a child together. By the way, has he seen Miranda yet?"

"No, he's been too busy but I promised to show him his daughter tonight."

"Just be careful that the other men, particularly the lieutenant, don't think you and he are too friendly."

"Why do you say that?"

"Because if things should turn about and the Royalists re-take the house it would not look good if you were reckoned to be a sympathiser."

"I can hardly be accused of such a thing when I was once betrothed to the man."

"That counts for nothing these days. All those considerations have been put to one side."

Nichola had sighed. "What a hateful situation this is." Then she had paused as a thought struck her. "My God, I hope Joscelin doesn't come back to this. He'd be walking straight into a trap."

"Word will be out already that we've been commandeered, never you fear. The servants must still go abroad upon their business."

"What about Mr Hollin?"

"If he's any sense he'll keep away, though as Michael is commander here I expect he would turn a blind eye to a pastoral visit."

"So our modest Christmas feast will not be served after all."

"The leaders of the Parliamentarians may well be Puritans," Emmet had answered, "but the common soldiery, or so I reckon, will be far from that. They'll enjoy the festivities as much as we."

Nichola had stood up. "If I cannot entertain my neighbours then the others can whistle for a celebration."

"With the exception of Michael, of course," Emmet had replied provocatively.

"With no exceptions," Nichola had answered and had walked from the room to avoid the girl's bright stare.

That night she had entertained him to a late supper, probably unwisely, possibly foolishly, but nonetheless because she had wanted to. Miranda, in her night clothes, had been brought to the room by a curious Emmet, who had been promptly dismissed. And then, in the firelight, his face softened by the glow, Michael had been reunited with his daughter. Nichola, watching them, had been moved by his joy in the child, by the love and affection which flowed out of him in so guileless a manner. Thinking of all the vile things she had read in newspapers, of the cases of incomprehensible child abuse, of juvenile crime so horrific that even to think about it made her ill, she was glad that she had, even if briefly, experienced another, more innocent, century, savage though it might be in many other ways.

Looking up at her from where he sat on the floor with the child, Michael said, "You have raised our daughter well, Arabella. And how much more beautiful you are for doing so, with your newfound wisdom and serenity."

"I, serene?"

"You sound surprised."

"I am. It is not a word I would ever have used to describe myself."

"Then you are mistaken," said Michael, and kissed her hand.

They went together to put Miranda to bed, Nichola feeling certain that tonight he should enjoy that privilege even if it should result in gossip amongst his men. And then they were finally alone, taking a repast in the dining room, watching each other in the candlelight.

Michael downed a glass of wine and recklessly plunged in with what he wanted to say. "Tell me, do you love the man you married?"

Nichola knew that it was vital she should tell him the truth. "I don't know. Others believe that I do but I am not sure enough of my own feelings. All I can tell you is that I am immensely drawn to him, that the fact he has vanished drives me to despair. So make of that what you will."

He laughed humourlessly. "Bodies and minds respond differently, as I have recently discovered. So I would hazard a guess that much as you admire your husband he has not yet awoken in you what I have done."

What could she reply but, "That is true, I suppose"?

He nodded. "And you do not deny that there is still a lot of feeling between us?"

"No," Nichola answered, experiencing an extraordinary moment of excitement and alarm.

"Do you realise that if it had not been for this war we would by now be husband and wife?" Michael went on.

"Are you trying to say that we should resume where we left off?"

"Why not?"

"Because I have married in the interim. Everything has changed."

"Has it? I think not. If this husband of yours truly satisfied you then you would not have kissed me the way you did."

"Michael, for God's sake . . ." said Nichola, rising from the table. But it was too late, he had also risen and, coming to her, snatched her closely into his arms before she could utter another word.

Beneath his kisses, the sweep of his hands, Nichola gave up the uneven struggle. Nichola Hall, who had once collected men, returned in full force, and took control of Arabella's body.

"Oh Michael," she gasped, "it's been so bloody long."

"Since you were with me or with another?"

"I don't know," she answered. "Don't talk. Just love me."

"I do, you know that."

And then, in the middle of a kiss, they somehow slithered to the floor in front of the fire and, with a sound like a moan, Michael was upon her, raising her beautiful silken skirts, his other hand releasing his breeches. Nichola arched her back as his hardness entered, threshing in its urgency, and, pushing deeply, instantly reached a wonderful draining climax.

"I was too quick," he gasped, his forehead glistening with sweat.

"We have all night," Nichola answered.

"Do you mean that?"

"Yes."

And she did, every word, that was the worst of it. After such a long spell of abstinence she was as greedy as a pauper at a feast, not able to have enough of lovemaking. They spent the night bedewed and bruised with passion, his lean frame wrapped round hers, his cock relentless. Nichola had laughed when her lover had referred to his penis like that, thinking that nothing changed, then realising that to him it was standard English as spoken every day and not a vulgarism. There was something amazingly straightforward about the directness of Michael's speech and she had found herself being swept along by it.

Morning found them satisfied at last, kissing each other goodbye and arranging that Michael should come to her again that night. Yet after he had gone and Nichola could think rationally again she began to wonder about the wisdom of what she was doing. If Joscelin were to return and learn through gossip that she had betrayed him, the consequences might be dire. And even as she thought this and wondered what would be the cleverest way to cover her tracks, another emotion stirred in Nichola's heart and was most ruthlessly pushed away again. For

Nichola Hall had never felt a pang of conscience as far as men were concerned and had no reason to start doing so now.

Within a matter of days, or so it seemed, Christmas was upon them. Michael and Lieutenant Field had kept very much out of the way while Nichola had entertained her neighbours to the humble feast, as prescribed by G. Markham, substituting one of the courses for a recipe of her own, which had been very well received. The visitors approaching the house had worn expressions of great trepidation, aware that Parliamentary soldiers were around if not actually about, but several glasses of punch had restored their spirits and soon they were toasting the health of their hostess and host *in absentia*. It was at that moment, sitting at the head of the table and looking at all the gleaming faces turned towards her, that Nichola suffered another terrible stab of guilt and had been forced to turn away. Joscelin had married her on trust, had refused to degrade their relationship by indulging in sex without love, and she had rewarded him by rank infidelity.

But that night, with the guests gone early, fearful to be out late, Michael had taken her superbly, having learned over the weeks what it was that pleased the new grown-up woman Arabella had become. His slim strong shanks straddling hers, his motion hard, deep, yet slow and restraining, Nichola had thought him one of the best lovers in The Collection. Why, then, when he had gone into the frost of the winter's morning had her mouth suddenly become dry and tears sprung into her eyes?

"Bitch!" she had said, loudly and fiercely, and hit the pillow with her clenched fists.

An hour later, washed, dressed and reasonably ready for the day, Nichola had tried to rationalise what was happening to her, asking herself why she should feel so guilty about a man who, technically, was nothing more than a friend. Yet the memory of that interrupted moment, of the carnal pleasure of Joscelin's kisses, would not go away. For the first time in her experience, Nichola knew what it was to worry about having two lovers at once.

She had arranged to ride into Rotherfield Greys that morning to see Mr Hollin for their weekly chat about the war and soon after breakfast Nichola set off, hooded and cloaked against the biting cold.

"You're very lucky," Michael had said to her on the previous evening, "that I allow you so much freedom. With Rupert and his men not far away it would be so easy for one of you to betray us."

"Why exactly *are* you here?" she had asked in return. "Are you really trying to stop the King leaving Oxford?"

"Not as such, he could go any time he wished, well garrisoned as the place is. No, the main aim is to protect the London road should Charles make another attempt to take the capital. I've heard it said that soon they are going to build a protective rampart right round the city so that London is completely fortified."

"It must matter a great deal to Parliament if they are prepared to turn the place into a fortress."

"It does. So now you know why there are small bands like mine dotted hither and thither to protect the roads and why it is imperative that our whereabouts remain secret."

"But how can they? Servants will talk to villagers and word will spread, it's the way of the world."

Michael had frowned. "And what of your rector friend? Would he betray us?"

"Not if I request him to remain silent."

"Then do so, my dear Arabella. For I would hate there to be reprisals against him."

It had been rather an alarming conversation, thought Nichola as her horse crunched on the ice of the track that led to the village. For news of the arrival of a troop of horse would carry regardless of whether there was local support for Parliament or King. And if Michael's men were ready to plunder the houses of her acquaintances as an act of revenge the results could well be most unpleasant both for them and herself. The full implication of what Emmet had said to her about being considered a sympathiser came home to Nichola. She might be seen as a traitor and worse, should it ever be discovered that she and the men's leader were engaged in an affair. Desperately worried, Nichola allowed her horse to pick its way slowly towards the rectory.

Much to his visitor's surprise, Mr Hollin was not at home, though his front door stood ajar and a fire burned in the hearth.

"Hello," called Nichola, "are you there, Rector? It's Arabella Attwood."

But there was no reply and after hesitating a moment Nichola decided to look for the cleric in the church. Leaving her horse tied to a post she walked the short distance to St Nicholas, wondering why Mr Hollin should have gone out in such biting cold.

All around her the Oxfordshire landscape stretched out bleakly, the scattered buildings throwing shadows on to the virgin white, the trees, dark at their base, raising aloft glistening arms and heads towards the pallid sun. The smaller streams and brooks were frozen and still, silver threads which glittered rainbows when that same sun struck them. In the distance at Henley, the Thames, flowing freely as yet, was as sombre and grey as sealskin. Looking about, Nichola was struck afresh by the beauty of the countryside in all its varied guises. The air, clear and cold and unpolluted, was like wine to her nostrils, the day, bitter and bracing, a tonic to the blood. Sweeping her eyes over the dazzling vistas of arctic splendour and feeling the taste of them upon her lips, Nichola went into the church.

It was shadowed and dark after the brightness of the snow. So much so that she almost stumbled as she went through the door, the noise of her fall attracting the attention of two figures who knelt before the altar. One she recognised, blinded as she was, as Mr Hollin but the other, heavily hooded and mantled, Nichola did not know. Both heads turned as she came in and after a moment's hesitation the rector got to his feet.

"Ah, Arabella my dear, I am so glad that you thought to look for me here."

"I went to the rectory but nobody was in." She thought at once how obvious this remark was but did not add to it, too intent on staring at the stranger.

"I see you recognise our visitor," Mr Hollin murmured.

"No, I don't."

"Nonetheless he would like to speak to you," the rector went on and began to propel Nichola down the aisle.

The stranger stood up, saying, "Good day, Mistress," in a soft voice.

The sound of it sent a chill through Nichola, glad though she was to hear it. For the owner of this particular voice was the one person clever enough and devious enough to discover the guilty secret of her bedchamber.

Not bothering with a single pleasantry, Nichola said, "Is Lord Joscelin alive? Just tell me for God's sake."

"Alive and well, my Lady," Caradoc answered, throwing back his hood. "I left him in Oxford this morning."

"Thank God. I have been so afraid."

The servant's eyes met hers in one of his strangely blank stares. "These must have been very difficult times for you, on your own."

Nichola looked away. "Why did you not send word sooner?" she asked, anger covering her other emotions. "Surely one of you could have written?"

"The battle at Edge Hill caused certain confusions..." He seemed almost deliberately facetious. "... and by the time we had withdrawn from Turnham Green it was to hear that Greys Court had fallen into the hands of the enemy."

"*How* did you hear?"

"There are spies constantly at work, Mistress. Unless one knows exactly what the other side is doing a war is as good as lost, believe me."

Nichola's heart sank even lower. "And do I guess correctly that Lord Joscelin volunteered you for such a role?"

Again the cool flick of Caradoc's eyes. "He was kind enough to suggest it to Prince Rupert, yes."

"So what happens next?"

"My task is to get you and your child and servant safely to Oxford to join your husband."

"And how will this be achieved?"

"I shall shortly appear at Greys Court in a guise which hopefully will not arouse suspicion. Then I will make a plan suitable to the circumstances."

She wanted to throttle him, his assurance infuriating her. And yet his ability to keep calm, to plan and execute with dexterity, ought really to be admired, she knew. Nichola did her very best to keep her voice even. "Will you return to Oxford in the meanwhile?"

"No, it is too dangerous. I shall remain based at the rectory."

"Very well. I await your visit."

It was only as Nichola rode back home that the full import of what was happening dawned on her. With Caradoc snooping round the place it would be impossible for her to continue her relationship with Michael, while her lover, for obvious reasons, would want to know why she had called such a sudden halt. Yet nothing like the truth dare escape her lips or Joscelin's servant would be a dead man and she would never see her husband again.

"Why can't I get back to my own time and away from all this intrigue?" Nichola said out loud, and then thought how difficult it would be to equate the feelings she was currently experiencing with those of her old hard-bitten life style. The notion struck her that to leave at this moment would be like missing the final episode of a TV serial and she smiled at how ridiculous the situation had now become.

Several days passed, days during which Nichola felt more and more on edge, and still there was no sign of Caradoc.

"You're ill at ease," Michael commented, watching her narrowly.

"Why do you say so?"

"When I made love to you last night I had the feeling you were thinking of something else. It was disconcerting."

Nichola seized the opportunity he had given her. "I am growing increasingly worried about gossip. If it were to be discovered that you and I are lovers it could be highly dangerous for both of us."

He took the point seriously. "Our meeting in this way should never have happened. Greys Court was chosen as a billet only because it was understood to be empty other than for a handful of servants. But I think you're right. I have started imagining that certain of the men are giving me sly looks."

"Does it matter to you what they think?"

"My private life should never be allowed to interfere with discipline."

"Then perhaps it might be safer if we stopped our liaison."

Michael looked at her earnestly. "Is that how you think of it, Arabella? As an intrigue? You seem to forget that we were once betrothed, that we are the parents of a child. I cannot speak for you, of course, but as far as I am concerned the emotions between us transcend some shabby dalliance."

Nichola felt desperately ashamed. The man was genuinely in love with Arabella, or the woman he considered her to be. "Remember that I am married," she answered lamely.

His eyes changed from iris to slate. "What are you saying to me? That you care for Lord Joscelin? Well, how can that be? It is perfectly obvious that your marriage was one of convenience only. I thought you loved *me*, Arabella."

Nichola simply did not know how to answer. For how could she explain to a man of integrity that she had been enjoying sex without actually being in love with him? Guilt came yet again and for the first time in her experience she cringed at the idea of what she had done.

"I *do* love you Michael," she said, too afraid to speak the truth, "but the fact is I owe Joscelin Attwood a great debt. He saved me, then took me on trust as his wife. In a sense I feel that I have betrayed him. Can you understand that?"

Michael sighed, his expression grim. "I cannot work out the rights and wrongs of it, but it seems, for several differing reasons, our intimacy must now end."

Nichola nodded. "It might be better, more sensible. At least for the time being."

"Then amen. But I would request that I still have access to my daughter."

It sounded just like the terms of a divorce, she thought.

"You lodge in the same house. Of course you can see her."

He stood up, looking down on her where she remained seated. "It would never surprise me if you vanished in the night, Arabella. I thought at first that my presence here would prevent you from trying to find your husband. Now I am not so sure. It seems to me that you have changed beyond recognition, that you can give me your body whilst retaining your heart, something that the girl I once knew could never have done. Why, if it were not impossible, I could almost believe your fanciful story that you became a different woman at the time of Miranda's birth."

Nichola smiled at him sadly. "It might be better for us both if you do believe it."

He stared at her darkly but made no reply and after a second or two of contemplating her in silence Michael left the room, the atmosphere stirred by his departure. Nichola did not move, thinking that if she kept very still the wave of pain that threatened to break over her might go away. But there was to be no avoiding it. This was the moment of truth and she must endure it in order to survive. Like a dying woman, her past flashed before her and Nichola tried to justify The Collection with the words 'experimentation' and 'looking for the right man'.

"Anyway I was about to finish with all that," she told herself. "Everything changed when I fell in love with Lewis."

But suddenly it was so difficult to remember him, even that most famous of faces refusing to flash up clearly on to the screen of her memory.

"What's going wrong with me?" Nichola whispered plaintively. "What the bloody hell is happening?"

In fact she knew; deep down, too low for easy acceptance, the truth was there. The past, or rather the present in which she now found herself, had become more important to her than her true past. This life, complete with its hazards and difficulties, was turning out to be more fascinating than the one she had lived before. Then Nichola performed the ultimate act of a true survivor. She finally admitted in her heart of hearts that the things she had done in her old life were neither admirable nor, indeed, particularly clever but, as they were done and nothing could undo them, now had to be cast aside so that she could begin afresh. Then a shadow fell over Nichola's mind as a question rose, unbidden. Would she still go back to the twentieth century if the opportunity presented itself? And though, of course, the answer had to be yes, for the first time there was a part of her that admitted she would miss the people she had met in the seventeenth, with the exception of Denzil Loxley, as acutely as she had at first missed Lewis Devine.

Michael's words had seemingly held a prophetic ring, for Caradoc appeared the next morning. Seeing him arrive from an upstairs window, Nichola momentarily did not recognise him, but when the long muscular frame swung itself from the seat of the cart he was driving there could be no mistaking the man despite the disguise he had adopted. The long reddish hair had been dyed black, even the skin tone altered to a more ruddy hue, while tied about him was a blacksmith's leather apron, the tools of that trade packed into the conveyance. It occurred to Nichola then that the mystery ailment which had struck the farrier low, so low that the horses had not been attended for several days, might not be quite the accident it seemed. She shook her head, thinking, My God, no wonder Joscelin uses him for all his dirty work.

At that moment it once more crossed Nichola's mind that, with his hair dark, Caradoc and his master were not dissimilar, and she wondered whether the servant might perhaps be a byblow of the noble house of Attwood. Watching, fascinated, she saw Caradoc unpack his tools and head towards the stables without even a glance in the direction of Greys Court. Wishing she could like the man more, Nichola went downstairs.

Over the last few days the snow had gone, leaving a countryside like mire behind it. Everywhere there was the bleak cold feel of cheerless winter and the actress could not help but admire the fact that, despite the conditions, Sir William Waller, MP for Andover, had successfully starved out Chichester in early January before leaving for his winter quarters in London. Since then there had been no further news, and with the new campaigning season not yet under way it seemed as if both sides were poised, waiting for the weather to improve, before either would fire a shot. The King had established new headquarters and remained in Oxford, surrounded by his loyal followers, while his Queen, Henrietta Maria, was in Holland trying to raise both men and money by selling her jewels.

Despite the slight thaw it was still bitterly cold and Nichola shivered as she made her way towards the front door, finding the house freezing, though hearty log fires spat and crackled in every room. Even as she stepped over the threshold, pulling on a thick cloak, Michael was making his way inside.

"Good morning, my Lady," he said, civilly enough, although every ounce of the hurt she had caused him showed on his face – which looked gaunt and drawn in the harsh light, his vivid eyes full of pain.

"Good morning, Captain Morellon," she answered, wishing there was something she could do to comfort him.

"The blacksmith is here from the village, the farrier being taken sick, and I wondered if it would be in order for him to come to the kitchens when he has done."

"Of course."

"It's not the usual smith," Michael went on, "but one I have not seen before."

His eyes met Nichola's in a compulsive stare and she knew, then, that he knew, was aware that there was something suspect about Caradoc.

"He is welcome," she answered shortly, and looked away.

Michael nodded. "Then all's well."

"Is it?" she asked, once more catching his eye. "Oh Michael, is it?"

"Only you can answer that," he said abruptly. "Goodbye, Arabella." And with that he turned and walked back to the stables, his footsteps ringing out on the frost-laden cobbles.

Chapter Fourteen

She had first seen Greys Court bathed in the soft shadows of late summer moonlight. Now as Nichola left the house, aware that she might never set eyes on it again, the place was once more illuminated by the light of moon and stars, though this time harsh with the stark cold gleam of winter. Turning to look back over her shoulder as the cart trundled through the woods, well away from the drive or any other area where the heavy horse's hooves might sound, her thoughts went briefly to Michael, innocently asleep in his bed – or so she presumed – and Nichola felt another wave of the guilt which, these days, seemed to beset her at regular intervals.

In the manner best favoured by Caradoc, the two women and the baby had departed Greys Court in the most subtle way. Nichola had announced her intention of going to have dinner with Mr Hollin, and then, as soon as darkness came, had ridden back to the home park to join Emmet and the child in a woodman's hut as it grew chill. The servant, meanwhile, had taken Miranda for a late afternoon stroll, both of them well wrapped against the cold, then had returned to the house by one door and walked out again by the other, skirting round one of the building's original towers and out to the woods that way. Caradoc, in his guise of blacksmith, had attended to one of my Lady's horses and then ostensibly left the estate. An hour later, all three adults were together and the journey had begun.

Over-riding every other emotion, Nichola had a feeling of raw excitement, as invigorating and daunting as the fearful elation she had experienced each night when first stepping on to the stage. At every performance her heartbeat had quickened and she had felt charged with adrenalin. And now it was the same, listening for the sound of pursuing horses, aware that the moonlight was dangerous, wondering if she would ever get as far as Oxford and, if she did, how Joscelin would react to her arrival. For she was still not certain whether Caradoc had overheard the soldiers' gossip about herself and their captain, and felt unable to trust him to keep silent if he had indeed done so.

Looking at him, his tall spare frame straight-backed upon the driver's seat, Nichola felt the customary surge of dislike, and wondered for the millionth time what it was about the man that had this effect on her. Almost because she felt so uneasy she spoke his name and, without turning, the servant answered, "Yes?"

"What time will we get to Oxford?"

"At dawn, my Lady. I shall not be taking the direct route but shall stick to the cart tracks. The less habitation we pass, the better."

"Is it true that the King intends to make the city his permanent headquarters?"

"That now seems certain. It is well protected by various surrounding garrisons, yet only the university is Royalist. They say the town itself largely supports the Parliamentarians, so His Majesty can never be entirely at ease there."

"I doubt he will ever be entirely at ease again."

"You do not hold out hope of his ultimate victory, then?"

"No," Nichola answered, and then regretted her frankness. If Caradoc had heard even the faintest whisper of scandal about her he would no doubt consider her a Roundhead sympathiser. Deciding that it might be wiser to keep silent for the rest of the journey, Nichola turned her attention to Miranda, who had woken, startled, and took the baby from Emmet's arms and rocked her until she fell asleep again.

Leaving the protection of the trees, the cart turned north-west, avoiding Henley which had fallen to Parliament shortly after the débâcle at Turnham Green, and picked its way beyond the hamlets of the Ewelme Hundred. Then it turned in a more northerly direction still, going past a number of distant scattered villages until the great loop of the River Cherwell finally came into sight. Craning to see it in the first red glow of dawn, Nichola suddenly thought her heart was going to stop. For there, rearing up into the lightening sky, was the tower of Magdalen College.

"Just as it was, is!" she muttered.

"You've been here before, my Lady?" asked Caradoc, overhearing her.

"Many years ago," Nichola answered, and ignored the fact that Emmet was staring at her in surprise.

The bridge over which she had driven then, sharing her car with three other actors appearing at The Playhouse, had vanished and in its place stood an ancient arched edifice over which the cart rumbled as it headed towards the town. And it was only now and for the very first time that Nichola took in the fact that Oxford had been a walled city, that Magdalen stood outside the boundaries, and that they were currently approaching a guarded gateway giving access within.

"The East Gate," stated Caradoc as he drew the horse to a halt.

"Will they let us inside?"

"Certainly. I have a signed pass in Prince Rupert's own hand. Lord Joscelin arranged it before I left."

Nichola said nothing, too overcome with trying to equate the Oxford she knew with what she could see as the big wooden doors were swung open and the cart passed through.

They were in a main thoroughfare which in length and contour strongly resembled the High Street along which Nichola had so frequently walked when she had stayed in the city during the run of the play. Nonetheless, St Edmund Hall was missing, though in its place there most certainly stood an academic hall of some kind, while Queen's, to the right, and University College, to the left, were both still there, even if not wholly recognisable. Looking over to where All Souls should be, Nichola saw a building on the site, though without Hawksmoor's Gothic exterior she found it difficult to be sure of its identity. The church of St Mary the Virgin with its great tower was easily recognisable, however, as the cart continued on its way past Brasenose to a place where four thoroughfares crossed.

"Is this Carfax?" Nichola asked.

"Yes," Caradoc answered, and with that swung the cart to the right up a street which Nichola thought must be Cornmarket, though it seemed wider than she remembered it.

"Where are we going now?"

"Past the Corn Market to St Michael's then out through the North Gate."

"Out?"

Caradoc looked at her for almost the first time during the journey. "Lord Joscelin has secured a house outside the boundaries, my Lady. He thought you might prefer that to being crammed within the city limits."

"That was very good of him. In what area does it lie?"

"Near St Giles church, not far from St John's College. By contrast to the city which daily grows more densely populated it has an air almost of rural tranquillity."

"I hadn't realised how small Oxford actually is within those walls."

Caradoc's eyes swept her once more. "I thought you said you had visited the city before."

"It's changed," Nichola said, and refused to be drawn further.

It was just as they drew level with the Corn Market, a long low building in the centre of the thoroughfare, open below but roofed above, the lead covering supported by wooden pillars, that Nichola saw the first signs of life. Despite the fact that dawn had scarcely broken, a party of horsemen clattered over the cobbles towards them, obviously having just ridden into town. They passed two abreast on either side of the market building so that Caradoc was forced to halt the cart and draw it to one side in order to let them by. Nichola stared, all eyes, at the first sign of war she had seen since the raising of the Standard.

"Handsome," Emmet remarked appraisingly.

Caradoc grinned, his face transforming. "There's a horde of them in town, all drinking and brawling and whoring. So just you watch yourself, my girl."

"There's no need to tell me how to behave," Emmet answered crisply. "I know what's what."

Caradoc burst out laughing, taking Nichola by surprise and making her realise he was human after all – it was only her he disliked. "Even the big rough pillicock hill climbers?"

"Don't be vulgar!" Emmet exclaimed, while Nichola could only guess at what the words meant.

The cart drew level with Jesus College, the only Oxford college founded in Elizabethan times, its brickwork looking amazingly fresh and new, and then the tower of St Michael's loomed before them. Nichola had climbed it during her stay, despite its rather alarming height. Now she saw it with new eyes as she realised that it guarded the northern entrance to the city. And the name she had sometimes heard it called by, St Michael-at-the-Northgate, took on true significance as the cart passed through the great wooden doors, thrown open when Caradoc showed Rupert's pass, and beyond the city limits.

Opposite and slightly to the right stood Balliol, looking completely different from the college that Nichola knew. Undistinguished Victorian architecture had long since replaced the original, which had become a permanent part of the University in 1282, but now she saw two soaring towers and a cloistered quad. Automatically Nichola's head turned to the left to look for the Apollo Theatre and the Oxford Playhouse but, of course, neither were there. Ahead of them, in the middle of the thoroughfare, stood the church of St Magdalen, to the left a long row of houses. Opposite, in the vicinity of Archbishop Laud's favourite college, St John's, and within sight of its huge garden, stood a building in grounds almost as lovely.

"That's it," said Caradoc tersely. "That's where Lord Joscelin is quartered."

"It looks fit for the King himself," Emmet remarked, large-eyed.

"Almost. It belongs to someone quite important, I believe."

With that the cart swept in through the gates and up the circular drive to the steps leading to the front door. Nichola remained silent, aware of the thumping of her heart. For though she was constantly reminding herself that she was a twentieth century woman and up to handling most situations, the thought that Joscelin might somehow be aware of her affair with Michael was more than she could cope with at this particular moment. By the time the cart had drawn to a halt and Caradoc had lifted her down before going to assist Emmet, the actress could feel herself shaking. Then, of course, came the inevitable anti-climax. Ushered into the hall by a yawning servant, Nichola was informed that Lord Joscelin had ridden out with Prince Rupert and was not expected back until nightfall.

"In that case I shall have something to eat then rest for a while," she said, relief tinged by the alarming thought that tonight she would have to go through the ordeal all over again.

"Certainly, my Lady," answered the servant and solemnly ushered the bedraggled party towards an anteroom. Nichola, however, hovered in the doorway and looked about her before going in, anxious to see something of the place in which she would now be living.

The house which Joscelin Attwood had somehow acquired for himself was indeed commodious. Built on classical lines, the feeling of space was enhanced by the fact that it allowed a great deal of sunlight in through its abundant collection of mullioned windows. The entrance hall, from which all the principal rooms led off, had a floor of black and white marble, a richly moulded plaster ceiling bearing a crest, and Ionic pillars on either side of the several doors, above which were triangular pediments. With her somewhat sketchy knowledge of period architecture, Nichola hazarded a guess that the house had only been built within the last fifty years.

The anteroom which she now entered, taking a seat on one of the high-backed chairs before the fire, was also very fine and endorsed that opinion. A tapestry showing the exploits of Venus and Vulcan, woven in bright reds and vivid greens and blues, dominated one wall, the other being taken up with scenes of the chase. While the fire, which had obviously been burning all night and on to which another servant hastily threw some more wood, flamed in a stone fireplace decorated with heraldic designs. Harmoniously, the reds in the tapestries were complemented by the colours in the Turkey carpet and the long heavy curtains.

"Well?" asked Emmet, who had been watching her mistress.

"It's gorgeous. I wonder who owns it."

"You'll find out soon enough when the Master returns."

"I'm surprised to hear you call Lord Joscelin that when you've never met him."

"He *feels* like the Master now that you and Michael have parted company."

Nichola leant forward and took Emmet's hands in hers. "I suppose you know that our love affair started up again, so I won't insult your intelligence by informing you of the fact. All I ask is that you don't tell my husband."

The servant looked at her closely. "*Why* did you do it?"

"Because of bodily needs I suppose," Nichola answered honestly.

Emmet made no reply, staring at her with such a shrewd, bird-like glance that Nichola was forced to look away and gaze into the flames. Fortunately, there was a tap on the door at that moment and two servants appeared, carrying trays of food which they proceeded to set out on the table, making further discussion of her wayward behaviour impossible. Despite her hunger, Nichola saw that the board was heaped with platters bearing quite the most unpalatable fare for that hour of the day: mounds of pickled oysters and anchovies, jugs of ale and wine. Feeling quite unable to stomach any of it, she asked for bread and marmalade to be fetched, promptly earning herself a reputation as an eccentric eater. Emmet, though, tucked in heartily and downed a great deal of beer from which Nichola narrowly rescued the baby, who from then on had to be content with small strips of her surrogate mother's bread and preserve.

"And now I'm going to bed," said Nichola, handing the child back. "Wake me if my husband returns."

"I will – and I won't say anything. I know the difference between lust and love, even if you don't," Emmet answered, wiping her hand across her mouth.

"How could you?" asked Nichola, genuinely astonished. "You're just a little country girl."

"So are you, come to that."

"Don't be cheeky," Nichola retorted sharply. "You don't know what I am."

"Well, you're most certainly not the girl I grew up with!"

Emmet replied angrily, and left the room, red in the face.

Sighing, Nichola drew her chair closer to the fire and promptly fell asleep. But almost immediately, or so it seemed, she was awoken by a tentative knock and the sound of the door opening. Looking round, she saw that a female servant had come in.

"Forgive me for disturbing you, my Lady, but Lord George Goring is here to see you. He says he has ridden ahead of Lord Joscelin and has a message from him."

"Ask Lord George if he will be seated and give him some refreshment. I must go and change. Oh, and later I shall require a bath."

"Yes, my Lady," answered the servant, looking doomed.

Having sent for Emmet to help her into the only item of clothing she had brought with her, a somewhat plain day gown, Nichola attempted to recall everything Mr Hollin had told her about George Goring while the girl struggled with the garment's complicated laces. As far as she could remember, the nobleman waiting downstairs had married money, an Irish heiress, and his career as a professional soldier had thereafter taken off like a meteor. His new father-in-law had purchased the command of a foot regiment in the Dutch army for the bridegroom, who had consequently seemed destined for great things. Then, tragically, Lord George had been severely wounded at Breda and his career as a fighting man had come to an abrupt halt. Disconsolate, Goring had returned to England, partly disabled, where he had in rapid succession become first governor of and then MP for Portsmouth. He had also been one of the conspirators in the plot to seize the port and bring French troops in that way, in order to aid the King, but the Portsmouth plan had failed and Goring had soon become involved in a new scheme.

This time it had been to replace the army commander, the Earl of Northumberland, with another Earl, Newcastle. The idea had been to march the militia on London in order to subdue Parliament, but at the last minute Lord George had traitorously informed John Pym, leader of the House of Commons, and the First Army Plot had been revealed.

"It was Parliament who re-appointed him Governor of Portsmouth," the rector had told Nichola, "and then he turned coat on them as well, by declaring for the King when the Standard was raised. The man is a double-dyed villain, I believe."

Somewhat intrigued, Nichola had gone downstairs to meet a real live character who had stepped straight from the pages of history, thinking that other than for her glimpses of the King, Rupert and the royal princes this was the first time such a thing had happened to her since becoming Arabella.

Lord George Goring rose from his chair as she came in and Nichola could not help but smile at how different the man was from her preconceived idea of him. She supposed that she had expected someone dark, saturnine and sinister, with a closed secretive face, but this fellow was candid looking, his widely spaced eyes clear and large. Those same eyes now ran over her appraisingly and their owner made a bow which revealed that his disability lay in a leg wound.

"Lady Attwood?" he said, and at Nichola's nod continued, "By God, friend Joss *is* a lucky man. I'd heard a rumour he had married a beauty, but never having been one for listening to gossip thought it probably untrue. Tell me, my dear, do you enjoy the pastime of tittle-tattle?"

He was obviously teasing and Nichola replied, "But of course. I learn so much that way."

"Then you will undoubtedly have heard that I am a drunk and a reprobate, of which only the former is true."

It was such a fascinating situation, to be actually speaking to someone who had achieved historical notoriety, that Nichola found herself smiling again.

"I see that you like me," Lord George stated boldly, winking one of his wide eyes. "So I'll drink your health for it." He raised his wine glass. "Will you join me in a toast?"

Nichola nodded, refilling his glass to the brim and pouring one for herself.

"To the finest beauty in Oxford whose presence amongst us is sure to raise the spirits of all who see her." He drained the glass and gave her another audacious look. "Tell me, Lady Attwood, are you as pure as you are lovely?"

In her old life Nichola would have answered him succinctly but somehow it was difficult to be rude to this swaggering cavalier with his long hair and laces. "Are *you*?" she asked instead.

Lord George roared and slapped his thigh. "By God, but you're a sonsy wench. I'd give a fortune for one sweet night with you."

"Would you now?" Nichola replied, still smiling. "Well I'm sorry, sunshine, but I'm not available."

George roared all the louder and downed another glass. "Fiery, too! By God's dear teeth, you're a woman to be reckoned with."

"I believe you have a message for me," Nichola countered primly, an emotion almost unknown to her in her old days.

"I have indeed. Joss's man Caradoc met us on the road and informed him of your arrival. His Lordship sent me ahead to tell you he'll be back tonight and will join you at the festivity."

"What festivity?"

"The Master of Revels has ordered a celebration to mark the fact that the campaigning season will soon be upon us once more."

Nichola stared in astonishment, having long since learned the function of such an office but unable to comprehend the presence of a Master in a town that had virtually become a garrison.

"You look surprised," said Goring, reading her expression. "The Master was appointed not long after His Majesty's arrival and has become a necessary feature."

"But what is the object of having him? To boost morale?"

"To make sure that court life continues," Lord George answered seriously. "There are all kinds of entertainment here in Oxford: plays, concerts, new fashions, to name but a few."

"That's outrageous. I thought the King was here to fight."

Goring waved a lace handkerchief about. "Indeed, but surely one doesn't have to be miserable whilst doing so. Besides, what would the ladies say?"

"Are there a lot of women here?"

"Of course – wives, mistresses, camp followers. The place is seething with 'em. You won't be lacking company, my dear."

"I'm frankly amazed," said Nichola. "I hadn't expected anything like this."

"Wait until tonight," George replied. "You'll be even more astonished, I swear."

"And where is the festivity to be held?"

"In the Hall at Christ Church, at which college His Majesty is in residence. You should dine lightly today for a supper will be served. You are to attend the King at eight o'clock." He leant towards her, his eyes gleaming with fun. "And if the question is already in your head as to how you will robe yourself and what you shall use for conveyance, let me put your mind at rest. The last incumbent of this house only took with him what he could carry conveniently and so, too, did his lady wife."

"Who was he?"

"Alderman Richard French, a wealthy merchant but one with Parliamentary leanings for all that. He fled from hence and into rebellion when news of the King's coming was mooted abroad."

"And Joscelin appropriated his belongings?"

"Indeed." Lord George rose to his feet. "The town is packed with strangers, billeted in private houses, in colleges, in taverns and inns, and the number swells daily. Let me hasten to assure you that not many dwell in such comfortable surroundings as you find yourself, my Lady. You must thank Joss for that. He was in here like a flash and had staked his claim before another could do so."

Nichola smiled. "I can imagine that quite easily."

Goring grinned, his large eyes full of mischief. "A good man is friend Joss, even though I covet his place in your bed. I will await both his pleasure and yours this evening."

Nichola curtsied, relishing the unreality of the entire scene. "Until tonight, my Lord," she said and realised with surprise just how much she was enjoying playing the role of Joscelin's wife.

An exploration of the house and offices revealed that when Alderman French and his spouse had fled from Oxford they had indeed left behind much that could be of use, though all truly valuable personal and household effects had been carefully removed. However, within the clothes press Nichola discovered several fashionable dresses, all somewhat large for Arabella's small frame, though none of them defying alteration. A sewing woman had been found amongst the servants, also abandoned to their fate, and hasty renovations were made to one particular gown while Nichola took her long-awaited bath. In the meantime Caradoc, who had returned during the afternoon, investigated the stables to see that the Alderman's finest coach was in place, having obviously been considered too delicate for headlong flight. There were also two rather elderly horses within, capable of pulling despite their years, or so he informed Nichola.

"So Cinderella shall go to the ball!"

"My Lady?"

"Nothing," she answered, not even wanting to enjoy a joke with him. As ever, Caradoc's taciturn manner irritated her and Nichola wished, as she went down the steps to where the conveyance waited, that the escaping family had left their coachman behind so she could have shared this momentous occasion with someone more congenial. As quiet and withdrawn as ever, Joscelin's servant sat on the driver's box and simply nodded to her as she climbed inside.

Retracing their steps of that morning, the coach entered the city by the North Gate then went straight on past the Corn Market to Carfax. Nichola, staring through the open window, still felt as if she were in fantasy land, gazing at an Oxford that had existed long ago. There were people everywhere; common soldiery spilling out of the taverns, gawdy whores loitering in doorways, ordinary townsfolk going upon their way, all of them lit by the flickering gleam of the torches attached by brackets to the exterior walls of the shops and dwelling places.

Away from this illuminated scene there was audible evidence of yet more people about, for from the darkened alleyways came the sounds of scuffle and affray, coupled with the gasps and laughter of hasty lovemaking. In spite of finding herself caught up by the excitement and romance of the spectacle, Nichola could not help but shudder at the thought of the state of the streets when daylight finally revealed the detritus of the night before. For amongst all the many unspeakable things that must run along the cobbles, blood was obviously no stranger. Two soldiers were clearly visible duelling outside an alehouse and one had wounded the other so badly that his essential fluids were pouring down from a gash in his arm. It was almost a relief to leave such a boisterous, noisy, noisome pageant and proceed into the quieter confines of St Aldate's.

Gone was the Town Hall which housed the Museum of Oxford, round which Nichola had once walked, tourist style, wearing a headset and listening to a recorded voice telling the tale of the city's past. Now she had seen that past for herself, had smelled its terrible, exciting smell, had been so close to one of the King's generals that she could have touched him. For the first time since the inexorable events which had begun at Lewis Devine's party, Nichola felt a sense of privilege.

The great wooden doors of Christ Church had been flung back to allow carriages to pass through, but just for a moment, as they drew level with them, Nichola did not know where she was, for the quirky splendour of Christopher Wren's Tom Tower was missing. In its place stood a typically Tudor archway with turrets on either side, under which the coach passed before it turned left and came to a halt before a doorway Nichola had never noticed when she had done her tour of the college in that other life so long ago. Through this open doorway came the sound of music and voices, laughter and the clink of glasses. Christ Church was *en fête* and King Charles I was receiving his guests.

A disappointingly small staircase led upwards, ascending which was a tightly pressed pack of people; Nichola smelt sweat and scent, felt the heat of bodies in beautiful heavy clothes. Suddenly very conscious of her own appearance she touched Arabella's fair hair, smoothed straight back from her forehead, the effect softened by a semi-circle of little curls, and brushed at the ringlets which fell on either side of her face. Then Nichola reached the top and stepped into the Great Hall of Christ Church as it had looked when the King had once held his court there, and instantly forgot about everything else.

Hundreds of candles burned, throwing their light on the great hammerbeam roof, the goblets and plate, and all the other fine things that had been mustered in order to make Charles's exile from London as harmonious as possible. On the raised dais sat a consort of musicians so that the Hall was full of the sound of viols and flutes and sackbuts, and the high bright voice of clarino trumpets. The effect was overwhelming, the reflected glow of the flames from the two great fireplaces merely serving to add to the heightened brilliance of the atmosphere. And in the midst of such great splendour, small and thin to the point of being haggard, the famous long hair just showing its first streaks of grey, stood the little Stuart monarch about whom this whole brutal war was being fought. Open-mouthed, Nichola joined the line of loyal subjects waiting to greet him.

What she had not expected was his charm, the genuine sweetness of personality which was so much a part of his character. Curtseying before him, then kissing his hand as she had seen the others do, Nichola frankly stared into the pale *triste* face with its large, rather protuberant, brown eyes.

"Lady Attwood," murmured a tall spare fellow, standing beside the King and considerably dwarfing him.

"Welcome to Oxford," said that voice from the past, that voice from history, never before heard by twentieth-century ears.

Nichola felt the room spin round her as the full import of what was happening registered in her brain. "Thank you, Sir," she managed to mutter, then moved away like an old woman, incapable of more.

The room about her was suddenly alive with smiling faces, with the sparkle of jewels, the sheen and swirl of satins and silks. Breathing slowly and deeply to calm herself, Nichola absorbed every detail, aware that whatever happened, even if she were to return to her own time this very night, she must remember everything and treasure the memory for ever. And it was then that she saw Joscelin.

He stood in the doorway, as dark and vivacious as ever, his thick curls falling about the lace collar of his elegant suit. In one ear he wore a pearl pendant which shone as brightly as his eyes as he gazed about him. Nichola felt that she had never been more pleased to see anyone, nor more terrified that he should discover her guilty secret. And these warring emotions caused her to stand stock-still, unable to make a move, and watch as this most fascinating of characters made his way into that glittering ballroom.

He was searching for her, that much was obvious, and yet could not see her. Just for another moment or two Nichola remained hidden and then she started to push through the crowd towards him. And it was like that, separated by several groups of carousing people, that their eyes finally met. For the first time in her life she knew what it was to experience those old clichés, fire in the blood and ice in her veins. Her heart had begun to quicken and her mouth felt like the Sahara desert.

My God, she thought, what is this? and was amazed that her lips were smiling, almost of their own accord.

"Arabella!" he called, and waved a greeting.

Nichola knew then, knew beyond any glimmer of doubt. She was so much in love that she could hardly speak. The miracle had finally happened and, in the face of it, what she had felt for Lewis Devine was reduced to what it had been all along, a silly self deception.

"Joscelin," she whispered, so softly that he could not possibly have heard her. "What have you done to me? What have you done to the woman who used to be Nichola Hall?"

Chapter Fifteen

They left the Hall of Christ Church beneath a sky that burned with starfire. While they had been inside that warm room, sensuous with perfumes, glowing with candles, a heavy frost had fallen, so that the roofs of the silent cloisters glistened like sugar plums and each blade of grass in the great quadrangle lawn was adorned with diamonds. At long last the teeming town had fallen silent, all abed, drunk or sober, and the only noise to disturb the empty streets was the clatter of the coach's wheels as their iron rims sparked against the icy cobbles.

Within its dark exterior neither of the couple spoke, so that the sound of their breathing, the beating of their hearts, seemed heightened to an unnatural degree. Nichola sat next to Joscelin, his arm holding her close to him, and listened to the rhythm of his blood, breathed in the very essence of him; the smell of his skin, the scent he wore, the fragrance of his dark and lustrous hair. She was bewitched now, utterly captivated, shaking with the shock of love, still hardly able to grasp the enormity of the sea change which had swept her up in its relentless current. Yet over the many and bewildering sensations all so new and so daunting, there loomed a dark shadow, the memory of her traitorous adultery with Michael Morellon.

Just for a moment, in the close confines of that trundling coach, the old Nichola Hall reasserted herself and thought, So what? Joscelin hadn't slept with me. I was free to do what I liked.

But somehow, even though it was true enough, the reasoning of the twentieth century did not apply to this other time in which she now lived. With a shudder of something approaching fear, Nichola realised that Nichola Hall the actress, the street wise woman of her times, was on the point of vanishing without trace.

"Why are you trembling?" asked Joscelin, so quietly that for a moment Nichola hardly realised he had spoken.

"I don't know. Perhaps because of the cold," she answered, drawing even nearer to him.

"Come under my cloak." And he pulled its folds round her shoulders so that she could feel the benefit of its thick enclosing velvet. For reply, Nichola kissed him on the cheek, feeling its smoothness, glad that Joscelin did not have the small beard and moustache which were so much a fashion of the times.

"You must be very tired," he said, still speaking softly. "This has been a long and weary day for you and the last few months cannot have been easy. Yet Caradoc tells me the Roundhead troop treated you civilly enough. Did you lie to him or is that so?"

Nichola stiffened. "Why should I lie?"

"I thought maybe to spare my feelings."

Nichola sat silently, wondering exactly what he meant by that. It suddenly seemed that the conversation was about to go down a dangerous path yet she could not see quite how to avoid it.

"In what way do you mean?"

He moved away from her very slightly. "Simply that if they had ill-used you I would have had no option but to lead a party to Greys Court to seek redress."

"There will be no need for that," she answered, almost curtly. "They kept themselves very much to themselves."

"Then all's well," he said, and drew her close once more.

Nichola's mind raced like a hare. How much had Caradoc actually said? Had he revealed the name of the Roundhead captain? If not, might he do so at some time in the future? Would it be better to mention Michael Morellon now or did Joscelin already know? It seemed that whatever she did was going to be wrong and yet again Nichola shivered.

"Still cold, my darling?"

She longed to tell him, then. To reveal everything and be given absolution. But her old instincts for self preservation were far from gone and she simply said, "No. Just exhausted."

"We're almost home."

"Then I'll go straight to bed."

And though she wanted to add, "With you, my love," Nichola remained silent, her earlier mood dispelled by the fear of how much Joscelin might already know.

The coach passed through the North Gate, the sleepy watch peering in through the window, grinning as he saw the couple sitting so closely together, then went on down St Giles. Nichola closed her eyes, feigning sleep, giving herself more time to think, and did not move as the conveyance drew to a halt.

Softly, Joscelin called out to Caradoc, "Open the door like a good fellow. I'm going to carry Lady Attwood within."

And Nichola felt herself lifted up like a child and taken inside the house. It was unashamedly romantic and she relished the sheer sentiment of it all. For never before in her experience had she been carried up a flight of stairs and laid gently upon a bed. She had been chased, laughing; she had been pushed, meaningfully; she had even been thrown down and jumped upon – but this experience crowned them all. Opening her eyes, she smiled up at him.

"I've woken you," said Joscelin.

"Yes, but in what a wonderful way."

He leant over her. "Arabella, when I left you last—"

"We had unfinished business."

"I have thought of it so often while we have been apart."

Nichola struggled upwards. "I too."

Joscelin's face was so close to hers that she saw a muscle twitch beside his mouth, momentarily pulling his lips into a quirky smile. "Even with Michael Morellon around?"

"So Caradoc told you?"

"Yes."

"What a bastard!"

"Why do you say that? My servant spoke in innocence. It is

you who have just betrayed yourself by uttering those words." Joscelin stood upright, suddenly very white and gaunt looking. "There's no need to tell me anything further, Arabella. Your face says it all. He made free with you, didn't he, you miserable little slut?" And with that he swept from the room, slamming the door behind him.

An enormous urge to protect the new-found love that had come to her engulfed Nichola so fiercely that she felt ready to fight almost to the death in order to secure it.

"Just a moment," she called after him, running into the corridor. "Just think, my Lord, before you condemn me out of hand. I am a normal woman with urges and lusts as strong as any man's. So yes, I did have intercourse with Michael Morellon, thinking I would feel no sense of betrayal as I was your wife in name alone. But how wrong I was. Guilt became my constant companion. And do you know why?"

Joscelin did not answer, taking a step back into the shadows so that she could not see his expression. Nichola, feeling she had nothing further to lose, continued to speak, recklessly now.

"Because I had fallen in love with you, that is the reason. As soon as I saw you tonight I knew it. And I can assure you this is the first time such a thing has happened to me, in this life or any other. Once I would have slept with any man that took my fancy, now I want only you."

"Do you expect me to believe that?" he asked softly.

"Whether you do or not, the fact is I left Michael and went with Caradoc to join you, and did not give my abandonment of him a second thought. Oh damn you, Joscelin. What have you done to me?"

She wept, then, hiding her face with her hands, wishing for the first time in weeks that the regression would end and she could get back to the comparative simplicity of her own century.

"Are you telling me that you are no longer in love with Morellon?" he persisted.

"I never was," Nichola answered wretchedly. "That was another girl, a young empty-headed creature. I am telling you the truth when I say that I am a different person. And that the real me loves you."

"Then why . . . ?"

"Did I sleep with Michael? Because I felt a physical need." She looked up at him. "And I'm glad I did because, at long last, it has proved to me that sex alone is not enough, not any more. All human beings change, Joscelin. Grant me the favour of believing that I have too."

Even while she was speaking, a remote part of Nichola's brain could hardly credit that the words were not only coming from her lips but that she actually meant them. And she knew then that she had gone beyond the point of no return. The darkly fascinating creature who stood in the shadows was undeniably the man she had always been looking for.

And I had to be bloody well regressed in order to find him, she thought with a flash of her old cynicism.

But there was no time for further soul searching. Like a torrent he had come out of the dark to be beside her, lifting her up so that her eyes were on a level with his own.

"Do you love me true then?" Joscelin asked tersely. "Is Michael Morellon now a creature of your past?"

"If I said to you that he was never part of it," Nichola answered seriously, "I doubt that you would believe me. So just accept what I tell you. I have fallen in love with you and have never been more shattered in my life."

He laughed. "Shattered?"

"Amazed, then. Oh Joscelin, haven't we wasted enough time talking? You said that you would never touch me until I came to you in love. Well, here I am – at last."

"Yes," he said, loosening his shirt at the throat, "so you are, my sweetheart."

In all her experience, bluntly remembering everything even though it gave her no pleasure to do so, Nichola had never known anything like it. It was not so much that Joscelin was well made and beautiful, that he thrust his way in deeper, that he appeared both demanding and unrelenting yet never for a second stopped considering her, in fact it was none of those things. It was simply that their bodies were like two parts of a whole, that they moved slowly and superbly together, that both physically and emotionally it seemed as if they had been made, one for the other. There were kisses, touching, hardness and softness, followed by a loss of control that was exciting beyond description. Then came the most profound climax Nichola had ever known, and as Joscelin gasped and released, his carnal movements at an end, she knew that he had delighted in the same sensation.

Afterwards they lay in each other's dew, silenced by the experience they had so recently shared.

"I love you," Joscelin whispered at last.

"And I love you."

He propped himself up on one elbow, his black curls falling over her brow. "You won't leave me, will you?"

"What a strange thing to say. Why do you ask?"

"Because you have an elusive quality."

"Have I?"

"Yes. I sometimes get the feeling that one day, and not just through the fortunes of war, you will go away for good."

Nichola turned her head so that Joscelin could not see her face. "We have only just come together. Don't let's speak of separation."

"Is that the only answer you can give me?"

"Without knowing where fate is going to lead us, I'm afraid it is."

"Then I suppose," he said, taking her into his arms once more, "that I must be content with it."

The fighting of the year 1643 broke out in February when Rupert of the Rhine rode forth from Oxford and stormed Cirencester. The Prince then advanced north towards Birmingham while the Earl of Northampton, the former Master of the Robes, headed towards Stafford, Lord Joscelin at his side. Coupled with this military activity came the news that the Queen, Henrietta Maria, had finally returned to England from her fundraising in Holland. This mission had been moderately successful, though Henrietta Maria declared by letter that the

Dutch merchants had given her but half of what the pieces were worth. In any event, Her Majesty had raised about £100,000, together with two thousand cases of pistols and the services of several soldiers of fortune. However, hopes that she would soon join the King in Oxford were dashed. Henrietta Maria remained in York at the home of Sir Arthur Ingram.

"I couldn't bear that," Nichola had said to Emmet. "Not after so long a separation. I'd have had to set out to join him."

"It's too dangerous for her, so they say. And anyway you're moonstruck these days and not thinking properly."

It was perfectly true. Nichola was now so profoundly in love with Joscelin that she could hardly concentrate on anything else. And yet, in the midst of this extraordinarily painful happiness – painful because they had been forced to part again – the old dream had come back to haunt her.

This time the sequence of events had started in Oxford, the Oxford Nichola had known in her previous life, and she had been able to vividly compare one with the other. Then the scene had changed to that dreaded hospital room, the sound of the ventilator the only noise to disturb its stillness. On this occasion the body had been alone other than for a nurse, until suddenly, or so it seemed to Nichola's sleeping mind, time had convoluted itself and Joscelin had walked in. Yet he hadn't been awake, that was the horrible part of it. He was sleepwalking or else he was a ghost, for the nurse did not look up or even notice his presence. In the chilling way that dreamers have, Nichola knew that he was dreaming too, that somewhere in some field tent he was dreaming of the body at exactly the same moment that she was.

She woke with a scream to hear that Miranda was crying aloud in her nursery and, without stopping even to put a shawl round her shoulders, Nichola had lit a candle and run down the first floor corridor of that elegant house in St Giles. Through the high windows the March moon was throwing light in pools of frosted milk on to the polished boards of the wooden floor. Caught up by its beauty, Nichola momentarily forgot about the child and turned to stare out of the window.

Standing on the lawn in a V formation, Lewis Devine at the apex, was every person who had been at the after-show party on the night she had been regressed. Unable to believe what she was seeing, Nichola plunged at the lead lighted casement, the palms of her hands flat against the glass, her eyes wide with horror. But not a single member of that silent, staring group made a move, all of them continuing to gaze straight in front. And then, as one, they looked up and right at her, their eyes black and sunken in their pale moonlit faces. Putting her head back, Nichola let out a cry of pure terror, then sank to the floor sobbing.

There was the sound of running feet and a pair of arms that Nichola recognised from the touch as Emmet's, flung themselves around her.

"Whatever is it?" demanded the servant, her voice harsh with anxiety. "Arabella, what has happened? What frightened you?"

"Out there, on the lawn. The people from the past. They've come to take me away. I know they have."

"What *are* you talking about?"

"Lewis and Glynda and all the others. They're here in Oxford. I've just seen them. They want me to go with them."

Emmet craned her neck, peering through the casement. "But there's no one there. You've been having a nightmare. Look for yourself."

Shudderingly, Nichola obeyed, slowly rising to her feet and then, with the greatest reluctance, turning her head to stare out. The garden was empty, only the shadows of the trees and shrubs throwing strange distortions over the empty moon-drenched lawn.

"Was it a dream then?" she asked hesitantly.

"Of course it was. Oh, you're such a funny one, Mistress! I often think you live in another world. Those strange names you said to me just now. You never knew anybody called that. You imagine it all."

Nichola laughed without humour. "Sometimes I could almost believe you."

"And so you should. Now off to bed with you. After I've seen to Miranda I'll bring you a hot possett."

"I don't know that I want to sleep again tonight."

"You must," Emmet answered firmly. "You can't let these nightmares of yours start to get the better of you."

"How do you know that I have them?"

"Because I do," the girl answered, and went away before she could be drawn further.

It seemed to Nichola that the entire city of Oxford was caught up in an extraordinary state of schizophrenia. On the one hand the place was rapidly and visibly being converted into a garrison town, on the other, despite all outward signs of conflict, court life continued to be conducted as if the war simply did not exist.

The daily influx of troops, supplies and prisoners, had necessitated the immediate strengthening of fortifications, and work had begun shortly after the King's arrival on the mammoth task of encircling the town with a series of ditches and ramparts. A Dutch engineering expert, Sir Bernard de Gomme, already fighting for the King, had been called in to supervise this vast project, while the labour itself had been provided, most unwillingly, by Oxford's citizens. The university students, however, who as Royalists were more enthusiastic, usually worked on into the night with mattocks and shovels, compensating for the others, and thanks mostly to their efforts the great earthworks were completed by April 1643. This had been just as well, for in February eleven hundred prisoners from Cirencester had come to swell the numbers contained in the city, some of them being housed near to Nichola in the church of St Giles, where they dwelt in miserable conditions.

Beside the massive fortifications of ramparts and trenches, storm poles and palisades, gates and drawbridges, circling the city at a discreet distance, there had been other changes too. The halls known as The Schools, where Law, Logic, Music, Astronomy and Rhetoric were studied, had been turned into warehouses, in them stored cloth and coal as well as food supplies. The Law and Logic Schools were now granaries, Rhetoric housed rope bridges and scaling equipment, while Astronomy and Music had been given over to the tailors who sat cross-legged on wooden benches, stitching uniforms for the King's army.

The colleges had also been commandeered. While the King took up residence in Christ Church, Prince Rupert and his brother boarded in St John's, and Jesus College became an up-market lodging house for persons of quality from Wales. Unfortunately, the other colleges suffered a less pleasant fate. All Souls became an arsenal, a cannon foundry was set up at Frewin Hall, and there was a powder and arms magazine in the tower and cloister of New College. Similarly the tower of Brasenose was turned into a food store, and the great quadrangle of Christ Church, a cattle pen.

Meanwhile soldiers, together with their wives and women, were billeted in the parishes of St Ebbe, St Aldate, St Michael and St Mary Magdalen. Every other bit of accommodation was snatched up by courtiers and noblemen, to say nothing of the high-ranking officers and King's servants, including his surgeon, his apothecary and sewing woman. And yet in the face of this hideous over-crowding, much to Nichola's astonishment, courtly life continued, and the Master of Revels organised a constant stream of entertainments.

There were musical extravaganzas and plays, new works of literature, songs and sonnets, while high cutting fashions were flaunted through the jostling streets, to be copied by the wives of those local burgers eager to keep up with London styles. Romance and sexual liaisons flourished in this hothouse atmosphere and passionate affairs were conducted by the riverbank as spring arrived. Listening to the gossip, Nichola thought that never a lover would have walked there again had not the river by now been cleared of its filthy detritus. For an extraordinary character called John Taylor, to her mind a forerunner of William McGonagal whose terrible poems she had recited together with her fellow drama students, had come to put all to rights.

Taylor, a humble Thames waterman, had arrived from

London to serve the King in any way he could, and for his pains had been given the grim task of clearing the waterways. He had then written a poem about it which had made Nichola quite hysterical, the only un-funny thing about the work being that it was true.

Then by the Lords Commissioners and also
By my good King (whom all true subjects call so)
I was commanded by the Water Bailey
To see the rivers cleansed both nights and daily.
Dead hogs, dogs, cats and well flayed carrion horses
Their noisesome corpses soiled the waters' courses;
Both swines' and stable dung, beasts' guts and garbage,
Street dirt, with gardeners' weeds and rotten herbage.
And from those waters' filthy putrefaction,
Our meat and drink were made, which bred infection.
Myself and partner, with cost, pains and travail
Saw all made clear, from carrion, mud and gravel.
Besides at all commands, we served all warrants,
To take boats for most necessary errands,
To carry ammunition, food and fuel,
(The last of which last winter was a jewel).

"And so are you a jewel," said Nichola, reading Taylor's ode for the hundredth time, wishing that Joscelin were there to share the joke with her.

She had received one letter from him, which informed her that though the Earl of Northampton had won the day when he had clashed with the enemy around the coal-pits of Hopton Heath in mid March, the Earl himself had been lost. Leading his men in pursuit of the Roundhead horse, the nobleman's mount had been shot from under him and, as the Earl had fallen his helmet had been struck from his head. Instantly he had been surrounded by enemy soldiers who had offered him mercy, almost begging him to become their prisoner. But the Earl, who up till the war had passed a life of unrivalled ease and luxury, had suddenly displayed his true steel.

"I scorn to accept quarter from such base rogues as you are," he had said, and been killed for speaking thus by a blow to the head. Joscelin, mourning his commanding officer, had gone on to join Prince Rupert's force, about to attack Birmingham.

There had been no further communication since then, but the talk in Oxford was that the Prince and his men had charged into the town singing, shouting and shooting, and then had fallen to plundering and had 'assaulted many women's chastity'. This was considered amusing to all who heard it, though it was something on which Nichola did not care to dwell.

Amongst Alderman French's abandoned belongings she had found a strange looking contraption which appeared to be the forerunner of a pram. It resembled a cradle mounted on wheels and had a handle for driving it along. Wondering whether it might possibly be described as a bassinet, Nichola had taken to pushing Miranda out in it now that the weather was finer, turning right out of the great house towards the North Gate rather than walk towards St Giles, for the smell of the wretched prisoners wafting from it was more that she could stomach. With Caradoc gone to be with his master, a fact that gave Nichola an enormous sense of relief, a man servant usually offered to accompany her as bodyguard. On this particular day, however, Nichola had dispensed with his services and was alone.

Just outside the gate at the top of St Giles stood a house which had always fascinated her, for at whatever time of day she passed by there invariably came the sound of music and laughter from within. Nichola discovered that it belonged to a Mr William Stokes and was a school of dancing, the arts of fencing and vaulting from horses also included in the subjects taught there.

In love she might be, surrogate mother indeed, but on every occasion she walked past it was a temptation to mount the steps and look inside. And today, on this fine May morning, with the birds in full throat in the gardens of the three great colleges, St John's, Balliol and Trinity, Nichola was yet again wrestling with the compulsion when a boy whom she had vaguely noticed riding through the city gate at speed, in company with an older man, suddenly appeared at her feet, knocking into the bassinet.

"A thousand pardons, Madam," he said, and made a bow which spoke well of Mr Stokes's tutelage.

His voice was delightful, at the lovely squeaky stage denoting puberty, in fact the word 'pardons' had plunged an octave even while he spoke it.

"Why don't you look where you're going?" Nichola answered, pretending indignation. "You could have tipped my daughter over."

For answer he bent down and tickled Miranda, who was wearing that expression poised between laughter and tears, and she instantly smiled.

"What a pretty child," he said, a courtier in the making if ever there was one. "If I may be so bold, Madam, this girl will one day break hearts as easily as does her beautiful mother."

Nichola laughed aloud, delighted with this imp of sauciness. "Are you taught the art of flattery as well?" she asked, indicating the school outside which they were standing.

The boy bowed again, his long black hair falling almost to his waist. "I have no need for that, Madam. Tis as natural to me as oratory."

The attractive voice had been ranging up and down as he spoke, and the dark eyes, the colour of which reminded Nichola of that extraordinary flower, the black tulip, were sparkling with fun. So much so that she laughed delightedly again.

"You're a cheeky monkey, that's for sure. Tell me, how old are you?"

"Thirteen, but for a day or two. My birthday is 29 May."

"A Gemini, eh?"

"Aye, a twin. My mother's astrologers cast a horoscope when I was born which said I would be the lover of many women. I don't think she was too well pleased."

"I should think not indeed. I hope she's keeping a strict eye on you these days."

The boy's face flickered and at the same time he looked at Nichola sharply. "She's away from Oxford at the moment so unable to do so. I am in the charge of my father."

Nichola felt a faint stir of concern. "She's not divided from you by politics?"

The boy positively gleamed. "In a sense I suppose one could answer yes." He changed expression and looked downcast. "She will not even be with me for my birthday, though my Papa is giving a small celebration." He paused, his white teeth glinting in his dark face, still exhibiting some youthful podge about the cheeks. "Will you come and join the company, Madam? I would deem it a great favour. I feel that we are already friends, don't you?"

"Where is this party to be held?" Nichola asked him cautiously, not wanting to commit herself.

"At my cousin's home in the High Street. He and his brother have been billeted elsewhere but now they are to share a new dwelling place. Yet they are both away fighting at present so the house is empty. I'll write the address down and bring it to you. Say you'll come."

He suddenly looked young and vulnerable, all his brashness vanished.

"Is it on the 29th itself?"

"Yes. We are not to sit formally to dine but will take supper early in the evening. I'll expect you there." And before Nichola could say another word, the boy had kissed her hand swiftly and vanished into the confines of the dancing school.

She stood staring after him, thinking him one of the most extraordinary and delightful children she had ever met, a true product of his era. For what boy of her own times, of an equivalent age to that one, would have possessed such charm and *savoir-faire*? But then all the young people of this century were little hothouse plants, forced into adulthood by the cruel war that raged around them. And then Nichola thought of the children of what had once been Yugoslavia, of the innocent victims of the Third World, and those mindless beings wandering the housing estates of Britain with no one to love or guide them, the hideous legacy of an uncaring society, and shuddered at the plight of the young and defenceless at any time in the planet's history.

The house in the High Street, to which she was taken by coach through the stifling streets, proved to be rather more elegant than its neighbours, a tall handsome building no more than a few years old. Studying it through the carriage's open window, Nichola thought there had been something decidedly mysterious about the way in which the facts of the place's location had been imparted to her. Firstly, she had not given the boy her address, yet during the night a note had been left with her porter, as if the child had known all along who she was. Secondly, after confirming the time and date of the party, he had signed his letter 'Gemini', though this was probably just a schoolboy's love of intrigue. Nevertheless, Nichola realised, as the coach's step was swung down and she dismounted, Gemini's father was obviously a man of substance, for the house was well lit by candles and there was the sound of music playing.

A bowing servant escorted her into the hall, where Nichola was greeted by a major-domo. But a glimpse up the staircase beyond revealed the boy himself, hovering excitedly and swooping downwards like a bird the moment he saw her.

"Mind your manners, Sir," said an invisible chiding voice, to which the child answered, "Tis all informal tonight, Papa. I requested it so and you gave permission as it is my birthday." He bowed before Nichola. "My dear and beautiful Lady Attwood, what a pleasure it is to see you. The court painter, William Dobson, is here this evening and I have told him to remark you well."

He was irresistible and Nichola smiled. "You are cheekier than ever – and also a very bright lad. How did you know who I was when I never so much as gave you a hint?"

"Because the lovely Lady Attwood, who dwells in St Giles

with her child and gallant husband and is something of a mystery into the bargain, is the talk of the town."

"Is she indeed?"

"Most certainly."

The black tulip eyes were gazing into her own and Nichola was just thinking what a sexy little creature this thirteen-year-old was when there was a rustle of satin behind her. Glancing up the stairs again, Nichola found herself staring into a familiar face. Hollow-cheeked, sad, with the air of his destiny already about him, she was gazing straight at Charles I. Seeing her jaw drop, the boy let out a giggle and allowed his deep sash, which he had been holding curiously high, to slip down to its normal place, thus revealing the fact that he wore an Order.

"You little devil..." Nichola exclaimed before she had had time to think.

And then she was back playing a part in a costume drama, curtseying to both royal father and son, realising that in a way she had betrayed the fact she did not come from this era by completely failing to recognise Charles, Prince of Wales.

The King's genuine charm, the reason why so many men had flocked to his side while not altogether agreeing with his cause, once more became apparent. "Lady Attwood, it is a pleasure to see you again," he said. "When the Prince told me he wanted you as one of his special guests I was delighted. Yet I sense he has played some kind of trick on you. Should I chastise him?"

"Not at all, Sir. It was my own fault to a certain extent."

"Then all is well. Let us go to the receiving room and leave him to greet his other visitors."

For all his melancholy air it was obvious that the King was not beyond appreciating a good-looking woman and was also clearly missing female company. For, with a dignified nod of the head, he escorted Nichola up the stairs, betraying the kind of nervous alacrity which showed most clearly how lonely he had been since the Queen's departure. Imbued with a sense of disbelief, Nichola went into the room where the Prince of Wales's birthday guests had foregathered.

There was an odd assortment of people within, all of whom made reverence as the King entered. Looking at them closely, not wanting to make the same mistake of not identifying someone she should know, Nichola saw several elderly men, all too old to be engaged in active combat, together with a younger, tall, comely creature with a mass of shining fair hair. There were also two others present, a lively fellow with a ready smile and laugh whom she guessed to be the court painter, Dobson, because of a slight smear of paint on his hands, and a dark and angry looking man addressed as Lord Henry whose expression was one of barely concealed superciliousness.

There were women and children there too, all of whom stared at Nichola quite openly, the ladies with that rapid look of assessment common to all centuries, the young people with no more than the frank curiosity of their age. Smiling graciously in their direction, Nichola allowed a servant to pour her a glass of claret and was just about to sip it when one of the women came towards her and swept a curtsey.

"Jacobina Jermyn," she said. "I have seen you about the city, my Lady, but so far have had no opportunity to speak with you."

She was gorgeous in an elfin sort of way, a cloud of red hair, strongly resisting being flattened and ringleted, surrounding a small white rosepetal face. In the midst of this face were goblin green eyes, in fact the whole effect was quite enchanting and charming.

Nichola curtsied. "You are in Oxford with your husband?" she asked politely.

"Not I," the newcomer answered roundly. "I find most men too pompous for my tastes. No, I'm here to await my brother Henry. He's in the north with the Queen. They're old friends, of course."

The elf girl said this last with an utterly straight face yet somehow managed to convey the impression of a *tendresse* between Henry Jermyn and his royal mistress. Nichola found herself warming to her.

"And what about you?" Jacobina continued. "You are

married to the scampish Attwood, are you not? Now there's one who would not know the meaning of the word pompous, or so I should imagine."

"You imagine correctly. How long have you been in Oxford?"

"Since shortly after Christmas. I came as soon as I received intelligence that Her Majesty and Henry had set sail."

"He was in Holland with her?"

"Oh yes," answered Jacobina innocently.

"Good gracious!"

Jacobina smiled. "Several of the Queen's friends went into exile with Her Majesty and, besides, she has now made Henry colonel of her guards."

"How intriguing all this is. I'd love to know more."

The other woman shot her a penetrating glance. "Do you lead a very sheltered life that you are not *au fait* with all the latest gossip?"

"It is true to say," Nichola replied carefully, "that where I once used to live I heard nothing about such matters."

"Then I shall make it my duty to catch you up."

"I would like that very much."

Jacobina glanced round. "But for now, that must be that. Here comes our birthday Prince, with his virginity bursting from his breeches."

Nichola giggled, reminded of dressing room bitchiness, even though it had been frequently directed at her. "What do you mean?"

The elf girl flashed her emerald eyes. "You can't be that innocent, Lady Attwood. Charles can't wait for his first sexual encounter. He's thirteen today and looking to make a conquest."

"I thought he didn't get going till he was fifteen."

It was out before she could snatch back the words, and Nichola only hoped that Jacobina had not heard, for the young man had arrived to bow before them and was offering Nichola his arm.

"My dear Lady Attwood," said the Prince of Wales charmingly, "will you give me the honour of allowing me to escort you in to supper?"

"Certainly, Sir," answered Nichola, paying him due respect, but only too well aware that with a barely noticeable movement of her lovely eyelid, Jacobina Jermyn had winked.

Chapter Sixteen

The summer of 1643 was destined to be one of death and despair for both sides in the great war between the King and his Parliament, death brought about not only by the fury of battle but also by the unseen enemy of disease. For as June came to the city of Oxford and the days grew warmer, the common soldiery took to sleeping upon the streets, careless about their sanitation. Whilst the other visitors, from great lady to lowly groom, crowding into lodgings too small to house them, suddenly felt stifled, found that there was no fresh air left to breathe, and choked on the stench of their close stools and chamber pots, and the foetid stink arising from the thoroughfares. Then, as the drains blocked through over-use and the stench became indescribable, fever finally broke out, the symptoms of which gave Nichola Attwood – as she had now begun to think of herself – much cause for concern.

She had always had scant medical knowledge, confined merely to glancing through her stepmother's copy of *Pears Medical Encyclopedia*. Yet it had registered in Nichola's mind that typhus was a disease prevalent in wartime and conditions of gross overcrowding, its carrier the louse, passed so easily from unwashed body to unwashed body. So, in her house in St Giles, strict orders had been given about personal cleanliness which had driven the servants to the point of such rebellion that they would have walked out, had not Emmet convinced them that her mistress had second sight, and had divined that it was lice which were the killers. In that age of extreme superstition, the girl could not have said anything better, and a routine of strip washing and inspection of the hair became a daily occurrence. Clothes worn to go into

Oxford were burned, and it soon became remarked that Lady Attwood's house was noticeably one of the few to remain free of infection.

In a panic, Jacobina Jermyn begged sanctuary there, escaping from her lodging in the High Street. But even she was made to bath in strong herbs and wash out her hair, while her dresses were beaten with a dust remover over the smoke of a garden bonfire. And all this time, as the death toll in every parish mounted, the courtiers were aware that the Queen was gradually making her way south to join them in that city of disease.

She had left York on 4 June, with a huge escort of men and dragoons, a hundred and fifty wagons bringing up the rear of her train. Henrietta Maria had ridden at the head of the column, styling herself Generalissima, flanked on either side by her two ardent admirers, Henry Jermyn and the Honourable Charles Cavendish, second son of the Earl of Devonshire, a man obviously deeply in love with his royal mistress.

"And is the Queen really so attractive to men?" Nichola had asked Jacobina as the two women ate a simple supper in the garden of the house in St Giles, their hair clean and flowing loose, their freshly washed bodies clad only in shifts.

Her new friend had considered this, her delicate face endearingly serious. "Yes, in a way. His Majesty most certainly adores his wife though, as my parents recounted to me, their marriage began badly enough. But yes, the Queen is a powerfully pretty little creature and it is quite the fashion for her gentlemen to be all at sea with love for her."

"Does she sleep with any of them?" Nichola had asked, half amused, half curious.

Jacobina had laughed and given one of the answers which endeared her to the twentieth-century woman.

"Gracious no, it's all a big tease, you know. The Queen loves a coterie of ardent young men around her but if one were so much as to suggest fornication she would have him on a charge of high treason."

"And what about your brother? Where does he fit in?"

"He has made himself indispensable to her. But, believe me, his is an unscrupulous friendship, for he is a committed self-seeker as you will soon see when you meet him. Prince Rupert loathes him, by the way." Jacobina had smiled ruefully.

"Then why have you come here to wait for him? Why not stay at home and avoid all this plague and danger?"

"Nowhere is safe in a time of war and, besides, I like risk. I think it keeps one alive. I hope that I shall be taking risks when I am an aged, aged woman."

Nichola had laughed aloud. "And how old are you, my dear?"

"The same as you I believe, nineteen."

Still she had not learned, despite everything, to control a lifetime's habit of the tongue. "But I'm twenty-eight," said Nichola.

Jacobina had frowned in bewilderment. "God help me, but that can't be true! Your looks belie such a thing. Besides, my servant told me you were but a few days from your nineteenth birthday in mid-June, and servants' gossip is usually accurate as you well know."

Nichola had sat silently, unsure quite how to answer, struck by the thought that, other than for Emmet, Jacobina was the first woman with whom she had ever shared anything approaching a friendship and aware she must say and do nothing to jeopardise it.

"Forgive me," she had said finally. "I sometimes feel a decade older. You are perfectly right, I will be nineteen on 16 June."

The white rose face flushed a little. "Is it true," Jacobina had asked breathlessly, "that you have the gift of sight? That you know things that are going to happen before they do so?"

Nichola had paused. "Who told you that?"

"It is the consensus that you are mysterious. And it is generally agreed you knew how to keep your house free of camp fever."

What a golden opportunity had presented itself. Nichola's longing to tell the truth, to perhaps gain one sympathetic ear, was overwhelming. And yet the thought of frightening Jacobina, of making her believe her new friend was deranged, seemed too great a risk to take. Sighing a little, she had said, "That was just common sense combined with a little medical knowledge. As to the other thing, the answer is no, I am not clairvoyant."

"Then why did you make that remark about the Prince of Wales not consorting with a woman until he was fifteen?"

"It was a guess; a guess which I am beginning to think was incorrect!"

And Nichola had smiled a little wryly, for the thirteen-year-old Prince had decided he was wildly in love with Arabella Attwood and was making a point of letting everyone know about it. Yet, according to history, Charles had not started what would prove to be a hectic sex life until the age of fifteen, when he had seduced or been seduced by a former governess. Nichola knew one thing for sure; she wasn't going to respond to the ardent little beast, though she had a very strong suspicion that somebody in Oxford would soon be persuaded to take her place vicariously – and that history was on the point of being wrong!

Jacobina had made a little noise of annoyance. "That is a pity."

"The fact that the Prince is precocious?"

"No, that you do not have such a gift. I was hoping you would read my future for me." Jacobina's eyes had brightened. "I've heard there is a gypsy woman at Wolvercote who can interpret both crystal and cards. As it is outside the city walls there should be no danger of contracting disease. Would you visit her with me?"

Relieved to find herself on safer ground, Nichola had nodded. "Of course. We can go tomorrow if you like."

"I would enjoy that greatly."

"Good. Now, will you keep your promise?"

"Which one?"

"To tell me about Prince Rupert, about the marriage of the King and Queen. In fact anything you feel I should know about the court."

The white rose had raised thin eyebrows. "Well, Rupert is something of an enigma. He's rude, arrogant, suffers fools not at all, yet it is my belief that this apparent harshness masks sensitivity and reserve."

Jacobina had coloured slightly as she had spoken and it had occurred to Nichola that the girl might have a passion for the maverick nephew of King Charles I.

"Are there women in his life?" she had asked, waiting to see the reaction.

"Only a few whores and casual liaisons. He is a fighting man first and foremost."

"And is it true that he always wears scarlet?"

"He invariably does, if not a scarlet suit then a sash of that colour. He dresses very fancifully, you know."

"I am surprised I did not see him about Oxford before he went off to fight."

"Oh, Rupert shuns court life and polite society. He hates mannered small talk. When he was a student he preferred discussing seafaring in the company of rough sailors and dockers to the latest gossip with his fellows. When frequenting the taverns in The Hague he would disguise himself in old canvas clothes in order to look like one of their number."

"I do believe," Nichola had said smilingly, "that you have a soft spot for him."

Jacobina had looked wistful. "Yes, I admit it. I have been in love with the Prince from the moment I met him, which was shortly after he arrived in England. That is really why I came to Oxford, to see him. So now you know the truth."

"And that is why you want to visit the fortune teller? To find out what is going to happen?"

"Yes, be it good or bad, I want to know it."

Nichola had shivered a little as an evening breeze had

caught her hair and blown it outwards. "I wonder," she had answered quietly, "what on earth she will say to me."

The outlying villages surrounding the city of Oxford had also been affected by the proximity of the King's headquarters. At Wolvercote, lying some miles to the north, a mill had been set up to grind the sword blades forged at Gloucester Hall, while at Osney the corn mills had been altered to accommodate the production of gunpowder. The woods of Shotover had been robbed of their timber for the city's defences and the white clay that came from the same area had been taken into Oxford to make pipes for the soldiers.

Yet it was not the sight of the lowering mill that unnerved Nichola as she and Jacobina Jermyn approached the village of Wolvercote on horseback, having ridden down St Giles past the church where prisoners lay dying of typhus and out into the open countryside, passing through the fortifications by means of one of the many drawbridges. Far more worrying was the possibility that the fortune teller might have a genuine gift and realise that the female consulting her had come from another century, even if the means of the transition were beyond her comprehension.

The directions given to the two women before they left Oxford had been precise. In the very shadow of the mill was a track leading to the right, which they should follow. This same track would take them to another, which would diminish to a mere footpath through the woods. Having gone down this for about half a mile they would see the gypsy's hovel standing in a glade. Picking their way carefully, bending low so as not to be hit by the trees, it was the noise of a tin whistle which finally told the couple they were going in the right direction. For as it was such a warm and pleasant day, the gypsy was sitting outside her dwelling on a wooden bench, playing a tune.

There was something about the creature that sent a shiver of instant alarm through Nichola. It was a hermaphrodite figure that sat in the sunshine, blowing its primitive wind instrument. For though long and voluminous skirts and a baggy shawl concealed whether it be man or woman, Nichola had already caught a glimpse of a pair of knowing eyes and a gnarled brown face, so harshly lined that it seemed more male than female, before the being pulled its hood up so that very little of the countenance was left visible.

"Good day," Jacobina called to the gypsy, boldly. "We have come from Oxford to know our futures. Will you tell them to us, my good woman?"

An extraordinary voice, half whisper, half chuckle, replied, "Cross my palm, lady. Cross my palm and you shall indeed be told."

It *was* a man, Nichola felt certain of it, and wondered about the reason for such a masquerade.

Definitely uneasy, she said, "I'll sit outside, Jacobina. It's not right that I should hear what is personal to you. But I'll be nearby if you should need me."

The dark eyes flashed her a glance but the fortune teller said nothing.

"Very well," her friend answered, and Nichola could tell by the nonchalant tilt of her chin that the girl was also nervous. Walking extra determinedly in order to mask her fear, Jacobina followed the gypsy into the hovel.

Sitting on a log at the edge of the clearing, Nichola closed her eyes and let the day consume her. The sun, at the high point of the heavens, was blazing down like a warm and comforting blanket, the song of the birds and their newly hatched chicks broke a silence that would otherwise have been profound, and a beautiful smell of flowers and herbs wafted from the small garden that the creature, somewhat surprisingly, kept carefully tended beside the run-down house. Without meaning to do so, Nichola found herself drifting into a doze.

The dream came at once, harshly and without warning, frightening her with its intensity. She was in the room with the body, staring down into its face, and realising for the first time how very much like her it was in appearance. Up to this moment Nichola had had no idea as to its identity, but now it looked so terrifyingly familiar that the horrible idea came to her that it might be herself, that while her psyche had been roaming free, her poor shell had been enduring months of hospitalisation.

Immeasurably sad, she reached out to touch the body's hand and take the fingers in hers. They were neither warm nor cold but somewhere in between the two. And yet it was an unearthly sensation, holding a hand identical to hers within her own grasp. The body moved very slightly, as if it was aware of its soul hovering so near, and this was too much for Nichola.

"Oh God!" she screamed. "Help her, please. Help us both."

She woke with a start to find that Jacobina and the gypsy had come out of the hovel and were standing a few feet away from her, staring in her direction.

"What is it?" cried her friend, running forwards. "Have you been dreaming?"

"Yes, yes. I'm sorry. I must have dozed off."

"Then step inside, my Lady," came that strange whispering voice, "and we shall look into the dream and see the meaning of it."

"I'd prefer simply to have my fortune told," Nichola answered, suddenly afraid and defensive, as she followed the stooping figure into the dim confines of the dwelling with a certain reluctance.

A table stood before the fireplace, where there burned a few miserable twigs and on which a blackened kettle boiled even on so hot a day. On the table lay a crystal and a worn pack of cards. Looking closely, Nichola saw that it was an early version of the Tarot and immediately felt curious as to how a creature living in so remote a spot could have come by them.

"Cross my palm," the fortune teller continued, and extended a hand along the palm of which ran a savage horizontal scar. Nichola took a coin from the bag at her waist and made a cross, following the line of the cut exactly.

"How did you come by that?" she asked.

"Savagely," answered the other and, picking up the crystal, gazed into it intently. The hood fell back as the gypsy did so and Nichola was left in no doubt as to the being's gender. It was a man who sat opposite her, staring into the twinkling glass.

"What happened to the real one?" Nichola asked softly.

He looked up at her, his eyes shrewd. "She died and I buried her in the forest. Oh, don't worry, the cause was natural. I merely acted as her gravedigger."

"Why did you take on her identity?"

The man laughed and threw the hood right back so that she could see the contours of a strong and weatherbeaten face. "Because army life was not for me, though not for the reasons you imagine."

"How do you know what I imagine?"

"Because we are both fugitives and instantly sensed it, one about the other." He stood up and gave a little bow. "Allow me to introduce myself, Pikeman Ditch, so named because I was born in one, late of the forces of Parliament, now a deserter and imposter."

He looked at Nichola as if he expected her to say something but she merely replied, "Do you have no other name?"

The dark eyes softened slightly. "My mother was called Emerald, so I have used that from time to time. Though it was not well appreciated in the army."

"I can imagine!"

He laughed shortly. "Emerald was a gypsy, who died from the exertions of her labour in that same sordid trench in which she gave birth. Fortunately, some others of her race heard my puny wails and took me as one of theirs. It was they who taught me to study the earth and the stars, and how to scry a crystal and divine the ancient cards."

"So at least you are genuine about that?"

"I probably have a greater gift than the poor creature whose personality I took on. But the destruction of life, particularly in a war as futile as this one, was abhorrent to me and did not fit with my Romany beliefs, so I deserted after Edgehill. I killed there for the first time and it was something from which I shall never recover. Thus I ran off and made my way towards Oxford, chancing upon this place on the way."

"And the owner was already dead?"

"Had been for several days. The villagers were too frightened of her to come near, you see. So she passed from this world alone and unaided. It was a simple thing to assume her identity. And yet, though many quality folk come to visit me from Oxford, you are the first one who has seen through the masquerade."

"How strange."

"Not at all. It is because neither of us is in our right place and know each other for what we are, mere play actors."

Nichola found that she was freezing despite the cramped and overheated room.

"What are you saying to me?"

"I'm not sure. Mine is a simple adoption of another's role. Your deception is more complex. The crystal shows me things about you I cannot understand. All I can tell is that you do not belong here."

Nichola leaned forward and grasped his scarred hand. "Will I return to where I should be?"

Emerald Ditch looked at her quizzically, his harsh feature creased by a cynical smile. "How oddly you phrased that. Who knows where any of us *should be*? Perhaps the other place was wrong for you, just as the battlefield was wrong for me, though not through any sense of fear my vanity bids me tell you. It is quite possible, is it not, that this is your habitat after all?"

"You are playing games," Nichola answered. "Just tell me if I will return."

Emerald dropped a kiss in the palm of her hand. "You will if you want to."

"Well obviously I do."

"Not obviously at all. Your mouth may speak those words – but to find the truth you should ask your straying soul."

"You still haven't answered my question," Nichola persisted.

"I did just now. You can return if you so desire it."

"But *will* I?"

He paused, contemplating his reply, and it was at that very moment that Jacobina appeared in the doorway.

"There's a troop of horsemen approaching. I wondered if they might be enemy soldiers."

Emerald, who had snatched his hood back round his face and adopted the same strangely sexless voice, said, "No, it will be just another delivery of swords for honing at the mill. They come through every day." He stood up. "I hope I have given satisfaction, ladies."

Jacobina frowned. "I could have wished for a future less complicated."

"Life *is* complicated," said Emerald Ditch. "No gypsy woman – or man – can alter that fact."

Nichola got to her feet. "I think it is time we took our leave. Thank you for an interesting half hour."

The fortune teller made a little bow. "You did not tell me about your dream."

She smiled at him. "I think you know enough about me as it is."

He shrugged and put his head on one side. "Possibly. But remember what I said to you. In the final analysis the path of destiny lies in your hands."

"I won't forget," Nichola said as she walked out into the sunshine.

The summer continued in cruelty and conflict. On 16 June 1643, while Nichola, most unwillingly, celebrated Arabella's nineteenth birthday, only to please Jacobina who knew no better and had arranged a supper party for her, the Roundhead and Cavalier forces faced each other outside Bath. And it was on that very night that the Royalist commander, Sir Ralph Hopton, wrote to his Parliamentarian counterpart and cherished friend, the brilliant, erratic Sir William Waller, suggesting that they meet under a flag of truce. Sir William's reply summed up the whole tragedy of the Civil War in a few sentences.

> The experience I have had of your worth, and the happiness I have enjoyed in your friendship, are wounding considerations when I look upon this distance between us. Certainly my affections to you are so unchangeable that hostility itself cannot violate my friendship to your person, but I must be true to the cause wherein I serve ... That great God, which is the searcher of my heart, knows with what sad sense I go upon this service, and with what a perfect hatred I detest this war without an enemy ... The God of Peace in his good time send us peace and in the meantime fit us to receive it; we are both upon the stage, and must act the parts assigned to us in the tragedy. Let us do it in a way of honour and without personal animosities. Whatever the issue be, I shall never willingly relinquish the dear title of, Your most affectionate friend.

A few days later the writer and the receiver of this moving document engaged in battle at Lansdown Hill, just north of Bath. The victory went to the Royalists but they paid for it dearly. Most of their cavalry were slaughtered and Sir Bevil Grenville, the mighty leader of the Cornish pikemen, a lover of learning and a genial host, lay dead. Meanwhile Waller, unscathed, had withdrawn his troops in the darkness and led them back to Bath.

The day after this bitter triumph a powder wagon exploded, killing all those who stood near it and wounding many more. Sir Ralph Hopton, already shot in the arm, was blinded by the blast and badly burned. Suffering greatly, he was taken to Devizes by his wretched troops and there learned that Waller, with reinforcements from Bristol, had marched ahead of him and set up his cannon on nearby Roundway Down, preparing to engage once more.

Grievously wounded as he was, Hopton had given orders from his sick bed. Prince Maurice, Rupert's younger brother, together with the Marquess of Hertford and the Earl of

Carnarvon, protected by what was left of the cavalry, were to ride to Oxford for reinforcements and they were to stop for nothing, even if their horses died beneath them. Yet Oxford, despite the pestilence, despite the horror, was *en fête*, for Queen Henrietta Maria was approaching fast and Prince Rupert had already left to escort her through the Midlands.

The riders reached Oxford on the morning of 11 July, grey as ghosts and falling with fatigue. They had not stopped at all and had nearly killed themselves and their horses as a result. Those who witnessed their arrival, including one of Nichola's servants, who had recounted the scene to her, said it was the most terrible sight he had ever beheld. The men had ridden in reeling like drunkards, begging for help, only to find Rupert gone. Maurice had wept openly, unable to take any more strain. Fortunately the King had not yet set forth to meet his beloved wife and was still in the city and able to send a second brigade to Hopton's aid, having already despatched one under Henry, Lord Wilmot.

The position in Devizes was now grim. Both provisions and powder were running out, it was pouring with rain, and Sir Ralph Hopton was suffering grievously from his wounds. Two days more would have seen the end of them all – and then the miracle had happened. Despite the fifty mile ride from Oxford, Wilmot had attacked like a fury, charging headlong through the enemy ranks and driving the Parliamentary cavalry before him. On and on he had forced them, until they had come to a hidden escarpment over which men and horses had crashed to their deaths. Meanwhile, the Cornish pikemen had come on the run from the town and seen off the Roundhead infantry. At least thirty Parliamentary Standards had fallen into the hands of the Royalists, together with field guns and ammunition, and there had been huge casualties amongst the Roundheads, to say nothing of the enormous number of prisoners taken that day. What had started out as pitiful contest between David and Goliath had ended as a resounding Royalist victory.

The Queen arrived in Oxford on 14 July, having been met by

her husband and by the Prince of Wales and his younger brother James, Duke of York, at Edge Hill. Several people, including Nichola, had thought the choice of rendezvous tasteless in view of the many who had lost their lives in that very place. But Charles had obviously not seen Edge Hill in this light and had gone out to greet his wife there, willingly agreeing to her request that her boon companion, Jacobina's brother Henry Jermyn, should be immediately ennobled. Therefore it was as the new Earl of St Albans that Henry had ridden into the city as part of the Queen's escort.

Risking the chance of infection, Nichola had gone to be amongst the courtiers waiting in the quadrangle of Christ Church to greet the royal couple as they had ridden side-by-side beneath the Tudor arch. Yet other than for a cursory glance at Henrietta Maria, an historical character of considerable fascination, Nichola looked only for one person, anxious in case ill should have befallen him. But a glimpse of a dark head, riding a pace or two behind Prince Rupert, reassured her.

For the briefest of moments, Nichola analysed her feelings, wondering why she should have allowed herself to become so enamoured with Joscelin Attwood when, if her eventual hopes were to be fulfilled, she must one day leave him behind her. But no answer came out of her seething thoughts other than for the certainty that she was unable to help the emotion he aroused in her, fine sentiments and base desires confused into one thrilling sensation, so powerful that all Nichola's sensible ideas were banished by it.

It was a rather public reunion, but then all the courtiers with wives or mistresses in Oxford were similarly placed. Dismounting, the men of the escort greeted their partners, many with an embrace, only Prince Rupert stalking past and through the door in his marvellously moody manner. Even Henry Jermyn who, according to Jacobina, was too busy paying court to the Queen to have any serious entanglements, was hugging his sister, delighted with his recent elevation to the peerage.

"And how, my dear love, have you fared?" asked Joscelin.

not kissing her but holding her at arm's length the better to see her face.

"I missed you more than I would ever have believed possible," Nichola replied honestly.

Joscelin grinned. "Didn't the attentions of the Prince of Wales compensate for my absence?"

"You heard about that?"

"I heard he was boyishly besotted."

"And that is all, I can assure you. I can truthfully say that I have been utterly faithful," Nichola Hall answered him wryly.

Chapter Seventeen

According to the fortune teller's prediction, it was Jacobina Jermyn's destiny merely to have an affair with Prince Rupert, who always made it a rule to love and leave his women – when he could be bothered with them at all. Her eventual partner, or so the gypsy had told her, would apparently be a man born beneath her, yet with the blood of a Duke in his veins.

"A noble bastard perhaps," Nichola had said, on hearing the story.

"Obviously. Yet I cannot countenance the idea of any man possessing me other than the Prince. The very thought is repellent."

"Then perhaps Emerald Ditch was wrong."

"Was that the woman's name?" Jacobina had asked, surprised. "She did not mention it to me."

Nichola had looked vague. "Maybe I am mistaken."

"I doubt it," her friend had answered, the white petal face suddenly merry. "You are not the kind of person who ever is, Arabella."

With Joscelin's arrival imminent, the girl had moved back into Oxford, probably to be nearer Rupert who was due to leave his lodging in the college and take up residence in the house in the High Street, or so Nichola had guessed. Thus it was to a place empty of all except the child and the servants that she and Joscelin were due to return that night, after the welcoming celebration for the Queen finally ended. Yet her husband was in a strange mood, restless and oddly alert, and Nichola was not altogether surprised when he asked if they could walk home, taking the route by the river so that they might enjoy the day to the last possible moment. Leaving the horses behind them, they set out into the dusk.

It was a delicious evening, the sky the colour of mulberries, suffused with radiance as the sun began finally to sink. Intensive efforts had been made to clean the streets and this night the smell on the light breeze was of lavender and flowers. A local doctor had announced that the recent epidemic of camp fever had been caused by the presence of the army and their "filth and nastiness of diet, worse lodging, and unshifted apparel", so the City Council had doubled the wages of the scavengers. And at long last, and not before time, the benefits could be felt.

Setting forth without the fear of infection, Nichola and Joscelin left the great quad of Christ Church, turned left, and passed out of the city by means of the South Gate. Normally, comings and goings were restricted at this late hour but the guards on duty, sitting in the place occupied in peace time by a porter, recognised Lord Joscelin as one of Prince Rupert's henchmen and opened the wicket for them. Soon the couple were beyond the city walls and could stroll freely in the meadows bounded by the River Cherwell. Walking slowly in the gathering dusk, Joscelin took Nichola's hand.

She knew then that he wanted her, could feel the quiver of desire running from his arm to hers, and finally understood his nervous energy, wishing they were at home and did not have such a long walk ahead of them. But Joscelin was to surprise her yet.

"How clean is the river?" he asked, smiling at her in the half light.

"Pure, thank God. That strange man they call the water poet has been hard at work."

"Then shall we sample its pleasures for ourselves?"

"Do you mean we should bathe?"

"Why not? There's no one about. I take it you can swim, Arabella?"

"Of course."

"Then I wonder who shall be first into the water."

And with that Joscelin began to strip off his clothes, throwing the beautiful lace-trimmed garments down as carelessly as if they were rags. His body was even better than Nichola remembered it, toned and fine with the hours he had spent riding, while his privy parts, hanging heavy in their dark surroundings, began to awaken as he looked at her. The habits of a lifetime re-asserting themselves, Nichola provocatively undid the laces of her sumptuous dress while Joscelin watched without making a move towards her. Rustling and swishing, the silken garments descended to the ground until at last she stood as naked as he.

"You're lovely, Arabella," he said softly.

For answer she held out her arms and the man from another century crossed the space between them in a stride. Then Joscelin pulled her close to him, covering her mouth with his, and Nichola opened her lips in a kiss so intense that it seemed to drag out her soul. His tongue sought hers and they tasted the essence of one another, until the great kiss finally ended and his mouth moved to her throat and shoulders and then her breasts, which were desperately begging his touch.

He was fully hard, and pressed close to him as she was Nichola could feel every quiver and stir. It was erotic beyond words, the two of them in the gloaming, the crystal river the only witness as Joscelin caressed her nipples, then ran his lips downwards.

"Make love to me," Nichola pleaded, feeling a thousand little darts of pleasure, and very slowly dropped to her knees, forcing him to do likewise.

They stared at one another, their expressions enraptured, their features sharp with passion. And then Nichola sank backwards, giving a great sigh as he lowered himself on to her and she felt his full crushing weight. Slowly, deliberately almost, he eased inwards, every demanding inch of him. Nichola hung on his neck, where his shoulders blotted out the dying sun, accepting him, wanting him, until finally Joscelin began to move in a calm but relentless rhythm. Then he fought to keep his iron control, as his motion became ever more powerful, merciless, and deeper still. Very quietly, her husband started to groan with the effort of holding on. Not wishing such an incredible sensation to end, for all that, Nichola longed for him to be driven to fever pitch, and she moved quickly against him, forcing him to the point of no return.

Culmination came quickly then. With a gasp Joscelin began to dig fiercely, rapidly, like a stallion covering a mare. Then he exploded into her, calling out that he loved her with all his heart, and at that Nichola, too, flew towards heaven and felt herself touch the stars.

"I have never known it like that," Joscelin panted, falling on to the grass beside her, like the weary soldier he suddenly was.

"Nor I, ever."

"Do you mean it?"

"I do," said Nichola.

They dressed slowly, relishing their nudity, splashing in the water to wash themselves. And then, handfast once more, they walked beyond Magdalen College and through its garden and grove, until they entered St Giles, passing the grounds of Wadham and Trinity and St Johns, without having to go back into the city, which lay sleeping and moonlit as Nichola and Joscelin finally made their way into the house.

It occurred to her in the days that followed that most of Joscelin's company of troops, including the King himself, had probably been about the same business as she and her husband that night. Though obviously not Prince Rupert. He had set off at dawning, heading towards Bristol, where Waller had taken the remnants of his hapless army. Then he had pursued the wretched Sir William as far as Evesham, attacking and fighting relentlessly every step of the way. Parliament's Western Association, as they called the military merging of the counties of Gloucestershire, Shropshire, Somerset and Wiltshire, had been both defeated and humiliated. And all this, plus the death in mid-June of John Hampden, the most attractive and dashing of the Roundhead leaders, had lowered the morale of the Parliamentarians to a devastating degree. Then on 27 July came word of yet another defeat; Bristol had fallen to Rupert of the Rhine. Finally, as that wicked summer turned to autumn, came the events of the vicious battle fought on 20 September at Round Hill, near Newbury.

Neither army had had more than fifteen thousand men and both were suffering from the effects of bad food and grim conditions, coupled with long and exhausting marches. The Prince had led the cavalry charge, driving off the enemy horse, but the Roundhead infantry had held position and fired relentlessly at them. Guts and groins, bowels and brains, had flown through the air, landing in the faces of those coming behind. Captain John Gwyn had seen "a whole file of men, six deep, with their heads struck off with one cannon shot".

The bloody affray had ended with both sides ordering a ceasefire as night fell. But the next day had seen mangled corpses, stripped of their worldly goods, being taken away in cartloads, at least thirty carts being needed to perform the grisly business according to an eyewitness. The King, sick at heart, had returned to Oxford, mourning the loss of his friend and Secretary of State, the beautiful Lord Falkland, who had committed suicide on the field by deliberately trotting at snail's pace past a gap in a hedge through which the enemy were firing a flurry of bullets. He had gone to his death "dressed in clean linen as one going to a banquet", declaring himself weary of the times in which he lived and known to be grief stricken over the death of his mistress, Mrs Moray, "whom he loved above all creation". What had distressed all those who heard of the tragic losses, particularly the courtiers dwelling in Oxford itself, was that though both claimed victory neither side had won and such terrible loss of life had served no purpose whatsoever.

Observing him on the occasions she attended court functions, Nichola could see the change in Charles Stuart. A sad tale was circulating that on his way to Newbury, even before witnessing the battle's pointless conclusion, the King had sat down on a milestone, his head bowed in despair, and when asked by his young son James, Duke of York, if they might not go home, had replied, "We have no home". And this mood of despondency was now quite apparent in him, despite the fact that the Queen was once again by his side.

In many ways, Nichola thought, the arrival of Henrietta Maria had only served to make the situation worse. For though the King obviously adored her and the couple pursued an active sex life – their frequent trysts made possible by means of a door which had been specially put in the wall separating the grounds of Merton College, where she was in residence, and those of Christ Church –

their reunion was causing rifts. The Queen's set, including Henry Jermyn of course, had started to quarrel with the King's party, rivalling one another for honours and favours. And the two people who were suffering most as a result were the King's nephews, the Princes Rupert and Maurice, whom Henrietta Maria pointedly disliked.

Reports from the front were also depressing the court that autumn. The Roundheads had scored victories in Yorkshire and Lincolnshire, while the Royalist siege of Hull had been relieved for Parliament by the Scottish professional soldier, Sir John Meldrum, together with Sir Thomas Fairfax and a Colonel Oliver Cromwell. Nichola had been wondering when that name was going to crop up and had heard the story with a gloom only relieved by the knowledge that Joscelin was in Sussex, second in command to Sir Ralph Hopton, whose sight had been restored and who was now fully recovered from the terrible injuries he had received at Lansdown Hill. Yet even the news from Sussex was not altogether reassuring and she found her thoughts turning more and more to the possibility of Joscelin dying in battle. Not quite knowing why she did so and this time deliberately going alone, Nichola set out one October morning to see Emerald Ditch.

It was a supreme day, the air heavy with the smell of recent harvesting, of ripe and ready fruit, the sky overhead translucent, the opulent blue of butterfly wings. The trees in the wood beyond the mill raged with colour, bombarding her senses with gawdy glory, yet piercing Nichola's heart was the thought that here were repeated the colours of the battlefield: the crimson of blood, the buff of soldiers' coats, the deep dark ochre of a gaping wound. Beneath her horse's feet the leaves were cracking like musket shots, and all her thoughts were of death and despair when she finally came to the clearing in which the gypsy lived.

As if to echo her melancholy frame of mind, Emerald, too, seemed in an odd trance-like mood, and it occurred to Nichola that he might be mixing something with his pipe tobacco, some herbal substance which might well have induced the dreamy state in which she found him. The rugged lines of the deserter's face, brought about by so many years of living with the elements, were strangely soft, and the dark eyes glittered like gems as he ushered her into the hovel and bade her sit down before the fire.

"Are you well?" asked Nichola, with a certain curiosity.

"In elation," he answered, and would not explain further.

"Then will you read the cards for me?"

Emerald shook his head. "Today I must scry, for in the crystal's heart I know that many truths will be revealed."

"As you wish," she answered. "As long as I can have some guidance."

The faraway look vanished and Emerald's eyes were suddenly sharp. "Where the guise of poor dead Meg daily sits more easily upon me, you are still struggling with your deception, are you not?"

"Struggling for my sanity, I'm beginning to think."

"Take the orb," said Emerald, and passed Nichola the crystal which gleamed in her hands as if it were made of mercury.

"How long must I hold it?"

"Just for a moment or two, until the perfume of your soul has entered in."

"How poetically put."

"We Romanys are all poets," Emerald answered. "The dark skinned children of the earth."

The old Nichola Hall would have laughed at that and commented, 'schmaltz', but now she just nodded her head, listening to every word. Emerald extended his scarred hand. "Now I'll take it from thee, Nichola."

"What did you call me?"

"Nichola, for that is who you are I believe."

"My God!" she said, her voice devoid of breath.

"You've travelled such a long way," the gypsy continued, his speech crooning now, "that no man could comprehend a journey of such magnitude. And yet you did not set out voluntarily, you were sent by a force too powerful to resist."

Nichola nodded her head silently, overawed by the energy of the psychic power she was witnessing.

"At first you hated your destination, screamed and resisted, longed to be set free. And those times were easy for you."

"Easy?"

"Oh yes, because then your desires were clear cut. You were a child, knowing what you wanted but unable to get it for yourself. But all that has changed. A woman has taken the place of the little girl."

"What do you mean?"

"A man has brought you to fruition and you no longer know what you want. You are wandering blindly in a maze, part of you wishing to escape, the other part longing to stay here forever."

Without warning, Nichola wept.

"You will have your chance," said Emerald, holding the glistening orb to his heart as if it were the supplier of his life's blood. "In fact you will have two chances to leave."

"And will I take them?"

"I have told you before, the choice is yours."

"But what about Joscelin? Will he survive this war?"

"The man you refer to loves you in every way it is possible for a man to love, with his heart, his body and his mind. He truly believes you to be his soul mate. Yet it is he who will open the door for you."

"How?"

"That I cannot tell." Emerald laid down the crystal and looked at her, and Nichola saw that his eyes were misty as black pearls. "Beware the dream," he said softly. "That is when they come for you."

She shivered. "I saw them on the lawn, here in Oxford, and I was terrified."

His dark brows rose capriciously. "But they are the people you yearn for."

"I know. That is why it's so nonsensical."

"You must find the truth," Emerald answered, his tone a whisper. "Then you will know what to do. Your husband will live, by the way, if you wish him to."

"I'm frightened," said Nichola.

"There is no courage without fear. Now you must go. Come and see me again before you leave Oxford."

"When will that be?"

"Soon, very soon." His words died away and she saw that he had either fallen asleep or into a deep trance.

Nichola rode back to the city through an afternoon the colour of plums, the sky tinged with the first fine threads of evening, the trees reflecting the shadows of the dwindling day. Taking a diversion and climbing to the top of a hill, Nichola looked down, seeing Oxford stretched before her, the zigzag line of its encircling fortifications resembling an extraordinary star. In the distance, just visible, lay the broad sweep of St Giles, the house in which she dwelled with the man she loved, a mere distant dot.

"Let me go back now," she said aloud, "before he makes love to me again. Because the time's not far off when it will be as terrible to leave as it was to get here."

She patted her horse's neck, once more blinded by tears, and at this signal the animal began to plod its patient way home, regardless of the fact that its rider wept not only for her past but also for the undiscovered future.

The dream came again that night, as Nichola had feared it would. This time she stood outside the hospital, then went in through the front entrance, confused by the number of people milling about before realising it was visiting time. There were throngs of children everywhere, none of them as nice as Miranda. This set up a strange sort of yearning in her and Nichola would have turned and walked out again had it not been for the fact that she saw Glynda Howard. Compelled to speak to her, to tell her what had happened, Nichola hurried after her, calling the actress's name.

It was nightmarish, for Glynda would not turn round, instead hurrying down various corridors with Nichola in hot pursuit, still vainly trying to make her hear. And then Glynda stopped before a door and Nichola shrank back in fear, knowing that the body lay within and not wanting to enter. But somehow she was swept inside by Glynda's air currents, as if she had no form or substance of her own, and was forced to look again at the sight she dreaded.

The body lay still and inert as the actress sat down on a chair beside it, her ugly-beautiful face serious, her cyclamen slash of a mouth drooping.

"I got my Damery thing," Glynda was saying. "Do you hear that, you little bugger? I'm up there with Judi and Maggie *et al*. What a laugh, eh? Don't you think so?"

The body lay motionless, nothing disturbing its sleep.

"Oh Christ!" the actress exclaimed dismally, her shoulders sagging. "I wish to God I hadn't come. You were a hell of a bitch, Nichola, but I wouldn't have had this happen for the world. You didn't deserve this lot."

Nichola froze, grasping the truth of what she had only guessed at. The body was her, or what was left of her when the regression failed – or worked too well! – and now she lay lifeless, in a coma, her spirit gone walkabout.

Glynda braced herself and stared closely at the body's face. "If only I knew where you were," she said. "Where are *you*, Nichola? Where is your psyche, your soul, while you lie here? You're not dead and yet you're not alive, so where have you gone to?"

"I'm here, Glynda," Nichola whispered. "I'm here. Standing right behind you," and very gently she laid her hand on the actress's shoulder.

Glynda jumped violently, her head spinning round. "Christ, I'm hearing things!" she exclaimed over-loudly. "And yet I could have sworn . . ."

"Glynda, it's me," Nichola went on, more urgently now. "Here! Look! Glynda, Glynda, I'm in the room with you."

And then Nichola began to fall, just as she had done at the start of the regression, down and down into darkness, screaming the actress's name over and over again. She would have gone on falling, she knew it, but someone caught her and stopped her and held her tightly as she sobbed and shrieked frantically. Even before she opened her eyes, Nichola knew by the very scent of him who it was.

"Oh Joscelin," she shouted wildly, "don't leave me again. I get so frightened sometimes."

He rocked her in his arms, stroking her hair. "I'm here, I'm back with you. Don't cry, Arabella. It was only a dream."

"But so vivid, oh so vivid," she wept.

"Was it about your past?" he asked quietly.

"Yes."

"Of Michael Morellon?"

"No," Nichola answered, sighing, "of something that happened long before I knew him."

Joscelin nodded but said nothing further, just sitting in silence, holding her close, until Nichola slept once more.

That October of 1643, King Charles I called a meeting of his Council of War, several of his commanders returning to Oxford in order to attend, Joscelin Attwood amongst their number. He had ridden through the night to be with her early, or so he told Nichola afterwards, only to find his wife in such distress she was unable to welcome him. But they had come together as a couple in the dawning, the power of his presence beside her arousing Nichola to a state where she had knelt above him and lowered herself on to the length of his penis, grown hard even while Joscelin slept. And then the pleasure had begun as he had woken, worked himself in more deeply, and started to thrust. Sighing and content, they had slept afterwards until the autumn sunlight had finally told them it was time to rise.

The Council of War was to be held in Christ Church and Joscelin and Nichola had ridden out into the crisp morning side by side, he to attend his King, she to visit Jacobina, who in turn was calling on her brother. Henry Jermyn had been fortunate enough to find himself accommodation in the same college that housed the King, and in this way Henry's guests were free to sit by a window, taking refreshment and playing cards, but still able to watch those going in to the meeting.

For Nichola this was yet another fascinating glimpse of men who had made history, and she had hardly been able to take her eyes from the great quadrangle where the Council members were arriving, either on foot or horseback, despite the fact that her host had just dealt a hand of piquet.

First to appear was Edward Hyde, the successful lawyer and Member of Parliament who had decided to support his King. Well aware that one day Charles's son James would marry Hyde's ugly daughter Anne, mainly because he had made her pregnant, and also that Hyde Park would be named after the family,

Nichola stared. Despite a good head of hair, Hyde had no looks to speak of, in fact was both red-faced and tubby. Nichola hoped for the sake of the Duke of York, at present a pretty, blond little boy, that the description of Anne Hyde as goggle-eyed and gross was exaggerated.

Seeing her fascination, Henry Jermyn said, "A jackanapes fellow, that one. Do you know, he used to claim that the Queen had too much influence over the King before he decided which way his bread was best buttered."

"Really?" answered Nichola, resisting comment.

"And there goes another I cannot abide," Jermyn continued.

"Who is he?"

"General William Legge, an Irishman, thick as thieves with Rupert. He was a prisoner of Parliament but escaped last year. It was he who set up the sword factory at Wolvercote."

It was obvious from the new Earl of St Alban's comments that he was violently partisan. Anyone who agreed with Rupert was socially unacceptable, the rest were automatically good men. Thus Baron Byron, elevated to the peerage after the Battle of Newbury, was out of favour.

"Who could befriend a fellow with such a preposterous moustache?" was Henry's comment as the gallant soldier went in.

On the other hand Henry, Baron Percy, the supercilious creature whom Nichola had met at the Prince's birthday, was considered sound, simply because the Queen approved of him and he and Rupert were bitter enemies. Glancing over to discover Jacobina's reaction to all this, Nichola saw that the rosepetal face was changing colour so rapidly that it must have been clear even to Henry, should he have cared to notice, that his sister was in love with the man he detested most.

The Lord Lieutenant General, the seventy-year-old Earl of Forth, went in next.

"What do you think of him?" enquired Nichola curiously.

Henry's debauched young features looked blank. "Oh that old dodderer! He's too old to count. They say he pretends to be even deafer than he is so that he can ignore Rupert when he's holding forth."

"Not stupid then."

"No, I suppose not," the new Earl agreed reluctantly.

Almost immediately behind Forth walked the handsome fair-haired fellow who had also been present at Prince Charles's party.

"That's the Duke of Richmond, isn't it? Where does he stand?" Nichola asked.

Jermyn put his head on one side. "James Stuart? Well, he's the King's cousin, of course, and very close to His Majesty. He's constantly acting as peacemaker when the obnoxious Prince Rupert ruffles feathers."

"And do you like him?"

"It's difficult not to. But if Stuart has a fault it is that he sides with nobody and everybody."

Jacobina spoke at last. "That's ridiculous, Henry. The Duke is a marvellous man with a great deal of integrity. He quite rightly refuses to join in with all this ridiculous Queen's party, King's party, manoeuvring. And we would all be getting on a great deal better in this over-populated city if the rest of the court followed his example."

Her brother stared at her. "And what do you know about it?"

"Enough," she answered crossly. "I have been in Oxford longer than you, remember, and can clearly see the divisions that have been caused since the Queen's arrival."

"How dare you."

"I dare because I'm right."

"Please," interrupted Nichola firmly. "Other families may be divided by the conflict but you are both on the same side."

They looked contrite, like a pair of squabbling children. "I'm sorry," Henry muttered.

"I too," Jacobina answered grudgingly.

"Now here's a truly hateful man in my view," Nichola said, drawing their attention to something different. "I cannot understand why such a monster was appointed Governor of Oxford."

"The Queen thinks well of him," ventured Henry.

"Then I believe she has been deceived," Nichola replied, hoping that this remark was reasonably tactful, for the truth was that Sir Arthur Aston was a sadist, as cruel as the commandant of a Nazi concentration camp.

The recent epidemic of typhus, euphemistically described as camp fever, had taken the life of the old governor, Sir William Pennyman, and in his place had come Sir Arthur, nominated by Henrietta Maria, a fierce, brutal Catholic, so obnoxious that other Catholics pretended he was not of their faith. Universally loathed because of his evil ways, Aston had once insisted that a soldier against whom he bore a grudge should have his hand sawn off at the wrist. And now he had brought all his spleen and malice to Oxford. Even as they watched the members go in for the Council meeting, a gallows was being erected at Carfax together with another form of punishment known as 'the horse'. This was made of two planks nailed together to make a painful ridge which perpetrators of petty crime were forced to 'ride', a musket tied to their legs.

Nichola knew from Emmet's gossip that there was an unofficial price on the governor's head, and that when he was on his rounds Sir Arthur had to be protected by a guard consisting of four men wearing long red coats for identification, all armed with the long-handled axes know as halberds.

"He is so terrible," Jacobina said now, determined to stand her ground regardless, "that I feel he will come to an equally terrible end."

"He keeps good order," answered Henry, but both women ignored him, for into the quadrangle, insolently last, was finally striding Rupert of the Rhine. Jacobina sighed, Nichola stared, realising that she was watching that most unusual of creatures, a genuinely brave man who, for all that, possessed the moodiness and sensitivity of a great actor.

Today the Prince wore sombre black, lightened by a sash of his beloved scarlet. On his head was one of his famous collection of feathered hats, worn into battle when all the rest were protected by helmets, while on Rupert's feet were a pair of the fancy fringed boots he liked so well. Observing the Prince as carefully as she could, for this was the first real opportunity Nichola had had to do so, she saw a shoulder-length mass of dark hair, a long straight nose, and a mouth so sensual she could scarcely believe that its owner did not spend all his time making love. Yet in that lay part of the enigma of this extraordinary young man, for nothing about him was as it seemed. For the creature who appeared on the surface to be little more than an attractive soldier of fortune was in fact something altogether different. Behind Rupert's dash and charm, his frivolous clothes and temperamental ways, lay a man of great intellect, of skill and artistry, of huge courage and fierce determination. And a man who also possessed an enquiring mind and lovely curiosity about both people and things.

The Roundheads, who feared him greatly, believed the Prince to be under the personal protection of the Devil, and considered Rupert's dog, a poodle called Boy which accompanied him everywhere, even into battle, to be his familiar. Indeed Rupert had trained his pet to jump in the air on hearing the word Charles and to cock its leg at the name Pym, short for John Pym the Parliamentarian, a fact which unnerved all those superstitious beings who beheld the trick.

Now, feeling so many eyes upon him, the Prince looked up and swept his hat off to the ladies in the window above, his own eyes bright as gemstones, a smile relieving the somewhat solemn cast of his face. Meanwhile Boy, obviously at some whispered command, rolled over and played dead.

"Good morning," called Jacobina boldly, ignoring her brother who was muttering "Precious popinjay," beneath his breath.

"Good morning," Rupert called back and treated them to another smile, this one even more dazzling than the first, before his features resumed their usual intent expression and he went inside.

"Did he notice me?" Jacobina whispered.

"Of course," Nichola answered, though she had an uncomfortable feeling that the Prince's gaze had been drawn more to Arabella's lovely looks than those of her elfin friend.

"Is that the entire Council assembled?" she asked Henry Jermyn, by way of changing the subject.

"Yes, it is."

"Then I suggest we continue our game."

And with that Nichola turned back to the hand of piquet and tried to forget the fact that Rupert of the Rhine had stared at her quite so long and quite so unashamedly hard.

* * *

The Christmas of 1643 was much enlivened by the fact that the Queen had discovered she was two months pregnant. It would seem that the door in the wall between the two colleges had done its work well. The sad King had obviously not been so sad that he had neglected his marital duties and Henrietta Maria, already the mother of six, and thirty-four years old, was beginning to get the bloom about her cheeks that in certain women denotes the early stages of pregnancy.

Yet it had been a strange festivity, the unease that possessed them all only just concealed beneath the surface. There were undercurrents and tensions everywhere, exacerbated by the boy Prince of Wales and his youthful cousin Rupert, constantly vying for Nichola's attention, which naturally upset both Jacobina and Joscelin. Long ago, Nichola Hall would have relished the situation, now, to Nichola Attwood, it was nightmarish.

Joscelin was like a coiled spring, an aspect of his personality that she had never seen before. The horrors of war and of killing had seen off the scampish rogue and in his place had come a serious man, a man who would regard her with thoughtful eyes, the emotions in their cool green depths hidden. In the end such a clinical regard so frequently given had become too much for her and Nichola had challenged him.

"Darling, why do you stare at me like that? Surely you're not jealous of Charles and Rupert? They play at flirtation and half their fun comes from challenging one another."

He had smiled, a flash of his old humour returning. "No, sweetheart. The special magic between us has convinced me of your love."

"Then what is it? You're not still worried about Sabina?"

"No, my daughter was fully recovered when I left Devon to return to you."

"Then I give up."

The dark cynical face had shadowed. "The truth is that I am haunted by a feeling so nebulous that to put it into words might invite your scorn."

"I could never feel scornful of you," she had answered, savouring the words, realising that Joscelin really was the first man she had not despised in any way. "So tell me what it is bothering you, please."

"I am continually seized by a premonition that you will leave me."

"How? Do you think I'm going to die?"

"No, it's not that."

"But you can't suspect another man. You've just said you know that I love you."

Joscelin had shaken his head, the thick curls, long as ringlets, tumbling round his face. "It's nonsensical, I realise it, yet I cannot shake the feeling off."

Fear had struck at Nichola's heart then, and she had thought of the gypsy's prediction, his words: "You can leave if you wish, it will rest in your hands."

"But I don't want to go," she protested, then realised with an enormous sense of incredulity the exact meaning of the words she had just said.

Chapter Eighteen

"I am not," said William Dobson, standing back from the canvas and staring at it narrowly, "too happy about the mouth. If you have the patience I would like you to grant me another sitting, my Lady."

"Then may I have a look at what has been done so far?" Nichola answered teasingly, somewhat amused by the artist's constant reluctance to show her the portrait of which she was the subject, yet in a way understanding why the King's Sergeant Painter was so protective of his work until it was complete.

"I would rather not do that," he said, smiling at her. "The picture isn't quite ready for criticism, if you follow me."

Nichola nodded, standing up. "Like an under-rehearsed play?"

"Precisely."

"Then come back tomorrow at this time if it would help you."

Dobson bowed and began to pack up his brushes.

The portrait had been commissioned in January, just before Joscelin had returned to the war, the wretchedness of parting heavy on them both and the idea of having Arabella's likeness on canvas a welcome diversion. So inundated with requests for portraits that he was now forced to ask for half his fee in advance, it was rumoured that Dobson was being given a substantial sum by Prince Rupert to make a copy. And looking quizzically at the artist now, Nichola wondered whether this were true.

As if reading her thoughts about the Prince, William Dobson said unexpectedly, "I recently finished a portrait of Prince Rupert and he, too, has a deep dark quality about the eye."

"What do you mean?"

"That, like you, his soul lies within his pupils but, no offence my Lady, also like you the Prince prefers to keep his secrets."

Nichola's brows rose in surprise but she did not answer.

"It might interest you to know," the artist went on, "that at one time I made it my habit to go into the House of Commons and paint or sketch the members therein. It was in this way that I caught the likeness of the member for Huntingdon, Colonel Cromwell. Now there's a man to be watched."

Nichola's spine grew cold. "Tell me about him."

"His eyes burn with a bright clear blue, the colour of fanaticism. He has found God but not God's favour."

"What are you saying, Mr Dobson?"

"That within his unattractive exterior – clumsy, wart-ridden, balding, slovenly – lies a ruthlessness, a dedication, that frightened me. He is here to establish God's Kingdom on this flawed earth and cares not who perishes in the attempt. To me, Lady Attwood, Colonel Cromwell is probably the most powerful of all the Parliamentarians because he is a horse in blinkers, he sees only his version of God's purpose and gives no quarter to the frailty of humanity."

"But as yet hardly anyone had heard of him," Nichola answered slowly.

The artist ignored the oddness of her phraseology. "It was only because I drew his likeness and heard him speak that I came to these conclusions."

"You are a very observant man."

"Painters are," said William Dobson, and left the room.

After staring thoughtfully at the closing door for a moment or two, Nichola followed him out, anxious to change her clothes before the evening's soirée with the Queen.

It was March 1644, only a few days away from Miranda's second birthday, a few days from the second anniversary of her arrival in the seventeenth century. When she thought of it in those terms Nichola's brain ached with the impossibility of the situation, but when she thought of Joscelin and the magical relationship they enjoyed it sometimes seemed as if she had always been there, that the act she put on had become reality. And now she was to play a part yet again, cheering the spirits of Henrietta Maria in company with various other ladies, brightening the hours of the depressed and pregnant Queen.

Nichola had, in the months following the woman's arrival,

rather grown to like the tiny creature who was wife to the King of England. So small was Henrietta Maria in fact that had the actress been in her own body, rather than the diminutive Arabella's, the Queen would have appeared almost dwarf like. And her lack of height was never more apparent than, when standing next to the King, himself only five feet four inches tall, the top of her dark head could be seen barely to reach his shoulder. Yet these little people were two of the principal actors in the great tragedy being played out on English soil, and Nichola thought about them yet again as Emmet helped her change for the evening.

They had been married when she had been sixteen, he twenty-five, virgins both, though Charles had been infatuated with his late father's homosexual lover, the glitteringly beautiful George Villiers, Duke of Buckingham. Nichola had asked Joscelin some searching questions about this relationship, but it seemed certain that it was platonic and the King heterosexual, merely responding with passionate warmth to the romance and glamour Buckingham brought into his lonely life. However, marriage had not provided Charles with the love he so desperately sought, for Henrietta Maria had burst into tears at the first sight of her new husband and for two years they had lived separate lives.

"Did they sleep together?" Nichola had asked her husband.

"I believe the marriage was consummated, with much pain on both sides. After that they shied away from something so abhorrent to them both."

"So how did the situation resolve itself?" Nichola had continued, intrigued.

"Well, first of all he sent home her French attendants, the Queen making such a to do when His Majesty told her of his intention that he was forced to pull her by the hand into his own apartments, push her inside and lock the door, in order to restrain her. Though to no avail, for the Queen smashed her fist through the window and the King had to drag her roughly from the glass, not minding his manners and bruising her in the process."

"My God!" Nichola remembered now that she had been amused though somewhat shocked.

"And then Buckingham was murdered, as so he deserved. The inevitable happened after that. Charles was distraught and turned to Henrietta Maria for comfort and they fell in love, physically, mentally, romantically. In fact they kissed a hundred times an hour."

"Gracious!"

"She who had found him repulsive was now unable to get enough of him. They spent every night together – with the usual result! Her first baby died, though, but the second is the little monster who runs round Oxford making sheep's eyes at you."

But not for much longer, thought Nichola as she was laced into her dress. For, if gossip were correct, the well-made boy, big for his age and shortly to celebrate his fourteenth birthday, had tired of Lady Attwood and was currently in hot pursuit of a certain well-used eighteen-year-old, companion of a corporal in the King's redcoated Life Guards, the lady apparently being more than willing to initiate the Prince into manhood.

And here, thought Nichola, as an hour later she walked into Henrietta Maria's apartments in Merton College, dwells the randy little devil's mother, pregnant again.

The Queen's house stood in the north-east corner of Merton's Front Quad, its tall Gothic window brimming with candlelight, indicating that tonight Her Majesty was receiving company. Standing in the doorway for a moment before she was announced, Nichola observed the woman whose influence over Charles was so greatly blamed for the predicament in which the country found itself, and thought that love could be a great undoing. Yet it was difficult to criticise the vivacious little creature with her fringe of dark kiss curls, her black eyes, her long nose and small full mouth with its set of projecting teeth. For Henrietta Maria was as staunch a Catholic as Cromwell was a Puritan, and who could deny either of them the right to their convictions?

"My dear Lady Attwood," the Queen said graciously, glimpsing Nichola in the gloom, "how delightful." And she extended a very tiny, very white hand.

Curtseying as she kissed it, Nichola hoped that Jacobina, who these days glowed positively green with jealousy, would not be present, only to realise a second later that her erstwhile friend was already there ahead of her. Suddenly rather irritable about the entire situation, Nichola determined to clear the air for once and for all, should the opportunity arise. At the moment, though, there was no opportunity for anything except the most delicate conversation, for the Queen's musicians had started to play.

Tonight none of Her Majesty's male courtiers were present and Nichola thought wryly that she was attending the forerunner of a hen party, with gathered females and gossipy conversation, some wine and supper and, inevitably, a discussion about men and babies. And, sure enough, after gazing round the gathering with a smile the Queen said, "How grateful I am for your company, ladies. This pregnancy has not been easy for me and I would be in such low spirits without your pretty selves."

She was delightful and charming, that could not be denied, and Nichola felt a terrific pang of sorrow at the thought of what lay ahead of the poor woman.

"May I say, Madam," said some flatterer, "that despite your problems you are in radiant looks."

Henrietta Maria made a petulant little mouth. "I cannot think how. All this talk of war is so depressing and now that His Majesty has called Parliament to Oxford the place seems even more packed with people."

And it was true. To add to the city's gross overcrowding, Charles had summoned all Members of Parliament to attend a free Parliament at his headquarters. Just over a hundred had responded and the King had opened this opposition assembly on 22 January 1644. It had met in Convocation House, beyond the Divinity School in the Bodleian Library, and several peers of the realm had also attended – including the recently ennobled Prince Rupert, now Duke of Cumberland.

Because of the increased density of the population, brawling and drunkenness had recently become so out of hand that the sale of liquor was prohibited after nine o'clock at night. Indeed, Rupert himself had been forced to rush out of his house and part, with a pole-axe, two furious contestants duelling over the ownership of a horse. The horrible Sir Arthur Aston had been wounded in the side during a scuffle and nobody in their right mind ventured forth late. It was at times like these that Nichola actually missed Caradoc, still attached to Rupert's troopers as a spy, wishing that he were there to escort her through the dark and dangerous pathways.

"But surely, Madam," Jacobina now said pointedly to the Queen, "Prince Rupert's successes in the Midlands must be giving you heart?"

Henrietta Maria shifted uncomfortably in her chair, putting her hand to her body. "All this war talk makes the little one kick," she answered. "Could we not speak of other things?"

It was a clever way out of replying, in view of her known and enormous dislike of her husband's nephew, and her guests had no option but to do her bidding and change the topic of conversation. Fortunately this was made easier by the arrival of a handsome young singer to whom they all listened with rapt attention. Nichola was much amused by the thought that, three hundred and fifty years later, he would have been replaced by a male stripper. Yet, like his later counterpart, the entertainer kept the company amused until it was time for supper and Nichola at last found herself face to face with Jacobina. The elfin girl would have moved away at the confrontation but Nichola put out a restraining hand.

"Listen," she said, in a quiet but deliberately compelling voice, "I cannot bear this coolness between us, especially as it is caused by a misunderstanding. It means nothing that Rupert has been staring at me, he only does it to annoy the Prince of Wales. He has no interest in me whatsoever."

That was a lie, because Nichola well knew her admirer's motives, but it was a lie spoken with every good intention.

"I find that hard to believe," Jacobina answered coldly.

"Well, you must. And when the man returns to Oxford I suggest you put the matter to the test. Draw attention to yourself in some way and he'll soon stop gazing at me. The trouble is, Jacobina, that you are so shy in his presence that he has not noticed how beautiful you are."

"I believe he is in love with you," Jacobina said, turning an icy profile.

Nichola snorted. "What rubbish! He knows damned well that my marriage is a great success. A man of Rupert's intelligence wouldn't even waste his time on such a forlorn hope."

"Do you mean that?"

"Of course I do. Let us plan together how you can capture his heart, for a flirtation if nothing more."

"Why do you say merely for a flirtation?"

"Because of the words of Emerald Ditch, whom I truly believe to be gifted. So if he – I mean she – is right it is inevitable that you and Rupert will come together."

Jacobina's features relaxed somewhat. "I'm sorry that I have been so unfriendly. I should have known better, I suppose. After all, it is obvious that you and Joscelin were born to be lovers."

"Is it?" asked Nichola, surprised.

"Oh yes," Jacobina answered with great sincerity. "You both have that destined look of permanence about you."

Her affection for Arabella's child was as deep as if she had actually given birth to her, in fact Nichola often found herself wondering if she had in reality done so. For through the misty memory of the regression came a recollection of vast contractions, of pushing and heaving, of hearing a baby's high, thin wail. And this posed the question as to where exactly Arabella's life had ended and Nichola Hall had entered her body, a body which Nichola had now come to enjoy owning, with its small curving contours and firm breasts, breasts which were quite extraordinarily voluptuous in a girl so delicately made.

Miranda had celebrated her second birthday joyfully, kissing her mother frequently, toddling about in her long dresses, an adult in miniature. Nichola had heard it said that the King had been unable to speak until he was three years old and his father, James I of England and VI of Scotland, had wanted the ligaments at the base of the child's tongue cut in order to assist his progress. Fortunately this terrible measure had been avoided, and with such barbaric treatments in mind, Nichola was only grateful that Miranda babbled away incessantly, though often incoherently. She had grown to look less like Michael Morellon and more like a little girl, though her eyes were the deep mauvish blue of her father's, auguring well for her future beauty.

Within a few days of the birthday, which was on 16 March,

news came through to Oxford of one of Rupert's most brilliant exploits. With only a scratch force to lead, he had relieved the siege of Newark, furiously attacking Sir John Meldrum, capturing his troops and sending the rest off in full flight. It had been a triumph for the Royalists but Parliament had promptly retaliated. On 29 March several London companies had attacked an encampment of Cavaliers in Cheriton Wood. Though at first the attackers had been driven off by musket fire, they had been reinforced by William Waller's infantry and Sir William Balfour's cavalry, together with Sir Arthur Haselrig's 'Lobsters', a troop of cuirassiers from Leicestershire, so named because of their shell-like protective armour. This combined force had routed the Royalists, who had scattered in disarray.

It seemed to some that the King's cause was beginning to crack in the south of England. Sir Ralph Hopton, who many believed to have never recovered his confidence after temporarily losing his sight at the battle at Lansdown Hill, had been one of the Royalists at Cheriton Wood, the aged Earl of Forth, described by the King as loyal, ancient, brave and bibulous, vastly experienced and seriously gouty, another. As a result of this defeat, morale was getting low and there were those who murmured that even Oxford itself was under threat.

So it was in a mood of unease, beset by a premonition that something momentous was about to take place, though whether to her personally or to the inhabitants in general, that Nichola left the house and walked down by the city walls towards Magdalen Grove, now being used for the storage of heavy guns, pulled there by teams of sweating horses or oxen.

It was a mild night, the soft feel of April already abroad. As far as her eye could see the gardens stretched away into moonlight, the dark shade of the trees criss-crossing the path she walked upon. At that moment Nichola felt as alert as a greyhound, as tense as if she were about to go on stage, and experienced a violent pang of regret, an inexplicable hankering to be Nichola Hall once more. And then, swiftly and without warning, it happened. A tall thin shadow detached itself from one of the trees and swept her into its arms, covering her mouth with kisses. Nichola smelt drink, warm skin and the lavender scent of long, newly washed hair. She also smelt the man's individual essence and was aware that it was not Joscelin.

"Please don't be angry," whispered a voice, "I can't help myself." The merest trace of an accent betrayed its owner. It was Prince Rupert of the Rhine who had come to her out of the darkness.

She should have turned and run, or raised her voice and cried for help, or ordered him to go away. But years of being a collector of men, of loving the risk of dangerous liaisons, suddenly seemed to die very hard. Almost without knowing what she was doing, Nichola stretched up her arms and clasped her hands behind his neck, returning Rupert's ardent kisses. And then as suddenly as the Prince had come up to her, he broke away.

"I'm sorry," he said, "that was unforgivable. The truth is I've had too much to drink and I forgot myself."

She was very slightly disappointed, Nichola had to admit it. "I didn't even know you'd returned to Oxford," she answered coolly.

"I've not, officially. I just had to come back to sort my thoughts out, but I shall be off again within the next few hours."

"What thoughts?" Nichola asked quietly. "What's troubling you?"

"The fact that I've never felt like this before," Rupert answered sighing and, sitting down on the stump of a felled tree, put his head in his hands.

She suddenly felt enormously sorry for him and, squeezing on to the stump, sat down beside him. "Tell me about it."

He looked at her, his features so softened by the moonlight that he seemed little more than the merest youth. "It may sound unbelievable to you but I know little about women, though my mother, of course, is a celebrated beauty, the King's sister, the Queen of Hearts."

"The Winter Queen," Nichola added quietly.

"Needless to say, I am not her favourite child, in fact she describes me as charming but uncouth." He pulled a face, his sense of humour not entirely banished. "Anyway, I was sent to university, at Leyden, when I was ten so I was quickly out of her way. To cut a short story even shorter, Lady Attwood, I joined the army when I was fourteen and went off to fight in the Low Countries. But, if you can believe it, my mother called me back on that occasion. She had heard rumours about the immorality of camp life and thought I might be corrupted!"

"Are you saying that you did not have much opportunity to meet the opposite sex?"

"That is an understatement. In fact it was a positive effort to get rid of my virginity." His eyes twinkled suddenly. "I managed it, however."

"Where is all this leading to?" Nichola asked incautiously.

"To the fact that I've never been in love. When I was sixteen I came to England, to the delightful court of my Uncle Charles. He was such a good man, and fond of me too, so I had the time of my life. I was utterly idle, in fact I did nothing more than enjoy a round of ceaseless pleasure. That was when I first began to indulge in *les plaisirs d'amour*. But I never loved one of the women I slept with at that time, it was carnal fulfillment, that is all. Anyway, the King mooted this brilliant scheme in which he would send me to Madagascar to colonise and rule it. I had even started to study navigation and ship building in preparation, and then once again my mother interfered and I didn't go."

"Poor Rupert," Nichola said, knowing none of this story.

"Yes, I grew depressed. When I visited my uncle again in 1637, I hoped I might have a hunting accident so that my bones could be buried in England at least."

"And in all this time you had not met a woman you admired?"

Rupert leant forward to give her a kiss, though this one was gentle and brotherly. "Christ, no! My mother wanted me to marry by this stage, a hideous girl, though very wealthy. I simply said no and went back to fight in the Prince of Orange's army, this time with my own cavalry regiment. And the upshot was that I ended up a prisoner. I was not quite nineteen years old."

"So the outbreak of the Civil War must have come almost as a welcome diversion?"

"It did. But I never thought an attraction like this one I feel now would result from it."

"Are you trying to say that you're in love with me?"

"I'm not certain. I don't know how it feels to be in love. But I am so under your spell, Arabella, that I think about you night and day. I'd been wandering from ale house to ale house tonight before I brought the dogs for their walk. I'd been trying to forget you, in a way, then when I saw you here I could not help myself and I kissed you."

"But I returned your kisses," said Nichola wickedly, the almost forgotten part of Nichola Hall's character returning in a sudden rush of physical wanting.

Rupert stared at her thoughtfully. "Yes, you did, didn't you." He slipped his arm round her waist. "May I kiss you again?"

She felt her mind split itself in half, Nichola Hall fighting Nichola Attwood tooth and nail, an extraordinary conflict overshadowed by the horrible certainty that soon she would be racked by regret.

"I was rather hoping you would," she said.

And then things happened quickly. Rupert pulled her to her feet, kissing her all the while, and very gently carried her to the shadow of the trees, where he laid her down on the sweet smelling grass. Then he raised her skirts to the level of her waist, lowering his mouth to kiss the delicate flesh thus revealed. His hand had gone to the fore-flap of his brecches, still known as a cod piece though that intimate bag had by now ceased to be part of a man's apparel, and Nichola had gasped at the sheer bulk of what was revealed, then gave a cry of delight as the Prince, taking his weight on his knees, entered her rapidly.

"Shall I stop?" he whispered in her ear, well aware that it was too late.

"No, it's wonderful."

Yet even while she said that, even while she pushed herself on to him as Rupert strove to gain even greater depth, Nichola knew that she was going to experience guilt as never before. Deliberately, she forced the feeling away, determined to enjoy every second of this wicked, sinful, marvellous transgression.

Rupert was losing control of himself, thrusting into her hard and ruthlessly, the intensity of his pressure divinely unbearable.

"Oh God, Arabella," he moaned. "It's never been like this, never." And then he drew breath as he drained into her at the exact moment Nichola yielded to his relentless rhythm and climaxed.

"That was the best I have ever had," he said, and Nichola thought she saw tears mixed with his sweat.

"It was amazing, but it must never be allowed to happen again." She was recovering herself, too quickly for comfort.

"Why?"

"Because I have betrayed Joscelin Attwood."

"But you can't love him. If you did you would never have allowed this to happen."

"Rupert, you're wrong. I *do* love him, that's what is so despicable."

He looked sad. "I know little of love, as I have already told you. All I can say is that when I first came to my royal uncle's court, my cock ruled me and has done ever since. Now, at long last, my heart is involved. So I suppose tonight your passions got the better of you, but your heart was elsewhere."

"That about describes it."

Rupert looked grim. "Then so be it. I am unlucky again." He stood up. "Let me escort you home. It is getting too late for you to be out alone." He smiled but without joy. "There might be unsavoury men about."

And with that he whistled to his white poodle, Boy, and his new black labrador, who had been asleep, side by side, under a distant tree.

"I'd rather go alone. It is my turn to sort out my thoughts."

"As you wish." Rupert sighed. "But remember that was the most splendid thing I have ever experienced. I only wish it did not have to end like this."

And with that he was gone, his dogs at his heels, his shoulders slumped and his whole bearing forlorn. Nausea came literally, then. Gasping and vomiting, Nichola sat beneath the tree and wept as she had never done in her life before. She was in love with Joscelin, she knew it, and yet she had allowed this raw sexual act to take place. And this time she had been unable to use the excuse that her marriage had not been consummated, for it had truly been sealed with splendour. Shabby and shamed, tears streaming down her cheeks, Nichola reached emotional bedrock and with it a realisation. Such agony as this, far worse than the anguish over her infidelity with Michael, could mean only one thing. The other Nichola Hall, the proud owner of The Collection, the bitch, had had one last fling but had well and truly gone away as a result.

"And gone for ever," Nichola whispered into the silence. "I was a cheap shoddy drab and I shall never let that side take hold of me again."

And with the thought that good might come out of evil, Nichola slowly made her way back to the house, unaware that Prince Rupert had returned to his home in the High Street and there fallen asleep weeping because, sensitive, contradictory, strange young being that he was, he had realised that at long last he was madly in love.

Chapter Nineteen

The pace of events was beginning to quicken. After his secret love-crazed visit to Oxford, Rupert had returned to Shrewsbury, where he had been quartered earlier in the year. Meanwhile the Queen took sick, complaining of a permanent racking cough which she believed to be caused by the damp air rising from the rivers surrounding the city. Henrietta Maria also became prey to sudden spasms of violent pain, which she felt certain were nothing to do with her pregnancy. To make matters worse, the King called a general rendezvous at Aldbourne Chase, north of Oxford on 10 April and found, to his horror, that his troops numbered less than ten thousand – a muster incapable of taking on either the Earl of Essex's army or Sir William Waller's. Suddenly the situation had become dire.

Inevitably, Prince Rupert was sent for but he, poor soul, was being demanded on every fighting front. The Marquess of Newcastle, the Royal Commander, wrote telling the Prince that if he did not "please to come hither and that very soon too, the great game of your Uncle's will be endangered, if not lost." Hoping "that his Highness would come and that very soon", he signed the letter, "Your Highness's most passionate creature, W. Newcastle". However Rupert ignored this heart-felt plea and galloped to Oxford to attend one of the King's Councils of War. Just behind him, though coming from a different direction, was Lord Joscelin Attwood, weak and ailing, his left shoulder bandaged and bloody, the watchful Caradoc, as if sprung from nowhere, once more in attendance on his master.

Nichola, seeing the maverick scamp who had saved her from Denzil Loxley sick as a dog, suffering from a musket wound in the shoulder, finally knew what it meant to feel one's heart bleed. She had betrayed Joscelin with that bright flame Rupert, she had allowed herself to be cheapened once more. Now guilt and love and tenderness were combined in one overwhelming emotion which demanded that she take him away from this festering, endangered city to somewhere where he could recover in peace.

"Your home in Devon," she whispered to him as he lay hot with fever, his thick dark hair clinging in tendrils to his dampened skin.

"Kingswear Hall?"

"Yes. We must go there as soon as you are fit for the journey."

Ill though he was, Joscelin smiled. "You order it?"

"I do. Surely you will be granted leave of absence while your wound heals?"

He nodded. "Of course, but they would rather I stayed in Oxford to be close at hand. The situation is deteriorating despite Rupert's mighty efforts."

Nichola flushed and turned away so that he could not see her reaction to the name. "I can't help that. Somehow I must get you out of this place."

And it seemed that she was not the only one thinking on those lines. Nichola's duty visit to the Queen had revealed that, with a great deal of heartache, she and the King had reluctantly decided to part company.

"My dear Lady Attwood, I am devastated," Henrietta Maria had begun. "You see, I must say goodbye to you. His Majesty believes it best that I should go to Exeter to await my confinement. For from there I can easily escape abroad should it prove necessary."

"But do *you* want to go, Madam?" Nichola had asked, shocked that such a happily married couple could even contemplate separation.

"I cannot bear to leave the King and yet I feel trapped in Oxford. Alas, my friend, I am weary. Not of being beaten but of having heard it spoken of."

Looking at her, knowing the Queen's destiny, Nichola had

nodded her head. "Then I think perhaps you should leave, Majesty. It will be for the best."

Henrietta Maria had hesitated, then seized Nichola's hand. "You would not consider coming with me, I suppose? Naturally Lord Jermyn is accompanying me on the journey, but his sister does not wish to be one of my ladies. She says she will take her chance in Oxford, I cannot imagine why."

"I can," Nichola had muttered beneath her breath. Out loud, she had said, "I would be delighted to step into her place, Madam, though there is one small condition attached, if I may make so bold."

"Which is?"

"As you know, Lord Joscelin was wounded at Cheriton Wood. I would request that he also accompany us in order that he may travel on to Kingswear Hall, his home near Dartmouth, the quicker to recover."

The Queen had made one of her familiar little sparrow-like movements. "Of course. I will happily grant you that."

"Then who will be making up the rest of the party?"

"My priest, my doctor, three other ladies beside yourself, and Lord Jermyn, of course."

"And when do we leave?"

"In two days' time. On 17 April," Henrietta Maria had answered, and Nichola had realised with a cold chill that, ten days after that, would fall the twenty-ninth birthday of the real Nichola Hall.

All the trauma of departure had been temporarily suspended by seeing her picture, for Nichola had recognised it at once. It was called 'Portrait of an Unknown Lady' and it hung in the library of her grandfather's house in Holland Park. He had bought it at auction before the war simply, or so he had told Nichola the child, because he liked it. Staring at it now, the paint still fresh, the beautiful face of Arabella Attwood in all her Stuart finery smiling teasingly from the canvas, Nichola wondered in astonishment why she had never made the connection before. She had seen the painting so often, had even been told that it was signed W. Dobson, but it was only now that she realised that the face of the sitter and the face that looked at her every day in the mirror were one and the same. Shocked, she stared at it in silence.

The King's Sergeant Painter stroked his chin. "I see you do not like it, Lady Attwood?"

"I do, oh I do," she answered hurriedly. "It's just rather a surprise to see oneself, that is all."

"We are never quite as we imagine ourselves, true."

"Yet you have caught the likeness superbly."

Dobson bowed. "Thank you, my Lady."

Nichola went closer to the canvas. "Is it true you have made a copy?"

There was a long silence before Dobson finally said, "Why do you ask?"

"Because in this portrait I have a red rose between my fingers. But in the other I believe I carry a forget-me-not."

Dobson gaped at her. "But how could you know . . . ?"

"Because I have seen it," Nichola answered, glinting mischief as she left the room to arrange for the painting to be packed and put with the other belongings on the baggage wagon.

But a million extraordinary thoughts were going through her head. If Arabella Loxley had died in childbirth, then who was the subject of the two portraits? Was it herself? Or had she once been Arabella and was now merely reenacting a life she had already lived? None of it seemed to make sense, none of it seemed quite real, and yet she knew for certain that her grandfather had the forget-me-not portrait which had presumably originally been the property of Rupert of the Rhine. Confused and uncertain, Nichola had ridden that day to see Emerald Ditch, as much for reassurance as to bid him farewell.

The house in the woods was empty, all signs of life gone. Yet there was no evidence of a struggle of any kind, in fact all was neat and orderly. Puzzled and rather frightened, Nichola climbed the ladder to the room above, only to see that that, too, was deserted, devoid of the few small personal possessions the gypsy had owned. So he had taken his cards, his crystal and his tin whistle and gone on his way. Nichola wondered what had persuaded him to leave such a safe hiding place, but the bare walls told her nothing and after another few minutes, she remounted her horse and returned to Oxford.

That night, almost inevitably, the dream came, only this time it was radically different. It began as it invariably did in the room where her poor body lay on its life support system. But on this occasion, after staring at herself for a moment or two, Nichola left the hospital and drifted on to a bus going to Holland Park. Nobody could see her so Nichola stood up throughout the journey, in order to avoid the embarrassment of someone sitting on her lap.

She not so much walked from the bus stop as glided over the pavements, and when she got to her grandfather's house she saw that he was in, because a light was glowing through one of the elegant Georgian windows and Nichola caught a glimpse of him, sitting in an armchair, reading a paper. She rang the bell and floated into the hallway when he opened the door. Grandpa did not see her either, because he merely let out an expression of annoyance and returned to his chair.

The forget-me-not version of the portrait hung over the fireplace and Nichola went close to it, staring up into that familiar face painted so long ago. The paint had darkened and cracked now, the pollution of time had left its mark, but the passionate loveliness of Arabella Attwood still shone from the canvas and one small hand twisted that symbolic flower, its meaning 'True Love', around a finger of the other.

"Grandpa," said Nichola, quite naturally and as if nothing strange was happening at all, "what became of Rupert of the Rhine?"

He jumped violently, that handsome old man doing the crossword, knowing he was alone.

"Nichola?" he said, his voice quivering and shaking in a way which upset her.

"Don't be afraid, this is only a dream. It's just that I wanted to see you," she answered, full of concern.

But he did not come to her, instead her grandfather crossed

to the telephone and dialled a number, then she heard him ask to be put through to a ward and knew that he was ringing a hospital.

"Oh, good evening, Sister. It's Philip Paget here. I'm sorry to bother you, in fact it's quite ridiculous really, but I can't get my granddaughter Nichola Hall off my mind. She's the girl who was admitted six months ago..."

His voice faded, then boomed, and the words "six months ago" echoed over and over again.

"But I have been here two years," Nichola shouted, "so that's impossible. Why are my body and I on different time scales? Oh my God!"

She woke, as always, in a sweat of panic, calling out for her grandfather and repeating, "Why six months?" until she was hoarse. And then her bedroom door opened.

They were sleeping apart so that Joscelin could get more rest but, despite his illness, he had come to her. He stood leaning against the doorpost for support, his face haggard against the white of his nightshirt. "What is it?" he said, and his voice was cracked and tired with suffering.

Nichola leapt out of bed and ran to him, her fear banished by her anxiety. "Darling, you shouldn't be up. It was just one of my silly nightmares. Let me help you back to your room."

"No," he said, and for a moment there was a faint suggestion of his scampish grin. "The fever's broken and I'm over the worst. I'd rather get in with you, pale shadow that I am."

"Shadow or substance," answered Nichola, "there is always a place for you in my bed."

And she hugged him to her, feeling at that moment as if she were the ghost and he the creature of reality.

They left Oxford on the morning of 17 April, a small train of carriages, wagons and horsemen. The King, the Prince of Wales and the Duke of York rode with the Queen, Charles sharing a coach with his wife so that they could say goodbye in private. But at Abingdon the moment came when they had to bid one another a final farewell and it was then that Henrietta Maria lost control. Crying aloud that she was going to die, that she would never see her husband again, the Queen became hysterical and fell fainting into Charles's arms, weeping and distraught. In the end it was her doctor who led her away, taking the pathetic little woman back to her carriage where he administered a powder for frenzy.

The King and his two sons rode off then, in a tragic huddled trio. Knowing that the Queen was right, that this was the last time she would see her beloved Charles, Nichola watched them go and discovered that tears were running down her own cheeks.

"What is it, my witch wife?" whispered Joscelin. "Do you fear the worst?"

She nodded. "Yes. I believe the King and Queen will not set eyes on one another again."

He looked grim. "Then if that is the case we are all in danger and the quicker I can get you to a place of safety the better."

"But what of yourself?"

"As soon as I am fit enough to fight I'll return to defend him. I told you once before, I may not agree with all he does but he has my oath of allegiance."

Nichola put her hand on his where they rode together side by side. "Wherever you go I'll not be far away."

Joscelin's golden eyes turned their full beam on her. "Do you love me then?"

"Oh yes," she answered simply. "Recently I discovered just how much."

Thankfully he did not ask her how or why, despite the fact that she had flushed again at the memory of that sinful interlude with the warrior Prince.

"Yet I still have this feeling that one day you might leave me," he said.

"Unless something drags me away I will stay," Nichola replied with passion.

Joscelin's naughty face definitely reappeared and she knew for certain that he was getting better.

"Then when I regain my strength how would you feel about bearing our child?"

Nichola smiled. "I never wanted to have a baby, but with you . . ."

Her husband looked at her oddly. "But you bore Miranda."

"Oh yes," Nichola answered hurriedly. "I did, of course. I was just thinking about having *your* child."

"I see," he said, but in the depths of his eye there was a sudden flicker of uncertainty.

The Queen remained unconscious for thirty miles, so by the time she had regained her senses they had reached the village of Wootton Bassett. Nonetheless Henry Jermyn, showing true steel, insisted that the suffering woman carry on to Bath, saying that it would be far safer for them to spend the night in a town. The next day he turned his party due south and again would not rest until he was in the protection of Shaftesbury. Jermyn's pace and determination were relentless, and when the Queen begged for respite his reply was that the safety of both her person and that of the unborn child was in his hands.

"At this speed," said Joscelin, as they settled for the night in a wayfarer's inn, "we will reach Exeter within the next two or three days. And then what? How are you going to break it to the Queen that I want you to continue on with me?"

"I don't know. But she has been very tolerant so far. She has allowed me my maid and you your servant, to say nothing of Miranda, remember."

Unfortunately, Henrietta Maria's patience ran thin as they reached Sherborne and she was subjected to another attack of excruciating pain. Despite all Lord Jermyn's words she insisted on being carried into Sherborne Castle, much to the surprise of the incumbent, Sir Lewis Dyve, Sergeant-Major-General of the County of Dorset. However, Henry eventually had to agree that they would be safe enough there and waived his plan to reach Yeovil before nightfall. Furthermore, after recovering from the shock of having a royal party as unexpected guests, Sir Lewis laid on such generous hospitality that to have refused his offer of overnight accommodation would have been churlish, to say the least.

Nichola found herself uncomfortably intrigued by the man's name and for the first time in months thought of Lewis Devine. Her mind raced on in the wretched way she disliked so much, to the notion that she might be transported back to her own century that very night and she shuddered away from the idea, clinging to Joscelin as they got into bed.

"What is it, sweetheart?" he said, holding her so close that she could hear the beating of his heart.

"I don't know, just a silly feeling I get sometimes about us having to part."

"You said the other day you wanted to stay with me."

"I do, you'll never know how much. But there are forces outside us, Joscelin."

He propped himself up on one elbow and looked at her where she lay on the pillow beside him. In the candlelight Nichola could see every contour of his face and the changes in it brought about by all that Joscelin had recently endured. He was thinner, more drawn, but still the ebullient hair curled and tumbled about his shapely head and the great eyes, amber in this light, were incredibly clear and deep.

"As always," he said softly, "you speak in riddles, Nichola."

"Why do you call me that?"

"Because it is your name. I know that you are both Nichola and Arabella in one, though I do not quite understand the meaning of it. But I will not remain in ignorance for ever. When we get to Kingswear, when I have recovered my strength, I will somehow solve the riddle of what it is that possesses you. And I will set your mind at rest for once and for all. I will drive your demon away, I promise you."

Nichola turned her face from him so that he could not see her sad expression. "I think that might be beyond even you," she answered quietly.

They reached Exeter three days later, Henry Jermyn slackening his pace as they moved deeper into the loyalist West Country. Henrietta Maria proceeded at once to Bedford House, already prepared by means of an advance warning for her and her entourage. And it was there on that first evening, when the Queen was rested and presumably in a better frame of mind, that Nichola asked if she might take her leave and go on with her husband to Dartmouth.

"But, my dear Lady Attwood, I thought the arrangement was that you attend me. I have honoured my side of the bargain by giving safe passage to Lord Joscelin, your daughter and your servants. I would frown upon your quitting now," Henrietta Maria answered.

It was the fact that the Queen had said this in sorrow rather than anger that gave Nichola a pang of conscience.

"Why don't you compromise?" Joscelin suggested when she explained the disappointing situation.

"In what way?"

"Ask Her Majesty if you can be released once the child is born."

"And how would you fare in the meantime?"

"I will make my way to Kingswear and let Meraud nurse me back to health. I think she might enjoy that."

A warning bell sounded in Nichola's brain. "Does she wait on you hand and foot then?"

Joscelin chuckled. "No, not exactly. But our mother died when I was a year old and Meraud six – there were two babies in between us, both of whom did not survive infancy – so she accordingly took over my upbringing."

A grim picture of a fiercely possessive elder sister flashed through Nichola's mind and she did not reply.

"Then," Joscelin continued, "when my wife died giving birth to Sabina, Meraud came into her own once more and took on my daughter's raising. She never married, you see."

Oh God, worse and worse! thought Nichola, but said nothing.

"So she would be quite happy to look after me while you attend the Queen."

I just bet she would, Nichola commented silently. Out loud she asked the question which had bothered her for a long time. "Joscelin, why didn't you marry long ago? You must have been a widower for years."

"Because I dreamt of you," he replied.

She stared at him. "You're saying that you hankered after someone of my type?"

Her husband shook his head. "No, I meant the words literally. I used to dream quite regularly about *you*. Sometimes I saw your face and sometimes the face of another, a boyish creature with short hair. But it was all you. I know you won't believe this, but when we met on the road to Nottingham I recognised you. I was in love almost before you had spoken."

"Why didn't you tell me this before?"

"Because it sounded so strange, so unbelievable, and yet it is the truth."

"Have we been searching for one another for centuries?" asked Nichola, bewildered and off her guard.

"Probably," he said, his eyes dark and secretive, and then Joscelin would say no more.

The next day he and Caradoc, who somehow seemed to have extricated himself from his spying duties, at least temporarily, set off on the road which led to the wilds of Dartmoor. Nichola, who had been granted the Queen's agreement to her plan, had ridden with them to the outskirts of the town. And there she had felt so determined to put a brave face on the situation that she had done little more than brush Joscelin's lips with her own.

"As soon as the child is born, send word," he had said. "Then I'll come for thee."

"But what if you have returned to the war?"

"Meraud will take my place," Joscelin answered.

And with that unsettling thought uppermost in her mind, Nichola had turned back to Exeter to await the birth of the child which, if her knowledge of history was correct, was destined to be Henrietta Anne, known to her family as Minette, future wife of the homosexual Duc d'Orleans and mistress of his brother, King Louis XIV.

Prince Rupert's plan that early summer of 1644 was to leave Oxford to defend itself behind its great star-shaped fortifications, to reinforce his brother Prince Maurice, currently in the

West Country, then personally march north to relieve York, under threat from twenty thousand well-armed Parliamentary troops. This Rupert did on 16 May, taking not only Boy with him but also his black labrador, the dog he had acquired at the time of the autumn Council of War, when he had first noticed Arabella Attwood observing him from an upstairs window. At first he had called the dog Beau, but had later secretly renamed it Shade, to remind him of the most exquisite lovemaking he had ever experienced in the whole of his twenty-four years – one blissful hour in a shaded grove when he had erotically possessed the woman of whom he was totally enamoured.

As he went northwards, the Prince joined forces with other Cavalier commanders and their men. At Chester, John Byron attached himself to Rupert's column, at Bolton, the rascally George Goring, recently released from Parliamentary imprisonment in exchange for the Earl of Lothian. The Earl of Derby, who had come over from the Isle of Man to be with them, also joined the troop at this rendezvous. Then they marched on to Lathom House, which had been besieged for over a month, but most ably defended by the stout and redoubtable Countess of Derby, a Frenchwoman, born Charlotte de la Tremoille.

At the very word of Rupert's coming the besieging force had fled, yet another example of how the Prince's name alone could strike fear into the hearts of the enemy. In a great twit of relief the Countess had flown out of the domain she had so nobly protected and hugged Rupert which, so he declared afterwards, was one of the most frightening things that had happened to him since the war began.

The King, meanwhile, left Oxford to "make a grimace" at the enemy. Sending a decoy force to Abingdon to draw out William Waller, Charles had sped through the gap the Roundhead general left behind him, with three thousand horse, eight pieces of cannon and thirty coaches. The King's enemy, Lord Essex, declaring loudly that Waller, whom he disliked, was well able to cope with the situation, began to march westwards. So with both the Prince, his royal uncle and their opponents on the move, June came to England.

During the first week, Rupert, sensing the impossibility of retrieving York, wrote to Charles and asked if he might call off the attempt to relieve the city. The King replied on 14 June from Worcester, where he imagined himself to be in serious trouble. Believing that Essex had been ordered back to the fray and William Waller was also on the attack, he considered both men to be closing in on the Royalists fast. The opening words of Charles's letter showed the depths of his depression: "If York be lost, I shall esteem my crown little less." Then he had gone on to say, "Wherefore I command and conjure you, by the duty and affection which I know you bear me, that, all new enterprises laid aside, you immediately march according to your first intention, with all your force, to the relief of York." Taking this to be a direct order to fight, Rupert immediately set off, while the King, learning that Essex was heading west after all, prepared to do battle with Waller's army.

Early in the morning of 16 June, Queen Henrietta Maria went into labour and by the afternoon had produced a healthy baby girl. Nichola, who was present at the confinement as custom decreed, was stunned by the miracle. Not so much at seeing a new life enter the world, though this was a revelation to her, but at the fact that she was eyewitnessing the birth of Minette, the Princess who for one dazzling summer would enrapture the great Sun King himself, while his pretty little brother pouted and pirouetted on his high red heels, unable to give her the love she needed.

That night Nichola wrote to Joscelin that the baby girl was finally here and that he should come to take her home. And yet what lies in wait there? she thought to herself. Suddenly the idea of Meraud and Sabina, the spinster and the spoilt daughter, seemed far too close for comfort, and the prospect of having to make their acquaintance and live among them seemed daunting indeed.

The atmosphere in Exeter was tense. Prince Maurice had arrived in the city the day before Minette's birth, driven from the port of Lyme which he was besieging, by the Earl of Essex's relentless approach. Rumour was flying that it was the Earl's intent to take Henrietta Maria prisoner, and the party at the cathedral, where the infant was christened within a few days of her birth, was almost literally glancing over its shoulder.

Maurice, a stolid unimaginative soldier, most unlike his sensitive elder brother, was present, while Lady Dalkeith, Minette's newly appointed governess, held the child in her arms throughout the ceremony. Nichola, about to say her farewells to all of them, found herself weeping, partly because she could not remember exactly what had happened to Henrietta Maria and her new-born daughter, and consequently was suffering from enormous anxiety. Stepping outside afterwards into the sunshine of Cathedral Close, the light mellowed by the glorious red stone houses, a wonderfully elegant mixture of both Tudor and Stuart architecture, she found that she was still wiping away tears and fought to get a grip on herself.

There were men and horses everywhere, the young Prince's troop having fled with him from Lyme, better known to Nichola as the setting for *The French Lieutenant's Woman*. But one particular horseman caught her attention, for he was heading straight for Nichola and dismounted within a few feet of her. Not really expecting to be fetched so soon, Nichola gazed in surprise at the tall supple figure of Caradoc Venner.

"Where's Lord Joscelin?" she demanded abruptly, her dislike of the servant rushing back like a torrent.

"He's in the inn in Frog Street, my lady."

"Why is that?"

"He thought it would be a more private place for him to take his leave of you."

"Leave?"

"Yes. He has received news that Prince Rupert needs every man he can get to help him relieve York. The master has decided to go to his aid."

"Is he well enough?"

Caradoc nodded. "Aye, thanks to Lady Meraud's loving care."

Oh Christ! thought Nichola, then was furious with herself. "So what is his plan for me?"

"I am to take you back to Kingswear Hall and then follow after him."

"Well that, my dear Caradoc," Nichola said succinctly, "is exactly where both of you are wrong. If Joscelin is going north, then so am I. I have been lonely here without him and I have no intention of going through it again. Don't even bother to argue, just take me to my husband so that I can inform him myself."

For the first time since she had met Caradoc he actually smiled at her. "Yes, my Lady," he said and, lifting her on to his horse, walked beside her through the crowded streets.

Chapter Twenty

The city of York was now deeply affected by the siege. Cut off from the world as it had been for the last two months, its citizens were nearing starvation and existed solely on a diet of bread and beans. Yet under the command of the Marquess of Newcastle, the man who had once signed himself Rupert's 'most passionate creature', they were in an almost impregnable position. Having withdrawn behind the ancient medieval walls, the inhabitants had then set light to the city's outlying suburbs and fields, thus rendering them useless to the enemy, while at the same time they had fiercely fortified the gates. They were also perfectly prepared to blow up the bridges over the Ouse and the Foss should the Roundheads attempt to cross.

On 14 June 1644, the Marquess had blatantly refused a call to surrender, despite the shortage of food supplies, and soon afterwards he had been rewarded by an attack on the North Gate, known as Bootham Bar, which he had repelled. Yet even a man of such grit could not be expected to hold out for ever and news that Prince Rupert was approaching York fast, in fact was now only four miles away, had been met with a joyful letter.

> You are welcome, Sir, so many several ways, as it is beyond my arithmetic to number. You are the Redeemer of the North and the Saviour of the Crown. Your name, Sir, hath terrified three great generals and they fly before it.

And it was true that the three besieging commanders, Sir Thomas Fairfax, with his army from northern England, the Earl of Leven with his Scots troops, and the Earl of Manchester, in command of the Eastern Association, the name given to the amalgamated fighting force from the Eastern counties of England, including Huntingdon and Lincolnshire as well as East Anglia, had withdrawn from the city walls. At this longed for event, the citizens had rushed out and helped themselves to the spoils left behind, which had included, amongst other things, four thousand pairs of new boots and shoes!

Nichola and Joscelin had caught up with the Prince's force on 30 June, finding it camped overnight between Denton and Knaresborough. Fortunately, the embarrassment of coming face to face with Rupert after such unrestrained carnality had been spared her, and it had been Joscelin who had gone to the commander's tent to report his arrival. Whether he had told the Prince that his wife accompanied him, Nichola did not dare ask.

"I suppose that you really ought to join the other women," Joscelin had said as they climbed into their shared truckle bed beneath the canvas of his spacious tent.

Nichola had looked at him in genuine surprise. "What other women?"

"Oh, they're a good hundred or so that march with the army, march with all armies to be precise."

"Who are they?"

"Baggage carriers, food purveyors, cooks, seamstresses, medicine women, to say nothing of the camp followers."

"Whores?"

"Yes, and wives too."

Nichola had grinned. "Which am I?"

"Both," murmured Joscelin, and as he had kissed her she had felt the stir of his shaft and strained towards it, as she always did.

It had been lovemaking that had won her this journey, for that afternoon in the inn in Frog Street, Nichola had set out to enrapture her husband. Drawing him into her as often as his newly returned strength would permit, she had, in a way, also been expiating her guilt over Rupert. Joscelin, knowing none of that, had believed she was making up for weeks of abstinence as her lips ran over his body and he responded in kind. Then had come the ecstasy of entry before the sheer bliss of pure sensation had driven him to frenzy.

"Don't leave me behind," Nichola had begged him then. "I

can't be parted from you for another endless spell of months."

"Neither can I," Joscelin had answered as ecstasy enveloped him. And so Nichola had got her way and had ridden northwards by his side.

That night while the army slept, Lord and Lady Attwood amongst them, one of Rupert's spies had returned to the camp and woken the commander, who was dozing lightly as was his habit, not yet aware that the woman he loved was encamped close at hand. Thus when that great troop of people rose the next day it was to find that orders had been changed, and a message was being passed down the line by word of mouth.

"The enemy know we're heading for Knaresborough, then coming in from the east, and subsequently have withdrawn their forces from the north side of York. They've crossed the Ouse on a bridge of boats and have formed up at Long Marston to block our approach. The new command is to bear due north after reaching Knaresborough and come down on the city's undefended side."

"He's clever, that Prince," said Joscelin, as he mounted his horse, as jet black in colour as its owner's mass of curling hair.

"Yes," Nichola had answered quietly.

Half an hour later, the vast train of foot and horse, of cannon and ammunition, over two miles in length, stood in as near to silence as it possibly could, only the stamp of horses and jingle of harness breaking the tense quiet. There were to be no drums to beat them off, nothing to indicate to the enemy that the brilliant young leader was aware of their movements and had ordered his forces to march in a different direction once having reached the town. Seeing that tall elegant figure ride out to take his place at the head, Nichola almost wished she hadn't come, for there could be no doubt about Rupert's physical attractiveness. The man with whom she had shared such a frenzied coupling was today as beautifully dressed as ever, a scarlet hat decorated with a great black plume on his head, his fringed boots polished and fine. Gazing at him, remembering, Nichola knew for certain that she did not love him, indeed that that was not the point. It was simply that he represented a shame Nichola had never experienced or acknowledged before she had begun her life in another century.

Unsheathing his sword, the commander pointed it forward, and at this signal the silent army marched off. Nichola turned her head to see the great horde of women walking behind and wished she, like them, had some function, some way of helping the fighting men should there be a confrontation. Yet for the life of her, she could not remember whether a battle was involved in the relief of the siege of York.

"Why didn't I pay more attention during lessons?" she muttered, then in normal tones asked, "Isn't there something I could do to assist?"

Joscelin's eyes, cognac cups in the morning light, followed her gaze. "Surely you don't want to be a cook?"

"Well, better that than nothing."

He looked serious. "Then it had better be nothing. I consider anything else too hazardous."

"Why?"

"Because working women go on to the battlefield and are in just as much danger as anyone else. And as for the scouts, they run the constant risk of being discovered."

"Is a scout the same as a spy?"

"More or less. Only the women lookouts used before a battle don't actually go behind the lines as Caradoc does."

A chill ran along Nichola's back. "What *do* they do, then?"

"Spy out exactly where the enemy lies and what kind of numbers they have."

"And how is this achieved?"

"By dressing one of them up as a farmer's wife and letting her trot past the enemy encampment as if she's about her daily business."

"I see," said Nichola and left the topic alone, determined to experience such a dangerous adventure for herself, yet aware of the look in Joscelin's eye and deciding on a more subtle approach than argument.

They reached York later that day, 1 July 1644, and marched past the city to make camp on Marston Moor. Hearing the name, Nichola remembered at last that a bloody and bitter battle had indeed been fought but could not recall who had won the day. But even while she took herself to task yet again for not concentrating during history lessons, events were beginning to take shape. The Marquess of Newcastle sent his letter of greeting to the Prince, which Rupert interpreted as an offer to serve under his command. Accordingly, the commander sent George Goring into the city with the message that Newcastle and his men would be expected at four o'clock the following morning, in order that their combined force could march against the Parliamentarians. That done, Rupert set off to tour his camp, checking yet again how strong his numbers were.

He came across Nichola quite by accident, walking round the corner by her tent and stopping to stare in blank surprise.

"What the Devil! My God, Arabella, what are you doing here?"

"I came with Joscelin. I felt I could not bear sitting uselessly at home any longer."

Rupert took a step towards her. "If I'd only known I would have sent word to you."

"Highness," said Nichola formally, "I am in this place with my husband and can only beg you to be discreet. What happened between us must be forgotten."

The Prince gave a bitter laugh. "How can you ask me to forget what I have thought of every day since it happened? You may look on it as a transgression, but to me it was an act of passion, a statement of the depth of my love for you."

She turned away, flushed and wretched. "Please don't say those words. It upsets me."

He snatched her hand to his lips. "I would rather die than do that. My only wish is to make you happy."

"Then do not let Joscelin suspect. Be normal in your behaviour towards me, I beg you."

Rupert looked grim. "Not to treat you as my beloved is the hardest thing you could ever ask of me."

"Please do it though, for everybody's sake."

"Very well. Yet do not believe that there will be a moment, a second even, when I will not be thinking of you."

"Oh God!" Nichola exclaimed, the irony of having a Collection in this century and not wanting it in the least, too much to bear.

She was saved further embarrassment, however, by the arrival of Joscelin, returning from his own inspection of the site. Seeing Rupert, he bowed, a reverence which the Prince acknowledged with a curt nod of the head. Despite this Rupert spoke affably enough. "I am expecting the Marquess of Newcastle in the small hours of tomorrow morning but until then intend to relax. I'd be obliged if you would bring your lady to dine with me, Attwood."

"Certainly," Joscelin answered, his face suddenly alert. "Will you then outline your battle plan?"

"My plan," said the Prince, turning to go, "is to trounce the vinegar pissers."

"Well, well," Joscelin commented, watching Rupert stalk away, "he's somewhat sour. One could almost believe he was nervous, if such a thing were possible."

"You make him sound like a machine," said Nichola, putting her arm round her husband's waist.

"That's what he is, a fighting machine without an ounce of sentiment or tenderness."

"Nonsense. He loves his dogs."

"And you I shouldn't wonder," Joscelin answered, winding her ringlets round his fingers. "I always thought his contest with his princely cousin, vying for your attention, was quite serious."

Nichola turned a blank face, thanking God for her theatrical training. "I can't imagine how you could think that," she said, and went to their tent to change her clothes.

They dined late that evening of 1 July, there being much to do beforehand about the encampment. A table had been placed in front of the Prince's tent, and round it were seated his loyal generals and companions, the Lords Byron, Molyneux and Attwood, Sir Samuel Tuke, Sir Francis Mackworth, Sir William Blakiston, Sir Charles Lucas, Sir Arthur and Marcus Trevor, and the Colonels Dacre, Carnaby and Langdale. Nichola was the only woman present and sat on the Prince's right hand, where she was uncomfortably aware of his presence, very close to her yet at the same time rigidly keeping his distance.

Shortly after midnight, just as the dinner party was about to break up, further guests joined the company. Four hours earlier than anticipated, the Marquess of Newcastle, in company with several prominent citizens of York, arrived to join them.

"My Lord," said Rupert, downing a glass of port and waving a casual hand. "I wish you had come sooner with your forces. But I hope we shall have a glorious day tomorrow."

"Sir," answered Newcastle, looking decidedly peevish, or so Nichola thought, "my forces are still in York under the command of Lord Eythin . . ."

"Christ's wounds!" the Prince interrupted with a groan.

". . . so I have come to offer you my advice instead."

If she had had any doubts about Rupert's fits of impatience, Nichola was about to lose them. "I don't need that, thank you," he answered peremptorily. "I intend to attack without delay while the enemy's armies are still unprepared. Why, they've not come on to the moor in full strength yet."

"But Lord Eythin . . ."

"Pox Lord Eythin," the commander replied rudely, "I've never liked the man nor he me. So, my Lord, I suggest we go ahead without even waiting for him. I have fourteen thousand men on Marston Moor, many of them the cream of my cavalry. If we go at dawning I can catch the bastards with their breeches down."

"How many troops do they have?"

"I'm not absolutely sure. I'll send a woman out early to give me a tally."

Nichola stood up, making a polite curtsey to her host. "If you will excuse me Highness, Gentlemen, I would like to retire now."

Rupert was very slightly drunk and therefore dangerous. With his soul in his eyes he leapt to his feet and kissed Nichola's hand.

"Of course, my Lady. Get some sleep before the fight and remember, on my orders, you are not to go near the field tomorrow."

Horribly aware of Joscelin's steady gaze, Nichola murmured something appropriate and withdrew to her tent, her mind teeming. The urge to participate in the battle of Marston Moor, to convolute time and be involved in an actual historic event, held her in a compulsive grip. Yet she had just promised Rupert not to play an active part when the battle began. That, of course, left her a loophole. If she were to go scouting tonight, to act out the role of simple country woman going early to market, she could taste the thrill of danger and still be back before daybreak to give the Prince the information he needed. Without stopping to think about Joscelin's reaction, yet knowing how furious he would be, Nichola threw on an old skirt and blouse given to her by Emmet, and made her way to the place where the horses were tethered.

The fine weather appeared to be on the point of breaking, some high nervous clouds scudding across the face of the harvest moon. Even so there was light enough to see to saddle her mare, a skill Nichola had been forced to learn even though she had until relatively recently been rather afraid of horses. Then, once mounted, the rest seemed simple. Heading off in the direction of the rye fields beyond the ridge at the summit of the moor, making her way past the tents of sleeping soldiers, Nichola was out of the encampment within minutes and heading towards the spot where it was believed the enemy were drawn up.

About two miles to the east of Marston Field lay the village of Long Marston and it was towards this that Nichola now trotted, certain that Roundhead soldiers were somewhere within the vicinity. And sure enough, as she crossed the ditch which separated the moorlands from the rye fields, she could hear the sounds of life. Yet the encampment, when she first caught sight of it, was much smaller than she had imagined, almost as if the main bulk of the army had moved on elsewhere and left behind them little more than a cavalry regiment. A fact borne out by the number of horses herded together in a makeshift enclosure. Fascinated, Nichola drew closer, the combination of moon and torch light giving her a clear view.

The men of the enemy camp had also retired for the night, though lanterns were still lit in one of the larger tents, from which came the sound of subdued voices. The Parliamentary generals were obviously discussing the situation as earnestly as their Royalist counterparts. Dismounting, Nichola crept forward, thinking what a triumph it would be if she could relay their actual words.

The hand that seized her by the scruff of the neck came so violently and so suddenly out of the darkness that she did not even have time to scream. It was not until she was hauled into the air, her feet swinging above the ground, that she first let out a cry, partly at the sight of her captor, an enormous creature of well over six feet, with huge fishy eyes which he fixed on her unpleasantly.

"And where, little lady," he said, "do you think you're going?"

Nichola had the wit to switch to 'stock rural'. "To market, Sir. I've just come from the village," she answered winsomely.

"Oh? And what market would that be?" he asked, not looking in the least convinced by a word she said.

Nichola thought wildly. York was under siege and she knew nothing about any other towns in the vicinity.

"To Knaresborough," she hazarded.

He guffawed. "But that's over twenty miles away."

"That's why I started so early," Nichola answered earnestly.

"I see. And what produce are you taking, my good woman?"

"Oh, eggs and vegetables from my husband's farm."

"Well, they could be useful to us. Let's go and fetch them."

Her bluff was being called and she knew it. When he found the horse with no provisions attached, the game would be up. Nichola tried one last desperate ploy.

"If you let me go home I can bring back a lot of things, chickens and bacon and all. It won't take above twenty minutes."

He smiled at her, his great moon face horribly close. "I think I'd better ask my commanding officer about that. He might want to put in an order like."

"Very well," Nichola answered nonchalantly. "If that is what you want."

"Aye, it is. Because we've heard talk here that that fancy Prince sends out women for his lookouts. Not that you'd know anything about such things, of course." His sarcasm was so laboured that Nichola wanted to scream.

"No, I don't, to be sure," she answered curtly. "And so I'll tell your officer if you'd be good enough to take me to him."

"The pleasure will be entirely mine," her captor answered, making a clumsy bow, and with that he frogmarched her towards the lighted tent.

There were two men within, that much was obvious from the voices, and Nichola, determined to talk her way out somehow, was still wondering which one might be the more amenable, which the more susceptible to female wiles, when she found herself thrust within the opening. Blinking in the light, she stared around her.

The men sat at a table, one with his back partly turned, the other facing the entrance and looking directly at her. Nichola saw the long dark hair and triangular eyebrows of a familiar face, a face dominated by a pair of cynical black eyes. Fairly certain that she was in the presence of Sir Thomas Fairfax, the great Roundhead general, Nichola dropped a humble countrywoman's bob.

"What's this?" Fairfax asked, obviously more surprised than anything else.

"A spy, Sir. Leastways I think she is. She was loitering near the camp then told me she was on her way to market."

The extraordinary eyebrows rose. "At this time of night? Come, come."

"To be sure, Sir, I am," Nichola answered, 'stock rural' working overtime. "It don't seem right to me that a body can't go about her business without being questioned like this."

"My good woman," Fairfax answered pithily, "you must know as well as the next that there's likely to be a battle fought here in the next day or so. You really can't expect anything else." He turned to her captor. "Was she carrying any produce?"

"I don't think so, Sir, but I'll get the horse checked."

"Yes, do that." Fairfax turned to his companion. "She looks like a spy to me. She's too pretty a creature to be wandering the countryside at this hour. God help us, do they think we are so easily fooled?"

The other man turned and stared straight at her and Nichola nearly fell to the ground. Yet again, Michael Morellon had entered her life at the most unexpected moment. However, the effect on him was equally staggering. His jaw quite literally sagged and his eyes bolted in his head.

"God's wounds!" he exclaimed.

Fairfax looked alert. "Do you know her?"

Michael floundered. "I'm not sure, it's possible that I may have seen her around the village."

"Then why the surprise?"

"It's her beauty," Michael answered swiftly, recovering himself. "It's really quite outstanding."

"This is war," Sir Thomas answered reprovingly. "We are here to fight, not to ogle pretty women." His face relaxed. "However, I do grant she's a lovely creature. What's your name, girl?"

"Betsy, Sir," said Nichola, and had the satisfaction of seeing Michael start to grin.

"You don't look like a Betsy to me," Fairfax answered coolly, then turned his head as the guard reappeared in the opening. "Well?"

"The horse is a fair groomed animal, expensively saddled, Sir. Tis no farm nag for sure."

"Well, well," said Sir Thomas, putting his fingertips together. "Rupert's getting careless."

A thrill of indignation shot through Nichola but she kept her mouth shut, having no desire to make things worse.

"Isn't he just!" added Michael meaningfully.

"You should be on your knees thanking your Papist God that we had exact intelligence of the enemy's strength, my girl," Sir Thomas went on. "Or else I should have sent you for questioning, not always altogether a happy experience."

"Then what *are* you going to do with me?" Nichola asked, with just a slight note of apprehension.

"You shall spend tonight in chains," Fairfax answered smoothly. "I'll run no risk of you escaping to tell your masters what you saw. As for tomorrow, well, we must wait and see."

Michael stood up. "Where do you want her put, Sir Thomas?"

"Anywhere, as long as she is securely bound."

"Would you like me to see to it?"

A smile played round the worldly mouth. "No need for that. I'll call the sergeant. Our conversation's not yet done, Colonel." Fairfax rang a bell which stood on the folding table he was using for desk. "Take the prisoner away," he ordered the trooper who came in response. "And chain her, wrist and ankle." The general gave Nichola one long amused glance. "Goodnight, Betsy," he said, and turned back to the papers lying spread out before him.

It was a terrible experience, probably the worst she had ever endured. Secured to a post near the horse compound, Nichola had barely enough slack to crouch when nature finally forced her to relieve herself, hiding in the shadows, hoping that none of the soldiers were about. Standing thus, she saw the harvest moon finally fade and the first skein of purple appear in the sky after the most wretched night of her life.

In the gloom, just before morning, Michael had come to her, leaning close so that no one could overhear their whispered conversation. First he had berated her furiously that she had been so cruel as to desert him at Greys Court, then he had asked, rather pathetically, after the welfare of his daughter. Finally, the man who had been Arabella's first lover had flung a kiss on to Nichola's lips which she, captive that she was, had no choice but to accept.

"I still love you, that's the devil of it," he had murmured. "By God, Arabella, I swear that if I see your husband on the battlefield I'll take his life."

Confident that he had absolutely no idea what Joscelin looked like, Nichola answered, "That must be between you and your conscience, Colonel Morellon."

He had looked her straight in the face. "What kind of magic do you possess that you have the power to haunt me still? I wish to God I could be free of your enchantment but now I believe that I never will."

To ask what plans had been made, whether she was going to be released, seemed too prosaic at such a moment and Nichola had kept silent as Michael had scowled and hurled away. Yet, afterwards, the memory had returned of Rupert saying something similar less than twenty-four hours earlier, and Nichola had dwelled bitterly on the fact that there was a new Collection, in this life, and that she detested it.

"I hate you, Nichola Hall," she said then, and hung her head forward and let the scalding tears make rivulets on her unwashed cheeks.

Daylight had brought the same sergeant who had imprisoned her, bearing the bunch of keys with which the locks on her chains could be released.

"You're to join the women," he said, loosening the fetters. "Colonel's orders. By the way, he told me to tell you not to say you're an enemy spy. Tell 'em you've come from the village, otherwise they'll have your hair out in lumps."

Oh God! thought Nichola, as she was marched to a tent where a lot of unfriendly females regarded her with a suspicious eye.

"Come to help?" asked one.

"Yes. What would you like me to do?"

There was a screech of laughter. "Clean out Sir Thomas's chamber pot, that's what. He's too refined to go outdoors like anyone else."

"And just where," said Nichola, putting her hands on her hips, exactly as the woman who addressed her had done, "would you like me to empty it?" And after that there had been silence.

At roughly ten o'clock, as far as she could reckon it and later than he had proposed, Nichola had seen from her vantage point cleaning round the camp that Rupert's cavalry had begun to draw themselves up on the ridge above. At this, riders had left the Parliamentary camp at great speed and shortly after that Roundhead troops had begun to appear in droves. It seemed that they had been marching away from Marston Moor, their vanguard nearly at Tadcaster, but that this order had now been reversed.

At approximately noon, the Marquess of Newcastle appeared with his own lifeguard, four regiments, two of them known as the Whitecoats, so called because of the undyed woollen cloth they wore. Meanwhile, Nichola observed the Parliamentarians getting into formation, Sir Thomas Fairfax drawing up before a wooded mount known as Marston Hill on which, she realised to her amazement, stood spectators – just as if they were out to watch a day's sport.

The weather had broken, a mixture of sunshine and showers, so that the men and horses manoeuvring themselves into position must have been getting uncomfortably damp. On the Roundhead left wing under Oliver Cromwell, too far away for Nichola to experience the shock of historical recognition, Parliamentary cavalry faced that of Prince Rupert. Staring amazed, the woman from the twentieth century found she could not count the number of soldiers, quite literally thousand upon thousand, who confronted one another that day over the ditch which divided Marston Moor from Marston Field.

She had been given a tray with various lotions and potions upon it and had been told to get out behind the men and tend to the wounded.

"No setting of bones, mind," one woman had warned. "The surgeons will see to that, if they have time."

"But how will I know the difference?"

"If their limbs are at a funny angle, that's how. Now get on."

Nichola had never experienced such tension as she listened to the sound of sporadic cannon fire throughout the afternoon. The man with whom she was in love and two others who loved her were all involved in this mighty, looming conflict, and she felt paralysed with dread at the thought that any one of them might very easily be killed.

Oh God help them, she prayed silently, and felt the cold chill of fear weigh down her heart.

The day continued in a strange kind of calm, the only sounds the snort and trample of horses, the occasional burst of hymn singing from the Roundhead ranks, the subdued undertone of voices. The sky had begun to darken, evidence of an impending storm, and Nichola noticed that most of the spectators had gone home for the evening, certain that no battle would take place that afternoon. And then came a roll of thunder accompanied by a sharp fall of hailstone. At this, as if it were some kind of natural signal, the Parliamentarian infantry under Alexander Leslie, the Earl of Leven, began to advance down the incline towards the ditch separating the two armies. In rapid response, the Royalist cannon boomed out several shots and the men vanished into smoke.

It was the sign for every man to make his move and, marching behind the infantry, Nichola went forward with them to encounter instant bloodshed. Lord Byron, seeing Cromwell's cavalry bearing down on him, disobeyed Rupert's orders and emerged from cover, only to be thrust back in confusion. Out of the smoke Nichola caught one glimpse of the Prince, galloping up to Byron's men, sword drawn, shouting, "'Swounds, do you run? Follow me!" And then he was lost to her view and she was left to tend the mangled men lying at her feet, while from all around her came the screams of horses and troopers.

The scene was one of total disarray and panic, with absolutely no indication as to who was winning. A young Roundhead died in agony in her lap, his belly broken and his bowels torn, his hip bone smashed by a bullet, all the fractured pieces still lodged in his bone and flesh. The sun went down as he passed out of life, the harvest moon rose, and by its light Nichola saw a sight that made her vomit: Sir Thomas Fairfax, bleeding freely from a cut in the cheek, was knocking aside the weapons of his own troopers with his sword, trying to prevent them from hacking Newcastle's Whitecoats to pieces. This regiment had stood firm, pikes at the ready, while darkness fell, refusing to move and preferring to die rather than surrender. Hopelessly and helplessly, Fairfax was yelling, "Spare your countrymen!" but all to no avail. As the poor mangled bodies fell one upon the other, the smell of blood and carnage became too much to bear and Nichola retched once more.

And then, very slowly, the smoke and noise began to clear and she suddenly found herself standing alone in the moonlight, deafened by the sudden silence, looking about her in horror. The dead and the dying lay in rows, the mobile wounded hobbling amongst them, the surgeons and women tending the rest with an air of utter hopelessness. Gazing down, Nichola saw that she was soaked with blood, as were her hands and arms.

Knowing that she must get away somehow, yet moving like a zombie, Nichola began to head off in the direction of what had once been the Royalist encampment, tripping over corpses as she went. And then she fell and found herself face to face with a dead Cavalier, his sightless eyes an inch from hers, his mouth twisted into the parody of a smile, blood that was still congealing running from one side of it.

"Help!" she screamed, though no sound came out. "Won't someone help?"

Nobody answered, and steadying herself on the dead man's shoulder, Nichola once more rose to her feet, nursing a vague hope of catching one of the many riderless horses and escaping.

And then, mounted and unwounded, and picking his way amongst the dead, each of whom he seemed to be examining closely, she saw Caradoc.

"Help!" she called again, trying to raise her voice above the level of a squeak. "Caradoc, for God's sake help me."

He heard her and looked over and she saw that he was weeping in the moonlight. A great fear gripped Nichola then, and she began to pick her way towards him, corpses clutching at her ankles.

"Where's Joscelin?" she called as she drew nearer.

Caradoc did not answer, instead he leaned down from his saddle and snatched her up in one great enveloping movement.

"For Christ's sake," she repeated. "Where is he?"

Still he made no reply but his heaving sobs told her everything.

"He's dead, isn't he?" she demanded.

"Yes, yes. I saw him fall and now I cannot find him."

"Oh no," Nichola shrieked, burying her face in her hands. "He can't be gone. I can't lose him having come so far to find him. Oh Caradoc, tell me it isn't true."

"Oh dear God," the servant answered, "if only I could."

"Then I must help you look for him."

"No, I forbid it. You will see sights you'll never forget and you've witnessed enough today, God knows. He told me what to do if I should find you alive. He said I was to take you to York and put you into the care of the Prince."

"But I can't leave his poor body lying here."

"You must," said Caradoc, and his face was like iron. "I will not disobey my Lord's final orders for you or any man living. You will be taken to York and put in the Prince's charge if I have to kill you to do it."

"You would, wouldn't you?" said Nichola, staring at him hard.

"Yes," the servant answered harshly. "I loved that man, I owed him my life, now I will carry out his instructions while I have breath in my body."

She could not argue further, nor had she the strength to do so, and it was in a state of collapse that they moved away from that scene of misery – not only confined to human suffering. For a small white corpse lay amongst all the others, blood spattered on its curling coat.

"Oh God," said Nichola, pointing. "Isn't that Boy, the Prince's dog?"

"Yes," Caradoc answered tersely, and wept afresh. "All is lost today."

"Including the Prince? But you said he was in York."

Caradoc shook his head. "I don't know whether he is there or not. I am taking you to find out."

"And if he isn't? What then?"

"Then," the servant answered falteringly, "I will accompany you back to Kingswear Hall as Lord Joscelin would have wanted."

"I don't know anyone there," Nichola cried hysterically. "Caradoc, I'm afraid to go. I fear this unknown future."

But he could no longer answer her, too shaken by grief, and their tears splashed down in the moonlight and mingled with the blood which soaked the earth of the slaughter house that once had been Marston Moor.

Chapter Twenty-one

The ride back to York had been like a scene from a nightmare. As far as the eye could see, the road had been strewn with bodies, the dying lying alongside the dead, moaning and holding up pitiful hands to attract attention at the sound of approaching hooves. The air was rank with the smell of corpses and though Nichola had longed to shoot past, to get away at all costs, the faint hope that Joscelin might be amongst this remnant of the Royalist retreat, slashed down even while they fled, had impelled her to ask Caradoc to slow his pace so that they could look into the faces of those who lay there. But the most careful search had revealed no sign of her husband, nor indeed of Rupert of the Rhine, and eventually and at what hour God alone knew, they had arrived at York's West Gate.

Here another grim scene unfolded. Those Royalist soldiers who had managed to get as far as the city were being turned away, so that the entire thoroughfare leading to the gate was packed with the wounded; groaning and crying and begging admittance.

"Oh God," said Nichola, beyond tears, beyond revulsion, beyond anything except a longing to go to bed, "we're not going to get in."

"I'd like to meet the man who'll stop me," answered Caradoc, and she saw that his skin had bleached to the colour of lightning, his mouth to a livid line of fury.

"Open up in the name of Prince Rupert," he roared, beating on the wicket with a fiercesome cudgel, pulled from his belt.

"Is that you, Highness?" came a voice from behind the entrance.

"No, I'm the escort to his woman, Lady Attwood. If any harm befalls her you'll answer with your life. Now let us in."

And with that Caradoc started such a relentless knocking that she wondered the wood did not splinter, reinforced with iron bars though it might be. There was the click of a peephole springing open and then the sound of massive bolts being pulled back. At this, those of the wounded fit enough to run hurried forward, and it was riding on a wave of human despair that Caradoc's horse thundered through the great gates and on to the cobbles beyond.

"Let them be," Nichola screamed over her shoulder at the guards. "They are your fellow human beings. For Christ's sake, show some pity."

Yet she never knew whether her words had been heeded, for Caradoc rounded a corner and the whole ghastly spectacle was lost to view.

"Where now?" she asked, suddenly so tired she could hardly speak.

"To the Marquess of Newcastle's house. If the Prince is alive that is where he will head for."

"And what about you?" asked Nichola, turning to look at her husband's servant.

"As soon as I've seen you safely indoors I'll return to the battlefield."

"But you must be exhausted."

"I will not rest until I've found Lord Joscelin. I'll not see him stripped and plundered. And, believe me, at first light the enemy will return and do just that."

"How can they be so heartless as to rob the dead?"

"They need food and supplies as badly as we do," Caradoc answered emotionlessly. "The valuables of the fallen are considered honest pickings."

"My God," said Nichola, "is there no decency left in any century?"

"None," he replied bitterly, and Caradoc's shoulders twitched in a humourless laugh.

The Marquess of Newcastle, or so they discovered when they finally found his dwelling, had not returned from the battlefield either, in fact nothing had been seen of him since he had departed at the witching hour to meet Prince Rupert.

"Well, his guest is here for all that," Caradoc informed the night porter.

"The Prince, has he come back?" Nichola asked anxiously.

"No, my Lady. Nobody had appeared since the battle."

"And probably never will," Caradoc put in tersely. "In any event now I'll away." He turned to the servant. "Lady Attwood is under Prince Rupert's personal protection, so mark her well, do you hear?"

"Caradoc," said Nichola, hardly daring to say it but compelled to do so. "You remember Captain Morellon, who was in command at Greys Court?"

"Yes, what of him?"

"He was in the Roundhead camp, I saw him for myself, promoted to colonel. If he's dead and you should find him, give him a burial. He once was a friend of mine."

"They were once all friends," Caradoc answered bleakly, and went out into the night.

She thought she would have slept at last but Nichola was too exhausted even for that. Instead she lay in what must have been the Marquess's guest room, staring at the hangings of the four-poster bed, thinking that Joscelin was dead, yet not really taking the fact in. Then, finally, when the room was full of light, Nichola fell asleep, only to dream of death. When she woke again it was to hear rain beating down on the window and at this she got up, wondering what to put on, for she had given the blouse and skirt she had worn on the battlefield to the servant, that he might burn them. Aimlessly, she wandered downstairs in the nightgown which one of the maids had found for her.

A figure sat huddled in a chair in the smaller parlour, a figure so mud-stained and blood-soiled that Nichola could not recognise it. And then she caught a glimpse of dark matted hair and was suddenly filled with hope.

"Joscelin?" she called and ran in, kneeling down by the chair to gaze into the figure's face.

It turned to look at her and she saw that the deathly white features, the sunken eyes and gaunt expression, belonged instead to Rupert of the Rhine.

"Oh Christ!" she cried, and did not know whether to rejoice or mourn.

"Arabella!" the Prince exclaimed harshly, and burst into tears, thrusting his face into his filthy hands and heaving with sobs, so painful a sight to witness that Nichola wept also.

He could not speak, choking and spluttering, every inch of his spare frame racked in agony, but from time to time he looked at her and shook his head as if he had so much to tell her he thought his heart would burst. Eventually, though, quite worn out with it all, Rupert slumped down on to the floor beside her and flung himself into her arms, where she rocked him to and fro for what seemed like hours. Finally, being the creature he was, the Prince wiped his eyes on his bloodied sleeve, drew a deep breath, and pulled his pride and manhood on to him like a tattered yet wearable garment.

"It was terrible," he said.

"I know. I was there," Nichola answered quietly.

He looked surprised. "Where?"

"On the field, behind the Roundhead lines."

"How much did you see?"

"Enough. I waded amongst the dead. If it hadn't been for Caradoc I'd be there still." She turned her head away. "Joscelin has gone, Caradoc saw him fall."

"Christ's mercy!" Rupert whispered, clenching his fists to knuckle white. "Is nothing to be spared us? That great, good man, whom I so cruelly treated."

"Don't," said Nichola falteringly. "Just don't, I cannot bear to think of it."

"When I left the field, the moon high overhead, I counted at least three thousand of our men dead, probably more."

"There were heavy losses on the other side, too."

"I know. A great many survived, though, and they were

after me, after my blood, threatening to cut me to ribbons, to throw my genitals to the crows. I had to hide in a beanfield for hours before the trail went cold. They captured my Standard and bore it away. But what was worse than that, Arabella, by far the worst..."

She looked at him and saw that tears were pouring down his cheeks again even though Rupert made no sound.

"Yes?"

"They killed Boy and captured Shade, my beautiful Shade, named to remind me of you, my darling. They took him captive and they cut his ears off and called him Roundhead."

"Oh no!" said Nichola, her hands flying to her mouth.

"Oh yes, yes. They butchered not only my friends and my gallant fighting men but also my dogs. My God, Arabella, they have broken me with this."

At that they both wept wretchedly once more, holding each other close, mingling tears and saliva.

"I cannot go on without Joscelin. I loved him, Rupert, do you understand?" Nichola whispered chokingly.

"I know you did. Do you think I didn't?"

Nichola made a restless movement. "I must go back to find him. I must dress and go back to the Moor."

Rupert shook his head. "Our enemies will already be there, stripping the corpses before they bury them. Anyone who ventures near will risk capture."

"But Caradoc's gone, he's searching for his master."

"That man is safe almost anywhere. But as for you risking your life again, I must forbid it."

"I've never been forbidden to do anything," she answered automatically.

"I'm quite sure you haven't," the Prince said wearily, "but on this occasion you must treat the direction as a military order."

They stared at one another in silence, then Nichola asked abruptly, "When did you last eat?"

"I had breakfast before the battle."

"That was it?"

"Yes."

"Let me fetch you something, or is the Marquess here? Should I ask him?"

"The Marquess has gone," said Rupert, with just the suggestion of a smile. "Both he and Lord Eythin, that traitorous bastard who did not bring his troops on to the field until late yesterday afternoon, and then not all of them, or so I am led to believe. Well, neither of them can stomach my command any longer, or so it seems. They have left in haste for Scarborough in order to take ship abroad. So there ends the tale of 'my passionate creature'."

"What happened to Fairfax?" Nichola asked, the memory of the man thrusting back the weapons of his own troopers in order to protect the Whitecoats coming back with all its cruel imagery.

"He believed the battle lost and fled to Cawood after having suffered many casualties, including the death of his own brother."

"He tried to save the Whitecoats."

"So I am told. But they fell for all that, in the same order and rank in which they'd fought. They were redcoats by the time they'd done," he added bitterly.

Nichola stood up. "We must not talk of it more. We must be practical like those who lived through the last war."

"Which war?"

She shook her head wearily. "It doesn't matter. Let me get you some food."

Rupert bit his lip. "No, let me just drink enough to give me sufficient courage to go back."

"To the field?"

"No, to round up the cavalry that escaped. Goring's Northern horse are hiding out somewhere. I must locate them and bring them here."

"To continue the fight?"

"Of course. I said I was broken and indeed I am. But they'll not put my uncle down until I've first put down every last one of them. Now, let me get drunk, then order me a bath. I stink of death." Seeing Nichola's anxious face he added, "I will eat tonight, I promise you."

She knew now, or thought she did, how the widows of the Second World War must have felt, with the fight still going on and the living to be cared for. Ringing for a servant, Nichola went upstairs and hurriedly dressed in the only garments the girl could find her, a plain skirt and bodice trimmed with white collar and cuffs, then went back to Rupert. As good as his word, he was downing brandy rapidly, the colour returning into his cheeks along with some of his old hauteur. Yet Nichola thought his handsome eyes too bright, too frantic, and was certain that the slightest thing could once more trigger off his mood of deep depression.

At two o'clock in the afternoon, bathed and dressed in some of Newcastle's clothes, he set off on his mission, breathing alcohol at her, promising to return before nightfall. And then Nichola was left to stare at the wall, trying to come to terms with what had happened, still awaiting the flower of grief to bloom inside her.

An hour later Caradoc came back, grey as a ghost, his exhausted horse reeling under him, and at the sight of him all Nichola's old dislike of Joscelin's servant vanished. Yet she busied herself with getting him food and drink before she dared ask a single question, even though the answer to the biggest question of all was written on his face. Caradoc was in despair.

"You found him?" she said eventually.

"No, not him. He's still lying out there somewhere. But I brought this for you." And from his pocket Caradoc fished out Joscelin's signet ring and dropped it into the palm of her hand.

She stared at him. "What are you saying to me? Is he dead or taken prisoner? Surely the fact that you couldn't locate his body must give us cause for hope?"

The servant looked grim. "I think not, Madam. Lord Joscelin would never have surrendered this ring while he was alive. Do you remember the story of Sir Edmund Verney?"

"The King's Standard Bearer?" Nichola went pale. "After Edgehill they found his ring but not him. Is that what you mean?"

"I do."

The unasked question hovered between them. "Are you saying that Joscelin was hacked to bits?" Nichola said finally.

"I could not find him," Caradoc repeated, his voice hoarse.

"Then he lives. Either that or someone else has given him a decent burial."

"The Roundheads have buried their dead, the Royalists are still lying there."

"Don't," said Nichola, "no more, Caradoc. If I hear one further thing I shall not be able to continue helping those who have escaped. Do you understand?"

He nodded and raised her hand to his lips. "You're a good woman, my Lady. A strong capable woman. At first I thought you naught but a pretty brainless doll, but at last I see you in your true light. It's small wonder that my Master cared for you so deeply."

At that, at Caradoc's kindness, so sincerely meant, at his use of the past tense when he spoke of Joscelin, Nichola finally broke down and wept for her dead husband, with no thought of Rupert's suffering or that of anyone else on that terrible battlefield.

"You must rest," said Caradoc, distressed and overwrought himself, "come, my Lady." And exhausted though he was, he picked up Arabella's small person and delivered her into the hands of the women servants, who fussed and pampered and put her to bed with much cossetting and affection. They also administered a good dose of potent sleeping draught which almost immediately sent Nichola into the deep sleep she so badly needed.

She was back on the battlefield, empty now except for the high wheeling birds in the blue sky above. All the graves and pits had been dug and covered over, the grass regrown strong and wiry, coarse as only moorland can be. William Dobson was there, standing on the skyline, working at a canvas which took up all his attention. Nichola called his name and he doffed his hat and waved in response.

"What are you painting?" she called out.

"Come and see," he shouted back.

She ran over the heath feeling like Cathy in *Wuthering Heights*. "Though not as stupid," Nichola said to herself, having always considered that particular heroine not only immensely irritating but spitefully thick.

"It's a portrait," the artist said, as she drew nearer.

"Of whom?"

"He asked me to keep it secret but you've caught me," Dobson answered. And he stood back from the canvas to let her have a look.

It was a picture of Joscelin, as fresh and vivid as if he were still alive. Nichola stared at the springing black curls, the golden eyes, the lovely passionate mouth.

"Is he really dead?" she asked herself softly.

But Dobson had overheard and enigmatically answered, "Ah?"

Looking at the portrait more closely, Nichola saw that in echo of the painting of herself, Joscelin carried a flower in his hand, a lily of the valley.

"Does that have a meaning?" she asked Dobson.

"Oh yes. It stands for 'Return of Happiness'."

"Thank God," Nichola answered, "then there is no need to mourn him."

The artist did not reply, continuing to daub intently at his work, and she turned away to search for her husband. And then, suddenly and from nowhere, he came to her and she felt the beloved warmth of his arms, the sweet sensual touch of his lips. Sighing contentedly, Nichola drew even closer and fell asleep in the embrace of the man who loved her.

Dream and reality must have become confused, since just for a moment she woke, seeing the curtains of the four-poster bed yet feeling a human presence next to hers. Warm and alive, a man lay there, his flesh firm and supple to her touch. As sleep poured over her again, Nichola drew off her nightdress so that she might lie naked beside him, aware that the man who held her loved her with all his heart.

She woke at dawn, trying to separate fantasy from truth, and then saw that it was Rupert who shared her bed, as naturally as if he belonged there. In the silence of that sleeping house, in the unyielding light of dawn, she studied that creature from the history books with a kind of loving fascination.

Against the white of the pillowcase the long silky black hair was spread like an intricate web and his dark lashes brushed slightly hooded eyelids. He was pale, as if memories of dead friends and animals had come to plague him once more, while the ardent lips had parted while he slept. He looked childish, vulnerable, younger than his twenty-four years, and it struck Nichola more forcibly than it ever had before that in the hands of this impetuous fearless sensitive boy had lain the future destiny of the crown of England. For surely it had been he more than any other who had striven to save his uncle, Charles I, from losing all that was supposedly his by hereditary right. Without waking him, Nichola dropped a kiss on Rupert's brow and felt a sense of privilege, rather than her former irritation, that he should have chosen her with whom to fall in love.

They breakfasted together, his eyes never leaving her face, until the time came for him to go. Then he said urgently, "Arabella, today I am forced to depart from York."

She had been half expecting it. "You have found the missing cavalry, then?"

"Not only that. I discovered yesterday that there are well over one thousand infantry here in the city, reinforcements that the bastard Eythin overlooked to bring with him. Also, I have received word that two thousand horse under Sir William Clavering are making their way towards me from North Yorkshire. I have an army again, small it is true, but for all that an army."

Just for a moment Nichola thought of a boy playing war games, but was forced to put the notion aside in the face of Rupert's military prowess.

"So you're on the move?"

"I must be, there's much to do." He leant across the table and took her hand in his. "Caradoc told me last night that Joscelin put you under my protection. Because of this I feel perhaps he knew how much I love you. And I do, Arabella. If this were not such a tragic and terrible time I would say more to you, but as it is I will leave it for now. Yet understand that I will never marry unless it is to you, I will never make love to a woman lest I pretend she *be* you. You are the ghost that has come from nowhere to haunt my days and nights, and I thank God for it. I would rather have known you – yes, in the carnal sense as well – and to suffer losing you, for that might yet be my fate, than to have lived comfortably without the knowledge of your rare spirit."

She could not answer, choking over the words she would have liked to say.

"And now," Rupert went on, "as your appointed guardian I decree that you go to Lord Joscelin's home in Devonshire. Caradoc will escort you there and will remain with you to keep you free of danger, I have so ordered him."

"A military order?" whispered Nichola, half laughing, half not.

"Yes. I have released him from his army duties until further notice."

"And what then?"

"We must await events. But until I see you again, you will be in my heart and in my thoughts every minute of the waking day, and at night my dreams will take command."

"God bless you," said Nichola.

"And you, Arabella. I shall not know a moment's happiness until we are together once more."

And with that, that gallant youth, the arrogant, complex soldier of fortune, left the room without pausing to look back.

A day later, Nichola and Caradoc rode out from York on the

start of their long journey to Devonshire, totally unaware that the Earl of Essex had approached so close to Exeter, repeating his vow to take the Queen of England as his prisoner, that Henrietta Maria had been forced to flee the country. Leaving three-week-old Henrietta Anne behind her, she had crept out of the town, ill though she was with puerperal sepsis, and had made her way towards Cornwall, accompanied only by one of her ladies and a doctor. They had walked most of the way, an agonising trip, but had eventually reached Falmouth from whence Henrietta Maria had sailed for France.

On the night before she left, the little Queen had written a letter to the King. "Adieu, my dear heart. If I die, believe that you will lose a person who has never been other than entirely yours, and who by her affection has deserved that you shall not forget her."

The next morning she had boarded ship, leaving behind the husband she adored, an emotion he fully reciprocated. That rare thing, a happy royal marriage, was being brought to a close by events too big for either of the loving partners to contend with, or ever to overcome.

Chapter Twenty-two

When the King had written to Rupert from Worcester, urging his nephew to relieve the city of York, thus bringing about the battle of Marston Moor, he had considered himself to be in deadly peril from the combined forces of Sir William Waller and the Earl of Essex. But this had not been the case, as Charles was soon to discover. The fact of the matter had been that Waller, with only a scratch force at his disposal, had found himself quite unable to keep up with the King who, having amassed a sizeable army around him, was heading straight towards Buckingham and the undefended Eastern Association. The two sides had eventually engaged at Cropredy Bridge, marching on either bank of the River Cherwell, in full view one of the other. Taking advantage of a gap that had opened up between the Royalist van and rearguard, Waller had poured his troops across the bridge. This gamble, however, had not come off. Though there had been Royalist losses, the Roundheads situation had been far worse. The London regiments, who had marched two hundred miles in four weeks, raised their familiar cry of "Home! Home!" and by 7 July 1644, two thousand of them had deserted, wandering off into the countryside. Much heartened, the King had headed for the West Country.

The Earl of Essex, meanwhile, jealous of Waller, had huffily disobeyed orders and marched west to relieve the siege of Lyme. He had then gone even further, by disregarding yet another command from London to return to the capital. Instead he had proceeded deeper into Devon. Learning of this through his intelligence network, Charles had gone in hot pursuit. And it was towards this highly volatile situation that

Nichola and Caradoc had headed as they finally left the county of Yorkshire behind them.

Rupert had departed the city of York on 4 July, Joscelin's wife and servant, the day after, travelling on the Great North Road as far as they could. Nichola, who had cut across country when she had travelled to Nottingham and who had only seen the road for the first time when she had ridden north with Joscelin, was once again impressed by its quality in comparison with the other miserable tracks. However, in order to avoid enemy territory Caradoc had turned west as soon as he could and headed towards Wales, preferring to cross the rough terrain than to run the risk of being caught.

They were now travelling exactly the same route as the one Nichola had taken with Joscelin, and every step served to remind her of him. Yet the dream, the message of the lily-of-the-valley, had had a profound effect. A part of her now refused to accept that he was dead, in fact she had quite convinced herself that he had been taken prisoner and would one day reappear, and this hope had kept her going throughout the many difficult miles.

In the end the journey had proved so long and so arduous, several minor mishaps causing them even further delay, that Nichola and Caradoc had not entered Exeter until 26 July, only to learn that the Earl of Essex, having heard of the Queen's disappearance, had by-passed the city and gone instead to Tavistock. The King, however, was only four miles away and expected at any moment.

"I didn't know whether to stay or run," Emmet had informed Nichola at their reunion, when she had kissed her mistress heartily, then made way for Miranda, who had walked unaided to her mother with arms outstretched. "When the Queen fled I was troubled, I can tell you. Though it seemed better here than going to strangers at Kingswear Hall. For I knew you'd come back for me somehow."

Holding the child tightly to her, Nichola had said, "There's some bad news I'm afraid. Lord Joscelin fell at Marston Moor, or at least so I am informed."

Emmet had stared into her face in that sharp, disconcerting

way she had always had. "Then why is gloom not sitting on your shoulder?"

"What do you mean?"

"That you don't believe it, do you?"

"Don't – or won't?"

Emmet had shaken her head. "I cannot answer that. I am only aware you cherish hope, Arabella."

"Michael survived the conflict."

"How do you know?"

"I saw him there, spoke to him even, then afterwards Caradoc found out that he was still alive."

"How was he?"

"In good health. Promoted to colonel."

"You don't still care for him?"

Nichola had shaken her head. "Only as a friend. As a lover he belongs to yet another of my many distant pasts."

"Oh you!" Emmet had said, and had gone about the business of retrieving her mistress's gowns from the clothes press and giving them a thorough beating with the dust remover.

When Nichola had left Exeter she had moved both the servant and her daughter into a small lodging house of their own, a few yards away from the Queen's residence, and now she had never been more glad to return anywhere, cherishing the freedom and security of the little dwelling. As if picking up Nichola's thought waves, Emmet had asked that very evening, "*Must* we go on to Kingswear Hall?"

"Why do you say those words?"

"Because there are two women there who might not like us, who might resent us, having had Lord Joscelin to themselves all these years."

"And him missing and not able to keep the peace."

"Just so."

Nichola had sighed. "Before my husband went into battle he left instructions that I was to be placed under the protection of Prince Rupert, should he fail to return. And now the Prince has ordered me to go to Kingswear."

"Why?"

"He believes I will be safe there. I don't think he is quite aware of how serious the position in the West Country has become."

"Well, the King's arrived unharmed, anyway. He entered Exeter about an hour ago and has sent word round that you are to dine with him. Informally, of course."

"I would be pleased to."

"He must be sadly broken hearted that he missed the Queen by only two weeks."

"Poor man," Nichola had said, for a moment forgetting that Emmet was still listening to her, "as if he won't have enough to bear, without that."

Emmet had shaken her head. "Talk about God's mysterious ways!"

Yet as Nichola entered Bedford House that evening, she found the atmosphere quite the opposite of gloomy, for in the reception room, sitting in a comfortable chair, one neat leg crossed over the other in order to make a better lap, was the King, his six-week-old daughter held securely in his arms.

Part of Charles Stuart's genuine charm lay in the fact that he was a wonderful father, caring for his three sons and, now, his equal number of daughters, with a delightfully spontaneous affection. Yet of this neatly matching brood only two were safely with him in Oxford; Charles, Prince of Wales, and James, Duke of York. The eldest girl, Mary, the Princess Royal, had married the Prince of Orange at the age of ten and was thankfully away from the conflict. Less fortunately, both nine-year-old Princess Elizabeth and four-year-old Prince Henry, Duke of Gloucester, had fallen into the hands of the enemy and were under house arrest in St James's Palace. And now here was Minette, protected for the moment, but obliged to stay in the care of Lady Dalkeith rather than her father because of her extreme youth.

The King looked up as Nichola came into the room and made a respectful curtsey. "What an adorable child, this new daughter of mine! She almost compensates for my having missed the Queen by just a handful of days, though nothing could ever quite do that," he said, smiling a sad smile.

"That fact was wretched," Nichola answered.

"You were not here at the time Her Majesty departed?"

"No, I had gone north with Lord Joscelin."

The King shook his head slowly. "Marston Moor. What an unmitigated tragedy." He looked at her, his eyes full of tears. "And how much I grieve for you, Lady Attwood, in your terrible loss."

"It is very strange, Sir," said Nichola, sitting down opposite him, having been waved permission to do so, "but I cannot believe that Joscelin is gone. You see, his servant could not find his body despite the most diligent search. So I am certain that he will one day come back to me."

"I pray you are right. Of course, prisoners *were* taken and I suppose he could be amongst them."

Nichola nodded. "I can only hope that. But let us speak of Minette. I was present at her birth, you know."

Charles's expression became careworn. "My poor wife's eighth confinement! You are aware, no doubt, that two of our children died, our firstborn the day after his christening and Princess Anne as a mere child."

"Yes," said Nichola.

"It must have been so hard for the Queen at her age to endure the rigours of yet another birth."

"Her labour was very quick."

"Then God be praised. And now this perfect little daughter to bring us joy."

But what joy? thought Nichola sadly. You are doomed, my little King, quite doomed.

Nevertheless she chattered away during supper, she and Lady Dalkeith the only two women amongst the King's fighting men.

"Is it true you are leaving us soon?" Charles asked, turning to Nichola during a lull in the conversation.

"Yes, I must go to Kingswear Hall. Though I dread it," she added confidingly.

"Why is that, my Lady?"

"Because of family reasons. My husband has two close female relatives who might well prove hostile to an intruder."

"Yet," the King said sensibly, "if Lord Joscelin is alive it will be there that he will undoubtedly try to contact you. If your belief is true then you must play your part."

"You are quite right," she answered thoughtfully, "thank you, Sir. You have given me a vital reason to go and now I have to stop making excuses."

The King smiled his sweet, *triste* smile. "That I fear is something of which we are all guilty from time to time." And with that he kissed her hand.

Nichola left Exeter at dawn the following day, Caradoc being anxious to avoid Dartmoor completely and make an early start in order to get his party of females to Newton Abbot before nightfall. They rode in a wagon, the extra space being needed for Nichola's clothes and personal possessions, to say nothing of William Dobson's red rose portrait of Arabella. Caradoc sat on the driver's seat, the two women and the child bouncing in the rear, everything rattling including, Nichola thought, her teeth, as every bump, however slight, shook the wagon's passengers forcefully. And the next morning the whole uncomfortable process began again as they clambered inside, hoping that the promise that they would reach their destination before evening would hold good. Yet sure enough, as the afternoon sun began to decline, the wagon reached Totnes and turned south to follow the winding course of the River Dart.

Nichola, who knew Devon only slightly, was enraptured by the beauty of the countryside. Dense dark woods and vivid pastures swept down to the very shores of the glassy river, which eased its tranquil way, every drop of water glittering beneath a delphinium sky, towards the sea. Here, no thought of war could interrupt the quiet pastoral scene, and even the sleepy little hamlets of Stoke Gabriel and Dittisham seemed to have the calm of an earlier time, as if their inhabitants had never heard of the strife that was ripping their country asunder.

"Not far now," called Caradoc into the shadowy interior. At that, Nichola, on a whim, demanded that he should stop so that she could have her first glimpse of Kingswear Hall from the driving seat, rather than the hooped peephole at the wagon's rear.

The sturdy horse, tiring now, plodded on as they slowly came round a bend on the approach to Dartmouth. And then Nichola saw the house, standing on the opposite bank amongst stately trees, its lawns running down to the water's edge. She turned to Caradoc. "Is that it?"

"Aye." He stared across the river, shading his eyes from its brilliant glare with a capable hand. "I thought I'd bring you this way so that you could get a better view."

"How do we get to the other side?"

"There's a ferry just below. It belongs to the house. If I ring the bell someone will come for us."

"It reminds me of a book," said Nichola. "Did Agatha Christie live round here?"

And then she remembered herself and grew confused, only to hear Caradoc say, "The Gilbert family are the only people nearby. They have built one of their many homes not far away."

"Draw up for a minute," Nichola said, "before we go down to the river. I'd like to take a really good look."

"Whoa there," called Caradoc, and they came to a halt, the horse sinking its head down between the shafts.

The house had obviously been built in the reign of Queen Elizabeth, probably by Joscelin's father, for it followed the traditional letter-form E.

He would think of it as modern, thought Nichola, and shook her head at the absurdity of it all.

At each corner of the vast building at which she stared, stood an octagonal tower, surmounted by a cupola and ball, a weather-vane swinging on each one, while between these two formidable extremities reared one of the most dramatic silhouettes Nichola had ever seen. Turrets, gables and chimney stacks crowded one upon the other, giving an impression of great size and magnificence. Even the porch, which rose two storeys and formed the small middle stroke of the E, seemed substantial and large enough to house someone. Yet the mansion's awesome effect of austere grandeur was softened by the warm mellowness created by the rose coloured bricks of which the house was built.

"Manderley!" breathed Nichola, and ignored Caradoc's inquisitive stare, asking him a question to fix his mind on other things. "How many rooms are there?"

He shook his head. "I've never counted, my Lady, but I reckon there must be upwards of fifty."

"A stately home indeed."

"Yes, it is that. Have you seen enough?"

"Yes, let's go and meet them." She gulped and turned to stare Caradoc in the eye. "I am more afraid now than I was on the battlefield of Marston Moor."

He gave her one of his rare smiles. "I will be there, never fear."

"Are they very formidable?"

"A little," he answered cautiously, and started a careful descent to the river.

On the opposite bank a large raft, big and strong enough to support a coach and horses, stood at mooring, and in answer to the ringing of a bell, situated on their side within a wooden hutch, a servant appeared from the house above.

"Giles," shouted Caradoc across the gleaming stretch of water, alive with leaping fish at this hour of golden sunset, "go and tell the Lady Meraud that Lord Joscelin's widow and her party are here."

The man took a good hard stare across the stretch of river, obviously anticipating questions as to the appearance of the newcomers, and hurried back through the iron gate which led to the landing stage, then went uphill through an avenue of limes.

"He'll return in a moment," Caradoc said calmly.

"How does he get across?"

"By hand. He pulls the raft along those iron chains that go from bank to bank."

"I'm sure it's the same book," said Nichola, and smiled to herself.

They waited in silence, watching the ferryman, who obviously doubled his duties with that of general handyman, reappear and methodically proceed to haul the raft across to the bank on which the new arrivals stood. Then, having loaded aboard the conveyance and its passengers, on foot now, he heaved the whole thing back over the glistening Dart without so much as breaking into a sweat. At the far landing stage, Caradoc climbed on to the driver's seat and drove the wagon off on a gentle incline to the right, leaving Nichola and Emmet, Miranda carried for expediency, to climb the narrow walkway between the elms alone.

"Oh my lawk, one of them's awaiting us," murmured the servant, and glancing upwards Nichola saw that a female figure had come to stand, in a perfectly composed manner, outside the large oaken front door.

"Lady Meraud?" she asked as they drew nearer.

"Yes," said the woman, and dropped a respectful curtsey which completely threw the newcomer off her stroke, since she had not been expecting that kind of greeting at all.

"Forgive me for arriving unannounced," said Nichola, speaking rapidly and taking refuge in courtesy. "The fact is that I have travelled from the north and had no idea when I would get here."

"Is it true that Joscelin fell at Marston Moor?" the woman asked, ignoring her apology, and Nichola noticed for the first time that Meraud was clad from head to toe in black.

"Well, yes," she answered, acutely aware that she was wearing emerald green and so far had not gone through even a pretence of mourning, being so absolutely certain that Joscelin was still alive.

"Then I grieve for you as I do for myself," Meraud said, and made another deferential gesture.

"Please," Nichola replied hastily, "we are sisters-in-law. There really is no need for you to do that." And she raised the other woman up by hand, taking the opportunity while doing so of having a long glance at her face.

The Lady Meraud Attwood missed being good looking by the merest thread, her heavy features begging definition, a rescuing from the bland impression she created. Her hair was the same shade as fudge, her eyes caramel, while her lips, drawn into the compressed line that denotes suffering, were the pallid tint of a marshmallow. She was a study in the colours of confectionery without any of the enjoyment and delight associated with them. In fact, Meraud seemed as devoid of vivacity and personality as it was possible for a human being to be.

Heaven help me, thought Nichola, almost losing hope but still smiling a friendly smile.

"There is every need to pay respect," Meraud continued. "As Joscelin's widow you are now senior member of the family. It is to you that we must look for direction."

It sounded like the script of a second-rate play.

"For goodness sake," Nichola put in, speaking instinctively and momentarily forgetting herself, "it isn't like that at all. I am the stranger, you have been running the place for years. If you imagine I'm here to make a take-over bid, you've another think coming."

The words must have been more or less incomprehensible but Meraud seemed to get something of their meaning, for she gave a somewhat laboured smile.

"You would like me to continue as housekeeper?"

"Please do," said Nichola, suddenly beginning to tire.

Joscelin's sister seemed to notice Emmet and Miranda for the first time and she frowned, taking in the fact that the child was at least two years old.

"But surely this cannot be Joscelin's . . . ?"

"No," Nichola interrupted firmly, "this is *my* daughter, Miranda."

Meraud's eyes swept Arabella's pretty figure. "And you are not carrying a child? I did so hope for a living reminder of my beloved brother."

"Unfortunately, I must disappoint you." Nichola paused, then plunged in recklessly. "Meraud, I do not believe Joscelin to be dead and that is why I have not adopted the trappings of conventional mourning. It is my honest opinion that he is a prisoner-of-war and until the day it is proved to me that he is not, I simply refuse to wear black. I hope this does not offend you."

A warmer smile lit Meraud's mouth. "If only I could believe you were right. If only Sabina could do likewise. My niece has always been a motherless child, and consequently doted upon her poor father. She has taken the news of his death monstrous ill. If you could persuade her otherwise it might do so much good."

"I will certainly try," Nichola said, as the four of them, dwarfed by the lofty porch, went into the house.

They had stepped through what was obviously the middle entrance to the entire building, for looking about her to both right and left Nichola could see the lofty ceiling and minstrel's gallery of a great hall. And then she blinked, trying to adjust her eyes to the light, believing that within the shadowy reaches of the hall she had seen a fox, a vivid vixen draped in jet, a fox with such extraordinary contrasts of colour about it that Nichola stared and stared again in disbelief. It was a girl, of course; yet a girl with a face so ivory pale, a head of hair so tawny, a body so completely clad in the colour of death, that Nichola could only gape at such a theatrical apparition.

"And this," said Meraud, sounding ill at ease, "is my niece, Sabina."

Just for a moment the vixen lingered in the twilight, and then she stepped forth, revealing herself in the light of the candles which had been hastily lit to greet Arabella Attwood's arrival. Aware that she was under full scrutiny, that the flickering illuminations would not flatter her, the girl nevertheless stood stock still.

The black veil she wore over her head, removed by its gauzy material from the confines of a cowl yet closely resembling one in shape, only served to emphasise, by means of stark contrast, the hair which blazed beneath. Where Jacobina Jermyn, the erstwhile friend whom Nichola felt she had most wretchedly betrayed, had been a white rose with an amber aureole, this girl's tresses glowed as if flames smouldered within them. Nichola had never seen anything of quite such an indescribable colour, and could only think of the words smoky red as being closest.

A pale hand, quite long and thin, appeared from inside the layers of black, and grasping Nichola's fingers, Sabina made a curtsey. "How nice to meet you at long last, Stepmother," she said.

Her voice was low, quiet, and yet there was something alarming about it. Almost before she had looked the girl full in the face, Nichola knew that Sabina did not like her at all, that much as she had feared, Joscelin's daughter resented the intrusion of a beautiful young woman into the household.

"I hope we can be friends," Nichola answered, doubting it even as she spoke, and then feeling Sabina staring at her, returned her glance.

It was a strange face she was gazing into, lovely in an intense, disturbing way. Yet it was the girl's eyes which arrested and held Nichola's attention for, like her hair, she had never seen anything quite so unusual. They were of a very pale clear blue, the colour of ice, but what made them so extraordinary was the fact that the pupils were ringed with black, while round the irises were dark stars of the same colour. They were as stunning to behold and as chilling in their aspect as a polar landscape.

"Indeed, yes," the girl answered softly and dropped her glance, afraid, perhaps, of revealing too much.

"And now," said Meraud busily, "let me show you to Joscelin's bedchamber."

Nichola decided on a clever move. "No," she said, "let that wait for his return." She raised her voice and looked in Sabina's direction. "Because he *is* coming back, I'm certain of it. Put me where I can be near my daughter and my maid and I'll be quite content. It really is not my wish to cause any of you any trouble."

Poor Meraud flushed, not quite sure of herself, but Sabina merely turned and glided silently away.

"I do hope you're going to be happy here, Lady Attwood," Joscelin's sister said as they climbed the huge staircase leading towards the first floor.

"I shall do my best," Nichola answered, "and please call me Arabella, I do not want our relationship to be formal in any way, truly."

"But you are mistress of the house now," Meraud repeated.

"No," said Nichola, stopping on the stairs and putting a hand on the older woman's arm to draw her to a halt. "I meant what I said. You must continue in exactly the same style that you have been used to. If I can help in any way, that is a different matter. But as for interfering, I have absolutely no intention of doing so."

"You are very lovely," Meraud answered earnestly, staring into Arabella's face. "But also very young."

"I can assure you," said Nichola with great emphasis, "that I am considerably older than I look."

[illegible]

Chapter Twenty-three

Nichola's initial guess had been absolutely correct, Kingswear Hall was not only Elizabethan but had been built at the time of the Queen's passion for Robert Dudley, Earl of Leicester, when she had been at the peak of her physical attractiveness. In fact the house dated from 1566, the year in which the French ambassador swore to his Spanish counterpart that Leicester "had slept with the Queen on New Year's night".

"Gracious," Nichola had said when Meraud, rather pink in the face, had given her this piece of historic tittle-tattle, "I always thought she was disabled in that department."

"Arabella!" Meraud had answered, looking shocked, which had given Nichola food for thought as to whether her sister-in-law might still be *virgo intacta*.

By Nichola's reckoning, based on what Joscelin had told her, Meraud must by now be forty-six years old, though the plain clothes and unflattering hair style she wore made her look older. Observing her in the brilliant August sunshine, Nichola longed to get at that bland face and give it the definition and colour it needed, using the cosmetics available to any woman who followed the exhaustive hints of the inimitable G. Markham. Yet at this point, only two weeks after her arrival, Nichola hesitated to say anything, feeling that she was slowly beginning to break down the barriers Meraud constantly put up, and not wanting to do anything to spoil that situation.

The house's elegant exterior beauty was echoed throughout the grounds. There was a paved terrace overlooking the river and in the back courtyard the theme of water was repeated by a fountain. To the west lay a dovecote, reputedly very old, beyond it a walled garden, though Joscelin had added some other conceits, including an attractive pair of twin pavilions which lay to the east, and a formal garden enclosed in yew hedges, centring on a classical cascade which emptied into a deep and beautiful pool. The stables and coach-houses formed the further part of the rear courtyard, all handsome buildings of rose brick, their doors made of gleaming oak, and the river bounded the house to the front.

As if all this were not enough, the interior proved to be an even greater treasure trove. There were quite literally dozens of rooms, every one furnished with beautiful objects brought from various parts of the world. A vast long gallery ran the entire length of the East Wing's first floor, a library almost equal in length underneath. Joining the two wings was a long corridor, one side a gallery from which one could observe the great hall from above, the other leading to minor bedrooms, presently occupied by Nichola and her daughter and maid. In the West Wing were situated the suite of rooms belonging to Joscelin, one of which, she was intrigued to discover, was a laboratory for scientific experiments.

It was quite obvious, even without asking, that the Attwood family had once been Catholics, for there were hiding places for concealing priests situated in the most unlikely places. A panel by the fireplace in the long gallery swung open to reveal a staircase with an exit to the grounds below. A window seat in the library lifted to disclose steps going down to the cellars. By pressing a particular piece of carving in the dining room, a floorboard moved back to reveal a tiny room between the floor and the cellar ceiling. Most intriguing of all, there was a panel in Joscelin's bedroom which, when sprung open, led to a tunnel below the grounds, emerging into one of the summerhouses.

"Which came first," Nichola had asked Meraud, "the tunnel or the pavilion?"

"The tunnel. Joscelin built a summerhouse over the entrance for fun more than anything else."

"And was that the way the priests escaped?"

"Yes. But after my father died my elder brother, the

present Duke of Avon, now residing in France, adopted the Protestant faith for reasons of political expediency."

"I thought Joscelin told me that you brought him up, that you two were the sole survivors of four children. So where does the Duke fit in?"

"We were the only siblings left at home. Our brother was fifteen by the time Joscelin was born and had gone out into the world."

"And then history repeated itself and you raised Joscelin's child."

"Yes," Meraud had answered, and sighed. "But how I worry about the girl. Why, she has hardly spoken a word since you came to the house."

"Are you saying that she does not like me?"

Joscelin's sister had given a smile of sudden heart-wrenching sweetness. "I think she finds you a challenge, Arabella. I must confess that neither of us were expecting anyone quite so young or so lovely. When Joscelin wrote to say that he had remarried I imagined it would be to a much older woman."

Challenge or not, it was true that, since Nichola's arrival, Sabina seemed to have little more substance than one of the great house's many shadows. She appeared every day to sit down for the formal dinner, clad in black as ever, picking disinterestedly at her food. And at supper time, Sabina would join them once more, drinking wine but eating no more than a wing of fowl. Nichola wondered if she had anorexia, but could ask no searching questions for the girl had put up a wall of silence that seemed utterly impenetrable. Yet uncomfortable though this was all proving, Nichola could not let Sabina's obvious dislike dampen her enthusiasm for the beautiful rambling mansion, the exquisite gardens, the riverside walks, and the general air of tranquillity and peace.

Despite this the war continued. News came through, mostly via Caradoc who rode into Dartmouth daily to pick up what gossip he could, that the King, having spent some time with Minette, had now moved on into Cornwall in pursuit of the

Earl of Essex. Rupert, meanwhile, had gone to Shrewsbury with George Goring, leaving the Northern Horse behind him. However, from what Nichola could gather, there was internal strife within the Royalist rank. The King had discovered that Henry, Lord Wilmot, Lieutenant General of Horse during Rupert's absence, had made secret overtures to the Earl of Essex regarding a truce, to be followed by a negotiated peace which, Wilmot suggested, should be imposed by force on the leaders of both sides if they refused to implement it.

Round about 8 August, according to Caradoc's sources, Charles had suddenly had Henry arrested, even while he rode at the head of his brigade. He had then been sent to Exeter under close arrest and the newly arrived Goring had taken his place. This affair had caused much unrest amongst the elite cavalry officers with whom Henry had ridden to victory at Roundway Down and Cropredy Bridge. Words of revolt and mutiny were muttered – and something even darker. It appeared that there were those who thought as Wilmot did, that there were now doubts as to how this war should end. Suddenly the idea of a negotiated peace seemed not such a bad one after all.

"Will it come?" Nichola had asked Caradoc.

"I doubt it, my Lady. There are those, like the Prince, who feel the conflict should be fought to the finish."

"I don't think he is right about that, do you?"

"Who knows? Men have had differing opinions since time began." And with that the servant had walked away.

He had been in a strangely introspective mood since his return to Kingswear Hall, a circumstance which Nichola had put down to his uncertainty about Joscelin, coupled with a longing to get back to the war. But when she had challenged him with these things, Caradoc had denied both.

"I am not as certain as you are about the Master, my Lady, though your conviction he is alive has influenced me to some extent. As for the war, I find the whole thing bloody and brutal. I saw enough horror at Marston Moor to last me a lifetime. Yet, for all that, I do wonder if my skill as a scout might still help to save lives."

"Then why don't you rejoin the King?" Nichola had suggested. "He's not far away in Cornwall. I can manage here quite well. Even though Sabina hates me, Meraud is getting more friendly."

Perhaps she had been a little tactless to speak of his lifelong employers thus, for Caradoc had flushed an uncomfortable red, the first time Nichola could remember seeing him discomfited, and muttered something about the young lady being shy.

"Really?" Nichola had remonstrated. "The truth is she can hardly bring herself to address a word to me. Do you call that shyness?"

"It might be," Caradoc had answered in the same tone of voice, and it had occurred to Nichola, then, that he could well be besotted with the extraordinary girl. Having once seen it, she looked for evidence, and came to the conclusion that Caradoc certainly had a terrific liking for his young mistress. Yet even in this supposition she was not quite correct.

Towards the end of August the rains had come to the Dart Valley, turning the meadows an even lusher shade of green. On a whim, wanting some air yet not wishing to get wet in the process, Nichola had gone to Joscelin's room, pressed the carving by the mantelpiece, and gone out through the sliding door. Descending the hidden spiral staircase which lay beyond, Nichola had made her way through the priest's tunnel towards the summerhouse.

At the end of the tunnel another set of steps led upwards to the pavilion's floor where, at the touch of a switch, a floorboard slid back and one could step up into the room above. Yet as she put her foot on the bottom of these stairs, Nichola stopped in surprise. There was somebody in there ahead of her, two people in fact, and the sounds they were making left her in little doubt as to what they were doing. Imagining themselves to be alone, the couple were indulging in intercourse. Nichola turned, greatly embarrassed, and would silently have retraced her steps had not the female voice caught her attention.

"Come on, harder! You know how I like it," it was saying in a low sibilant tone incredibly like Sabina's.

The man did not reply but Nichola heard him gasp as he increased the power of his stroke, pushing so rhythmically that the padded seat on which they were lying creaked in time.

"That's *better*!" the girl called out. Now there could be no doubt. It was Sabina.

Still the man remained silent but Nichola, feeling horribly like a voyeur, found that she could hear every other detail of what was taking place above, creating an alarmingly explicit picture. She listened to Sabina's buttocks thumping down on to the seat, the thud of the man's frenetic thrashing as he strove to satisfy her, until he suddenly groaned, "I can't help it. I've got to..." But his next words were drowned by Sabina's shrill scream of pleasure, to which the man added his own a second later. Nichola was now in no doubt whatsoever. It was Caradoc who lay in the summerhouse above, pleasuring his Master's daughter.

She turned to go, not wanting to hear anything more, but Joscelin's servant, watchful even at a moment like the one he must be experiencing now, had obviously detected the faintest sound from beneath the boards, for he said, "What's that?"

Terrified, Nichola sank back down on the stone steps, knowing it would be worse to be caught than to remain eavesdropping.

"I didn't hear anything," Sabina answered lazily, and Nichola had a vivid mental picture of her, hair like a forest fire, pale face animated, legs spread voluptuously.

"Was that all right for you?" Caradoc asked softly.

The vixen considered. "Reasonable. I've known you be more exciting."

So this relationship is no new thing, Nichola thought.

"When was that?"

"When both you and Father were last home, before the advent of the bitch. We did it on the stairs behind the long gallery chimney while Papa had company, sitting just on the other side of the wall. It was wonderful. Do you remember how we giggled?"

"I felt ashamed afterwards."

"Oh you would, you great pillicock. Rogering is no fun without risk, you ought to know that by now."

Caradoc sighed. "You're totally debauched, for all your youth."

Sabina shifted on the seat. "That's what you said when you relieved me of my virginity all those years ago. I could have had you castrated for doing that, you know. I was scarce above a child."

"But I had loved you for years, even then."

Nichola, who had once considered herself quite unshockable, felt utterly appalled by what she was overhearing, and yet, horrified as she was, a certain sympathy for Caradoc tinged her other emotions. She could imagine him, rescued by Joscelin from some unpleasant situation not as yet explained to her, and brought into a household where a depraved little girl ruled the roost.

She's a dangerous slut, Nichola thought, then wondered how Joscelin could possibly have sired such a creature. But Sabina was speaking again, wheedling now.

"And do you love me still? Just as much?"

"You know I do."

"Then are you going to help me see off that bitch?"

Caradoc paused. "I can't, Sabina. I was so full of your prejudices when I first met her that I had branded her a money seeker and parven . . . what's that word? . . . before I had any right to make such a judgement."

"A parvenue *arriviste* is what you mean. And that's exactly what she is. She's years too young for my father and married him solely for what she could get out of him."

"I no longer believe that," Caradoc answered uncomfortably. "You should have seen her at Marston Moor. Arabella is a woman of great courage. I do wish you'd believe me."

Sabina's voice fell slightly and Nichola had to strain to hear what she said next. "She is here to get her hands on what should rightfully be mine. If my father really is dead then Kingswear belongs to me."

It was not difficult to imagine Caradoc's face. "Arabella thinks he is still alive – and I pray that she is right. Besides, this house would revert to the Duke in the case of Lord Joscelin not leaving a male heir."

"I know that," she answered contemptuously. "But my uncle would let me live here for the rest of my days or until I made a brilliant match."

"And where would that leave me?" Caradoc asked sadly.

"Where it always has, as my provider of thrills and danger."

"Is that all?"

"Yes, all. And it won't even be that much unless you help me."

"Then I'll have to do without," Caradoc answered angrily. "Even above you I love your father, remember. And he cares for Arabella deeply. I'll make no move against her."

"Then I'll have to do so alone," Sabina answered chillingly as Nichola, no longer caring whether she was heard or not, finally turned and fled.

The rain had lasted all day, increasing in intensity towards the evening. Dinner, which Meraud preferred to serve as late as possible, usually at two o'clock, came and went without any sign of Sabina, a fact for which Nichola was grateful, giving her time, as it did, to collect herself.

"Where can the wretched girl be?" Meraud asked anxiously, signalling to the servants to start serving, murmuring that she could not wait any longer.

It was on the tip of Nichola's tongue to say, "Out planning my downfall, I expect," but she restrained herself. Instead, she said, "She probably went for a walk and got caught in the rain."

Meraud peered towards one of the many square-paned

windows which let light into the gracious dining room. "Is it falling as hard as ever?"

"Pouring," Nichola replied certainly and raised her wine glass in the direction of her sister-in-law. "In a way I had been hoping that the fine weather might end so that I would not feel guilty about remaining indoors and talking to you, my dear. Something I have wanted to do for a long time. I drink your health."

Meraud looked pleased. "I thought perhaps you might be bored in my company. After all, you are far nearer Sabina's age than mine."

"In actual years, maybe, but mentally I am much closer to you."

And so Nichola went on, smiling and flattering, until the meal was finally cleared and they retired to Meraud's own withdrawing room. Declaring herself to be in a mood for port, Nichola made quite sure that a servant followed them with a tray bearing a decanter and two glasses. Then, having dismissed him, she poured her sister-in-law a generous glass while Meraud went to the window to gaze out.

"Oh dear, I do hope the child is all right," she repeated, surveying the miserable day.

"You refer to Sabina as that quite frequently, yet surely she must be eighteen," Nichola answered.

"Very nearly. Her birthday is in late November."

"Then she is a young woman of marriageable age, is she not?"

"Indeed she is, but all the elements of decent courtship have been shattered by this horrible war. With families divided and friends on opposing sides, the choice of eligible young men is severely curtailed."

"So what are you going to do?"

"Pray that the conflict ends soon. And pray, above all, that you are right, my dear Arabella, and that Joscelin will come back and take the problem off my hands."

"Poor Meraud," said Nichola, without stopping to think, "you can't have had an easy life acting as mother all the time."

Her sister-in-law's plain features grew even more drained. "I knew I had to do my duty."

"Yes, but at what cost to yourself? Did you not want to marry and have a child of your own?"

Meraud sat down opposite her and sipped the port. "It's true, alas. I was in love once and would have married the man concerned, even though my elder brother, the Duke of Avon, considered him beneath me."

"Why was that?"

"Because he was the son of a local landowner, nothing more. Though the fashion for cold-blooded arranged marriages is starting to diminish even amongst the aristocracy, I still fell victim to it."

Fascinated, Nichola refilled Meraud's glass. "How are things changing?"

"Naturally, young people must still obtain their parents' consent before they can be wed, but even in society circles the tendency is now – or was until the war – for children to be allowed greater consideration in matchmaking."

"You mean provided that the young man or woman is fit enough and wealthy enough, it's take your pick time?"

"How sweetly put, but yes I believe that is the coming trend."

"The war will bring about further change," Nichola said thoughtfully. "They always do."

Meraud stared at her. "You are indeed wise for your years, my dear. It is small wonder that Joscelin loved you."

"Loves," corrected Nichola. "He isn't dead, Meraud. I know it."

"But how?"

"If I mentioned gypsy fortune tellers and dreams you would laugh at me."

"No I wouldn't," said Meraud seriously. "Years ago I went to just such a one in Dartmouth..." She gave a start and her voice trailed away as a recollection came to her.

"What is it?"

"She predicted *you*, all that time past. She said my happiness would come about when I heeded the words of one who seemed naught but a girl, but who had the wisdom of centuries within her soul. It *must* be you, Arabella," Meraud added excitedly. "She said you would cross my threshold, and so you have."

Nichola smiled wryly. "I don't know about the wisdom but I am certainly centuries old."

But Meraud was not listening, remembering the prediction and flushing with pleasure. "She said Ralph – that is the man I once loved – would come back to me, free to ask for my hand, and that I should go with him."

"Well, you must. But where is he now? Have you lost touch with him?"

Meraud's sudden animation disappeared abruptly. "He long ago took horses and men to join the ranks of the Earl of Essex. He sat as a Member of Parliament, you see."

"I do, very clearly, but don't let that deter you. If fate has decreed that he will come for you, then he will. So why don't you prepare yourself in the meantime?"

"What do you mean?"

"You have sacrificed yourself too long. My dear, the time has come to concentrate on yourself. Now listen to me. With your light hair and darker eyes you could be beautiful, I mean it. But you must highlight your good points and disguise the bad. There is no sin in using cosmetics, Meraud. All women do."

"And you are a shining example of how to apply them. But I would have no idea."

"Well, let me show you. It would give me enormous pleasure and be of such benefit to yourself. So if Ralph comes calling he will be delightfully surprised."

"He's more likely to come and lay siege to us," Meraud replied dourly.

"Then he can carry you off as his prize, can't he? Now, what do you say?"

"I say thank God you've come to us, sweetheart." And rising from her chair, Meraud gave Nichola a hug of genuine affection. "You don't know what the last few years have been like," she added quietly.

"Sabina?"

"Sometimes I fear for her," Meraud went on, bending low so that only Nichola could hear her voice.

"Why?"

"All was not well on her mother's side of the family. We discovered, too late for they were wed, that Joscelin's bride's brother had whipped his own wife to death and was kept under restraint by his father."

"Oh my God!"

Meraud dropped her tone even lower. "I am glad Catherine died, may God forgive me. Hers was bad blood and I did not want the taint to go any further."

"And Sabina?"

"Wilful, headstrong, of violent moods, but not evil."

"You're certain?"

"As far as I can be."

"Does Joscelin know what she is like?"

"No, nor will he while I have life. The best thing that could happen now is for the girl to marry a man with a will of iron. And soon at that."

"But there's no chance because of the war?"

"The only young men left are those too weak or too simple to fight. Until the conflict ends she must remain under her father's roof."

"Then let it be hoped he comes back soon, for surely Joscelin will be able to keep her in check."

Meraud shook her head slowly. "He dotes on her, I fear. But now that you are here things could be very different. He may no longer indulge her whims and caprices."

"I think she may well be thinking the same thing," Nichola answered thoughtfully. And with those words a thrill of unease laid a cold hand on her, causing her to give a violent and involuntary shudder.

Chapter Twenty-four

In the calm autumn days that followed, the River Dart became a sheet of glass, another world of green banks and crimson trees reflected in its clear crystal depths. As Nichola walked along its shores, hand in hand with Miranda, she stared about her at the golden weather, the rains long since dried up and gone, and thought that it was time now for Joscelin to come back, so that she could share the beauty of the changing season with him. Down by the water, the plums in the riverside orchard were adding their darkening purple to the red and russet tints that fired the leaves of the woodland, in the farming country between the Dart and Plymouth, the wheatfields were bleached with harvest gleaning. The savage year of 1644 was drawing to its close and Nichola, whose faith in Joscelin Attwood's survival had never been shaken, now felt her confidence start to diminish with the shortening of the days.

Yet while she had grown more anxious and depressed, the reverse had happened to Meraud. A few lessons in the basic arts of presentation and dress had seen Joscelin's sister emerge transformed. Never a beauty by anyone's standards, nonetheless a woman with an individual style had taken the place of the boring housekeeper. There had also been a resultant change in Meraud's attitude to life which had, of course, included Sabina, who was no longer treated as a being of fragile temperament to be handled with care, but had actually been subjected to a lecture about her behaviour towards her stepmother.

It had been well meant, naturally, but Nichola had caught the quick glance the girl had shot her and read such hatred in the extraordinary ice-blue eyes that she had experienced another moment of spine-chilling fear. It seemed to her that the vixen was beginning to bare its teeth.

"What shall I do about her?" she had asked Emmet. "I sometimes get the feeling she'll have a knife in my back one of these days."

The servant had not smiled. "I think you must have it out with her, my Lady. Remind her who is mistress here."

"That could do more harm than good."

"What do you mean?"

"The Lady Meraud told me that there was instability in the family of Sabina's mother."

"I don't doubt that for a moment," Emmet had replied with a swiftness which showed the idea was not new to her.

"Then in view of that, what is my best move?" Nichola had repeated desperately.

"Perhaps to pray that Lord Joscelin comes back quickly."

For the first time, Nichola faced the horrible truth. "Supposing I've been wrong all along? Supposing he really did die at Marston Moor?"

"Then I'd go to find the Prince," Emmet had answered practically. "I wouldn't rot away here, lovely though the place may be. Why, I think in view of what you've just told me, you'd be safer on a battlefield than getting on the wrong side of that girl."

It had all been so full of countrywoman's sense that Nichola had smiled. "I believe you're right, but that must be the last resort. If he is alive, Joscelin will come looking for me at Kingswear Hall."

"Aye, he will," Emmet had said, nodding. "You must be strong, Arabella."

Yet the fact was that with each passing day Nichola's strength was diminishing, worn down by uncertainty and the brooding atmosphere. Other than for Meraud's transformation, the only bright spots in her life were her conversations with Caradoc, in which they discussed the progress of the war, for Charles Stuart was having his fair share of success and it was heartening to hear of them even though Nichola knew that all would, inevitably, be lost.

Having pursued the Earl of Essex down the Fowey peninsula, the King had finally surrounded his arch enemy who, on the night of 31 August, had ordered his cavalry to escape under their Dutch commander and had then made a personal disappearance in a fishing coble. His infantry, Essex had abandoned to their fate, and they had surrendered to Charles, who had found them drenched to the skin and half starved. This débâcle, known as the Battle of Lostwithiel, had resulted in ten thousand muskets, to say nothing of other guns and ammunition, being handed over to the King's troops. Many thought that Charles had made a grave mistake in allowing the infantry to go free and march away to Portsmouth.

"And where's Prince Rupert now?" Nichola had asked the servant.

"In Bristol. They say he is delighted by the fall from grace of Lord Wilmot and the consequent resignation of Lord Percy. It's believed the Prince has got his eye on becoming Commander-in-Chief. It is also said that he has only just got his nerve back after Marston Moor."

The very mention of the place had sent a shudder through Nichola. "Tell me something truthfully," she had asked, looking Caradoc directly in the eye. "So much time has passed since then, is there a chance Lord Joscelin survived or am I just deluding myself?"

He had shaken his head sadly. "If only I knew, my Lady."

Nichola had frowned. "I would send you to search for him but for one thing."

"Which is?"

She had been on the verge of telling him all her fears, but remembering that the man loved Sabina, had hesitated. But Caradoc was ahead of her.

"You don't want to be left here without my guardianship, is that it?"

"Yes."

The servant had spoken very softly. "She won't touch you, you know. She'll try to drive you away with a war of nerves, but she'll go no further."

"Oh my God!" Nichola had exclaimed. "I didn't want you of all people to know about this."

"Because you think I love her?"

"I'm aware that you do, yes."

Caradoc had looked away, his features taut. "Love is not the right word, my Lady. I am besotted, infatuated, crazed by the power of my feelings for her. I was ten when Lord Joscelin brought me here and she still a babe in arms. I worshipped her, adored her, and then, God help me, I seduced her as soon as she had her first moon flux. I've never forgiven myself for that and yet I could not help it. Nonetheless over the years I've been aware of what she has become and I have sworn to watch over her and never let her act too wildly."

Nichola had repeated a question she had asked Meraud, though in another form. "Does Lord Joscelin know how depraved Sabina is?"

"He thinks her virgin still. It has crucified me, my Lady, that I could have betrayed him so basely and yet I was so mad with desire that I felt compelled."

"Then how is it that you are not totally in her thrall and can speak to me like this?"

A single tear had sprung from Caradoc's eye. "Because I would rather kill her than let her stoop too low. My goddess fell long ago, but she must never be allowed to enter hell."

Nichola had gazed at him silently and then had put her arms round him, Arabella's small stature only reaching to his waist.

"Poor Caradoc," she had said, "you must have endured a life of misery. If ever I have been sharp with you or rude in any way, I want you to forgive me. It was just that I believed you had no liking for me. But now I understand the reason why."

"I knew in York, after that terrible battle, what a good

woman you really are, my Lady," Caradoc had answered simply. And Nichola had marvelled to herself that the words 'good woman' had actually been applied to her.

The mellow autumn grew richer, the days shorter, and the King finally began to move northwards, taking with him an army of ten thousand men. On 10 September he left Plymouth with his mighty column, and on the following day the rider came, ringing the bell at the ferry so violently that Giles, harvesting apples and grumbling about the disturbance, was beaten to the raft by Caradoc. He brought the man across, horse and all, and there was a certain gleam about the servant of which Nichola was instantly aware.

"Is there good news?"

"Aye, there is. This man is the King's own messenger, my Lady, with a letter direct from His Majesty."

The oppressive atmosphere of the last few weeks seemed to be lifting and Nichola broke the King's seal impatiently.

"What is it?" asked Meraud, who had hurried in, in order not to miss anything.

"The King wants to stay here with a dozen of his officers. The army will camp outside Totnes, but he asks our permission to rest at the Hall for a night or two."

"When will they arrive?"

"The day after tomorrow."

"God's life, there's work to do," Meraud exclaimed, and broke into a run as she headed for the kitchens.

"I'll write a quick reply," Nichola called after her. "Caradoc, can you organise food and drink for the messenger?"

"Let me," put in a low voice, and Nichola saw to her surprise that the fox girl had come into the room and had stood silently listening to every word. Nichola's eyes went from the rider, who was a well set up muscular young man, to Caradoc, then back again.

"I think perhaps, my dear, you could be of more use to your aunt," she said sweetly, and turned away.

A wonderful bout of organised chaos ensued as soon as

the messenger had left. A great feast, as prescribed by G. Markham, was set in train with every member of the household playing their part in the preparation. Fresh lobsters were brought in from the Dart estuary and further supplies of food obtained from Dartmouth. Even the youngest member, Miranda, was given the task of washing fruit. Meanwhile, all the bedrooms were cleaned and aired and bed linen seemed to be hanging out of every window.

"I shall put the King in Queen Elizabeth's chamber," Meraud had announced to her sister-in-law.

"Did she stay here?" Nichola had asked in wonderment, cold with the sense of England's mighty past being only a hair's breadth from her grasp.

"Yes, my father entertained her at Kingswear Hall towards the end of her reign."

"What was she like, did he say?"

"It's strange. My mother declared, she being young and beautiful herself, that the Queen wore a great red wig, had black teeth with such gaps in them that it was hard to understand what she said, and that Her Majesty's bosom, much on display, was wrinkled and low. Yet my father, equally young and discerning, swore that she was as fair as a goddess."

"What an extraordinary thing."

Meraud had laughed. "I think perhaps Elizabeth had the power to dazzle men, whereas women saw her more clearly."

"And where are you going to put the rest of the King's party?"

"I would like to use the bedrooms you are currently occupying. May I move you into Joscelin's room and put Miranda in the nursery suite?"

"Of course."

And yet it had been an eerie experience to move her things into the apartments where Joscelin had slept and worked, his laboratory presenting yet another side of her husband's many faceted personality, the man of science, the being who spent hours poring over old books and manuscripts in the pursuit of knowledge. Tossing restlessly in the bed where once he had slept, Nichola had experienced the recurring dream and had woken afraid yet full of a burning and inexplicable elation. Shaking with the power of her feelings, the girl who had been Nichola Hall had got out of bed and walked to the window.

Dawn was breaking over the Dart, the river clear and lucent in the soft, spellbinding light. Down on the banks, clearly visible from this high vantage point, presenting a far better view than Nichola had had from her old room, she could see the curving hollows made by the nests of king-fishers, the tracks left by a jolly otter, the foam of a leaping fish. And she could also see the wake in the water created by the ferry. Even at this early hour, somebody was coming across. For no reason that she could explain, Nichola threw a cloak over her nightdress and ran from the house, over the dew-filled lawns and down through the lime walk towards the river. And with every step she took she felt a lift of her heart that could mean only one thing. Wrenching open the gate, she hurried through and stared towards the stretch of gleam-ing water.

The raft was half way over, its occupant hauling him-self across as if he had been doing it all his life. The early sun picked up the gleam of black hair, the elegant shape of the shoulders as they strained against the chain.

"Joscelin?" called Nichola, her voice a shadow.

The man looked up, even though he could not possibly have heard her. And then she saw the gleam of a smile lighten that dark mischievous face.

"Oh thank God," she said, not sobbing with relief as she had imagined she would be when this joyful moment came, but instead brimful with bliss. Rushing on to the landing stage, Nichola stood with her arms outstretched, waiting for the man from the seventeenth century who had taught her what it was to love.

They exchanged no words, only a kiss that seemed to last

for all those centuries. Then, having tethered his horse to the post, Joscelin walked up to the house with her, his arm round Nichola's waist, dashing his hat from his head as they entered the great hall, turning to look at her in its dim and shadowy light.

"I have imagined seeing you here so often," he said. "The mistress of Kingswear Hall, finally in her rightful place."

"Oh my darling," Nichola answered, "I have imagined being here with you so often, all the while hoping against hope."

"Don't speak of it now, we have days in which to catch up with everything. Let me simply tell you, without explanation, that I have rejoined the King's troops and that His Majesty will be here in a few hours."

"I won't say another word," answered Nichola. And she kissed him again, in the Hall of his father's house, wishing they could be alone together instead of in the midst of the bevy of delighted people who at any moment were bound to burst enthusiastically in upon them.

They had had no time for private conversation after that. Just as Nichola had imagined, they had been seen returning to the house and several of the servants had come running, others being despatched to wake the Lady Meraud and her niece. Then there had been uproar as Joscelin's sister had hurried in, flushed and pretty-looking, in fact so markedly changed in appearance that my Lord had shot Nichola an amused and quizzical glance. Of course Sabina had made a wonderful entrance, sinking to her knees in front of her father and repeatedly kissing his hand. Somewhat sickened, Nichola had been forced to look away, catching Caradoc's eye as she did so, and just for a moment their expressions must have been apparent before they quickly masked what they were thinking for Joscelin's sake.

Then there had been further celebrations as every member of the household had been called in to drink a toast, and by the time all this had been done and the place made ready once more, the King and his generals had arrived.

It had been a day which Nichola felt she would never forget, as the full import of what was happening had come home to her. She, who had once been Nichola Hall, was acting as hostess to that small grave-faced man, the creamy lace of his collar and cuffs resplendent against a suit of wine coloured velvet, who was to become known to history as King Charles, the first to bear that name, the man who was later to be called the Martyr. As they had walked on the river terrace after dining, his head covered by a wide-brimmed feathered hat, the single pearl earring he wore pale against his long hair, a sense of unreality had swept over her as the King turned to smile.

And he must have noticed something of this reaction for Charles had said, "You look startled, Lady Attwood. Is anything amiss?"

"No, Sir. I was simply thinking how strange everything is."

"You mean the miraculous return of your husband?"

"That – and other things, Majesty," Nichola had answered, and would not be drawn further.

Evening had brought a lighting of fires, precluded earlier because of the warmth of the fruit-scented day, together with the sound of musicians and jovial laughter. There had been a gay informal atmosphere and even the abstemious King had taken a little too much to drink. And then, amidst the sound of contented drowsiness, the company had broken up, repairing to their various rooms, the King to the Queen's Chamber, and she and Joscelin had at last been alone.

They had lain side by side in the candlelight, staring up at the bed's green damask tester, lined with the finest sarsenet, and felt the glow of companionship, the harmony of being together once more.

"Are you tired?" Nichola had asked.

He had turned his head towards her, his hair dark against the white of his nightshirt. "Aye, too tired even to play the husband's role I fear. Do you forgive me?"

She reached for his hand and brought it up to touch her cheek. "We have all the time in the world for that." Then a chill of fear had gone through her. "At least I hope we have."

"Why do you say that?"

"Only because I sometimes get nervous. Pay no heed to it. Just tell me, because I won't sleep otherwise, how you got away from Marston Moor and how you came to lose your ring, which I now return to you."

And Nichola had taken Joscelin's signet ring from the chain on which she had worn it round her neck and slipped it back on to his little finger.

"The answer is very simple as far as the ring goes. It fell off during the battle, so smeared with blood and sweat were my murdering hands. The miracle is that it was discovered at all amongst so much filth and on such terrible ground."

"That was Caradoc's doing. Yet he searched and searched, hour after hour, and still found no trace of you."

"That was because I lay beneath a pile of bodies, some dead, some dying. I was covered with the blood and urine of my companions, and was quite unrecognisable I should imagine. I would have died myself, not from my wounds which were slight, but from the terrible conditions I was in. Then an extraordinary thing happened. With the scavengers, who crept on to the field like rats as soon as they thought it was safe, came a man whom I thought at first to be one of their number. He drove a cart and on to it heaved those of us who showed any sign of life. Then he drove away, not to murder and rob us after all, but to hide us while he restored those of us he could save to health."

"How extraordinary. Was he some kind of doctor?"

"No, not he. Just a gypsy fellow with a face hard as leather. He had no allegiances either, because he took both Cavaliers and Roundheads on to his wagon. He applied those herbs and potions his Romany people must have taught him to use. And at night, while we lay in his hovel, he would sing to us or play on his tin whistle. A strange being to whom I owe my life."

"You say he played a tin whistle?" said Nichola incredulously.

"Yes, why?"

"Did he have a colourful name, this man?"

Joscelin laughed in the shadows. "It was Ditch. Emerald Ditch."

"Then there is a strange thread running through this," Nichola answered wonderingly. "For I met him at Oxford when he was telling fortunes for those who dared to venture to his dwelling at Wolvercote."

Her husband stared at her. "How odd that you should know him, too. And what did he say to you when he read this future of yours?"

"That I won't want to go back," answered Nichola sleepily, insinuating herself into Joscelin's arms, suddenly tired out.

"Back where?" he asked softly.

"Just back," she said, and kissed his cheek.

That morning found both partners in the marriage which spanned three hundred years, ready to consummate their love once more. It began with kisses, kisses that flowed from mouth to hips and slowly back again. And then Nichola and Joscelin touched each other deliciously, taking a phial containing attar of damask roses and rubbing the contents into one another's bodies in a slow and sensual way. "Sweet life, but I've wanted you," he whispered, close to her ear.

But she could not speak, holding on to him, pressing the soles of her feet against his thighs, as her husband pounded to culmination, then lay between her breasts gasping with joy. Nichola, though, was not satisfied as yet and still clung to him, eager for more. And as the sun came into the room, throwing pools of light behind the curtains, Joscelin took her again, his seed flowing into her as she had never known it do before.

"That was incredible," she breathed.

"And for me, for you are the woman I have been seeking all my life," Joscelin replied quietly, and held her closely against his heart.

Two days later, Charles Stuart and his generals, the genial Lord Digby trotting at his side, left Kingswear Hall and set out for Salisbury. The King had granted Joscelin a fortnight's leave of absence by way of a gift, though with the injunction that my Lord should join him and Prince Rupert in Sherborne in Dorset at the beginning of October.

"And I pray you enjoy this time with your wife," His Majesty added as he made his farewells.

"It will be the happiest two weeks I have ever spent," Joscelin answered as they waved the royal party farewell and turned back to the house.

"Wasn't that a little fulsome?" Nichola said, laughing.

"No, I meant it. But delightful though the time will be, there is still something important I intend to do in the coming days."

"And what is that?"

"To solve your mystery," Joscelin answered, his face suddenly serious.

"What mystery?" asked Nichola cautiously.

"You know full well, my dear. The fact that you call yourself Nichola as well as Arabella, the odd mistake you made when first I met you and you let slip that you were in your twenties, the terror you are sometimes subject to when you dream. All along I have called you witch wife, for you sometimes seem to know what is going to happen next. And now it is my intention to find out why."

She looked at him earnestly, placing her hands on his arms as if she could restrain him in some way. "Joscelin, I beg you not to do this. There are some things that are beyond even your comprehension, and I could not bear it if this determination to discover them caused a rift between us."

"But how could that be?" Joscelin answered. "My one aim

is to help you. I want to find out the cause of your nightmares and relieve you of their burden. Nichola, Arabella, wife, we live in an age of discovery, impeded though it might be by this damnable war. How do you know that I will not understand what it is you reveal to me?"

"Because I do," Nichola replied desperately. "Leave it alone, Joscelin. No good will come out of this."

"Let me be the judge of that," he answered firmly, and taking her by the elbow propelled her up the stairs and into his laboratory.

It was as mysterious as an alchemist's den, lined with shelves on which stood rows of jars, made of both glass and earthenware, their contents highly coloured pastes and liquids, to say nothing of oil of *prima materia*. Retorts and crucibles crowded alembics, the early form of distilling apparatus, and matrasses, the long necked chemical flasks, while on a central table stood a pestle and mortar, scales and an oil lamp, a pewter pan lying beside it. There were books everywhere, on the floor and piled on yet more shelves, some of them very ancient, others bound in opulent leather.

"My God!" exclaimed Nichola, staring round.

"You have not been in here before?"

"No. It seemed an intrusion somehow."

One mobile brow flew up. "Was that stroke meant for me?"

"It wasn't as it happens, but if you think it describes the situation, who am I to disagree?"

He smiled, gently taking hold of her hands. "Nichola, if you want me to stop now, I will. I have no wish to invade your private territory."

She paused uncertainly and turning from her, Joscelin struck a tinder and lit the oil lamp, placing the pan upon it and measuring some coloured liquid into a jug before pouring it in and setting it to heat.

"What are you doing?" Nichola asked, intrigued and curious.

"Following an old recipe for a sleeping draught. I thought

that if I could not cure your bad dreams any other way this, at least, might help you."

Nichola shook her head and slumped down on the bench that stood beside the table. "We will never be at ease together unless I tell you everything, I can see that. But please be warned that by the time I have finished speaking you will think me totally insane."

Joscelin smiled. "I doubt it."

"Then so be it," said Nichola miserably. For how could one explain to a man who would not even understand the meaning of the word hypnosis exactly what had happened on the fateful night of Lewis's party? Completely uncertain as to where she should begin, Nichola sat in silence.

"Who is Lewis?" her husband said suddenly, taking her totally by surprise.

"Why do you ask?"

"Because you sometimes call his name in your sleep."

"He's the cause of everything really," she answered hesitantly.

"Then tell me about him."

"That would be too simple. First I must try to explain that there exists a state which can be induced by one person but which affects another. In this state the subject is asleep yet awake, can talk and answer questions, yet his or her sleeping mind has been released and can relive experiences from the past. The name of this effect is hypnosis."

"From Hypnos, the Greek god of sleep?"

Nichola stared at him open-mouthed. "Yes, I suppose it must be. You've heard of such a thing?"

"Not exactly, but it is not difficult to imagine."

"Then visualise one step further. The sleeping mind, having been set free and allowed to travel, is told by the instructor to go back into the past, to dredge up memories from childhood, in fact to go even beyond that and to regress to a life before childhood, before birth, to the last life it led before it died."

There was a profound silence during which Joscelin stared at her thoughtfully.

"Is it believed in such a concept that there is no heaven or hell, then? That the soul continues on a never ending journey, inhabiting body after body? That, surely, is an Eastern philosophy not a Christian belief."

"I think that there is an end, when the spirit reaches perfection. But I don't know enough to discuss it. All I'm going to tell you is this. I volunteered myself for just such an experiment. I was hypnotised, as it is called, and was told to go back in time. To put it simply, Joscelin, and this is the part that you are not going to believe, the whole thing worked only too well. My mind, soul, psyche, call it what you will, ended up in the body of a woman in labour, a woman just giving birth to a child. It was that of Arabella Loxley. From that moment on I became her, unable to get back to the century I really come from."

"And when is that?" he asked gently.

"I was alive in the year 1994. My real name is Nichola Hall and I am an actress, a woman who appears on the stage, something you have yet to see but which will come about as a theatrical reality when the present Prince of Wales ascends the throne as Charles II."

Joscelin said nothing, rising to his feet and going to one of the retorts from which he poured himself a glass of brownish liquid which he downed in a single gulp.

"Is this the truth?"

"Yes."

"You come from a time so far ahead that I would be but dust?"

"Yes, if you must put it like that."

"And you are marooned in this century like a shipwrecked sailor on a deserted isle?"

"Yes, I suppose I am."

"And Lewis, I take it, was your lover in this time?"

"He was the man who hypnotised me, who sent me back. He didn't know what he was doing, he was playing a game. That's how the mistake arose. He got me here then couldn't retrieve me."

Joscelin shook his head. "And to think I wedded and bedded you when you belonged to another, when you were a virtual prisoner with no say in the matter. How abhorrent that must have been."

"Oh for Heaven's sake," Nichola interrupted, jumping to her feet. "You just don't understand, do you? I may have got here by accident, and as God is my judge and witness I swear that is the truth, but now that I have settled, I like it. I've fallen in love with you Joscelin Attwood, only eleven years your junior as I really am, and no simpering child bride. I think you're a cracker, to use an expression you will never have heard of. I want to stay in this century and be your wife, do you hear?"

He looked at her very seriously. "Are you sure? Because if not I could learn this art, hypnosis, and try to send you home."

"But *this* is my home," said Nichola, and started to cry, racked with uncontrollable sobbing.

He folded her into his arms, stroking her hair. "But, sweetheart, I only want to do what is best for you. It is such a strange tale, such a fanciful concept that you have told me, it is hard for me to know what to say."

"Say what you would to a woman who loves you, regardless of where she comes from or who she is."

"I would tell her in that circumstance that I never want her to leave me."

"Then don't try to make me."

"Is *that* what you dream about, that you have to go away?"

"Yes, of course it is. And the more I have grown to love you the more terrible it seems. My one fear is that I will slip back by accident, back into the body that lies waiting for me, and that I will never see you again."

"God's life, Nichola," said Joscelin, the tears springing into his own eyes, "if that were to happen it would be the end of me. You may have travelled hundreds of years but so have I, in a manner of speaking. I used to dream of you, remember, and I knew then that when I found you, you would be my soul mate. That's why I wouldn't consummate our marriage all those months ago. I wanted you with love or not at all."

"And now you have me, with love and more."

"Then we must do all we can to make you stay."

Even as Nichola nodded she remembered the words of Emerald Ditch. "You will have two chances to leave. It is the man you love who will open the door for you."

"Never offer to hypnotise me again," she said passionately, certain that that had been her first chance. "It could be so dangerous."

"I swear I will not do so."

"Then perhaps we are safe," Nichola answered, holding him tightly. But somehow, in a quite intangible manner, she remained uneasy.

Chapter Twenty-five

The first severe frost of the winter of 1644 came to the Dart Valley in the middle of December, laying its pale hand on the bleakened landscape, if not the fast flowing waterway itself. For though the river continued to run deep and silent, too strong for ice to form upon its surface, its banks sparkled silver and the paths that ran alongside them glittered with rime, most treacherous to those on foot. The trees, stripped of their autumn jewels, stood dark and looming, casting harsh shadows upon the hardened earth, while at night a black sky that seemed to go on for ever was spangled by stars molten with a fiery brilliance.

The great house that stood by the water grew cold, though logs burned in all the rooms. And Nichola, walking to and fro through the corridors, wore a cloak lined with pelts of red fox and pulled a matching hood over her head when she went out of doors. Every night before she slept, alone in the big four-poster, she snuggled beneath the clothes, watching the shadowy flames dance upon her ceiling as the fire consumed the wood that had been stacked on to keep it alight through the hours of darkness. And it was at these times, despite Joscelin's absence, that she thought she had never been happier. For with each passing hour, each waking morning, she was becoming more and more convinced that she was no longer alone.

She had not menstruated for nearly three months now, the last time being a fortnight before he had come back to her, crossing the rushing river on the dawn ferry, on his journey home. And there were other signs, too. Arabella's beautiful breasts were tender to the touch, already enlarged, and Nichola remembered them as they had been when she found herself obliged to feed Miranda, at first so very much against her will. Now all she wanted to do was cuddle the child close to her, longing for the day when she could whisper in her ear that she would soon have a baby brother or sister.

Emmet, of course, already had an inkling of the truth. Helping Nichola to do up her laces, she had paused and looked at her closely. "Thy veins are blue," she had commented, and the very fact that she had used the endearment form of address had said it all. And now, with Christmas so near and Meraud so busy in the kitchens, Nichola thought that even if Joscelin were detained with the King and his court in Oxford, where they had retired as the winter campaign drew to its annual close, she had something of him with her and could enjoy the festivity more with this unknown, unseen little being.

Her husband, knowing nothing of what was happening to her, had set out to join His Majesty on the last day of September and had arrived in Sherborne on 2 October, a few hours behind the King. According to Joscelin's letter, Rupert had joined them there for a Council of War, and then His Majesty's troops had marched to Salisbury to relieve Basing House, only to find it hedged in by three enemy armies. Accordingly, the King had proceeded onwards to Donnington Castle, near Newbury.

Royalist spies had now confirmed rumours that the Parliamentary leaders were falling out among themselves. The Earl of Manchester, who disliked both Cromwell and William Waller, was becoming increasingly convinced that to continue the war was a futile gesture. The Earl of Essex, who also hated Waller, marched grimly through the pouring rain. Cromwell, who was deliberately filling the ranks of his cavalry regiments with religious fanatics and was disliked by most of his fellow commanders, had quarrelled bitterly with Major-General Lawrence Crawford, of whom he was jealous. Waller was an outspoken critic of them all.

Yet, so Nichola's husband had written, these reluctant allies had been finally forced to agree a plan to engage with the

King's troops while they still outnumbered them. Reinforcements of four London Trained Bands – those men of the capital who trained and drilled in peace time, had other trades besides soldiering, and who were originally raised to maintain law and order in the City at the behest of the Lord Mayor – were sent for, the scheme mooted to block the King's advance before Prince Rupert could rejoin him. In this manner both sides had eventually drawn up to engage in the second battle of Newbury, the first having been fought at Round Hill in 1643.

Seventeen thousand Parliamentarians had faced a Royalist army numbering less than half that amount, but the Earl of Manchester, losing all heart for war, had arrived and attacked late, with resultant heavy losses. Cromwell's cavalry were too slow and had been driven back by George Goring. Prince Maurice had then got his second wind and had flown at the Roundhead infantry, who had ended up marooned in Newbury village. At dusk the fighting had ceased and the King and his generals had sped off to Bath to rendezvous with Rupert. According to Joscelin, Sir William Waller and Sir Arthur Haselrigg had wanted to pursue Charles Stuart and call him out to battle on, but the Earl of Manchester had screamed at Sir Arthur, "Thou art a bloody fellow!" and had refused to take part. At this, the King and the Prince had moved on to Burford where, on 6 November, His Majesty had named his nephew, still a month off his twenty-fifth birthday, Commander-in-Chief. This done, they had departed in triumph, accompanied by the beating of drums, aware that Manchester had no intention of doing battle with them. Two weeks later they had marched cheerily into Oxford and thus ended the 1644 campaigning season.

"My Lord says in his letter," Nichola had told Emmet, "that the Roundhead generals were ordered by London not to go into winter quarters, but that every one of them disobeyed. All but Cromwell, of course. He wanted to continue fighting."

"He's very harsh for a man of God, isn't he?" Emmet had commented.

"I expect he prays as he kills," Nichola had answered, thinking of all the twentieth-century atrocities committed in the name of religion.

"That's not what Christ taught us, is it, though?"

"No," Nichola had answered firmly, "it most certainly is not."

By the middle of December Nichola felt positive she was pregnant. Confident enough, indeed, to mention it to Meraud. A week after the arrival of the severe chill, with rims of white by the river and frost frilling the window panes, she had therefore sought her sister-in-law out, drawing her from her household duties into Nichola's own withdrawing room and making her take a seat by the fire, then pouring her a glass of claret.

"I have some news for you," Nichola had started to say, but the sparkle in Meraud's eyes had forestalled her.

"I think I know what it is," the older woman had replied, patently glowing.

"Do you? What then?"

"You are getting plumper, my dear Arabella. I could swear that you are rounding to a child."

"I think perhaps I am," Nichola had answered, smiling.

Meraud had got to her feet, and had crossed over to her sister-in-law's chair, kissing her warmly. "What a wonderful gift for Joscelin, in fact for us all. When will the babe be born?"

"In June, I imagine. Obviously it was conceived this September..."

Meraud flushed a little.

"...so I think it will be due then."

"Round about the time of your own birthday?"

"Er ... yes," Nichola answered, never able to come to terms with the fact that she and Arabella had been born at different times of the year.

"To you, my dear," Meraud had said, and raised her glass.

They had sat in silence, looking at one another, the glow from the fire lighting their faces, echoing the contentment that both were feeling. And then, as if to break that comfortable spell, Nichola had heard a faint noise coming from Joscelin's laboratory, the door of which opened into the withdrawing room, the two rooms, together with the bed chamber, forming his own private suite.

"What was that?"

"I don't know," Meraud had answered, looking uncertain.

"It sounded like someone in the other room. I do hope it's not one of the house cats, it could cause chaos amongst all those glass vessels." And Nichola had jumped up and hurried to the door, throwing it open and staring inside.

The laboratory was in darkness, night falling early on such deep winter evenings, the only illumination coming from the window, already filled by the shimmer of frost-filled stars. Nichola tensed, peering into the gloom, then took a few cautious steps into that cavern of alchemy. And then she heard the sound of rapidly indrawn breath and the next moment something caught her a stinging blow to the head and she fell silently, glass flying as she crashed into one of the many laden shelves.

The dream came at once, cruelly, harshly, the worst she had ever known it. Her parents stood by the body, their years of mutual acrimonious dislike written all over their faces. A doctor was with them, a senior looking man, white coated and professionally grave.

". . . no hope," he was saying.

Nichola's mother gave a heaving sob at that and her daughter thought this outburst, for a woman as cold as she was, extraordinarily emotional.

"None?" asked her father.

"In my opinion, no. I would advise that the machine be . . ."

But Piers Hall, looking stiff-upper-lip, cut straight across him. "We will discuss it, that's all I can say."

"Very well," answered the doctor, frowning.

"Oh my poor body!" Nichola called out.

At that, the other her, the thing lying on the bed, suddenly seemed to shudder.

"Look!" shrieked Nichola's mother, "oh look, look, look!"

Then the scene faded, receded far away, just as if she were looking down the wrong end of a telescope, and Nichola felt a pair of arms around her and the sticky warmth of blood about her head. She opened her eyes and saw Meraud gazing at her, her expression frantic, while just behind her, storming into the laboratory like an oak tree in a gale, came Caradoc.

"What's happened, my Lady?" he was asking, gasping as if he had been running upstairs.

"I don't know, I really don't know. Lady Attwood thought she heard a noise in here and then there was the sound of splintering glass and I found her lying on the floor."

"Did someone attack her?"

Meraud looked startled. "No, of course not. She must have fainted and thus cut her head as she fell."

Caradoc pushed Meraud to one side, almost brusquely. "Here, let me lift her."

"Be careful, my Lady is with child."

"Then pray God the babe be unharmed."

And then she was up in the air, as light as a feather to that powerful young man, who carried her, cursing beneath his breath, into the bedroom and laid her carefully down on the bed.

Nichola looked at him earnestly. "There *was* someone in there," she murmured, too softly for Meraud to hear.

"Who was it?"

"I don't know. I couldn't see. Yet for sure I was struck on the head."

But her sister-in-law had come into the bed chamber and they could say no more.

"I'm going for the physician in Dartmouth," Caradoc announced forcefully, staring belligerently at Meraud.

"No, wait. It's a bitter night," she answered anxiously. "Emmet and I can treat Lady Attwood ourselves."

"If anything happens to her or her baby it will be our

responsibility. That's Lord Joscelin's child she's carrying, remember that. May I take the carriage?" he added, just as if he hadn't heard her.

"Of course. But be careful. The ways are like sheets of glass."

"And you be careful of your charge, Lady Meraud. I am her guardian in my master's absence. Make sure that she is not left by herself."

She stared at him. "What are you hinting at?"

"I don't know quite. All I ask is that my Lady is attended."

Then he was gone, hurling out of the room and leaping down the great staircase several steps at a time. As the sound of his footsteps died away, Meraud sighed.

"What a strange young man he is, but I suppose he's right. I'll get Emmet to sleep in the room with you." And with that she rang the bell for the servant to attend them.

Things began to blur and slip after that, the shadows in the room growing denser, the firelight gleaming on the oak of the bed and its elaborate hangings. Just for a moment it seemed to Nichola that she was alone and unguarded, and that one of the shadows detached itself from the far corner and came to stand by the bed, gazing down at her with a look of such intense hatred that Nichola literally shivered with fear. It was Sabina, as drained of colour as ever, her glacial eyes alight with loathing.

"Go away," Nichola whispered, "go away, go away."

Then Emmet stirred in the chair by the fire and called, "What is it, Mistress?" and the shadow slipped from the room, as quietly as it had come in.

The next thing she remembered was that the physician was there, kindly and rather ignorant as they all were, but at least bringing with him a rosy little woman who laid her hands on Nichola's abdomen, then felt between her legs for any trace of blood, and finally announced that the babe was safe at present but that my Lady must rest.

"Is there really a baby there?" Nichola asked her with as much trust as if she were addressing a modern qualified midwife.

"Aye, there is, my Lady."

"Then how big is it?"

"Big enough."

"Big as a nutmeg?" Nichola persisted.

"Nay, big as a pear."

Nichola had smiled at that and fallen asleep, her drink laced with the dried juice of poppy seeds, and this time she did not dream at all.

When she woke again it was to see a bright white day and frost patterning the windows. Emmet had obviously gone off duty and now it was Meraud who stood looking out, turning swiftly as Nichola called her name.

"My dear, how do you feel?"

"I've a thumping headache, but other than that no ill-effects."

"Then God be praised. Here, let me help you sit up. The physician is still in the house, it being too cold and too late for him to return last night."

"Does he want to see me again?"

"Oh yes, I'll warn him that you can receive him soon."

Nichola smiled at her sister-in-law. "Would you mind if Emmet helped me get ready? There's something I want to say to her."

"Not in the least. I'll go and see if she's awake. She sat up all night with you."

"Then perhaps you shouldn't bother her."

"I doubt she's more than dozing. She's extremely concerned for your welfare, as is Caradoc."

And with that Meraud bustled away, leaving Nichola alone once more. But this time there was no shadow, in fact nothing sinister at all, and Nichola was just beginning to wonder if she had imagined the whole episode when Emmet came in, her face pale and her oddly coloured eyes darting round the room.

"Are you safe?" she asked in an undertone.

"Yes, why?"

"I spoke with Caradoc last night. He said you believed you had been attacked."

"I was, there can be no doubt of it. And then I thought I saw Sabina."

Emmet looked thoughtful. "Caradoc didn't say that, but then of course he wouldn't, would he?"

"You know about him and the girl?"

"Of course I do."

And the servant described, rather graphically, how she had come across the pair of them in the woods, Sabina sitting in Caradoc's hands, her legs on either side of his thighs, he wearing nothing but a shirt, lunging and plunging into her as wildly as a mating stallion.

"Did they see you?"

"Of course not. They were too busy about their business."

"They've been lovers for years, apparently. He is utterly besotted with her, you know."

"But not so besotted that he isn't alarmed. He told me, quite fiercely at that, to keep you under my eye."

Nichola fell back against the pillows. "Why do you think she's doing this?"

"Because you're expecting a babe, Mistress. She thinks she might well be cut out."

"Of Joscelin's affection?"

Emmet gave a contemptuous snort. "I shouldn't think she gives a tinkard's culls about that. No, her sole preoccupation will be with her inheritance."

"But this house is entailed."

"It's the gelt she's worried about. Another child and her marriage portion could be less."

"If she marries well, would that matter?"

"Mistress, thou art a fool!" Emmet exclaimed impatiently. "With all the great families tearing at one another in this war, what will be left for girls to marry? Old men and enfeebled boys. The rest are probably dead upon the battleground."

"Meraud said something like that."

"Because it's the truth. I think it would suit Sabina right well to see you and the child you carry, out of the way for good. Then she can go back to all she enjoys. Ruling this house and family unhindered."

Nichola put her arms round the girl's waist, where she sat beside her on the bed. "Then we must be very careful. I really want this baby, Emmet. I know I hated the idea of having children once. But that was in the past, before I met Joscelin."

Emmet stared at her. "You're rambling again. When the betrothal bed of you and Michael bore fruit, you didn't seem to care."

"Ah well," Nichola answered hastily. "I was very young then."

"Oh, just you stand mum, Arabella!" Emmet exclaimed briskly, and with that she set about helping her mistress to rise and prepare for the visit of the physician.

Towards Christmas it grew even colder, though no snow fell. On Christmas Eve, celebrated on 5 January under the Julian calendar, Meraud had yule logs brought into the great hall and their heat most certainly warmed the company of masters, servants and guests who drank hot punch and toasted the Yuletide. Nichola, fully recovered by now, had cherished hopes of Joscelin's return almost until this moment, but the worsening weather had finally convinced her that he would remain in Oxford to keep his Christmas with the King. Standing by Meraud, only too aware of Sabina's shimmering presence on her left-hand side, Nichola raised her glass with the others and drank to the eve of the Nativity. Then, this done, all sat down to feast before going to the chapel, set in the grounds of the mansion house, to pray as midnight came.

There were still faint signs of Popery, of the things that Parliament and all it stood for had turned against. When the events which had finally led to the Civil War had yet been fermenting, Canterbury Cathedral had been cruelly vandalised, the window images of Becket and the Virgin the first to suffer desecration. Then later, from all over the Kingdom, had come reports of other outrages, of altar rails being ripped, of altars overturned. In one church the parishioners had kicked the communion bread from out of the curate's hand, using it as a football in the chancel. In another, the

Church of the Holy Sepulchre without Newgate, a mother had mouthed encouragement while her child passed urine on the communion table.

And Nichola, modern woman, learning of it, thinking of it, had once again been sickened by the evils of sectarianism. So this, then, had been the work of those who had found God, the zealous Puritans, Mr Cromwell among them, who wished to bring the people out of darkness and into their own perceived image of the light.

Yet in the gentle, careful service conducted by a minister of the Church of England who then suggested that the congregation should each go to his stable to see the cattle kneel, Nichola had found some consolation and the act of communion, conducted almost covertly, had for the first time become an uplifting experience.

However, the fact that Sabina sat in the same pew, clad in scarlet, a colour completely at odds with her glorious hair and for that very reason wildly exciting, served to cast a dark reflection over that cold crystalline midnight. Holding her hand to her body, as if to protect the precious life that was growing within, Nichola had walked back through the starlight, gripping Meraud's arm, aware of the present that was the past, of the past that was the future, and wondering where within the bold sweep of the universe, one truly began and the other ended.

Chapter Twenty-six

The first days of the New Year, 1655, had seen a wave of unbelievable cruelty perpetuated by the puritanical men of Parliament. First to go to the block had been Archbishop Laud, who would have made a dignified exit had it not been for the interference of a swaggering Irishman, suitably named, or so Nichola had thought reading Joscelin's latest letter, Sir John Clotworthy. This despicable being had actually pushed his way on to the scaffold to try to trick the Archbishop into eternally damning himself. But to all his bullying, Laud had merely replied, "I have always lived in the Protestant religion as established in England and in that I come here now to die." Then he had laid his head upon the block and escaped Sir John's vile attentions.

A few days later, Henry Morse, a Roman Catholic who had worked amongst the poor and plague-ridden of London, had been awarded a traitor's death for his beliefs. He had been stripped and hanged, his body suffered to swing naked before it had finally been lowered. His heart had been torn from his flesh, his entrails burnt and his body quartered. The huge crowd, witnessing the acts of those who took issue against these individuals in the name of their God, had remained silent. Though the Lord Mayor had gone as far as to apologise to both the French and Spanish ambassadors that they had seen so savage a thing. "My Lords," he had said, "I regret that you should have witnessed such a spectacle, but such are our miseries that it must be done."

Nichola had read these particular pages of the letter and thought of the ethnic cleansing of Bosnia and realised for the millionth time that nothing ever changed.

The harsh and bloody winter had seemed to drag on interminably after this hideous start, but spring had finally come to the Dart Valley and wild violets and daffodils had once again swept the banks of the river. Sitting in her favourite spot beside the cascading fountain, Nichola had read and re-read Joscelin's letter.

> My beloved Nichola, how strange it must be for you to carry the child of a man who, in your terms, has long since departed from this world. Yet your experience makes me question the whole concept of time. Is it possible that somewhere, still, the mighty beasts of the past are roaring in the primeval swamp? The more I think about it the less certain I am. Yet of one thing I *am* positive. My love for you may cross centuries but, for all that, is the strongest emotion ever to confront me. I earnestly pray that you remain in good health and are happy throughout your pregnancy and confinement. Please be aware that I would sacrifice years of my life in order to be at your side.

Nichola had smiled and wept, echoing the month of April, then had read on.

> There is much news to give you. The King has sent the Prince of Wales forth from Oxford to set up his own court in Bristol. His Highness left here during the first week of March, large, lusty and immoderately lively, his companions Edward Hyde and John Culpeper. It is widely rumoured that the Prince's virginity is a thing of the past and judging by the look in those brilliant black eyes of his, I tend to believe it. Meanwhile, the enemy sent a peace delegation to Oxford, upon which the Princes Rupert and Maurice looked with supercilious contempt. Nothing will come of these negotiations I fear.
>
> The reports from London are that Parliament has recently passed a Self-Denying Ordinance which obliges Members to lay down their military commands. The Earls of Essex and Manchester have complied, not without a great deal of

> wailing on behalf of the former. Friend Cromwell, naturally, is havering, but as it is an open secret that he would be recommissioned at once, as Fairfax's Lieutenant-General of Horse, such reticence makes a mockery of the entire Ordinance. It is commonly said that Cromwell's role at Westminster is now something of an embarrassment. All this while George Goring has been leading both him and Sir William Waller a merry dance in the west.

Joscelin had added a post script: "Parliament's new army, under Fairfax, is to be called the New Model. Here in Oxford we call it the New Doddle."

Nichola had folded the letter up and sat in silence, listening to the soothing sound of the bubbling waters. At that moment the war seemed a thousand miles away, the atmosphere in the gardens of Kingswear Hall outwardly so calm and so tranquil. And yet she was well aware that this was merely an impression, for the mansion once again possessed that air of brooding menace which she had sensed on her arrival. Very subtly yet very surely, ever since the night of the accident in the laboratory, everything had changed.

Meraud, though not giving up the little artifices which had so enhanced her appearance, had reverted to her former role of busy housekeeper, companionable with Nichola, daily asking after her welfare, yet avoiding the intimate chats which had started to bind her sister-in-law and herself so closely together.

"It's as if she is avoiding me," Nichola had said to Emmet. "Is it because she fears the truth?"

"Aye, that's for sure. She brought that bitch Sabina up and now can't bear to face reality about the girl."

"Poor Meraud," Nichola had answered, and meant it.

Yet the omnipresent cloud which hung over them all had affected Caradoc in a different way. He had now become conspicuous by his presence. Almost without anyone noticing, he had got into the habit of shadowing Nichola wherever she went, making it quite clear that he had taken the threat to her safety very seriously indeed. It was unnerving, knowing that even if she could not see him he was around somewhere, silently observing.

I've got a minder! she had thought.

And yet in a way this was a relief. Emmet had given her opinion that Sabina was merely biding her time before she made another attempt to rid herself of her two rivals, her stepmother and the unborn child destined to be her brother or sister. And indeed there had been a minor incident at Christmas. An incident which could have been a coincidence and yet which had raised alarming questions in Nichola's mind.

A dish of sweetmeats had been the cause, a dish left lying beside the silver punch bowl, garlanded with holly and ivy and long red ribbons and constantly topped up with its spicy contents, enhanced by the roasted apples stuck with cloves that floated within. Nichola had taken a bite from one of the sweets but its strangely bitter taste had been repellent to her and she had thrown the rest of it on to the fire. Nevertheless that night she had suffered severe stomach pains and had vomited violently. Of course, the upset had been blamed on her pregnancy, but when she had gone downstairs next morning it was to hear that one of Meraud's spaniels, a greedy old soul of nearly fourteen years, had died in the small hours. The odd thing was that the dog had been lying in the great hall beside the empty dish of sweetmeats, which it had presumably knocked over, then scoffed.

"God's heart!" Emmet had said, her eyes widening. "Did you not eat one of those last night, Mistress?"

"I had a quarter of one then threw the rest away."

"I reckon you owe your life to that."

"But they can't have been poisoned. I mean anyone could have taken one, even Caradoc."

"Perhaps he was warned."

"I won't think along those lines," Nichola had answered firmly. "One could suspect everybody and go quite mad."

Emmet had narrowed her eyes. "Maybe only the green ones were tampered with."

"Why do you say that?"

"Because anyone who has observed you will have noticed that you always take a green sweet if there is one available."

The logic and truth of this had set alarm bells ringing in Nichola's head and she had not helped herself to sweets or fruit thereafter. Yet since then, whether because of her own precautions or whether just by chance, there had been no further misadventures. The remark about Caradoc had worried her, though, and Nichola often caught herself wondering whether to trust him or not.

Despite his apparent loyalty to Joscelin's wife, despite the fact he constantly watched over her, Nichola knew perfectly well that his affair with Sabina was continuing. It seemed to her that they nugged, to use Emmet's basic word, everywhere; in all the secret places of the house and garden, some of which were not quite secret enough. She was beginning to tire of the glimpse of thrusting buttocks and the cries of culmination. And in the end, when she was particularly tired one day, when the child seemed extra heavy, when she was missing Joscelin and just beginning to wonder what she was doing in this ridiculous situation, Nichola finally snapped.

She had been sitting in the long gallery, one wet and dismal afternoon, trying her hand at some tapestry work and realising, much to her surprise, that she really was quite good at it. Seated at the far end by the windows to get as much light as she could, she had not at first noticed the figure that had appeared in one of the wide arches giving access to the gallery, standing one hundred and forty feet away as it was. Yet some slight movement must have attracted her attention, for Nichola had looked up and peered down the length of the enormous room.

Sabina was instantly recognisable by the waterfall of her smoky red hair, by the pallor of her ivory skin. Today, the girl wore hyacinth blue, a perfect colour for her, and as she stood, silent and watchful, Nichola found herself thinking how beautiful her stepdaughter was, and was at once reminded of the vivid and glorious markings of an adder.

Sabina had turned to go but Nichola had called out, "No, don't leave. I want to talk to you."

Just for a second the girl had hesitated, torn between ignoring the summons or exercising common politeness. In the end some innate sense of duty must have won, for Sabina turned back again and began to walk down the gallery towards the place where Nichola sat. She moved silently, the only sound the rustle of her dress, and her gait was that of a stalking cat, controlled, elegant yet prepared at any moment to let loose its violent power. When she came to within a foot or two of her stepmother, Sabina halted and dropped a straight-backed curtsey, her eyes never leaving Nichola's face.

"Yes?" she said.

It occurred to Nichola at that moment that this was the first time she and Sabina had ever actually spoken without someone else being present and she smiled in as pleasant a way as she could manage.

"Why don't you take a seat? We could move nearer the fire if you prefer."

"I am quite happy standing," Sabina answered, her eyes still keeping their strangely hypnotic regard. "What is it you wanted to say to me?"

"I would like to talk about our relationship," Nichola threw at her, hoping to see the girl react.

Sabina regarded her impassively. "It is that of stepmother and daughter, is it not? I hope I do my duty in this regard. All I believe that can be expected of me is to show you respect. Have I not done so?"

"You have always been polite."

"Then do you have any other cause for complaint?"

It was on the tip of Nichola's tongue to say, "Yes. It's simply that you're trying to kill me", but she controlled the urge. Deciding to play Sabina's game, she said with an utterly expressionless face, "I feel, my dear, that your politeness could be extended a fraction further."

"What exactly do you mean, Madam?"

"That you could conceal the fact of your liaison with Caradoc just a little more cleverly. For a girl of your intelligence, I am frankly astounded as to just how careless you can be."

Sabina's face bleached from ivory to snow and Nichola saw that it was the insult to her intellect that had hurt her more than the realisation that she had been discovered.

There were a few moments of silence while the girl considered her answer, then she said, "I am of marriageable age, in fact well over the age of consent. I confess that I have pleasured myself with a servant – many a lady does so and most certainly that fashion will continue in the future – but I regret that I have been indiscreet. It will not happen again, I assure you."

"You mean you are going to give him up?"

The cold blue eyes glittered ice. "Whether I do or not is hardly your affair, is it? I am in control of my life and as long as it does not affect yours, I cannot see why you are concerning yourself."

It was so much like an answer that she might have given her own stepmother at eighteen, that Nichola felt her blood grow chill. All of a sudden she was blustering.

"I think it is your father who should be considered, not I. How would he like it if he knew just how badly you behaved?"

"I would imagine, Madam," said Sabina, her freezing glance penetrating Nichola's soul, "that you have been a woman of varied experience in your time. Perhaps he would not like to hear about that either."

"What are you inferring?"

"Caradoc mentioned, in all innocence, how you had had a child by one of the Roundhead captains. And how that very captain returned to the place where you were living. Don't tell me that you did not enjoy him again. I have a woman's instinct about these things and can just imagine you playing the whore."

Nichola rose to her feet. "How dare you, you evil little slut."

"I've hit home I see. Well, my dear Stepmother, I'll make a bargain with you. I'll keep my lips sealed about your adultery if you will do likewise about my intrigue."

Sabina had almost got the better of her and Nichola was aware that she had gone red in the face. "My adultery, as you call it, was in fact no such thing. It occurred before your father and I had consummated our marriage and he now knows all about it. You cannot blackmail me with that, my dear."

"But there's something of which you *are* ashamed, for all that," said Sabina, and the vixen grinned within her face. "I feel it. And I know that if I question Caradoc hard enough he will let the information slip. You'll not outwit me, Madam, be assured of that."

Nichola took a deep breath and regained her poise. "You may run to your father with all the salacious tales you wish, but there is one thing you still haven't taken into consideration."

"And what is that?" asked Sabina, glowing like a Christmas rose.

"The fact that you are trying to kill me and I know it. You are not just a depraved little bitch you are also a potential murderer."

A muscle twitched by the girl's eye. "Do you think Lord Joscelin would believe one word of your slanderous ravings?"

"If you put me to the test, I intend to find out," Nichola answered, and with that she carefully put down her embroidery and, walking past Sabina, traversed the entire length of the long gallery without giving her another glance.

She supposed in retrospect that she had probably put her life in even greater danger and Emmet, on hearing the story, grew very grave. Nichola would have liked to have run to Meraud, to Caradoc even, and to have asked for their advice. However, considerations of kindness, of relationships formed that must not be jeopardised, began to weigh heavy with her and she kept her own counsel. And yet, through all that treacherous April, Nichola hardly knew a moment's peace.

The news from the front, still faithfully reported by Caradoc and by the sporadic letters received from Joscelin, did little to raise her spirits. The Committee for Both Kingdoms, the name by which the organising body of the Parliamentarians was known, had sent Fairfax, he of the triangular eyebrows, to relieve the siege of Taunton, and Sir Thomas had duly marched westwards at the end of April. Cromwell, meanwhile, was patrolling Oxfordshire, confiscating every draught horse he could find. Despite his presence the King and Rupert, together with Lord Joscelin Attwood, had managed to slip out of Oxford to rendezvous with George Goring at Stow-on-the-Wold. Thus, the eve of May Day had seen all the enemies out of their headquarters, busy at various locations throughout the country.

"It's getting near the date of my confinement," Nichola had said to Emmet that night, feeling the size of her abdomen and suddenly growing alarmed.

"When do you think the child is due?"

"It must be by the middle of June at the latest."

"Aye, if you count up from September when Lord Joscelin was here."

"Do you realise that that was the last time I saw him?"

"I do indeed. Now just you be careful, my Lady. I reckon that baby could well be born on 16 June, your own twenty-first birthday."

"I wish I knew a bit more about the mechanics of labour," Nichola had found herself saying thoughtlessly.

"You'll remember when the time comes," Emmet had answered briskly. "Anyway, I'll be with you. 'Twas me that revived you after Miranda's birth, if you recall."

"You and Bill Cosby both," Nichola had said, smiling.

"Now don't start. You'd best get some rest if you're going to rise early to gather flowers with me."

"I might not," Nichola had answered, giving a lazy yawn. "I'll come if I wake up in time."

"Very well. I won't disturb you."

And with that Emmet, old friend that she was, had kissed her mistress goodnight.

It was the custom on the first day of May for all young men and maidens, who did not always return home as innocent as they had left, to go into the woods before dawn to pick flowers and branches to decorate the house. Nichola, waking early and remembering from her days at Haseley Court how much Emmet enjoyed this kind of thing, had gone to the window only to see the servant already stealing out of doors. Opening the casement, she had called out, "Wait for me!" and Emmet had looked upwards.

"Well, hurry then, Mistress. I want to wash my face in morning dew. Half an hour more and it will all be dried away," she had shouted back.

"I won't be a few minutes."

The heavy burden of pregnancy, the fact that she was living a sparrow's life with no husband and few friends, to say nothing of the feeling of being under constant threat, had vanished, and Nichola felt more like her old self. Putting on a flowing shift, one of the most comfortable things to wear in her present condition, she had gone out into the morning.

It was almost conventionally fine, the sky rose pink and full of early bird song, the grass lush and wet where they walked.

"Let's go barefoot," suggested Emmet, giggling. "Here, I'll make thee a daisy chain, Mistress."

And with that she had taken off her shoes and started to pick the little white flowers, not yet opened by the sun's rays.

"Where are we heading?" asked Nichola, doing likewise.

"I thought to the woodlands that go down to the water's edge. There's a profusion of wild flowers there."

"Shall we walk through the gardens?"

"Aye, that will be a pleasant path to go."

They had set off via the grounds, traversing the paved river terrace and making their way towards the formal garden. Drenched with early light, the tall yew hedges which enclosed it threw indigo shadows on to the lawns which swept downhill to the river, striking a slightly menacing note on such a lighthearted morning. For no reason at all, Nichola quickened her pace very slightly.

There were two entrances to the garden, one giving access to the house and the outbuildings, the other to a path leading down to the river, both entrances consisting of a tall iron gateway set in a stone arch, flanked on either side by the high yew hedges. Yet as Nichola put her hand on to the latch which clicked the gate open, she distinctly heard the sound of the far gate being similarly set ajar.

She turned to look at Emmet. "Who's about at this hour of the dawn?"

"Somebody else going a-maying, I suppose," Emmet answered uneasily.

"Did you see who it was?"

"No."

Shrugging her shoulders slightly, Nichola opened the gate wide and went within, her eyes taking in the lovely complex pattern of the garden, a dazzling kaleidoscope of interlocking flower beds bordered with low hedges, fanning out from the circular centre, in which stood two shaded marble seats. The cascade, though the pivotal feature of the garden, was not centrally placed but had been created over an artificial rock staircase, down which the water rippled and shimmered as it tumbled into the large basin beneath, sending plumes of spray back into the air under the weight of its impact. Around this artificial waterfall the atmosphere was always cool, dewed by the veils of foam which rolled constantly below. And this morning, with the early sun reflecting on them, it seemed to Nichola that these same sheets of water had been transformed into bales of silver taffeta, each one shot with iridescent rainbow colours. Just for a moment she stood listening to the fountain's soothing sound, admiring the beauty of her surroundings, and then her eye was drawn to the pool at the cascade's foot and she suddenly started to run forward, as quickly as her bulky body would allow. For there, unbelievably, floating in the water, her golden hair spread out around her, was Miranda.

Afterwards, Nichola supposed she must have acted out of pure instinct. Leaning over the rim of the basin, she grabbed Arabella's daughter by the heels and swung her out, holding the child upside down so that the lungs would empty themselves of the fluid that was filling them. Then, she flung both herself and Miranda flat and gave the child the kiss of life, pulling the girl's tongue forward and pushing her head back, jaw upwards.

"Oh my God, is she dead?" shrieked Emmet.

Nichola could not answer as she applied cardiac massage, giving eight hard pushes on to Miranda's breastbone, then once again frantically administering artificial respiration. And it was at that moment, without a word, that Emmet suddenly sped off, sprinting across the garden and out of the far gate as if the hound of hell were in hot pursuit of her. Too nonplussed to wonder why, Nichola continued to try to revive the child that she had almost brought into the world. Then she saw the chest wall rise of its own accord and, spluttering and coughing up more water, Miranda came back from the brink of death.

"Oh my darling, my baby," said Nichola, rocking her to and fro, "how did this happen to you? What were you doing up so early on your own?"

Too weak to speak, Miranda merely looked at her, and it was then that Nichola knew the truth. The child had not fallen into the water at all, she had been deliberately pushed. A recollection of the far gate clicking came back and Nichola could almost see the murderous figure, its horrible task accomplished, hurrying through the river entrance and making its way down to the Dart, to be well away from the scene by the time the tragic little body was discovered.

"Sabina," she said certainly, and knew that Emmet had come to the same conclusion and gone in pursuit.

Moving awkwardly, not quite sure how best to rise, Nichola got to her feet, still holding Miranda in her arms, and turned back towards the house, walking slowly through the intricate pattern of the lovely flower beds. Then from somewhere hidden, somewhere that Nichola judged to be near the river bank, she distinctly heard Emmet give a shriek. Torn between her instinct to get help for the child and the urge to go to her servant's assistance, Nichola hesitated, then hurried towards the house as quickly as her aching limbs would permit. Whether Meraud, too, had risen early to go flower gathering, Nichola was not sure, but as she left the garden behind her, to her relief she could see that her sister-in-law was not only out of bed but standing on the river terrace, her attention also caught by the scream.

"Meraud," Nichola called to her, "for God's sake help me. Somebody tried to drown Miranda but I found her just in time. She must be put to bed, though; she must be nursed and cherished. Here." And without waiting for an answer she bundled the pathetic child into Meraud's arms and, going past her sister-in-law, hurried down the lime walk towards the river.

The gate leading to the landing stage stood open, as if somebody had been there before her, and Nichola plunged through it and on to the jetty, staring out over the rushing Dart. The ferry was half way across the river, though by what means Nichola was not quite certain, as neither of the two people aboard seemed as if they could have heaved it this far. For rolling on its wooden platform, striking one another as harshly and cruelly as any men, were Emmet and Sabina, engaged in what looked like a fight to the death.

Nichola stood watching helplessly, her child leaping wildly within, unable to do anything to help her servant who was definitely getting the worst of it, her face raked by nails, bleeding copiously, her legs and genitals subjected to a flurry of vicious kicks. And then Sabina's intentions suddenly became horribly clear. Slowly and systematically, she was pushing

Emmet towards the edge and it seemed that there was nothing anyone could do to stop her.

"Leave her alone," screamed Nichola, "I can see what you're up to. I'll bear witness against you, you murderous bitch."

But Sabina ignored her, or rather seemed to grow worse at the warning. Swinging her fist into Emmet's face, she rendered the girl practically unconscious. Nichola longed to look away, then, dreading the moment when her servant would be tipped into the water and wondering if she would have the strength to jump in and save her. In fact she was almost hiding her eyes as Sabina stood up, hauled the ferry into the centre of the river, the deepest part, then quite casually kicked Emmet off the raft and into the swirling stream.

"Oh Christ!" Nichola yelled, and started to strip off her shift. And then she heard a shout come from somewhere close by, and saw Sabina look up in surprise as a rock came hurtling through the air, catching her on the side of the head. Her beautiful hair was matched by the streak of blood gushing down the side of her face as silently and slowly her stepdaughter fell to the deck below. Faint and dizzy, Nichola slumped to her knees as Caradoc, wearing only a pair of light breeches, ran past her and dived into the river.

He's going to save her, Nichola thought wildly, he's going to save that terrible girl.

But there she was wrong, for it was Emmet that Joscelin's servant carried on to the landing stage, an Emmet limp and spewing up water from purple lips, but an Emmet who was still very much alive.

"Thank God," said Nichola, and shook with bitter sobs of relief and sorrow.

Thus she did not see Caradoc look towards the silent form of Sabina, lying as still and white as any swan, nor did she understand when he kissed her hand and said, "May God bless you, Lady Attwood." In fact the first thing that Nichola was aware of was that he was no longer standing beside her where she huddled over Emmet's prostrate form.

Looking up through a mist of tears, Nichola saw that Caradoc had once more dived into the river and was swimming out towards the raft. And then she watched, frozen to her heart, as he gained the ferry, took his beloved in his arms, and with Sabina clutched to him, her hair spread out over his breast, jumped down into the swiftly flowing stream and let the waters close quietly over their heads.

Chapter Twenty-seven

As evening began to fall, they brought Sabina and Caradoc up out of the Dart. They had gone down on the current to just below Bearscove Castle, a small fort built during the reign of Henry VIII as part of the King's coastal defences. A fisherman had spotted them there, still side by side, just below the surface of the water, and it was he and his two companions who had brought them in. So it was that the lovers were returned by boat to Kingswear Hall, where they were laid to rest in the cool of the chapel.

An hour later, the parish constable from Dartmouth had come to see the Lady Meraud, but when she had assured him that her niece had fallen into the Dart and Lord Joscelin's servant had drowned while attempting to save her, no further questions had been asked.

"And will that be that?" Nichola had asked her sister-in-law cautiously.

"Oh yes, as far as the world is concerned that is the truth about what happened today." She had turned to look at Nichola. "But it isn't, is it, Arabella?"

Nichola had gazed at her, not knowing what to say, longing to keep the facts from Meraud but not seeing how she could.

"There's no need to protect me," her sister-in-law had continued. "I have been aware of undercurrents in this house for some months now, but I closed my mind as to what lay behind them. Yet now I want to know. Am I right in thinking Caradoc was Sabina's lover?"

"Yes," Nichola answered quietly.

"I see," said Meraud, and had turned to stare out over the river.

It was nearly night, the Dart dark as blood, picking up the

colour of the crimson sun sinking behind the trees, etching their outlines sharply against the deepening sky behind them. And now, despite the warmth of the evening, a little breeze had come up off the surface of the water, chilling the two women who stood on the paved terrace, watching one of the most terrible days of their lives draw to its close.

"Then it is as well they're gone," Meraud went on.

Nichola looked at her but said nothing.

"They were related, you see, any carnal knowledge between them was prohibited by both the laws of God and man."

"What do you mean?"

"That Caradoc was our brother, Joscelin's and mine. No, don't look startled. The facts are quite simple really. After my mother died, my father, in his old age, had an affair with a fisherman's daughter, a Dartmouth girl. It was all highly unsuitable, she but twenty, he forty years older. Prohibition of class forbade him from marrying her, though he was smitten enough, God knows. Anyway, Caradoc resulted from their union. Of course, my father left enough money to the Venners for them to raise the boy, but what we didn't know was that both the girl and her father had died and the man's second wife was in charge of him. She brutalised the child, treated him like an animal, kept him in a coop in the garden amongst the hens. That was how Joscelin found him and that is why he brought Caradoc here."

"Poor devil. Did he never know?"

"The truth about his background? No. It would have been too cruel. We treated him as a respected servant, nothing more. But you know how much he loved Joscelin, always said he owed him his life. That is the reason why."

"So Sabina was his niece?"

"Oh yes, though in her defence she did not know either." Meraud had turned to look at Nichola, her face tired and plain once more. "She was evil, wasn't she, that girl I raised?"

Nichola nodded. "To lie to you would be to insult your intelligence. She tried to kill both me and Miranda. And then, when Emmet guessed, attempted to silence her as well."

"And Caradoc realised all this?"

"Meraud," Nichola had said, taking her sister-in-law by the

shoulders, "he drowned her and killed himself as well. They died together. That is the terrible truth of what happened today."

The tears sprang silently from the older woman's eyes. "How cruel a finish for two such beautiful people."

"Tragic. But is that ending not the best one? The girl had bad blood, or so you told me. And Caradoc was unknowingly committing incest. How could they have gone on like that?"

"They couldn't. And as black deeds beget black deeds, then I suppose it was inevitable that violent death would be the outcome."

"I think it was. Now we must, for the sake of our sanity, try to come to terms with what has happened."

A look of determination had crossed Meraud's face. "They shall both be buried here in the chapel, in the family vault. It is only fitting that poor Caradoc takes his place at last."

"So you do not hate him for killing her?"

"No," said Meraud, sobbing aloud, "he was my brother and must have lived a life of misery. How could I turn against him now?"

Nichola spoke out of the darkness which had engulfed them within the last few minutes. "Joscelin must never know of this. He has to be told the story that all the world will hear. He will be quite unable to cope with a truth of such magnitude."

"Is Emmet to be trusted?" Meraud had asked wretchedly.

"Totally."

"Then there are no other witnesses to the tragedy except yourself."

"And I saw Sabina fall into the water and Caradoc drown as he tried to pull her out."

"Amen," said Meraud, and in the darkness held Nichola close to her.

Five days later, despite the fact she was eight months pregnant and as big as a barge, or so she thought and felt, Nichola left Kingswear Hall to go in search of Joscelin. Thankfully, the double funeral was over and done. The two coffins, a red rose in each from Meraud, had been placed together in the family vault and prayers had been said for the immortal souls of Sabina

Attwood and Caradoc Venner. After that all the mourners had trooped into the great hall for a light repast, and then a profound silence had fallen over the house, as if the very stones had absorbed the nature of the tragedy and been stunned by it. To Nichola, that silence was broken by whispers and she could have sworn that she had seen a glimpse of smoky red hair in the shadows, heard a light footfall in the corridor at night. The house was too full of memories and she had known, quite certainly, that she must leave if she was to keep her nerve during these vital last weeks leading up to the birth of her child.

Meraud had thought her completely mad. "But how can you travel in your condition? And where are you going to anyway?"

"I'm going to meet up with Joscelin. I want to be with him when the baby is born."

"Do you know exactly where he is, then?"

"I received a letter from him this morning. The King has been advised by his astrologer that he will shortly win a great victory. He is therefore leaving Oxford in order to hold a grand review at Stow-on-the-Wold."

Meraud had looked askance. "Was it not indiscreet of Joscelin to inform you of this?"

Nichola had shaken her head. "No, when the King's army goes on the move everybody knows about it. It is only details of their actual plans that they must not reveal in writing."

"But did he say when he would be there?"

"Not exactly, but I shall catch up with him, never fear."

"Then you must have a coach and coachman."

Nichola had kissed her. "No, my darling. Let Emmet and I look like two country women about our rural affairs. In that way we can travel without attracting attention to ourselves."

"Surely you don't intend to journey in that horrible wagon?"

"Yes, I'm afraid so. But I won't sit in the back and be jolted into having the child too soon. There will be room on the driver's seat for all three of us."

Meraud had frowned. "Three? I trust you are not subjecting Miranda to such an ordeal?"

"I never want to be separated from her again. I know you would look after her, that she would be safe and comfortable here at Kingswear Hall, but I want to keep Miranda with me. You see, when she nearly drowned that day I felt as if the child were really mine at last."

The words had come out too fast to be checked and Meraud's expression had changed from one of annoyance to one of bewilderment. "But she *is* yours. Isn't she?"

"Yes, of course," Nichola had answered swiftly. "It's just that Joscelin's baby is so important to me I sometimes believe it to be my first."

Meraud's face had softened. "Dear Arabella. What a wonderful wife you have made for him."

"And what a wonderful sister-in-law you are to me. Now, don't cry. I'll come back I promise you."

"Will you? Will you really?"

"Yes. After all this is my baby's rightful home."

Yet Meraud had wept for all that and Nichola had felt guilty about leaving her alone in the vast empty house, so full of ghosts and sadnesses.

"You won't be nervous here, will you?"

Her sister-in-law had shaken her head. "Sabina did not hurt me while she lived, she certainly won't do so from beyond the grave."

"Nonetheless, could you not consider going away for a while?"

"No," Meraud had answered determinedly. "I must see that the place is kept clean and comfortable for when you and Joscelin return."

"I shall worry about you."

"And I about you."

They had reached an impasse and both knew it. Further argument was pointless. So it was with brave faces that they bade each other farewell the next morning, saving their tears until the wagon, driven by Emmet and superstitiously avoiding the ferry, had trundled up the track and gone out of sight as Nichola and her party set off to rejoin the Civil War.

They travelled in a straight line, even though it meant passing through enemy territory. Carefully avoiding Taunton, a Parliamentary garrison under siege from the Royalists but about to be relieved by Sir Thomas Fairfax, or so rumour maintained,

Emmet picked her way carefully from Exeter to Bath. Troops of both armies were glimpsed as the wagon crossed country but no questions were asked of the two farmers' wives, one of them fast approaching her time, going about and minding their own business. However, so long a journey conducted at so leisurely a pace was bound to take a while, and when Nichola and Emmet finally arrived at the village of Stow-on-the-Wold it was to find that the King and his generals had gone.

Joscelin's wife, tired beyond measure of camping in the wagon, took rooms for them at The Eagle and Child, quite literally showing her money first in order to get accommodation, and it was there that she discovered to where all the troops had vanished. It seemed that a fairly large muster had been achieved, roughly six thousand; three hundred horse, and five thousand, three hundred foot. Yet at the Council of War, George Goring and Prince Rupert had apparently disagreed about their deployment.

"The King and the Prince were for heading north. They stayed here, you know, and the Council meetings were held within these very walls," the landlord's wife informed them proudly, putting a large meal down in front of them, which Nichola devoured with no thought of good manners.

"What about Lord Goring?" she asked, her mouth full.

"Well, he being sober, which makes a change, for he did lose consciousness one night right here on my parlour floor, wanted to go back west. One of his troopers told me my Lord has a good time there, living upon free quarter and plunder and the like."

"He behaves like a robber baron," Nichola commented over her chicken bone.

"Anyway, they went their separate ways in the end. My Lord returned to the West Country and the King's army headed off for another muster."

"Do you know where?"

"Oh yes. It was to be held at Market Harborough."

"My God," said Nichola, groaning. "How much further is that?"

"Miles," answered Emmet. "Miles and miles and miles. Shall we not just stay here and wait for them to return?"

"But how do we know they're going to return?"

Emmet looked alarmed. "You don't mean . . ."

"No, I don't. I simply meant how do we know they are going to come back this way?"

Emmet sighed. "You're right of course. It's just that the wagon has shaken me up so bad I doubt I'll ever get back to normal."

Nichola stared at her in amazement. "Are you saying we should have stayed at Kingswear Hall?"

Miranda, sitting up on her chair and speaking clearly, as Nichola had taught her to do, answered for her. "No, that's a bad place."

"It isn't any more," Nichola informed her daughter firmly. "All the bad people have gone away." She smiled at Emmet. "But the child is right. It was best to leave when we did."

"I suppose so," Emmet answered, and sighed again.

The next day saw them back on the road, intent on travelling as fast as they could so that the appalling discomfort of the journey should at least be lessened in duration. And by pushing themselves to the limit the two women and the child clattered into Market Harborough during the morning of the last day of May, only to learn that the main body of the King's troops had moved on to Leicester.

"But there's women camped not far away," Nichola was told as she sought accommodation, once again having to show her money in advance, and realising that such a disreputable wreck as she must now look could easily be mistaken for a gypsy.

"The army women?"

"Aye, the whores and mistresses, wives and camp followers. Prince Rupert has gone to Leicester to demand admittance in the name of the King, and so the leaguers have mostly been left behind."

"We're not going to see them now," Emmet announced firmly. "We're going to eat and sleep and wash, in that order. Tonight we can go to the camp and see if anyone we know is there."

"But many of the leaguer ladies are staying in the town," the landlord put in. "It is mostly the bitches who are encamped."

Despite the strangeness of his terminology, Nichola knew

exactly what he meant. The leaguer ladies were the wives of officers or, at the very least, the mistresses of gentlemen, the leaguer bitches was the term applied to the rest.

"We'll call on them this evening," Emmet reiterated firmly.

"But one of them may well be able to give me news of Joscelin," Nichola protested.

"She can do so just as well later."

Yet despite the fact that she was exhausted by having travelled throughout the night, Nichola found it difficult to rest. During the afternoon the sound of heavy guns being fired awoke her, even though several miles separated Market Harborough from the town of Leicester, and this relentless battery kept up until nightfall. Having managed an hour or two of sleep, Nichola finally rose at dusk and asked for the wooden tub, which poor Emmet and one skinny maidservant filled between them. Then, after what seemed like months without washing, she carefully lowered her swollen body into the soothing water and scrubbed away the ingrained grime. Looking at her abdomen, as she lay back for a moment or two, Nichola saw her baby move from side to side and wondered how much longer it would be before it decided to be born.

She had missed the main meal of the day but was served a light supper and after this, having seen Miranda safely bedded for the night, Nichola and Emmet set out on foot, their hope being that one of the Oxford ladies of their acquaintance might be staying at one of the other hostelries, namely The Bear or The Angel – Nichola's own inn being The Three Swans. Yet as it transpired it was while walking past the ancient grammar school that Nichola heard a voice call, "Arabella?" and then add the words, "but it can't be!"

She spun round with a delighted smile on her face and saw that there in the darkness, regarding her by the light of a flickering lantern, stood Jacobina Jermyn, the girl she had most despicably betrayed by her behaviour with Prince Rupert of the Rhine. However, Jacobina had either forgotten this or had never been sure it had happened in the first place, for she flung herself into Nichola's arms and greeted her as a long lost friend.

"My dear, I hardly recognised you, for you are indeed huge

with child. Lord Joscelin, of course, had told me you were *enceinte*, but I had never imagined anyone quite as small as you are, could be so *big*."

Nichola smiled ruefully. "I shall be thinner in a fortnight or so. But that's not really important. Have you seen Joscelin, is he here?"

"He was until yesterday when he marched with the King and Rupert to Leicester. This morning, Rupert's herald was going to demand that the gate be opened to admit His Majesty and, if they refused, would give them fair warning that the Prince intended to attack. And judging by the sound of the guns, this is precisely what has occurred."

"Do you think the city has fallen yet?"

"I don't know, but I intend to ride there in the morning and find out."

"Then I shall go with you."

Jacobina ran her eye over Arabella's enlarged shape. "Do you think that is entirely wise?"

Nichola burst out laughing. "It wasn't wise of me to come this far so I'm damned if the threat of imminent childbirth is going to stop me now."

"You haven't changed," Jacobina answered smiling.

"And neither have you."

With linked arms, they set forth for The Angel where they gossiped for several hours, Emmet tactfully excusing herself and returning to The Three Swans. But a sad story emerged which once again caused Nichola pangs of conscience. It seemed that Rupert had finally noticed Jacobina during the Christmas season just past and had taken her to bed, robbing her of her virginity almost callously, or so she said.

"He apologised, Arabella. He said he didn't expect to find me untouched and if he had known he would have controlled himself."

"That doesn't sound callous to me."

"He said it so casually. He didn't really give a damn and he still doesn't. When he takes me carnally he often closes his eyes and I know perfectly well he is thinking of another woman. Rupert is in love with some jade or other, though I cannot for the life of me discover who it is. At one time I foolishly suspected you, but when you disappeared to Devon I knew I had been wrong about that."

"So what are you going to do? Surely this arrangement can't be satisfactory to you?" Nichola asked carefully.

"I am resolved to give him up, because it is more painful to proceed than to forget. The worst of it is that that will mean quitting the army, for when I see him I am lost and become besotted once more. Short of escaping abroad to join my brother, I am at my wits end as to what move to make."

"Poor Jacobina," said Nichola.

The elfin girl sighed. "Aye. Being in love is the most cruel thing I know."

"Not necessarily. It just means finding the right man and Rupert is obviously not the one for you."

"No, indeed."

"Then let us speak of other things," Nichola suggested, and moved on to different topics as skilfully as she could. Yet there was a saddened air about her friend, whose face, if anything, had grown even more attractive since her doomed affair, and Nichola's feelings of guilt magnified and would not go away. A dread of the next day, when she would see Rupert as well as Joscelin, started as a small cloud on the horizon and refused to shift. And even though she had a good night's sleep and awoke refreshed, the uneasiness was still there in the morning.

Leicester had clearly reeled under the assault that the angry Prince had hurled at it. There were jagged breaches in the walls through which the invaders had obviously poured, and there were still one or two scaling ladders in position, showing the Royalists' other means of entry. Yet despite the bitter fighting there were no bodies in the streets, though the cobbles were bloodstained and slippery, bearing silent witness to the fact that lives had been lost. There was also evidence of something else, almost equally unpleasant. Houses had been pillaged from roof to cellar, the cottages of the ordinary folk ransacked. Even churches and hospitals had not escaped the attentions of the plunderers. There were signs, too, of mindless vandalism. Shop shutters had been splintered and the tools of honest tradesmen tossed into the street.

"Wholesale looting!" said Nichola with disgust.

"It's always the same story, and on both sides too. The King will express regret, Rûpert will turn a blind eye, just like the Parliamentarians."

"They ought to have more control over their soldiers."

"Once the troops become enraged and greedy there's nothing that can be done with them."

"It's reprehensible," Nichola answered angrily, and even while she spoke a cart packed with plunder rolled past and out of the city gates.

The two women had brought the dreaded wagon to Leicester, since by now it was impossible for Nichola to travel any other way. Yet as they proceeded deeper into the city it occurred to both of them that the shocked and terrified citizens might think that they, too, were potential looters, and after a while decided to abandon their vehicle at a hitching post and proceed on foot. Still nobody spoke to or smiled at them, and Nichola was just thinking how few people there were about, when she suddenly saw a great horde of Cavaliers, all swaggering boots and beautiful plumes, bright as popinjays, and every one of them proceeding in the same direction.

"What is this?" she asked Jacobina.

"The King and his gentlemen are obviously off to morning prayer to give thanks."

"Will Joscelin be there?"

"Of course he will. And Rupert."

"Then what are we waiting for?" said Nichola in modern idiom, and taking her friend's arm walked with her towards the ancient looking church in the direction of which everyone seemed to be heading.

"They're going to St Mary de Castro, where King Henry VI was knighted."

"Oh, so it's even old by your standards," Nichola remarked thoughtlessly.

"What *do* you mean?" Jacobina answered, surprised, as they passed beneath the historic entrance arch.

Despite the hypocrisy of those who had just killed and witnessed such appalling pillage now bending the knee to God, the very thought of which bred rebellion in Nichola's soul, the church's ambience, its warm and mellow atmosphere, had such an instantly calming effect on her that she found herself taking a seat in a back pew in good heart.

Right at the front sat the King, surrounded by local dignitaries who, as a man, looked thoroughly wretched and depressed. Next to him, clad in blue with a vivid scarlet sash, was Rupert, staring about him as if he were very slightly bored. Beside him, in turn, was Joscelin, his black hair cascading to his shoulders and on to his lace collar. Nichola felt her heart leap that the two men who loved her so dearly were so close together, their shoulders even touching as they squeezed up to make room for latecomers.

"You're very pale," whispered Jacobina, shooting her a glance.

"It's this," Nichola whispered back, and laid a hand on her body.

She had not said the words above a murmur, having adopted the usual solemn church voiçe common to all on entering a holy place, but something of the sound she made must have carried for Joscelin turned his head, followed a second later by Rupert doing likewise.

"They've seen us," said Jacobina triumphantly.

They hadn't, of course. Instead the eyes of the two men raked the congregation as if they were seeking someone, though both of them were apparently unaware that the other was searching too.

They know I'm here, thought Nichola, before she dismissed the idea as being too foolish.

Yet the evidence of what she was seeing told her otherwise as Joscelin and Rupert looked all about them, then finally settled their gaze, almost simultaneously, on her.

How blind is love, for Jacobina said excitedly, "Rupert's picked me out. See, he's staring."

Yet it was not for her that the warrior Prince's somewhat solemn face was suddenly lit up by a spectacular smile. And it was most certainly only for Arabella Attwood that Lord Joscelin stood up in his pew, gazing as if he could not believe the evidence of his eyes, and then blew both hands towards Nichola in the gesture of a loving kiss.

Chapter Twenty-eight

They had been reunited outside the ancient church of St Mary de Castro in the sunshine of that first day of June 1645, Joscelin throwing his head back and laughing with pure joy at the sight of his wife so great with child that she seemed almost as broad as she was long. After that, whenever they were apart, that was how Nichola remembered him, his dark curls tumbling round his shoulders beneath his plumed hat, his teeth white in his darkly attractive features. Rupert had stood a pace or two away, his expression unreadable, his manner polite. Just for a moment, Nichola had seen his eyes sweep her body and two different looks cross his face in rapid succession, and she had realised that for a second or so the Prince had wondered if the child was his, before his brain had worked and he had realised it was utterly impossible.

"But how, why, are you here, when I thought you safe at Kingswear Hall?" Joscelin was asking.

And then had come the drawing aside, the carefully worded explanation, the helpless watching while sobs shook her husband's elegant body. The King, chatting with his companions, must have seen what was going on out of the corner of his eye and never had the little monarch's gentle sweetness been more apparent to Nichola. Crossing the space between them, he reached up on high to put his arm round Joscelin's shoulders.

"Dear friend," Charles said, "I do not know what grieves you, but be strong I beg you. There is so much sadness in this saddest of times, pray walk with me to my lodging and let us share your burden."

"Madam, may I escort you?" Rupert added quickly, bowing to Nichola and offering her his arm.

Stealing a glance at Jacobina's face, she answered, "It is kind of you, Sir, but do pray join His Majesty. I must confer with my friend about our arrangements. We had not come to Leicester intending to stay."

"Then let it be hoped," Rupert replied, his eyes not leaving her face, "that you will change your plans." And with that he bowed again and went on his way.

"I must be mad," said Jacobina, almost under her breath, "to hanker after him. He scarcely noticed me."

Nichola felt a rush of twentieth-century honesty coming upon her. "Have you ever heard the expression 'There's as good fish in the sea as ever came out of it'?"

"No."

"Well, it means don't be disappointed if one fish gets away, there are a lot more swimming around. And it particularly applies to men. I believe you're right. Rupert's a non-starter."

"And to think he robbed me of my virginity," Jacobina said angrily.

"Somebody had to," Nichola replied bluntly. She changed the subject. "Now, what's to be done? I can't leave Miranda and Emmet stranded in Market Harborough, yet equally, I don't want to abandon Joscelin."

"Do you want me to go back and fetch them?"

Nichola looked unsure. "Might it be better to tell them to wait there for me? After all, I have no idea of his moves which, no doubt, will be governed by the King in any case. What do you think?"

"They've done enough travelling, particularly the child," Jacobina answered practically. "Let them stay where they are comfortable."

"Then tell them I will either be back or send a message through. Do you mind doing that for me?"

"Of course not."

Nichola gave her friend a kiss on the cheek. "And will you afterwards return here to me?"

Jacobina shook her head. "I think I'll stay with the leaguer ladies. The less I see of the big fish the easier it will be for me to think about the shoals."

"Then I will meet you very soon."

"Very soon," Jacobina echoed as Nichola hurried to catch up with the royal party as best she could.

In the event things were not to work out as either of the women had planned. Having stayed in Leicester for two days the King, well pleased with the fall of that city into his hands, decided that it was time for some pleasure and withdrew into Warwickshire, to Fawsley Park near Daventry, in order to go hunting. There was other cheering news as well. Fairfax, who had been on his way to relieve the siege of Taunton when suddenly ordered to besiege Oxford instead had, according to the Royalist intelligence network, withdrawn from the city, thus removing the King's headquarters from danger.

"My affairs were never in so fair and hopeful way," Charles wrote to the Queen and repeated as much to his generals when he suggested the hunting trip.

"But what of you?" Joscelin said to Nichola. "I can't ask you to journey even further in your condition."

"Why not? The only alternative is for me to go back to Market Harborough and be with the other women. Darling, I want you to be present when I have my baby. It is the custom in my time if not yours. So that means I'm going to stay by your side until it is born."

Her husband loosened his lace collar. "My God! I shall most likely faint."

"Oh don't be such a wimp!"

"And what precisely is that?"

But they were laughing, teasing one another, and had set off for the hunting expedition in fine fettle. Yet there was an aura of melancholy about Joscelin that no outside diversions could dispel. Though he said nothing about it, Nichola knew that he mourned Sabina and Caradoc with an aching grief he found impossible to share, even with her. Eventually, somewhat diffidently, she broached the subject.

"I think I know something of what you're feeling. Once, when Miranda was in great danger and I thought her dead, I briefly felt the pain of loss. And as for Caradoc, he was more than just a friend to you, wasn't he?"

Joscelin looked at her sharply. "What do you mean by that?"

"That I know he was your brother. Meraud told me."

"Did she? Why?"

"Because she suffered as wretchedly as you over his death, and probably felt the need to confide."

Joscelin sighed. "And did she suffer equally over Sabina?"

It was a curious question but Nichola answered it as honestly as she could. "She was devastated that the life of such a beautiful young girl should have ended so tragically."

Joscelin stared out of the window. "I pray that my daughter's soul lies quietly," he said.

It was a very odd remark to make, so odd that Nichola felt she did not dare question him further. For something in the way her husband spoke gave her the uncanny feeling that, even if only briefly, he had actually glimpsed the blackness of Sabina's heart. Thinking to herself that the least said about it all the better for everyone concerned, both living and dead, she dropped the subject.

They reached Fawsley Park, a great house still loyal to the King, on 10 June, Nichola having written to Jacobina to tell her where she was and ask for the message to be passed on to Emmet. Then she took the precaution of engaging the services of a midwife, who fortunately dwelled in one of the cottages on the Fawsley estate. And with this reassuring thought, Nichola settled herself to enjoy the fine weather while the King and his generals went hunting. However, any idea she might have had of giving birth in the comfort of the mansion was to be rudely shattered.

A servant had come hurrying in while they were dining on the evening of 11 June to tell the King that Sir Thomas Fairfax's army had been spotted a mere two miles away. And while His Majesty immediately sent out spies to discover if the news were true, it had been abruptly confirmed before they had even returned. Strange horsemen had been seen at the Royalist army encampment at nearby Burrow Hill, all of whom had galloped off at full speed when challenged. The worst of it had been that the Cavalier army had been caught sunbathing, the horses contentedly at grass.

"They'll report back that we were in disarray," Joscelin had said grimly when he had returned to Fawsley Park an hour later.

"So what will happen now?"

"The King has decided to strike camp at once. We're to head for Market Harborough at full speed."

"Oh God!" said Nichola, rolling her eyes.

"Do you want the midwife to travel in the coach with you?"

"No, I shall be fine as long as we're reasonably quick. Once I get to Emmet she will organise me."

"Well, we leave just as soon as the army has got itself in order."

But it was in an extraordinarily tense atmosphere, aware that the enemy was right behind them and far too close for comfort, that they set off an hour later. Nichola, feeling so heavy that she did not know how to sit in any position for long, was handed into the royal coach, loaned to her for the purposes of travelling, by Prince Rupert, Joscelin being called at that moment to attend the King.

"I'm sending a rider to Market Harborough to fetch your maid," the Prince murmured. "The girl can meet us half way."

"That's very good of you."

"If that were my child you were carrying it would be the least I could do."

"But it isn't," she said, giving him a very direct look.

He flashed his expressive eyes. "I know that. But just supposing something had happened on one of those nights, Arabella."

"What do you mean, *those*?"

He looked away. "Never mind. Remember I remain your loyal servant, always." And with that he was gone to the front of the column, his scarlet hat picking him out from all his fellows even in the distance.

They travelled for a day and a night, each bump of the coach giving Nichola the certain feeling that she would go into labour at any second, and as evening came on 13 June she did indeed feel a low dull ache in her back. They had reached the village of Naseby, two miles south of Market Harborough, from whence had come the remainder of the King's troops and the great mass of army women. Yet Nichola had received the shock of her life, for Jacobina and her servant, to say nothing of the child, were not amongst the horde.

"Where's Jacobina Jermyn?" she asked one of the officers' wives as they made camp for the night.

"I believe she has gone searching for a midwife to bring with her, but is having some difficulty in locating one willing to come on to the battlefield."

"Are we at battle tomorrow then?"

"Yes. The Prince wanted to wait until Lord Goring could join us from the West Country but now believes, like everyone else, that it is better to stand and fight than be pursued."

"Oh dear. I just hope they manage to get through."

The other woman looked sympathetic. "Somebody will deliver you, don't you worry."

"But I'd rather it were Emmet," Nichola answered miserably, and repeated the same phrase to Joscelin when he finally came to her side as darkness fell.

He looked grim. "I can't risk you and the child like this. I'm sending you on to Market Harborough. At least you can get proper attention there."

"Supposing I pass Emmet on the way?"

"That's a risk we'll have to take."

Yet much as Nichola longed for him to stay with her on this night when she ached everywhere and would willingly have let the earth open and swallow her, it was just as it had been before Marston Moor. Rupert sat up into the small hours, discussing tactics, drinking, boosting morale, and all the King's men, including His Majesty himself, sat with him. So it was that Nichola saw the dawn come up without having had a wink of sleep, the pain in her back unrelentingly acute, her body too big to get any rest in the narrow truckle bed, only to see that Joscelin had thrown himself down fully dressed on the bed beside hers.

He woke and looked at her. "I must get you away from here, sweetheart."

Nichola bit her lip. "I couldn't bear the journey. That bloody coach is a nightmare over bad roads. Just let me stay here and wait for Emmet."

"And what if she doesn't come?"

"Then one of the medicine women can do the necessary."

He put his arms round her. "Are you in labour, my darling?"

"I don't think so. My back aches like hell but I've got no other signs."

"Then let me take you to the baggage train. At least you'll be safe there. I can get someone to sit with you."

Thus, in the early morning light, Nichola walked past the King's army, already starting to manoeuvre into position, towards the baggage train, parked a mile behind the lines and consisting of royal coaches, sumpter wagons, and carts for carrying equipment and luggage. The baggage commander, on seeing Lord Joscelin, whipped his cap from his head and looked respectful. Then his eyes went to Nichola.

"Has my Lady's time come?" he asked anxiously, obviously not wanting any more trouble than was absolutely necessary.

"Not quite," Joscelin answered tersely. "But I'd like her made comfortable in one of the wagons and a medicine woman kept on hand to attend her should it be necessary."

"Very good, my Lord," the commander replied, glancing at the coin Joscelin had slipped him and growing more co-operative by the minute. "If my Lady would just like to wait a moment, I'll get some fresh linen for her."

He bustled away and, in that final moment of privacy, Nichola, recalling the facts of the Battle of Naseby and who had been the victor, could only turn to Joscelin with tears in her eyes.

"Take great care, my darling."

He looked at her perceptively. "We're not going to win this, are we?"

"No."

"Is the King. . .?"

"No, neither he nor Rupert." She smiled at him. "Nor any other great men."

"Then I will see you tonight."

"Yes, my darling." And with that they kissed and parted company.

Unwilling to confine herself inside the wagon too soon, Nichola stood watching the Royalist troops form up, a gleaming exhilarating sight in the sunshine, the light breeze whipping their colours and pennants, their helmets and breastplates glinting brightly, the little King a tiny gawdy figure in his glittering suit of full armour. Of Joscelin she could see no sign, but shortly after ten o'clock the maverick Prince who also loved her, led the opening cavalry charge, obviously determined not to repeat the mistakes of Marston Moor. With his brother Prince Maurice beside him, Rupert appeared atop the slopes, sword unsheathed, thundering down towards the enemy and gaining momentum with every stride his charger took. And it was then, with her eyes fastened on this brilliant bloodthirsty sight from the past, that Nichola felt a cascade of water gush down her legs and form in a great puddle at her feet. Simultaneously she had a violent contraction and knew that two battles had begun together, both hers and Joscelin's.

"God help us," she prayed, and began to stagger into the wagon.

Yet somehow she still did not want to enter its stuffy confines, believing she could conduct herself better standing up. Quite blindly, not knowing where she was going and not really caring, Nichola began to walk towards the open country-side beyond the baggage train.

Behind her, in the distance, the battle gained in savagery, Rupert sweeping through the ranks commanded by Henry Ireton, recently appointed to the position of Commissary General over the heads of more experienced men because he was the friend and protégé of Oliver Cromwell. Meanwhile, Cromwell himself had led his Ironsides in full charge against the Royalist left wing so that all was confusion, smoke and bloodshed. Though Nichola, toiling onwards with no goal in sight, knew none of this.

The contractions were now coming frequently, more regularly than she would have imagined possible. So much so, indeed, that she began to wonder if she had been in labour for most of the night and was now much further on than she realised. Panic gripped her then, and she began to look round desperately for some sign of life. But there was no one about, the only living creatures visible beside herself, the birds wheeling in the sky above. And then she heard a faint sound, the dull thud of wheels crossing rough terrain. Thinking that perhaps the baggage commander had noticed her absence and had sent someone to fetch her, Nichola looked over her shoulder.

A cart was trundling slowly towards her, a lone driver sitting on the seat, his brown hands loosely gripping the reins, in no hurry to get anywhere.

"Help," Nichola called. "Please help. I'm having a baby and need assistance."

He looked up and saw her, flicking the horse's rump so that it would speed along. And then another contraction gripped Nichola, this one so blindingly strong that she fell down on to the earth, gripping her body, letting out a cry.

"Easy now," said a voice, and she felt rather than saw the cart draw to a halt and a man jump down and kneel beside her.

"Oh God," she moaned, "please take me to a midwife. I think my time's very near."

The man chuckled, a shocking sound at that moment. "Well, well, to think we meet again like this. Now don't you worry, my Lady. You've put yourself in safe hands I assure you," he added soothingly.

With a groan of gratitude, Nichola opened her eyes and stared straight into the face of Emerald Ditch.

He gave her raspberry leaves to chew, then examined her intimately in such a matter of fact way that Nichola cared nothing.

"You'll be pushing soon," Emerald said certainly. "Reckon you've been in labour a while now."

"I had back ache all night."

"That's it then. Now, girl, don't fight the next one. Swim like a fish right over the wave, d'ye understand?"

"But how?"

"Breathe shallow, don't mix your breathing with your guts. Now come on."

It was wonderful, just as if he had magic in his fingers. Sitting behind her, holding her securely, Emerald rubbed her back, relieving the pressure with every touch of his fingers.

"Now, how d'ye want to deliver?" he said eventually.

"What do you mean?"

"Do you want to stand, squat, lie? What?"

"How do the gypsy women give birth?"

"They stand. But I'll prop thee up, Nichola, 'twould be better I think. If we put these old blankets behind you that should do the trick."

She had forgotten that he knew her real name and found it comforting at this moment of extremis. With her back supported by a pile of blankets, smelling strongly of both horses and men, Nichola lay in a corner of the cart and felt the mighty contractions focus into one overwhelming urge to rid herself of the child. Gripping her legs tightly under the thighs so that she could raise and pull them apart, Nichola started to bear down. And then, suddenly, all the brightness of the summer day vanished and she was in a tunnel, a narrow tunnel like the ones used by the old canal barges of the past. Staring towards its end, Nichola was almost blinded by the light that lay there.

But with every push she gave she took an inadvertent step forward, a step nearer to the brilliance, a brilliance so intense that it was starting to make her eyelids flutter and her eyes roll in her head. Then, almost accidentally, Nichola gave a mighty heave, bigger than the rest, and approached so close that she could actually glimpse what lay beyond the light. Much as she had suspected, the body was there, lying in its hospital room like the Sleeping Beauty, its chest rising and falling, only separated from her by that flimsy, tissue-thin gauze of radiance.

Far, far away, a voice she dimly recognised as Emerald's spoke to her. "Nichola, where are you?"

"Going back," she answered dreamily.

"Nichola," said Lewis, so close to her ear that it made her jump, for she hadn't realised he was there. "I am going to count from ten to one. When I reach one you will awake refreshed and well."

"Where are you?" Nichola asked him.

"Just here, give me your hand." She could see him now, standing beside the body, taking its fingers and grasping them in his own. "Come on, darling," he said.

The distant voice spoke again. "Give me thy hand, girl."

"But Lewis has it."

"Nichola," Lewis murmured urgently, "you're so near now. Just one more effort and we'll be together again."

And she saw that he was right. One heave and she would step through the brilliance and into the world that lay just beyond.

"What shall I do?" she called out uncertainly.

In the dim distance, Emerald answered her. "Do you want to go, Nichola?"

She hesitated.

"Well?"

"Come *on*!" urged Lewis.

But she had done too much, had known too much love, had changed too drastically ever to return. "No, I don't," she shouted. "I want to stay here!"

"Then don't bear down. Just let me have thy child," whispered that voice from the past.

Trying to obey, Nichola panted and gasped and restrained herself as something slipped and slithered and slid from between her legs. Then there was a high thin cry which echoed and reverberated so loudly that it brought the walls of the dark tunnel crashing down to allow daylight to come pouring in on every side. And as the tunnel vanished so the radiance shattered into a trillion pieces like fragments of splintering glass.

Nichola opened her eyes and saw that Emerald Ditch was cutting the birth cord of the infant which wriggled in the blood-soaked straw between her knees.

"I have a son!" she gasped.

"Aye. A perfect specimen at that."

And he handed her the little naked creature, Nichola marvelling delightedly that his black hair hung almost to its shoulders just like his father's.

She looked at Emerald directly. "Something strange happened during his birth. Did you know?"

"Oh yes. The circle completed itself."

"What do you mean by that?"

"A baby brought you in, another nearly took you out."

Nichola nodded slowly. "I see. So was it you who kept me here?"

"It was what you wanted," the gypsy answered, shrugging laconically.

She smiled at him before dropping a kiss on the baby's brow. "Yes," Nichola Hall stated quite positively. "It was what I really wanted."

Chapter Twenty-nine

The aftermath of the Battle of Naseby had been a full retreat by the Royalists towards their stronghold, the city of Leicester. Between four and five thousand of the King's troops had been taken prisoner, while the bodies of the dead and wounded lay in a line four miles long, all of them stark naked, their clothes stripped and plundered by the enemy as they left the field.

It had been Oliver Cromwell himself who had put Charles Stuart under direct threat while the battle still raged. He had broken through the ranks of the Northern Horse and suddenly appeared before the King's Life Guards, a small reserve force of nine hundred cavalry and three hundred foot. With Rupert disappeared into the thick of the fight, Charles had suddenly been forced to use his own initiative. Bracing himself, the King had been about to lead his Life Guards directly into the fray when the Earl of Carnwarth, a northern nobleman, had grabbed his bridle swearing a foul-mouthed rollicking Scottish oath and exclaiming, "Will you go upon your death?" Most unfortunately, this action had startled His Majesty's mount so greatly that the terrified animal had wheeled to the right, and seeing the King leave the field, the Life Guards had followed suit en masse.

When the Prince, who had got as far as Fairfax's baggage train, returned to the battle, it was to find his forces in disarray. Appalled by what he saw, Rupert had nonetheless tried to rally his exhausted troops and winded horses but had found it impossible. He had therefore had no choice but to cover the retreat of the King who was by now galloping headlong towards Leicester. With the departure of the commander, those left alive had fled the field.

* * *

Presumably guided by some sixth sense, Emerald Ditch had not even attempted to return Nichola and her son to the scene of such a rout. Instead he had turned his cart in the direction of Leicester and, proceeding not too rapidly but steadily enough, had started to drive the mother and child towards the city. Inevitably, though, it had not been long before the King's baggage train, the furthest away from the field and subsequently the first to retreat, had caught them up. And there, amongst all the women hurrying alongside the royal coaches, the sumpter or packhorse wagons, and the loaded carts, had been Jacobina and Emmet.

Nichola, lying very still, her son at her breast, felt almost in a dream and did not even see them. But Emmet, her face black from the smoke of recent gunfire yet still searching for her mistress, gave a shriek of joy as Jacobina Jermyn glimpsed Arabella Attwood bumping along in a gypsy's cart. And then many willing hands had lifted the new mother on to one of the wagons, padding her all around with blankets and sheets to lessen the jolting, and it was the moment for Nichola to say goodbye to the man who had delivered her child.

"Emerald," she whispered to him urgently. "Will that ever happen to me again?"

He smiled his leathery smile. "If you mean birth, aye I expect it will. If you mean the tunnel, I reckon not."

"How did you know about that? About the tunnel?"

"I've known of it for a long while. Since the second time you came to see me."

"And can you promise I'll never have to go down it again?"

Emerald nodded. "Yes. Things will change now that you have made your choice."

"What things?"

He smiled. "Who's to say? I only know what I know. And now I must leave you. There'll be poor souls lying dying who could do with my tending."

Nichola snatched his hand, holding it against her cheek. "You saved my husband's life after Marston Moor, did you know that?"

"Yes, I knew," he said softly, and with that turned his cart and plodded towards the battlefield with nothing more than a wave of his hand.

"What an extraordinary fellow he is," said Jacobina, watching him go from her place beside Nichola, where she sat holding Miranda, while Emmet continued to march alongside.

"I believe him to be very enlightened."

"Well, he was right about myself and Rupert."

Nichola looked guilty. "I still haven't asked you about Joscelin. Is he safe and well?"

Jacobina smiled at her quizzically. "I think you must have known that through some clairvoyant means of your own, otherwise you would have been beside yourself with worry. But yes, he came through the battle unscathed then acted like a being possessed when he could not find you where he had left you. I swear to God he searched the contents of every vehicle in this train before he went galloping off to Leicester to continue the hunt."

"But that is where we are heading, isn't it?"

"Yes," said Jacobina reassuringly, "you'll be together again before long."

"Thank God," answered Nichola, kissing her son, who had fallen asleep as he sucked.

Jacobina smiled delightfully, looking almost amusing as her teeth flashed in her battle-darkened face. "He's a beautiful child, the image of his father. Have you a name for him yet?"

"Well, as Emerald delivered him and Emmet is such a good friend, I thought perhaps Emlyn. Also a great Welsh actor, of course."

Jacobina shook her head. "I don't think I know of him. But it's a strong name. Emlyn Attwood. Yes, I like it."

"Then that's settled, provided Joscelin likes it too."

"I'm sure he will agree with anything you suggest," Jacobina answered with a hint of a smile, then closed her eyes, suddenly exhausted by the events of the day.

"What's the date?" asked Nichola wearily.

"The fourteenth of June 1645. Why?"

"I remember reading about it somewhere."

"What did you read?" asked Jacobina, now too tired to notice the oddness of the remark.

"I read, 'It was more than the end of an army; it was, for all practical purposes, the end of a reign".'

Fortunately for Nichola's friend, she had already gone to sleep and so the harsh cruelty of those words was entirely lost on her.

Since it was not in the nature of a baggage train to travel quickly, they were still several miles off Leicester as the light began to wane from the day. Then, in the uneasy shadow of dusk, came the first intimations that something had gone badly wrong. The coaches and wagons had gone on the beaten track, not daring to risk a more difficult terrain, so it was no surprise to hear the thunder of hooves behind them. And yet there was something about the way in which these horsemen were approaching, so fast and so frantically, that sent a chill of unease through all the women, some several hundred of them, who marched with the train that twilight.

"What is it?" said Nichola, waking from a deep and restful sleep.

"I don't know," Jacobina answered, as she did likewise.

But poor Emmet, still on foot and hobbling a little, had already let out a shriek. "It's a whole host of riders, my Lady. They're coming at us like the wind."

And the next moment all three women saw who it was approaching. Dressed in buff coats and helmets, their features protected by menacing face bars, at least two regiments of Roundheads had come out of the evening with swords drawn.

"We're under attack!" Jacobina exclaimed.

"No, we can't be," Nichola answered, horrified. "We're just the leaguer ladies and not armed."

A second later the words died on her lips and she saw that the baggage train had been surrounded, that officers' wives and mistresses had swords at their throats, while the poor slatterns with no money were being set upon where they marched, their noses and cheeks mercilessly slashed to the bone, others simply being done away with and allowed to die in the dust. And there were other horrors. Some of the women who were offering money and jewels in return for their lives were not being spared. Ladies of quality were dying alongside their poverty-stricken sisters.

"Our turn," said Jacobina, and snatched a bag from round her waist so quickly that Nichola did not realise what she was doing. But Jacobina had seen what Nichola had not. A mounted Roundhead trooper had drawn alongside their wagon and was peering inside, having first grabbed Emmet by the scruff of her neck and put the point of his sword to her nostril.

"Don't touch her," screamed Nichola. "I'll give you anything you want."

"Here, take these," said Jacobina, shoving the bag into his hand. "They are my mother's emeralds. They're yours if you'll spare our lives."

The soldier laughed, raising Emmet into the air. "Perhaps. But I've a mind to pretty this one's face a bit."

The wretched girl screamed and closed her eyes, while Nichola dragged her wedding ring from her finger. "It's all I have on me but it's gold. Don't touch her, I beg you."

And then another male voice spoke from across the wagon. "One move, trooper, and I'll cleave the cods straight from your body and follow them with your prick. Now what say you?"

It was Michael Morellon, looking just as sinister as the rest with the triple face bars hiding his expression, yet at that moment the most superb sight Nichola could have wished to see.

"But, Colonel . . ." the man protested.

"Oh damn you," Michael answered, and shot him with the wheellock pistol he was carrying at his waist.

Nichola had never known anything happen so fast and she could scarcely keep up with what took place next. Dismounting, Michael hurled the soldier's body to one side and picked up the hapless Emmet who had fallen beneath the dead man.

"Oh, it's you, Master Michael," she sobbed, leaning against him.

"Yes," he answered grimly. "Now I'm commandeering this wagon and taking you all away. There's murder and disfigurement afoot and I cannot guarantee your safety." He called to the terrified man holding the wagon's reins. "Driver, head for Market

Harborough. I'll ride escort so you'll not be molested further."

And putting Emmet into the conveyance, Colonel Morellon remounted and set off at a brisk trotting pace, the wagon rattling along beside him.

"Who *is* he?" asked Jacobina, thoroughly intrigued.

"His name is Michael Morellon and I was once betrothed to him before our families took opposing sides in the war. As a matter of fact he is Miranda's father."

Jacobina put on her gossip's face. "Is he now! No wonder he smiled on her so fondly."

"Yes, that's the reason why. And now he's protecting her more than the rest of us, I'll warrant." In a louder voice, Nichola called, "How can you countenance this atrocity, Michael? I thought you would be above seeing innocent women killed and maimed."

"It's abhorrent to me," he called back curtly, "but what can I do? The soldiers will excuse themselves by saying that most of the women are Irish and Catholic and would murder God-fearing Protestants at the ring of an altar bell."

"What rubbish!" Nichola retorted furiously. "The majority of those poor souls are the wives of the Welsh recruits, and if this is an example of the action of God-fearing men then Christianity is a farce."

Michael shook his head. "Don't say any more. It cuts me to the quick that my daughter had to witness such things. And now I'm risking court-martial by taking you to safety. In fact as soon as I've seen you settled, I must make haste to Leicester."

"Why? What are you going to do there?"

"We are to retake the city before we turn west to deal with Goring."

The cold chill of fear held Nichola in its grip. "But Joscelin is in Leicester. He has gone there to look for me."

"I doubt the King's men will stay in the city long. They'll soon have intelligence that Sir Thomas Fairfax is after them."

Nichola wondered if she looked as desperate as she felt. "Then how can I get a message through to him? I've just given birth to his son, for God's sake, and he doesn't even know."

Michael stared at her bleakly. "This is war, Arabella. There is little hope of any contact in the state of chaos that always follows a battle."

Jacobina interrupted. "For all that, it would be worth writing a brief letter."

"But who will take it?" Nichola asked miserably.

"Perhaps you," said Jacobina, turning to Michael with an elfin smile.

He shook his head. "You must appreciate that I would do most things to help the mother of my child, but if it were to be discovered that I was carrying a communication for one of the enemy generals, the consequences would be unthinkable."

"He's right," answered Nichola. "We simply couldn't ask him to take such a risk."

"Then I don't honestly see," said Jacobina, looking genuinely perplexed, "how you are going to let Lord Joscelin know where you are."

"Unless we go to Leicester ourselves."

"That I forbid," stated Michael fiercely. "You have only just given birth to a child. Do you want to kill both it and yourself from sepsis?"

And Jacobina's voice cut across his. "Arabella, for the love of God be sensible. You have a son and a daughter as well as a husband to consider now. The needs of the children must come first."

She knew that both of them were right. "Very well," Nichola said, and noticed that for the first time Jacobina and Michael not only looked at one another properly but exchanged a conspiratorial smile she was not meant to see.

There was plenty of room at the inns of Market Harborough, the leaguer ladies and bitches now having departed, many never to return. Nichola thought of the poor unburied corpses, of the girls wandering the countryside, their faces disfigured, their looks destroyed for ever, and cried as Jacobina put her to bed in The Angel, before sending for a midwife to give mother and child some after care.

"What will happen to them, do you think?"

"The army women? God knows. I suppose those fit to walk will try and find their husbands and lovers."

"Perhaps to be rejected because now they are ugly."

Jacobina shuddered. "Don't speak of it. It's too cruel a concept."

"I would rather be dead than maimed so horribly."

"Yes," said Jacobina, "so would I."

Nichola slept after that conversation, surprisingly peacefully, only waking to feed her baby and appreciate the warm herb-filled solution with which a tall thin woman bathed her vulva. When she woke again properly it was to find that she had slept right through Arabella's twenty-first birthday, that the date was now 17 June, and that Leicester was about to fall into the hands of the Parliamentarians.

"So what are we going to do?" she asked Jacobina, as she consumed the meal that her friend had brought for her, glad to see Arabella wakeful at last.

"It is all arranged. Before Colonel Morellon left for Leicester we decided what was best for everyone concerned."

"Did you now?" asked Nichola, amused.

"Yes. You and I and the two children are to travel to Devon by coach in the wake of the Parliamentary forces. The colonel says that that is the only way he can guarantee us safe passage. And before you open your mouth to ask for Joscelin, let me tell you he is with the King and is heading for Raglan Castle in Herefordshire, or so rumour has it. It is believed, too, that the royal party will then proceed on to Barnstaple to join the Prince of Wales who has moved there from Bristol. So, the colonel's idea is that if we can all get as far as Devonshire, you will be able to link up with your husband who is also making his way there."

"How very considerate of the colonel."

"I am glad you approve because I have gone so far as to hire a coach and horses, and a man prepared to drive us, risking his skin in exchange for a large sum of money."

"Well, that's settled then."

Jacobina frowned. "Our one fear is that you might not be well enough to travel. Apparently, Sir Thomas Fairfax is becoming famous for his punishing forced marches. It will mean many hours of discomfort in the coach."

"I'll be fit, never fear," Nichola answered with determination.

"What other option do I have?" She paused. "You have not mentioned Emmet in all this."

"Because the conveyance is not large enough to accommodate her, Colonel Morellon has infiltrated her into the ranks of the Roundhead army as a cook. In fact she has already gone."

"Couldn't we all have done that?" Nichola asked. "Wouldn't it have been simpler?"

"Oh no," said Jacobina, and burst out laughing. "You see, the Parliamentarians only allow women who work to follow their troops. Whores and hangers-on are forbidden."

"But they work too," answered Nichola, and they both giggled.

That night she got out of bed, looked at her figure and sighed, thinking there would be little chance of an exercise programme until she got to Devon. But all the while, as these silly superficial ideas floated through her brain, she was pushing away other more serious notions: the realisation that she could have returned to her own time while she was in labour, that one further step down the tunnel and she would have been back in her old body. And the resultant, rather frightening, thought that now she had finally burned her boats.

Having retaken Leicester on 18 June, Sir Thomas Fairfax, Commander-in-Chief of the New Model Army, headed westwards and arrived in Taunton in Somerset on 5 July 1645. He had stopped on the way only to parley with leaders of the Clubmen, those bands of country vigilantes, armed with cudgels, formed to resist the plundering of their goods and property by both Roundheads and Cavaliers alike. Twice, at Salisbury and at Dorset, Fairfax had been confronted by huge groups of them, but had managed to talk his way out of the situation on each occasion. Other than for that, his men had marched steadily onwards in the boiling heat, achieving a remarkable seventeen miles a day.

Behind them at a discreet distance, forced to keep up because they dare not lose contact with Colonel Morellon, Nichola and Jacobina had suffered gross discomfort in the close confines of the stuffy coach, and could only look forward to the evenings, when they would put up at an inn and, more often than not, Michael would slip out of camp for an hour or so and come to see them. Miranda, at over three years old, now understood that he was her father and had taken to calling him Daddy, a word he did not fully recognise.

"What does she mean?" he asked the two women as he sat at dinner with them.

"It's her word for Papa. Don't you like it?" Nichola answered.

"I love it that she even knows me, and as far as I am concerned she can call me anything at all. I wish I could see more of her, Arabella."

"Perhaps when all is finally resolved you will be able to."

"If anything were to happen to Joscelin," said Jacobina, who had had far too much wine and had suddenly lost control of what she was saying, "would you two marry one another?"

"No," Michael answered swiftly, "we were youthful lovers, that is all. Since Arabella went to Oxford she has changed completely. Now that I have seen her so radiantly happy with another man I would not presume to ask for her hand. Besides," he added, "she is no longer what I am looking for."

There was a fractional pause. "Go on," said Nichola, very slightly annoyed.

"This war has taught me that there is something even more important than love," Michael continued, downing a whole glass of claret and suddenly looking incredibly like Michael York.

"And what is that?" asked Jacobina.

"Companionship and a willingness to share. I want a woman who will throw in her lot with mine, come what may. Who knows what the outcome of this conflict will be, who knows how many of us will survive? I want someone who will live recklessly from day to day and worry about the future as and when it happens."

Jacobina said nothing but drank another glass and Nichola put in rather caustically, "The whole thing is hypothetical anyway, my dear. Joscelin *is* alive and I hope will join me soon. There is no question of anything happening to him."

"Brave words," said Michael softly and changed the subject. "Sir Thomas's intelligence network informs him that the King is still at Raglan Castle taking his ease. Apparently, though it is hard to believe, he spends the days playing bowls or discoursing with friends, even reading poetry. I wonder whether the man has taken leave of his senses."

"I think," answered Nichola thoughtfully, "that it is very easy for the King to get lulled into a sense of false security. He was rather like that at Oxford. But if Joscelin is with him, he won't care for such inactivity at all."

"Nobody has yet left the royal party, it's said, so your husband must still be in attendance."

"Then I wish he'd get a move on. I want to show him his son."

"I think you'll have to go to Barnstaple and wait," Michael said consideringly. "And if I were you I'd proceed there in the next day or two. Sir Thomas is keen to meet George Goring head-on. He won't delay much longer."

"Where is Lord Goring now?"

"He has abandoned the idea of besieging Taunton and is encamped somewhere to the east."

"Is Prince Rupert with him?" Jacobina asked, her cheeks flushing at the very name.

"No, he has been to Barnstaple and has gone again. He sailed for Bristol a few days ago."

"How is he?" asked Nichola, full of a strange concern.

"More moody and irritable than ever. It's said that the defeat at Naseby wears heavy on him. Do you know, I believe he is beginning to lose heart for this fight."

"He is," said Nichola.

They both turned to look at her. "How do you know?" asked Jacobina.

"There was something odd about his demeanour when last we met, just before I gave birth to Emlyn. I think he is turning into a very unhappy young man."

"Perhaps because he won't take what is offered him," the elf girl said sharply, and Michael shot her a penetrating glance.

"Perhaps because that which he wants has never been offered at all," Nichola answered. And was acutely aware that a sudden and profound silence had fallen over the other two people seated at the dinner table.

Chapter Thirty

It was hot by the time the townsfolk of Taunton raised themselves from their beds. Above the swelling contours of the Black Down Hills the sky was a whitish blue, heat-bleached and limpid, the earth below shimmering and silent, nothing moving in the breezeless landscape that by afternoon would be fiery as a furnace. This was a day for sitting in leaf-dappled shade, for slipping into the cooling current of a deep flowing river, a day for laughter and flowers and wine. But it was 10 July 1645, and so was a day for savagery and killing, for soaking the parched earth with showers of blood, for leaving the bodies of horses and men to gaze sightlessly at the white-blue sky as it slowly, slowly, turned to crimson.

Nichola was up before dawn, aware that Michael was once more breaking the rules and coming through the darkness to bring Emmet to her, putting his future in jeopardy, risking all to see his daughter's family complete again.

And he will be left with nothing, Nichola thought, and tears filled her eyes as the first rays of that brutal white day spilt over the hills like droplets of milk.

Michael was looking the most handsome she had ever seen him on that particular dawning, his squarish actor's face tanned from hours spent riding in the sun, his tall body elegant in its buff coat and golden sash, a fresh stock, lace trimmed, at his throat. Emmet, however, looked thin and drab, an air of melancholy about her, her pert sharpness completely vanished.

"Oh, my dear girl," Nichola said, and took her servant in her arms, wiping the tears from Emmet's oddly matched eyes.

"Arabella," Michael interrupted her urgently, "I must go again. The camp will be stirring at any moment and though I can excuse an absence of half an hour I dare not be missing any longer. So listen to me well. You must go to Barnstaple as soon as you are ready. Take the high track skirting Exmoor and journey as quickly as you can."

"Is there to be a battle today?"

"I must not discuss such things. I merely tell you to go, swiftly."

An enormous fondness for him filled Nichola's heart. "You have been very good to me," she said, and impulsively flung her arms round him. He kissed her, of course, but she knew from the very nature of the embrace that his passion for her had indeed come to its end.

"I am good to the mother of my child," Michael answered simply.

"I shall keep Miranda safe, I promise you."

"And Lord Joscelin, will he still love her now that he has a son?"

"His attitude to her will not change. He married me, daughter and all, and he is a man of much honour."

"Then I am satisfied," Michael said, and with that turned to go.

There was a rustle in the doorway and Nichola saw that Jacobina had come in and was standing listening to them, dressed in a dark blue riding habit, the velvet tunic encasing her so tightly that she no longer looked elfin but fairy-like, her rich amber hair dazzling beneath the little round hat she wore.

"Good morning," she said quietly, smiling at the startled expression in the three pairs of eyes that regarded her.

Amazed by her friend's sudden enchanting loveliness, Nichola said, "I'm so glad to see you dressed, and so beautifully at that. It means we can leave almost straight away."

Jacobina's gloved hands clenched together. "That is why I have risen early, my dear. To tell you I have decided not to come with you to Barnstaple, that today must see the parting of the ways."

"But why?" Nichola asked, perplexed.

Jacobina turned to Michael. "Colonel Morellon, the other day at dinner, when I had consumed too much to drink and asked some rather impertinent questions, you told me that you no longer sought love but companionship. Afterwards, when I was sober, it occurred to me that the reason for this might be that you had loved then lost Arabella. Well, I too have loved and lost and know the pain of it."

Michael merely stared, saying nothing.

"On that same occasion," Jacobina continued, "you said that you wanted a woman who would throw in her lot with yours, come what may. If you were in true earnest, then I would like to be that woman. I will go with you, sharing whatever fate has to offer, living for each day as it comes."

Nichola stood transfixed, thinking how war changed people, how matters of civility and custom were dispensed with entirely in the urgency of the moment. Stealing a glance at Michael's face, she wondered how he was going to reply.

"But you are so beautiful," he said eventually.

"And what has that to do with it?"

"You could have your pick of anyone. Why choose an enemy soldier?"

Jacobina's face hardened. "I am sorry, Colonel. Either I was mistaken about what you really meant or obviously I do not suit you. I hope I haven't given offence." And she made to sweep out of the door.

At last Michael acted, taking her by the wrist to stop her going. "I *did* mean what I said, but how could I involve a glorious creature like you in such a wild adventure?"

"Oh for heaven's sake, Michael," Nichola put in, not able to bear another minute of such word games. "For all her fragile looks, Jacobina is as tough as boots. Now are you going to accept her offer or aren't you?" A thought occurred to her. "And by the way, do you have the blood of Dukes in your veins?"

Jacobina stared at her in surprise and Nichola mouthed the words, "Emerald Ditch's prediction."

"My maternal great-grandfather was the Duke of Norfolk," Michael answered, looking startled. "I thought you knew that, Arabella."

"I'd forgotten," Nichola said, brushing the matter aside. "Now, what about Jacobina's offer?"

"If she is willing to choose such an uncertain future, I can think of nothing I would like better than to have her as my companion."

"Then we should leave at once." Jacobina said in a business-like manner.

"No, you are to wait for me here in Taunton," Michael replied, equally firmly. "Blood will be shed today and I refuse to involve you in it. I will come back for you as soon as the fighting is done. But if by any chance I do not return, then you must go to join Arabella in Barnstaple."

Jacobina's face fell. "I had hoped our relationship would begin immediately."

"It *has* begun," answered Michael. "I will come back for you, I swear it."

And with that he kissed her, and Nichola, watching, knew by the way his mouth sought hers, by the way Jacobina's lips parted beneath Michael's, that it would not be long before they found magic in bed together and all their past unhappinesses would be forgotten.

She turned to Emmet. "Go and fetch Miranda quickly. She must say farewell to her father." Then, seeing Jacobina and Michael gazing at one another, added, "On second thoughts, we'll both go," and hurried from the room.

Her last glimpse of the man who had once been her lover and the girl she had once betrayed was unforgettable, for they seemed set apart already, dream figures caught in a landscape in which everything else had substance and reality but they alone were frozen into the glittering heart of a diamond.

An hour later, Nichola had parted from them both, waving goodbye to Jacobina as the coach took the rutted road to Barnstaple. Michael had long since gone to join Sir Thomas Fairfax at the Roundhead headquarters near the village of Long Sutton, and already through that broiling white hot day there could be heard the distant sound of musket shot, the boom of heavy guns and the high-pitched neigh of frightened horses.

"Oh Arabella, how I've grown to hate that noise," said poor thin Emmet, snuggling as close to Nichola as Miranda, who was sitting upon her other side. With a brief image of herself as Mother Courage, Nichola held them tightly while still keeping a watchful eye on Emlyn, who slept in his basket.

They had followed Michael's instructions and taken the road that ran near Exmoor, thus avoiding the scene of the conflict. But as she journeyed, Nichola's thoughts were full of the Roundhead colonel and his new love, glad that this terrible Civil War, which divided most, had in fact brought about their unlikely union, promising both people involved a chance of unique happiness.

Yet all these ideas were tinged with sadness for Nichola knew, sketchy though her knowledge of the period was, that the first Civil War was now drawing to its close and that it would not be long before England lay under the sole domination of Parliament. And this, of course, would mean that life would become very harsh, particularly for those who had supported the Royalist cause.

I wish I could remember what became of everyone, she thought.

But with the sure knowledge that the King was going down very soon, a premonition that something might still prevent her from being reunited with Joscelin caused Nichola to shiver involuntarily.

Emmet, sitting so close to her and knowing her so well, read her mind and said, "Will Lord Joscelin be waiting for us in Barnstaple?"

Nichola shook her head. "I have no idea. All I know is that he was with the King at Raglan Castle but I haven't a clue where he went after that."

"To think he still hasn't seen his son."

"Don't remind me," answered Nichola, and suddenly began to feel enormously depressed.

The sweltering day continued, tiring both horses and passengers, so much so that Nichola, having stopped for a change of animals at midday, decided that they should rest overnight at the market town of South Molton on the southern edge of Exmoor. So it was in slightly cooler weather that the two women and their coachman reached their destination the next morning, feeling that at last they were back in Royalist territory and hopefully could discover the current whereabouts of Lord Joscelin Attwood.

There had been a community at Barnstaple since the days of the Saxon Kings and, seeing its sheltered moorings nestling on the tidal River Taw, it was not difficult to understand why this was so. Looking round at the town's delightfully quaint buildings, its ancient church and, unbelievably, original Elizabethan theatre, Nichola felt her spirits rise again. Having found lodgings at The Black Swan, an inn standing right on the water's edge, she immediately changed her travelling clothes and made her way to the house situated just above Merchants' Walk where Charles, Prince of Wales, no doubt preferring the luxury of a merchant's home to the starkly cold comfort of the ruinous Norman castle, had taken up residence.

To call on a Prince without so much as an appointment seemed at the very least impolite, at the worst presumptuous, but Nichola was in no mood to bother about decorum. Her only concern was to make contact with her husband and talk to him about their future together, a future that at long last seemed assured, as she had finally come face to face with the reality of returning to her own time, and escaped its danger.

A servant answered the door, a servant who informed her that the Prince of Wales was in Council with his advisers and could not be disturbed. Somewhat disconsolately, Nichola told him she would return within the hour and went to stroll beside the lively river.

An elegant arched bridge, dating from the fifteenth century, spanned the Taw from east to west, the town having been built on the east bank at the point where the river broadened into the estuary. On an impulse, Nichola walked across, peering down into the waters below to see the reflection of the bridge's curving arches.

It was high tide and the river was filled to the brim, ripples of silver foaming over its surface where the wild blue sea called to it at the estuary's mouth. Turning her head in that direction, hearing the shriek of the gulls, smelling the tangy salt that hung like grains of crystal on the breeze, it suddenly came to her that going by water had been the Royalists' principal means of escape. As Henrietta Maria had already done, like the Prince of Wales would do shortly, it was by decamping across the Channel that most of the Cavaliers had survived. Knowing what she must do in order to protect the little family who now meant so much to her, Nichola returned to Merchants' Walk.

The Prince who received her graciously some thirty minutes later was much changed from the little devil who had so teasingly deceived her outside Mr William Stokes's dancing and fencing academy in Oxford. The young man who rose from his chair to greet her as Nichola entered the room had by this time celebrated his fifteenth birthday and was already over six feet tall, almost at the full height that she knew he would achieve in adulthood. Charles had slimmed down too, his face thin and well boned, so that for a moment she caught a glimpse of his father behind the dark swarthy features that the Prince had inherited from his Medici ancestors and which so dominated his appearance. It really was incredible that two such tiny people as the King and Henrietta Maria had produced this elegant young giant, Nichola thought as she made a polite curtsey.

"My dear Lady Attwood," said the Prince in a voice that for some reason shook very slightly, "I cannot say how relieved I am to see you. This is a miracle I had not hoped for."

"Miracle?" Nichola repeated questioningly.

"Yes. We had all believed you dead. My father wrote to me from Raglan that Lord Joscelin had put on mourning clothes and was inconsolable."

She stared at him uncomprehendingly. "I don't understand. Why does everyone think that?"

"You were reported slain during the assault on the women of the baggage train after Naseby, for which I shall never forgive those bastard Parliamentarians, never."

"But I did escape it, thank God."

The Prince smiled charmingly. "Thank God indeed. I must communicate to His Majesty immediately that all is well."

Nichola asked the question for which she had travelled so long and so far. "Then where is my husband? Do you know, Highness?"

"Yes, I do. He left Raglan several days ago and sailed for Bristol to join my cousin Rupert, who has promised to hold that city for our cause. Rupert himself has only been gone from here a short while. You've just missed him."

"How is he?"

"A much changed man, alas. He, too, put on mourning for you and became as moody as a bear. He seems to have taken the defeat of Naseby and the subsequent attack on the women entirely on his own shoulders."

Nichola caught the Prince's eye. "Do you mean that he is blaming himself for my death?"

"Yes." The knowing cynicism that would mark the man, peeped out from the eyes of the boy. "He is much taken with you, Lady Attwood, I believe. I think you are the Achilles' Heel of my dashing young relative."

"I hope Lord Joscelin doesn't agree with you."

Prince Charles smiled. "Your husband keeps his own counsel, as do all wise men. However, why don't you sup with me tonight? In the interim I can write to Bristol to give the joyful news that you are still alive."

Nichola looked at him with a slightly wry expression. "Could you also put in your letter, Sir, that Lord Joscelin is the father of a son, one Emlyn Attwood, born in a cart even while the battle raged."

The Prince's black eyebrows flew about. "You have had another child? My felicitations. May I offer to stand as godparent?"

She stared in wonder. "Can this really be happening to Nichola Hall?" she said under her breath.

Charles looked mystified. "To whom?"

"A slip of the tongue, Sir. That would be an honour indeed for both Lord Joscelin and myself."

"Then would you like me to request the vicar to baptise the boy soon?"

"Thank you, Highness," said Nichola, and shook her head incredulously at the wonder of it all.

Later, she walked back to the Prince's house in the gentle glow of a fine summer's evening, watching the shafts of sun strike the river and turn it into a shimmering carpet of pure daffodil. On the landing stages, the fishermen were unloading the day's catch so that the silvery satiny scales reflected buttercup gold. It was a glittering sunset in every way, for at last Nichola understood why Joscelin had gone to Raglan Castle so obediently when his King commanded and had not come in search of her. And though she had trusted him, had never for a moment thought the worse of her husband for not seeking her far and wide, Nichola was reassured to have the true explanation of events.

The young Prince who had once believed himself childishly infatuated with Lady Attwood, had dressed in his best to receive her. Dramatically clad in wine-coloured satin, his lace collar and cuffs very white against his dark skin, Charles already had something about him of the fatal attraction he would one day hold for women. Regarding him closely, Nichola felt sure that Joscelin was right and that some willing wench of Oxford had granted the youth her favours – and that several more had probably done so since. Indeed, his gaze was sufficiently adult and appreciative for Nichola to feel a sense of relief that Arabella's body was once more tightening into its usual nubile shape after the birth of Emlyn.

To add to the sensual atmosphere, the dining room of the merchant's house, into which the Prince ushered her, was musky with the gleam of candles and the scent of flowers, their light and colour reflected in a mirror that hung above a cabinet inlaid with ivory, its whiteness dazzling to the eye against the dark rich panels of the walls. Tapestries, too, enhanced the feeling of richness, the gleaming gold and mint green, the carnation reds and cornflower blues of their threads, their scenes of goddesses at play, all adding to the beauty of the surroundings.

"Would you like wine, Madam?" said the Prince, and poured it for her himself from a tall crystal jug crowned by a solid silver lid and gleaming spout.

And it was at that moment, as Nichola and Charles, Prince of Wales, clinked glasses, toasting the health of His Majesty the King, that the room's harmonious ambience was rudely shattered. From the street below came the sound of clattering hooves, of men dismounting, this followed by a thunderous knocking on the front door.

The Prince and his guest looked at one another. "Trouble!" he said curtly.

The major domo appeared. "Lord Goring is below, Highness."

"Send him up," answered Charles with an air of resignation.

George Goring had been the first person to greet Nichola when she had arrived in Oxford and she had liked him at once. Since then his terrible reputation for drunkenness, his awful behaviour in the West Country, where he had ravaged the countryside, allowing his men to rape and rob, to say nothing of killing those who stood in their way, had tarnished his image in Nichola's eyes. But still, as with all genuine rogues, there was something likeable about the man and to see him now, standing in the doorway of that most lovely of rooms and swaying, not through inebriation but with sheer fatigue, was heart-rending. Rubbing a filthy hand across eyes that seemed the only visible thing in his travel-stained face, Goring said, "We've lost, Sir. We're done in. I engaged with Black Tom Fairfax at Langport and the bastard trounced me. Two thousand of my men have gone for prisoners, the rest deserted as I retreated here from Bridgewater, and those that did not were cut down by the Clubmen. Over a thousand horses perished in the fray."

Charles looked at George Goring mutely, then pushed the elegant wine jug towards him, saying, "Here, help yourself." He turned to Nichola. "So we have no army left in the West."

She shook her head. "It would appear not."

The veneer of handsome Prince, of young man of the world, stripped away upon the instant and a frightened child looked out of Charles Stuart's face. "My God, Arabella, what is going to happen to me?"

"You must be as courageous as a lion," she answered, "and you must also be equally clever. I think perhaps soon your royal father will tell you to leave the country. When he does so, you must obey at once."

"And what of him?"

Nichola did not answer, staring round that harmonious room, seeing George Goring with his head sunk into his hands, the wine jug already empty, the dirt on his face streaked with tears.

"Well?" asked the Prince.

"I fear the worst," she found the courage to say, and the next moment held the future Charles II, one of the wisest and most skilled kings that England was ever to know, in her arms, as he shivered uncontrollably at the thought of all the dark days that lay ahead.

Chapter Thirty-one

Two days later, Nichola sailed from Barnstaple on the morning tide. The fisherman she had hired to take her had navigated his craft down the estuary, then out into the open sea, where he had hugged the coastline past Saunton Sands and Baggy Point before turning eastwards at Morte Point into the Bristol Channel. Nichola had sat on deck, thinking that at long last the end of her journey was in sight. With each sea mile Bristol grew nearer and with it, Joscelin.

The day before she had left, Emlyn had been christened in the early morning, the ceremony conducted in the ancient church of St Peter's, parts of which dated back to 1318 and whose dark interior still contained the heady smell of centuries of incense. The Prince of Wales had stood as one godparent, Emmet as the other, a fact which had appealed to Nichola's twentieth-century equal rights outlook.

After this little ritual had been performed she had paid off Jacob, the coachman who had so carefully brought her to her destination. In a flurry of gratitude, Nichola had given him far more money than he had asked for, enough to allow the man to travel back by boat; coach, horses, and all. He had promptly announced his intention of going up the Severn as far as was navigable for a vessel of the size he had hired, then making his way overland to his home in Market Harborough.

"These are not good times for travelling the countryside, my Lady," he had said heavily as they parted.

"I know. From now on I'm going by water as much as possible."

"And very wise too."

After she had waved him farewell, Nichola had sent the children back to the inn and gone to the royal residence where she had dined with the Prince and George Goring, the conversation over the meal being mostly about Bristol and the perilous position in that city.

"As you know," Charles had said, "my royal father sent me there from Oxford to set up a court of my own. Eventually, though, it was decided that the situation was becoming too dangerous and I was moved on here."

"Why was it considered so unsafe?" Nichola asked.

"It is a fortified town with no means of escape. Not the sort of place to leave in haste."

"Surely one could always get out by water?"

"I imagine the Avon Gorge would be blockaded. One or two people might slip through but it would be very difficult for me and the members of my entourage."

George Goring had refilled his wine glass.

"In my honest opinion, Lady Attwood, the situation there is dire. I doubt if even Rupert can hold out long."

Charles had spoken again. "My cousin assured His Majesty that he can keep going for four months. And when Rupert sailed from here he took a mass of supplies with him, food for the citizens, cattle and corn, and some mighty cannon with which to defend the walls."

Nichola had turned to George. "Then why are you so pessimistic, my Lord?"

He had looked at her gloomily, his equilibrium far from recovered since his defeat at the Battle of Langport. "Because Black Tom Fairfax is unstoppable in his present mood. His men are tough and well disciplined, he has a constant supply of money and equipment from London, and his own ruthlessness is in the ascendant. Bristol is England's second city. He'll not leave it alone for long."

Charles had shaken his head. "I pray you're wrong, Lord Goring."

"I think the time for prayer will soon be past," George had replied bitterly.

And it was towards this situation that Nichola was now heading, taking her hapless children into peril once more, along with the long suffering Emmet.

"You're weary to the bone, aren't you?" Nichola said, patting the girl's head, where she sat at her feet, staring out over the calm blue waters of the Bristol Channel.

"I am that, my Lady," the servant answered with a sigh.

"I feel so guilty about you sometimes. I've dragged you from pillar to post, taken you from family and friends, and subjected you to all kinds of danger. And you've nothing to show for it except to look worn out." A thought struck Nichola. "And talking of friends, do you know in all this time we've been together you've never mentioned a sweetheart to me. Has there never been anyone?"

Either a slight flush had come into Emmet's cheeks at this or else the sea breeze was finally doing its invigorating work. "There was a fisher lad who used to come to the kitchens sometimes at Kingswear Hall, selling his catch. I did quite fancy him."

"And was the feeling reciprocated?"

"Yes, I think so. He used to say he liked my funny eyes."

Nichola smiled. "Well there's a compliment!"

Emmet echoed the smile, though wistfully. "I always thought I could settle there. In one of those little cottages near Dartmouth. It would be a pleasant enough life."

"As pleasant as anywhere when this war ends and Parliament takes over."

Emmet narrowed her eyes. "Do you think that is going to happen?"

"Yes."

"And will they be very strict?"

"I've always had a fear of regimes based on religious fanaticism, but it will probably be the poverty brought about by the war which will cause the nation to suffer, more than anything else."

"Then maybe," Emmet answered shyly, "I should try and get back to the Hall once you and Lord Joscelin have met up again."

"Emmet," said Nichola firmly, laying her hand on her servant's shoulder, "when that day comes we are *all* going back to Kingswear and we're not going to split up ever again. We will stick together come what may."

"But Lord Joscelin's not the kind of man to give up on a fight."

"Then somehow he will have to be persuaded."

Not wanting to push his lady passengers too far, the captain of the fishing vessel put into shore that evening, mooring at the stone quay in the snug harbour of Minehead, where his humble craft nestled alongside larger ships, trading with such distant places as Portugal, Africa and North America. A row of colour-washed cottages with thatched roofs stood behind this jetty, and it was in one of these, an inn called The Mermaid, that Nichola and her family stayed that night, the sound of the restless ocean singing in their ears even while they slept. Rising at dawn and setting off early next day, the vessel and its passengers entered the twisting grandeur of the Avon Gorge later that afternoon and headed for the docks tucked neatly away inland, six miles from the actual sea itself.

The Saxons had been the first people to trade from Bristol and the port had continued to play a vital maritime role throughout the centuries until, in 1552, the Society of Merchant Venturers of Bristol had been granted a royal charter. Then world trade had boomed until now when, as a result of the Civil War, every kind of business dealing was adversely affected.

To Nichola, who loved the city, drawing into ancient docks she had never seen before, yet had known to have once existed, was a sight that even in her extraordinary state of mind, desperate for news of her husband, she still found quite enthralling. Yet again, though, came the shock of seeing a town so much smaller than its modern counterpart; in fact a compact walled city outside which lay its many bustling wharves.

They had arrived at a quay situated to the west and Nichola's startled eyes took in the fact that there had once been water lapping at Bristol's very feet. When she had appeared at the Theatre Royal there had been no sign of this prominent waterway and she presumed, now, that the river, which had stopped abruptly at the south end of the new City Centre, had been filled in to make way for the development. Delighted to see the Avon back where it should have been, Nichola bade farewell to the captain, paid him generously from her rapidly diminishing supply of money and, drawing her family round her, passed through the West Gate and entered the city.

An enquiry to the guards revealed that Prince Rupert could be found either at the garrison in the castle, which lay by the East Gate, or at his house in Wine Street. Staring around her, hardly able to recognise a thing, Nichola made her way up Corn Street to where an ancient cross stood at the junction of four thoroughfares. Just as with Carfax in Oxford, this was obviously the centre of the walled city and, sure enough, she saw that Wine Street ran off immediately opposite.

Rather as she had feared, the Prince was not at home, but his major domo revealed some worrying information in answer to Nichola's anxious questions. Lord Joscelin Attwood was not staying at the Prince's house nor, as far as the servant was aware, was he even in the city.

"Oh God," said Nichola, looking round at her tired brood and wondering what to do next.

"But if my Lady would care to wait until His Highness's return, I am sure he will be able to clarify Lord Joscelin's whereabouts."

"I will gladly do so," Nichola answered thankfully, and was delighted to be ushered into the smaller parlour and served light refreshments.

"Are we staying here?" whispered Emmet as the servants withdrew.

"It all depends on where Joscelin is. Why?"

"Because if my Lord is not about, I don't trust that Prince with your virtue."

"Oh for heaven's sake," Nichola answered impatiently. "Rupert is a gentleman when all is said and done. And have you no faith in me?"

"Rupert loves you," the girl stated simply. "And as for you, you've a kind heart."

"And what exactly do you mean by that?"

But Emmet would not answer, tucking into a sweet tart and stolidly munching and shaking her head when Nichola repeated the question.

The Prince returned at dusk, walking into the hall with his booted stride then, after a murmured conversation with his servant, bursting into the parlour, all eyes.

"Arabella," he said, and went down on one knee before her, the better to gaze into her face.

Emmet shot her a look which said, "I told you so", but Nichola ignored her and gave him the lightest of kisses on the cheek. "Highness, it is so good to see you again. We are here in search of my husband."

"Before I talk of him," Rupert replied, "let me say how great was my joy when I received Cousin Charles's letter. I had thought you dead and gone and had put on black clothes for you." In an undertone, he added, "I died myself at the news, if you but knew it."

Seeing his expression, and knowing that Emmet was watching her with the piercing glare of a hawk, Nichola said, "We all of us escaped the aftermath of Naseby, thank God. Jacobina Jermyn included."

"Oh yes?" answered Rupert, not betraying by the merest flicker that it was he who had deflowered the girl. "Is she here with you?"

"No, she has struck out on her own, but is perfectly safe I can assure you."

In the same low voice, Rupert said, "It is only your safety that concerns me." His eyes moved to the basket lying at Nichola's feet. "I see you have had your child."

"Yes." And she picked Emlyn up so that Rupert could look at him.

"Is it a boy?"

"Yes."

"A fine son indeed. Lord Joscelin is to be greatly envied." He stood up and his tone changed completely. "And while we await his Lordship's arrival I must insist that you stay here as my guests."

"I find it very strange that he is not here already," Nichola answered, also rising. "The Prince of Wales assured me that Joscelin had left Raglan Castle and was on his way here to help you defend the city."

"Then the Prince is mistaken," Rupert said shortly. "There has been no sign of your husband. But as soon as word reaches him that you have arrived I am sure he will hasten to your side."

Was he being sarcastic, Nichola wondered, shooting Rupert a sideways glance. Once again, there was no flicker on that handsome sensitive face and she was left to ascribe to him whatever emotions she thought fit.

Aware that Emmet was still staring at her, Nichola said, "I would welcome the chance to remain here, Sir. It has been very tiring for my children to be taken from once place to another without respite."

"They are the victims of war, alas," Rupert answered. "For it is my belief that there is nothing more harmonious in this world than a settled family life, particularly with the woman one loves at one's side."

"Then I pray you one day find such joy," Nichola said steadily, more than aware of all the messages, barely concealed at that, that he was sending her.

"Amen," Rupert replied. "And now, Madam, I will show you to your quarters. This house is large and comfortable and there is what I believe was once a nursery wing on the top floor. Would you care for your maid and children to be housed there?"

"That sounds wonderful," Nichola answered, and could not resist pulling a face at the hovering Emmet as the Prince courteously bowed her out of the room to start a tour of his home.

They had supper alone that evening and then retired to the withdrawing room where they sat, saying little, on tall-backed chairs before the fire, for the late July evening had grown cold and dismal with rain. As the great clock in the hall struck nine, Nichola rose to her feet.

"Where are you going?" asked Rupert, looking at her through the blue smoke of his long pipe.

"To feed my baby."

"Bring him down here, let me see such a sight."

"It is a very personal thing and you are not my husband."

"Arabella," said the Prince, leaning forward and catching her hand, "do you remember what I said to you at Fawsley?"

"About what?"

"About the child. How I knew he could not be mine but wished he could have been. Well, I meant that. And I meant every word of our conversation in York when I told you that I would never get married unless it could be to you."

Nichola looked away, suddenly confused.

"So in view of that," the Prince went on, "I am going to ask you a favour. Let me, just for the few days until Joscelin comes, pretend that I am your husband. Let me sit here in the evenings with you like this, let me see you feed your son, let me talk and eat and live comfortably with you. It will be the only chance I shall ever get, I know it. Do this one thing I pray you, if you have any feelings for me at all."

Nichola stared at him. "You are not asking to share my bed, I trust?"

"Of course not. You have made your feelings about that crystal clear."

"So you just want to play Happy Families?"

Rupert shook his head. "I do not know what that is. I was brought up very formally. But perhaps it is what I mean."

A sudden love for him constricted her heart, far removed from her passion for Joscelin but real enough as regarded her empathy with this extraordinary, temperamental, ruthless young soldier-of-fortune.

"Very well," Nichola heard herself say.

It was as well that Emmet was already abed, for Nichola brought Emlyn downstairs and sat before the fire, the reflection of the flames gleaming on Arabella's breasts, heavy with milk, as she suckled her son, Rupert sitting at her feet, gazing in wonderment.

"Have you never seen this before?" she asked.

"Never. Such things were strictly forbidden. Besides, my mother was too anxious to resume her normal life and keep her breasts beautiful to feed any of us."

"I thought like that once," Nichola answered dreamily.

"You? Such a womanly woman?"

A vision of Nichola Hall, slim and chic and sexy, flashed through Nichola's mind and she felt as if she were remembering a being from another planet.

"Yes, me. I've changed out of all recognition."

It was a feeble joke but she smiled at it for all that. And seeing her happy, Rupert kissed her hand, then returned to his seat, his booted feet thrust out before him, his glass of wine at his side, and watched her until the feed was over and Emlyn slept in her arms.

"And now?" he said softly.

"I will put him to bed and go myself. It has been a very long day. Goodnight, Rupert."

He stood up and kissed her on the cheek. "I will stay here and finish my pipe. Sleep well, sweetheart."

As she left the room, Nichola thought that if it hadn't been so touching, so pathetic, his game of Mothers and Fathers could have been hilariously funny. But the war had taught her too much about the frailty of others ever to let her laugh at them again. Walking quietly, she went up to her bedroom and set about getting herself ready for the night and then, when she had settled the child down and just before she blew out the candle, took the precaution of locking her door.

July turned into August and still there was no sign of Joscelin, a fact which Nichola found utterly extraordinary in view of the news which arrived for Prince Rupert, telling him that at the end of the month the King had finally left the tranquillity of Raglan Castle and was heading northwards.

"Then where *is* Joscelin?" she asked her host anxiously. He tried hard to appear concerned. "He must have marched north with the King. Oh, sweetheart, don't look so downhearted. Perhaps Cousin Charles's letter didn't get through. I'll write again, I promise you. Now, do you want to hear something to cheer you up?"

"Yes," she answered, trying to disguise her nagging worries.

"Do you remember old Meldrum who captured our great siege cannon, the Queen's Pocket Pistol, at Hull? The same fellow I trounced at Newark."

"Yes."

"Well, he's dead at last, the wily bastard. While he was laying siege to Scarborough – a siege that was successful, most unfortunately – he got shot in the cods." The Prince slapped his thigh and chortled like a schoolboy. "Right in them, can you imagine? Then he fell off the cliffs and descended two hundred feet but was saved by his cloak which ballooned out and eased the fall."

"First use of the parachute?" Nichola murmured.

"But finally, they got him in the guts and that was the end of him."

"Do you always laugh like that when people die?" Nichola asked acerbicly.

Rupert looked contrite. "No, I don't. But I did despise that particular old fart catcher. He was a professional soldier and took arms for the other side, would you believe it?"

"Well, you're a professional soldier and took arms for the King."

"He *is* my uncle," Rupert replied grandly, and ended the argument at a stroke.

He was very good company, Nichola had to admit it. And her presence had restored him to such good humour that it soon became the talk of the city as Rupert walked amongst his soldiers, affably swapping jokes with them and clapping them on the back.

"People are gossiping," said Emmet.

"Oh let them," Nichola answered crossly. "I am the Prince's guest and nothing more. And you can tell them that from me."

"One of the men who's been with him since Naseby said the Prince went mad when he thought you were dead. Weeping and carrying on and making their lives a misery."

"Emmet," said Nichola firmly, "once, at Kingswear Hall, when I was under threat and we all thought Lord Joscelin killed at Marston Moor, you advised me to go to the Prince and place myself under his protection. So what do you want? I wish you'd make up your mind."

"I don't want Lord Joscelin done down."

"He won't be. Now go away."

Yet the girl had a point and Nichola knew it. The very fact of constantly being in Rupert's company in such very domestic circumstances, was having its subtle effect. Very slowly, almost imperceptibly, they were growing closer.

Please hurry, Joscelin, Nichola thought urgently, or at the very least send me word.

Yet still there was no communication, and reports that the King, having got as far as Doncaster had now turned south again, only served to confuse her.

"Are you sure Joscelin was safe at Raglan?" she asked the Prince for the hundredth time,

"Listen," he said, rather irritably, "I did not see him with my own eyes but all my intelligences said it was so. What more can I tell you?"

"Why are you so angry?" she answered.

He was instantly repentant. "I'm sorry, sweetheart. Have I given offence?"

"No, of course not. But there is something the matter, isn't there?"

He nodded, refilling his wine glass. "There's an outbreak of plague in the city and the colonel of my guards, Sir Richard Crane, has been took sick."

"Does he have it, do you think?"

"I don't know, but I'm a mort worried."

"If it's what I believe it is," Nichola said thoughtfully, "we'd better start hunting for lice."

"Why, are they the carriers?"

"Of one type of plague called typhus, yes. But there are many different sorts of plague. The Black Death, for example, was caused by the fleas of infected rats."

He leant across the space between them, sitting together as they always did after supper. "You are so wise, Arabella, so clever. I have never met a woman like you in my life. Oh God's heart, how I wish you were single."

"But I'm not and I love Joscelin, you know I do. I only want him to come back."

"I don't," said Rupert honestly, risking her wrath. "Because every day I have alone with you is a treasure beyond price."

"Oh stop it!" Nichola snapped, and suddenly wept, the strangeness of her situation too difficult to cope with at that moment.

The Prince did not answer and when she regained control of herself and looked in his direction, Nichola saw that he was staring into the fire with such a pitiful expression on his face that it was all she could do not to take him into her arms. Somehow she managed to get out of her chair and make her way to her bedroom, thinking that she must soon move to other lodgings if the state of affairs between them was to be prevented from finally exploding into passion.

Help came to calm things down, but help of a nature that was the last thing Nichola would have wished for. Morale in the city was appallingly low, for the plague had spread, Sir Richard Crane was dead, and rumour coming from every front maintained that Sir Thomas Fairfax was ruthlessly closing in on them. Rupert spent more and more time patrolling the city, checking the defences, talking to his men, and would often come in so late that the entire household had retired to bed. Nichola wondered if he was doing it on purpose, deliberately putting a brake on their predicament by keeping away, yet the situation was unarguably deteriorating and it seemed that it would only be a matter of days before Black Tom laid siege.

On 3 September Rupert came in later than ever, but not so late that Nichola did not see him. Emlyn had been crying dismally most of the evening and finally, in desperation, she had started to walk about the house with him. Thus she was in the withdrawing room, the fire rekindled, when the Prince stormed into the room and then stopped short.

"Arabella, my dear, why are you still up?"

"Would you believe that this little wretch has been crying non stop?" and she showed Rupert the contentedly sleeping child.

He grinned, the lines of weariness on his face suddenly abundantly clear. "It's hard to I confess." But he could not be jocular a moment longer and sank down into his chair, pulling off his boots.

"What is it?" said Nichola.

"Get me some brandy and I'll tell you."

He downed a goodly glass in one gulp and refilled it from the decanter she had brought him. "Fairfax has written to me and I'm damned if I know how to answer."

"I beg your pardon?" she said, unable to believe what she was hearing.

"Black Tom has written to me. One of his troopers brought the letter to the garrison under flag of truce." And Rupert produced a parchment from his pocket and passed it to her.

Nichola stared at a document that was part of history. "I take into consideration your royal birth and relation to the Crown of England, your honour, courage and the virtue of your person," she read. "Sir, we fight to maintain; but the King, misled by evil counsellors, hath left his Parliament and his people."

She looked up at Rupert in horror. "What does he want?"

"For me to surrender Bristol. He promises me that I will be restored to the endeared affection of the Parliament and people if I do so." He swallowed another glassful.

"What are you going to do?"

Rupert shook his head wearily. "That's the devil of it, Arabella. I don't know. I've no stomach left for this futile war. An honourable truce is the only way it can end without the useless taking of yet more life. But I promised my royal uncle that I would hold Bristol for him, so I suppose I had better put up some sort of fight."

Nichola stared at him in disbelief. "Did Prince Rupert of the Rhine, the bravest soldier of them all, lose heart, then?"

He looked at her quizzically. "You speak as if it's all in the past."

"It is in a way. But ignore that. What do you intend to do?"

"Immediately, to stall him. In the longer term, I'm not sure. Oh Christ's wounds, Arabella, what a pass we have come to.

We're hopelessly outnumbered and I know it. Do I let men die just for the showing? Oh God, guide me." And he thrust his head in his hands.

Yet again, Nichola walked away and left him, too afraid of the genuine rapport between them even so much as to lay a finger on the man upon whom the King's last hope, the holding of Bristol, now rested.

Exactly as he had planned, Prince Rupert played for time, sending a reply to General Sir Thomas that he might indeed be willing to negotiate, but being decidedly vague as to exactly when. Fairfax responded by surrounding the fortifications outside the citadel, built somewhat after the manner of those encircling Oxford, with a mighty army which stood silently at the ready.

Within the walled city, tension rose as the epidemic continued to rage and trade with the outside world to diminish. Within Prince Rupert's home the situation reached fever pitch as he agonised to the point of drunkenness as to what he should do. Nichola meanwhile worried herself to tears both over him and the mysterious disappearance of her husband. Then, at last, the brewing storm came to culmination on the night of 9 September.

Rupert had yet again been round the fortifications, both within the city and surrounding it, and had seen the size of the force drawn up against him. He had returned home blind with fatigue and despair, too tired to do more than pick at the supper that was served.

"If Fairfax moves he'll nail us to the cross," he told Nichola, drinking yet another glass of wine and wiping his hand across his eyes. "We can't hold out, we simply can't."

"Then would it not be wiser to surrender and save the lives of the ordinary folk?"

"But the King would take that as a gross betrayal."

"Which is better? To see soldiers and citizens die? Or to please him?"

"I don't know," Rupert answered wearily. "I simply don't know." And folding his arms on the table, he sunk his head down into them in a gesture of total defeat.

This time she could not walk away, there was too much anguish and despair, too much responsibility on one young pair of shoulders, for Nichola to remain cold any longer. Getting up from her place, she walked round the table and gently took him in her arms.

"Oh help me, Arabella," he said, and she saw that he was weeping.

"No, Rupert, don't. You are the greatest fighter of them all. Whatever you decide to do will be right. I know it," she replied soothingly.

"Oh my God, I pray that is so," he answered and, pulling her on to his lap, kissed her.

The sexual chemistry between them flared instantly and, just for a moment, Nichola forgot everything as she returned his kiss. Then, unbidden, a picture of Joscelin came into her mind, an image of how he had looked on that first time she had ever seen him. She saw again the dark curls sweeping his lace collar, the diamonds that blazed about his person, but most of all she saw the look in his spectacular eyes as he had gazed at her.

Very gently, Nichola said, "No, Rupert, no." And stood up to escape his ardent embrace.

He stared at her, his gaze a blaze of blue anguish. "But I love you."

"And I love you, too."

"So why reject me?"

"Because everything has changed. I am no longer the woman I was. I have turned into a different person, a new woman who adores her husband."

Just for a moment a wry smile crossed her features as Nichola Attwood witnessed the final death throes of Nichola Hall.

"Then there is no hope for me?" said Rupert, getting to his feet.

"Not of that kind, no. But as to loving you as a friend, that I will always do."

The Prince walked to the door, every line of his body weary. Then he turned. "I accept your friendship because I have no choice," he said bitterly. "But know, and know well, that it will never be enough for me. I have given you my heart, Arabella, and now it is yours for ever. I shall not marry unless it be to you. Goodnight." And with that he left the room and she heard him slowly make his way upstairs.

Sad beyond words that she should have spurned so wonderful a man, yet simultaneously proud of her strength of character, Nichola blew out the candles and fell asleep in the chair by the fire.

At exactly two o'clock, for the hall clock was striking, she was awoken by the distant boom of mighty cannon. Jumping to her feet, Nichola was rushing to the door when it flew open and Rupert appeared, dressing himself as rapidly as only a soldier can. In one move he pulled on his boots then buckled his sword into place.

"It's started," he said grimly, and then a wonderful boyish grin transformed his features. "I'll wager that bastard Fairfax knew I was asleep and did it on purpose."

Nichola flung a rapid kiss to his cheek. "What should I do?"

"Wait for me here. I'll get back somehow, though God knows when. But if I don't return by midday get down to the docks and hire a boat to take you home to Devon. Have you enough money?"

"Probably not."

"Then help yourself from the bag I keep in my red hat, which is as good a hiding place as any."

And with that he was gone, out into the black night, leaving Nichola to go to her room and change, horribly aware that she might never see him again.

By dawn, the sound of distant fighting had filled the walled city, and it soon became obvious that the Roundheads had broken through the chain of elaborate outer fortifications and were pouring towards the citadel. Then, at about ten o'clock, filthy dirty with cannon smoke and blood, Rupert returned to the house, his expression very grim. Seeing the servants huddled in anxious groups in the hall, he dismissed them, turning to Nichola and drawing her into the library where they might speak privately.

"Have we lost?" she asked as Rupert closed the door.

"Yes. I did not have enough men even to cover the perimeter

of the fortifications, which stretches three whole miles. As soon as we'd formed up to repulse one lot, another would attack the part we'd left unprotected. Anyway, Rainsborough broke through on the east and captured Prior's Hill fort. Then Cromwell's cavalry came charging in and cut off the castle garrison from the men on the walls." He paused and drank the brandy Nichola handed him. "I could have retreated into the city, Arabella, and fought him street by street. But it would have meant the end of Bristol, this fine place. It would have been razed to the ground. So I said I would surrender. It seems to me I had little choice."

She went to him and put her arms round him. "You have done the right thing. Nothing is worth the total destruction of a beautiful city and the massacre of its inhabitants."

"The King will condemn me for a coward."

"Let him. You and your men know the truth." She smiled at him sadly. "So is this the parting of our ways?"

"I think it would be safer if you go now and return to Devon. God knows what will happen to me. You realise that we're losing this war, don't you, Arabella?"

"Yes," Nichola answered, "I do."

Rupert's manner became brisk. "Well, I'll to my bath and a change of clothes for the surrender. Black Tom and that cursed Cromwell shall have a sight, I can tell you. Will you stay to wave me off?"

"Of course."

He kissed her gently on the lips. "Once I've gone, take that bag of money and leave immediately. Get down to the wharves before they enter in force. Do you understand?"

"Yes."

"Then I'll prepare for my part in the charade."

Half an hour later everyone gathered in the hall to see the Prince go to surrender. Nichola and Emmet were already dressed discreetly in order not to attract attention to themselves, even Miranda wearing a gown of roughspun cloth. Thus, Rupert of the Rhine, flamboyant to the last, outshone them all, sauntering down the stairs as if he hadn't a care in the world. Nichola drew breath at the sight of him, clad in his favourite scarlet, very richly laid in silver lace, the most dashing Cavalier of them all.

"You look magnificent," she whispered.

"Fittingly dressed for the occasion," he answered wryly. He lowered his voice. "Now get away, my darling, before it is too late." They exchanged a public, formal kiss. "Forget me not," he added.

Then that most excellent Prince doffed his hat to the assembled company and was gone, mounting the black barbary horse which stood awaiting him, and galloping away to his destiny.

"What a brave man," sighed Emmet, weeping.

"I thought you didn't trust him?"

"I don't, but that doesn't stop him being the most stout-hearted creature who ever lived."

And so, yet again, they were moving on. Nichola could only be thankful that the children were quiet and behaving themselves as she hurried them over the cobbles and out through the West Gate, declaring to the Roundhead guard that she was going to the jetty to meet her husband who had been fishing at sea and was bringing his catch in.

"Tell him to bring some of it to General Sir Thomas Fairfax later tonight."

"Aye, Sir. And where's he to come?"

"To the garrison in the castle."

"Thank you, Sir. I will, Sir. And thank God for stock rural," Nichola added in an undertone as he opened the wicket and let them pass.

The docks were strangely quiet and, staring down river, Nichola could see why. A ship, presumably belonging to the enemy, had positioned itself crossways over the Avon so that all craft passing on either side of it could be carefully scrutinised.

"How are we going to get out?" asked Emmet, frantically.

"I don't know," Nichola answered her. "There doesn't seem to be a thing for hire."

And then she saw her salvation. A fishing smack quite capable of ocean going, and flying the Welsh Dragon of all things, was moored up at a far wharf, its captain sitting on the stone wall beside it.

"Hey you," Nichola called out. "Can I hire your boat for a good wage? I want to go to Dartmouth."

He looked up and Nichola gazed at a mat of black curls, a dirty stained face, and a great broad smile of strong white teeth.

"How much?" the man shouted.

"Eight pounds." It was a fortune.

"Right," he said, scrambling to his feet and bowing as they hurried towards him. "Welcome aboard, ladies, welcome aboard. And you there . . ." He playfully smacked Nichola's bottom. ". . . shall have a decent bed in which to lay your pretty arse."

She turned on him furiously and a great roar of laughter came out of the grime. "Would'st strike me?" he said.

She was looking straight at Joscelin.

Chapter Thirty-two

Like a train of clamorous attendants, a plume of gulls followed them as they slipped slowly from their moorings and made their way down the shadowy waters of the treacherous, twisting, spectacular gorge that led the River Avon towards the open sea. High in the air, the rush of their wings, their strange remote lonely cry, speaking of distant oceans and the sting of salt spray, echoed in the narrow confines of the towering cliffs. But they served their purpose, this horde of swooping, diving, wave white escorts, for as Rhys ap Richard passed the Roundhead ship, calling out to them in Welsh and holding a fish in his hand as he pointed a craggy finger towards Wales, the presence of his aerial following said in any language that there went a genuine fisherman.

Joscelin and Nichola stood together at the ship's rail, saying nothing, both smoking clay pipes, a touch that appealed to the theatrical in her. In her arms she held their baby, blatantly at the breast, to add to the fisherfolk image that it was so vital for them to portray convincingly if they were to pass unhindered. Emmet, drinking from a tin cup, wiped the back of her hand across her smacking lips and then offered beer to Miranda. who stood staring at the Parliamentarians open-mouthed, a piece of acting which delighted her mother, for she was not at all that kind of child.

"On your way," was the shouted instruction, and Rhys pulled his forelock, grinned, and called back something unintelligible.

"Done it," said Joscelin beneath his breath, smiling and nodding as he passed the enemy ship and puffing on his pipe as though completely unconcerned.

And even though they had soon gone out of the Parliamentarians' range of vision and could have demanded explanations of one another, still Nichola and her husband stood in silence, looking at the miracle of their child, feeling nothing except the intense happiness of being together once more.

Nichola, remembering how close she had grown to Rupert, said only one thing. "It's dangerous for us to be apart. We musn't do it again."

Still leaning on the rail, not looking at her, Joscelin answered almost as if he had guessed her thoughts. "From now on we will stay together, I promise you. Whatever happens, wherever I go, I will keep you at my side."

"Thank you," said Nichola, and meant it sincerely.

The sun began to sink as they reached the mouth of the River Severn and stared out across the open waters of the Bristol Channel, the ember red disc lowering itself slowly into the sea, transforming the ocean to a glittering crimson lake. On the starboard side Nichola could see the wild cliffs and lonely bays of the Welsh coastline, but much to her delight Rhys took the boat south and eased into the small port of Watchet. There he moored up and, still posing as a fisherman and his wife, Nichola and Joscelin went ashore for provisions.

They spent that night beneath the stars, just talking, nothing more. They had given up the only cabin to Emmet and Miranda, keeping the baby with them, wrapping him up against the September wind that blew in sharply from the sea once the sun had gone down. Rhys slept in a hammock rigged in the prow and Joscelin and Nichola, hugging one another for comfort, finally caught up with all the many missing days. She told him of Naseby, of the birth of Emlyn, of Michael's intervention during the attack on the baggage train, and of how she had gone to Barnstaple and Bristol in search of her husband.

"If only I'd known," Joscelin said. "I believed you dead and gone."

"Were you sad?"

The cognac eyes glowed in the dirty fisherman's face. "That word is inadequate, Nichola. I thought I had found my soul mate, then lost her again. Had it not been for Meraud I would have ended my life. But somehow it seemed so cowardly to leave her with no one when she had lost so many who were dear to her."

"Thank God you reasoned like that. So did the Prince's letter not arrive at Raglan?"

"Which Prince?"

Nichola stiffened slightly. "The Prince of Wales wrote to you from Barnstaple that I was safe and well."

"That letter never came. But I did hear from Rupert."

"Rupert?"

"Yes. He wrote that you were with him in Bristol, that it was his view the city would fall at any time and so could I please get back to Kingswear Hall, where he would send you as soon as he was able."

Nichola remained silent and Joscelin turned from his contemplation of the galaxies to look at her. "His love for you spilled from every page. That foolish, incredible, tempestuous boy can hide nothing. So it was from him, who probably wishes me dead at the bottom of his heart, that I discovered you were alive."

"Where were you when this letter arrived?" she asked him slowly.

"At Raglan Castle. I had been there earlier with the King, then marched northwards with him until he was forced to retreat. But after a flying visit to Oxford we returned to Raglan. I think His Majesty is soothed by its apparent tranquillity."

"Is he really so unconcerned about the situation?"

"I'm not certain. When we were going north he stopped at Brecon to send the Prince of Wales sealed orders as to what to do if the enemy should triumph. And this is obviously weighing on his mind, because just before Rupert's letter came he asked me to go to the West Country, it being my territory, to help Prince Charles cope with the situation. It seems that the local commanders, Goring and Sir Richard Grenville, are at each other's throats. Grenville refuses to obey George's orders and they are fighting between themselves instead of concentrating on the common enemy."

"Oh, what fools!"

"Love and war make fools of us all," answered Joscelin. "Now let me tell you the end of my story. As soon as I received his letter I left Raglan and went to the nearest fishing village and there hired Rhys ap Richard and his boat."

"Joscelin," said Nichola firmly, "please keep the Prince of Wales waiting a little longer. I really do need to get to Kingswear Hall and settle down. I have been dragging these poor wretched children half way round the country trying to find you. They need some stability."

"You're a good mother," he answered softly.

"I can't think how. If you had known me as I used to be you would never have believed it."

Joscelin looked haunted. "What will happen to her, to Nichola Hall, to the part of you that you have left behind?"

Nichola trembled violently. "I don't know. Emerald Ditch said there would be changes but he didn't tell me what they would be."

"Is she dying out there, somewhere in time, do you think?"

Unable to help herself, Nichola started to weep. "Yes, yes, I think she probably is."

"Poor Nichola," said Joscelin softly.

"No," she answered, shaking her head. "She is happy, for she is me. It is only her shell that is going to suffer."

"I shall pray for both of you," he said as he pulled her even more closely into his arms.

A week later, having carefully hugged that most beautiful of coastlines, they sailed into Dartmouth. It had been a journey unsurpassed in Nichola's experience, from the mighty cliffs where Exmoor drops down to the ocean, past wild headlands, jagged rocks, into the rolling swell of Cornwall's rugged coast, past magic Tintagel, and the booming surf and clear waters of the Penwith peninsula, and on to glimpse the mystic St Michael's Mount. Then had come the home stretch, past the Lizard Point lighthouse, built in 1619, past Falmouth and Plymouth, and finally into the mighty sweep of Start Bay to catch that first lovely glimpse of Dartmouth Castle.

"Home," said Joscelin.

"Home together," answered Nichola.

They had made love by now, having adopted their own personalities as soon as they were back in Royalist country. They had put in for the night at the deep narrow inland harbour of Boscastle, the sea having been like a millpond, and they had moored at the inner jetty rebuilt by Sir Richard Grenville, the captain of the *Revenge* who had gone down fighting the Spanish. And it had been there, in an inn called The Fisherman's Rest, that Nichola and Joscelin had at last spent a night together in privacy.

The sea had been everywhere, from the distant sound outside the window, to the blue hangings on the simple bed and the shells that stood on the mantelpiece above the fire that burned wood washed up upon the shore. The breath of the ocean had been almost tangible in that room, salt and clear, lapping about their nakedness as they had become one with the rhythm of the sea, their movements echoing the relentless pounding of the mighty rolling surf. And so, as they were dragged together into the swirling, demanding, clamouring undertow of flood tide, old emotions were washed away and they emerged from the cresting wave of their passion, dedicated to one another as never before.

And now the two of them were home, sailing into Dartmouth, bidding farewell to Rhys ap Richard and boarding a smaller river craft to take them the last step of the journey. Then came the one evil thing left to endure. The passing of the spot where Sabina and Caradoc had vanished into the water and Emmet had nearly drowned.

"You're shivering," said Joscelin to the servant.

"Only because I'm cold, my Lord," Emmet answered, determined as ever to keep the secret, and there the matter was allowed to drop.

There was such an air of stillness about Kingswear Hall, such an air of listening quiet about the place, that Nichola was forced to make as much noise as possible about her entrance in order to chase away the ghosts. And immediately Meraud came at the run, crying and laughing and asking how long they would be staying.

"As long as the war will let us," Joscelin answered.

Then Emmet came in with the children and Meraud was lost to

them as she took Emlyn in her arms and let Miranda climb on to her knee.

They dined very formally, at Meraud's insistence, in the great hall, Joscelin sitting at the head of the table, his two ladies flanking him. A cradle which had once been Joscelin's was found for the baby and Nichola had been on the point of placing Emlyn in it when an odd idea occurred to her.

"Sabina didn't sleep in this, did she?"

"No," her sister-in-law had answered very quietly. "All her things have been burnt, every last one of them. It was a hard thing to do, but it was for the best."

"A ritual cleansing by fire?"

"I thought so."

And so, sleeping comfortably, probably for the first time in his life, Joscelin's heir was present at the meal, and Miranda, now referred to as 'my daughter' by her adoptive father, yawned her way through as many courses as she could manage before Nichola sent her to bed.

Afterwards, the three adults retired to the withdrawing room, lit by the soft glow of candles reflecting from silver sconces around the walls.

"When do we go to see the Prince?" said Nichola.

"In a day or two."

"But what of the children?" asked Meraud.

"I shall take them both, tired though they are. I have promised myself that from now on we shall remain together as a family."

"I see." Meraud paused, swallowed, then said, "Joscelin, I feel I should tell you before you find out by some other means. Sir Ralph Welles called upon me the other day."

Joscelin stared. "Welles? But surely he's with the Parliamentarians?"

Meraud looked thoroughly discomfited. "That is true. He was fighting with the Earl of Essex but since the Earl's death has joined the New Model Army. He has returned here on compassionate leave. His wife died most suddenly and he has come to see to the allocating of his children with various relatives. The youngest is only six years old, poor little thing."

Nichola paid sudden attention. "Ralph? Is this *the* Ralph you told me of once?"

"Yes, it is he." And Meraud gave a small sigh that revealed everything.

"You shouldn't have received him, he is an enemy of this house," Joscelin put in abruptly.

Nichola assumed a thoroughly aggrieved expression. "Really! How can you be so stuffy? I never thought to hear you say such a thoroughly narrow-minded thing."

She sounded so vehement that he looked at her in alarm. "Well, I . . ."

"There's no well about it. Meraud has every right to receive an old friend. I hate this sword divided business." Nichola turned to her sister-in-law. "In fact, my dear, I think you ought to return his call tomorrow. Where does Ralph live?"

"In Dartmouth, in Bayard's House."

"Then go and see him, be assertive. Put your cards on the table."

They both stared at her dumbfounded.

"What do you mean?" asked Meraud tentatively.

"That you should tell him you still care for him. You do, don't you? Call and say that you are available if he is interested."

"Arabella!" said Meraud, shocked, while a reluctant smile was creeping over Joscelin's features.

"Well, where's the harm? If you don't say something how is he supposed to know?"

"But he probably lost interest in me years ago," Meraud protested.

"If so, why did he call? Tell him you'll move in straight away as his housekeeper but that you want to be married, and not before too long either."

"Arabella! His wife has only just died."

"This is war," said Nichola impatiently. "People don't muck about in situations like these. Go on, Meraud. Because if you don't, I will."

"You wouldn't dare."

"Oh yes she would," said Joscelin, and he was openly laughing now. "I married a very determined woman, I'll have you know."

"Yet, Brother, how could I? You yourself said Ralph Welles is our enemy now."

His smile vanished and Joscelin looked at his sister seriously. "Nichola is right and I was wrong. The war doesn't matter a damn. Go and see him and good luck to you."

"I'll think about it," answered Meraud. She frowned. "Why did you call Arabella Nichola just now?"

"Because it's my nickname for her," Joscelin answered, and taking hold of his wife's hand, he kissed it fondly.

Three days later the unheard of had happened. A Royalist woman of mature years had proposed marriage to a Parliamentarian widower and had been accepted. And, strangely, it was Ralph who had insisted that they marry before his leave was over.

"He says that were he to be killed in action my position would be invidious. We are to be wed by special licence, very privately, in St Petrox Church. Ralph has asked me to tell you, Joscelin, that he is also making a will in my favour," Meraud said, blushing like a girl.

"I think he's behaving very honourably," Nichola stated firmly.

Joscelin nodded thoughtfully. "He is, he is. Nonetheless Meraud, I hope you understand that there is no conceivable way in which I can attend the ceremony. I am too close to the King, would be fighting at his side now if it weren't for my mission to aid the Prince. I hope that you appreciate my position."

She nodded, just a shade sadly. "Of course, my dear. Even Ralph is taking a risk by lingering in Royalist territory."

Joscelin's elegant shoulders rose in an eloquent shrug. "The King's cause in the West Country is falling apart after the ravages of Goring and Grenville. There's not a man in Dartmouth who would lift a hand against your future husband."

"Oh, where will it all end?"

"In defeat," Nichola answered her sister-in-law. "It's only a matter of time." She turned to Joscelin. "I take back what I said earlier despite my vow. Go to the Prince alone. I'll stay with Meraud and attend the wedding. She can't possibly be expected to go through a memorable day like that without one of us being present."

The older woman turned a delighted face on her. "Would you really make such a sacrifice for me? I should be so delighted."

Nichola kissed her. "You deserve all the happiness in the world and I fully intend to play my part. As long as Joscelin doesn't disappear again."

He looked at her, his scamp's face very sober. "Whatever happens, whatever the delays, I swear that I will be back here for Christmas. Does that put your mind at rest?"

"Christmas Eve at the latest."

"I give you my word on it."

A few days later, on 1 October, 1644, the Lady Meraud Attwood married Sir Ralph Welles in the ancient church of St Petrox, standing within the shadow of Dartmouth Castle. It was the oldest place of worship in which Nichola had ever stood, its beginnings believed to go back to the sixth century. And it was in these mystic surroundings that she saw Meraud's journey to happiness begin.

The bridegroom, a vast, broad shouldered, amiable man in his late fifties, not yet fat but on the very edge of it, kissed his new wife so tenderly that Nichola knew all would go well for them, and she raised her glass with the half dozen or so people present at the modest wedding breakfast, in a toast to their future. And yet, ever uppermost in her thoughts, was the knowledge that time was now running out for the King, for the Prince of Wales, for Rupert, for them all, and that however well suited the newly weds, however good the portents, there was nothing that could guarantee their sweet and rather sentimental joy would last for ever.

Chapter Thirty-three

Shortly before Christmas, 1645, a spell of bitterly cold weather gripped England, the climate being so severe that the Thames, the Severn and the Dart froze over, to say nothing of many other rivers, both large and small. The frost that had accompanied Nichola's first winter at Kingswear Hall seemed negligible in comparison to this one and, passing from one room to another, all the occupants of the house wore cloaks and furs to combat the freezing temperatures of the corridors and passages. Yet, despite these savage conditions, the Roundhead army did not go into winter quarters but instead fought on, its soldiers crippled with frostbite, Black Tom Fairfax having announced his intention of crushing the last Royalist stronghold and marching ruthlessly ever deeper into the West Country.

Nichola, who had once obtained this kind of information from Caradoc, was now obliged to go into Dartmouth to learn things for herself. Though as she combined such trips with a visit to Meraud and her new brood of five stepchildren, their ages ranging from six to sixteen, she enjoyed her weekly visits to the town. Talking in undertones, the two women would discuss the worsening situation and make intelligent guesses as to where exactly Joscelin might be now.

He had been gone since early October, yet in all that time there had been only one letter from him, though this was hardly surprising in view of the fact that the ways and tracks were frozen solid. Disappointingly, however, that sole communication had contained little information other than for a veiled reference to the Prince's having to move on, as Barnstaple no longer seemed safe. Still, her husband had repeated his promise to be back for the festive season, and it had been left to Nichola and her sister-in-law to make their plans accordingly. They had decided that Meraud would come to Kingswear Hall for the Twelve Days, bringing her stepchildren with her, as there was no hope of Sir Ralph being released from his army duties.

"Why Fairfax has to keep going, particularly in view of this terrible weather, I'll never know," Meraud had said with a sigh.

"Because he wants to finish the war. The rest of the country has capitulated and now there's just this one pocket of resistance left. He's got to crush it."

"What will happen then?"

"The conflict will be over and Parliament the victors," Nichola had replied bluntly.

"But what of the King and the Prince of Wales? What will their futures be?"

"I think," Nichola had answered, choosing her words carefully, "we may have to resign ourselves to the King not having a future."

Meraud had looked horrified. "Do you mean he might be *killed*?"

Nichola had nodded. "Yes, I think so."

"How awful! And how grim to live beneath the rule of such cruel Puritans as men like Cromwell. Did you know, Arabella, that when he ended the siege of Basing House, so gallantly defended by the Marquess and Marchioness of Winchester, he put a hundred men and women to death, many of them unarmed and defenceless? Then he declared that as most of those people were Papists, muskets and swords could not be expected to show compassion. I should not tell you this, but Ralph informed me that General Sir Thomas would never have permitted such an atrocity and is greatly angered by it."

"I believe that one day he and Cromwell will fall out. Do you?"

"I wouldn't be at all surprised," Meraud had answered, nodding. But there, as Nichola had sensed her sister-in-law's reluctance to betray marital confidences, conversation about the war had ceased and they had gone on to the more interesting topic of Christmas.

Snow had now added to the bitingly cold conditions, making it almost impossible for anyone to get about, and it was therefore arranged that Meraud and her stepchildren should set out as soon as the ways became a little clearer. Yet every day seemed to bring a further fall and Nichola, cut off from the world completely by this time, resigned herself to a celebration with just Emmet and the children.

"I think we're going to be on our own," she said to the servant sadly.

Emmet shook her head. "No, my Lord will be here."

"What makes you think so?"

"He won't let a little thing like the weather stand in his way. Why, my friend Will from Dartmouth, that fisher lad I told you about, is going to skate here to see me. Well, he's not as fond of me as Lord Joscelin is of you. So I reckon if he can do it, so can his Lordship."

"I hope you're right," Nichola answered, trying to come to terms yet again with another of Joscelin's absences.

By the night of Christmas Eve, 5 January, her husband still had not appeared and there was another very heavy snow shower which came falling out of the sky like a veil, rather than blustering in on the bitter wind. The flakes had come so silently and so consistently that, by the time Nichola got up in the morning, the grounds and gardens were virtually unrecognisable, the different level of lawn and bushes smoothed into a sparkling plain out of which rose the trees, bedecked with white plumes as profusely and gaily as a Cavalier's hat.

The riverbanks were glittering slopes of treachery, where snow had fallen over ice, while the Dart was made of blue glass burnished with silver, a coating of crystal, formed as the snowflakes had settled and hardened, gleaming on its motionless surface. Above this fairy kingdom glowed a deep red winter sun, low in the sky, throwing a carpet of rose in its majestic wake.

"Beautiful," breathed Nichola, and staring up into the purply blue sky wished Joscelin were there to share such a splendid day with her.

And then quite suddenly and for no explicable reason, she knew that he *was* there, that sometime during the night he had arrived and, not wishing to disturb her, was waiting for her downstairs. Throwing a fur-lined cloak over her nightrail,

Nichola left her room and hurried along the freezing corridors, making her way towards the great hall.

A scene of brilliant colour lay waiting for her. In the huge hearth a fire, recently stoked and rekindled, shot sparks up the chimney as it consumed logs the size of tree trunks, while holly berries shone against the dark wood of the panelling. Mistletoe abounded and the minstrels' gallery was hung with greenery, its verdant shade reflected in the great silver punchbowl, itself decorated with trailing ribbons of red. Before the hearth, his stockinged feet turned towards the flames, a child on each knee, sat Joscelin, his black curls transformed to mahogany by the light of the fire.

"You're here!" Nichola shouted, and ran to kneel by his chair.

He smiled at her, as mischievous as ever. "Did you doubt me?"

"Of course I did. With the weather as bad as this I thought you might have holed up somewhere."

"With you as the prize," Joscelin answered, "any man would come through snow and ice."

"Flattery will get you everywhere."

"It was ever thus."

And then they stopped bantering and exchanged a loving kiss.

It was an occasion that Nichola would never forget, the first Christmas she had kept with all her family about her since she had left the twentieth century behind, an event destined to become a cherished memory as Nichola and her husband and children put the war from their minds and concentrated entirely on celebrating. Then, after the feasting was over, the fiddler – who had been plucked out of the servants' hall in lieu of musicians – grown silent, they stepped out together into the bitter night. Before them the river valley lay utterly still, nothing stirring, all creatures hushed.

"Will you be going again?" whispered Nichola, watching her breath plume like mist as it rose into the ice laden air.

"Only with you and the children."

"What do you mean?"

"I now know the King's orders. Come within and I'll tell you of them. It is too cold for conversation out here."

The memorable day grew even more special as they went back

inside and said goodnight to Miranda and Emlyn, then retired to bed themselves, not only to make love but also to sit watching the flames of the bedroom fire, drinking wine and conversing, enjoying each other's company.

"So tell me of the King's instructions," said Nichola.

"It's odd," Joscelin answered reflectively, "on the one hand, he sometimes seems unaware of the gravity of the situation, on the other he is acutely concerned for the Prince's safety. The orders are that if the enemy should triumph, Prince Charles is to sail immediately for France. As I told you, he has already been moved on to Tavistock and will be moved again should it prove necessary."

"Where to?"

"Truro, whence he can easily reach the Scilly Isles."

"Are we to accompany him?"

"Yes, I have given my word to protect the boy so protect him I will."

Nichola drank her wine. "Does that mean all of us will go with him to France?"

"Yes, should the need arise."

"I'm afraid it's going to."

"I know," Joscelin answered heavily, "we haven't a chance. Almost every major city has now fallen into enemy hands, the King has alienated himself from Rupert, the most capable soldier of them all, Goring has resigned his commission and gone abroad. There's no hope for His Majesty's men I fear."

"Nor for him either."

"Do you mean that he will pay the ultimate penalty for his foolishness?"

"Yes. King Charles I was executed by the Roundheads."

"And the Prince of Wales?"

"Escaped, gloriously. But he will return to claim his birthright, I promise you that."

"Thank God."

There was a small silence, then Nichola said, "What happened to Rupert after Bristol?"

"The King, to his shame, treated him like dirt. He said the surrender of the city smacked of treachery and sent the Prince a letter telling him to consider himself dismissed from the country."

Nichola drained her glass. "Has he gone?"

"Not he," said Joscelin, smiling. "Rupert insisted his uncle grant him an audience so that he could explain what had happened, and they eventually came face to face in Newark where the Prince and his brother Maurice had gone together to plead Rupert's case before a Council of War. There was a terrific scene, several in command, including Rupert's colonels, being on the Prince's side. Anyway, first the King wouldn't utter a word, cutting Rupert dead throughout supper, then he finally ordered them all to leave the room saying that the whole thing smacked of mutiny. Then he sent the lot of them packing."

"Where are Rupert and the King now?"

"Together again, though barely speaking, both of them at Oxford. The King is busy plotting and planning with foreign powers, Rupert is relieved of his command, which makes precious little difference as there are hardly any forces left for him to lead."

"Dear God, what a mess!"

"Let us not talk of it further," said Joscelin. "It's a gloomy prospect and one which does not do to dwell on. This has been the best Christmas I have ever enjoyed. I won't ruin it now with miserable conversation."

"Poor Rupert," Nichola murmured as she blew out the candle and snuggled down next to her husband.

"He'll survive," Joscelin answered. "He's too bright a flame to be extinguished."

And with that he drew Nichola close against him and everyone else was forgotten in the enchantment with which every embrace they had ever shared had always been so rapturously filled.

The bad weather persisted throughout the Twelve Days and Meraud, much distressed, sent a letter via Will, Emmet's fisher lad, to say that she would not risk bringing the children out in such hazardous conditions. Nichola wrote back that Joscelin had arrived and longed to see his sister, but that they quite understood her predicament. Thus on Twelfth Night, which fell on 17 January, Joscelin wrapped his family up against the cold and took them into the orchard, even Emlyn, to wassail the apple trees, a ritual much enjoyed by the servants who sang lustily, pouring buckets of hot cider over the roots, imbibing a great deal of it in the process, and leaving cider-soaked toast in the apple tree branches to placate the guardian birds.

"Does that ensure a good crop?" Nichola asked.

"Oh yes," Joscelin stated seriously. "The trees will be heavy with fruit, though I doubt we'll be here to see it."

"No, I don't suppose we will," she answered, and sighed at the prospect of leaving such a beautiful house, however full of sad memories it might once have been. However, her thoughts of the future were interrupted at that moment by a loud howl from the servants, denoting the end of the wassail, coupled with one or two gun shots. The sleeping baby, perfectly peaceful until then, woke and cried with fright, at which Joscelin, who had not yet been enlightened about sharing the responsibility of child raising, handed Emlyn back to his mother.

"I'll take him in and feed him," she said. "Are you coming, Miranda?"

"No, I'll stay with Joss," her daughter answered, slipping her hand into that of her stepfather.

So it was walking alone that Nichola began to climb the slope from the orchard, following the path that led to the house, and had almost reached the top before she identified the distant sound she had been aware of for the last few seconds as one of rapidly approaching hooves. Suddenly nervous, Nichola drew into the shadow of a tree and watched as a solitary rider, coming from the high track which led to Dartmouth, approached the house at speed. As the horseman drew nearer, Nichola realised that he rode side saddle and was actually a she, and hurrying from her hiding place, saw Meraud hastily hitch the horse to a post and make for the front door, on which she pounded frantically with the great lion's head knocker.

"Meraud," called Nichola, running up behind her, "what brings you here at this hour? What is wrong?"

Her sister-in-law turned a startled face towards her. "Oh

Arabella, it is you. Thank God for that. Where is Joscelin?"

"Wassailing the apple trees. He'll be back in a moment, the ceremony has just finished."

"There is no time to lose," Meraud answered desperately.

"Why? What's happened?"

"I had secret word from Ralph tonight. Fairfax has surrounded Dartmouth and will storm it within the next day. As one of the King's men, Joscelin will be taken prisoner, if not worse. You must leave Kingswear Hall as soon as possible. Ralph says so."

"But where are we to go?"

"I have arranged for Job Atkin, the father of Emmet's fisherman friend, to put his boat at your disposal. You can sail wherever you see fit."

"These are the death throes, aren't they?" Nichola said, almost to herself.

"Yes," answered Joscelin, coming up to the two women out of the darkness, "this is the end."

"My dear brother," said Meraud, throwing her arms round his neck, "you must take with you everything of value that you can. I fear that it may be a long time before you return."

A memory came back to Nichola. It was the date, such an easy one to learn, of the Restoration of the Stuart monarchy.

"It will be 1660," she stated quietly. "Another fourteen years."

Joscelin stared at her, aghast. "Do you mean that when we come back my son will be a youth?" He indicated the baby in her arms.

She nodded. "Yes, that is the truth of the matter, I'm afraid."

He drew her to one side, out of Meraud's earshot. "Nichola, are you sure you want to proceed with this? I could still try, if it is what you desire, to send you back to your own time. It will mean an easier life, I don't doubt."

She turned to him, putting her hands on his shoulders. "I made that decision at Naseby. I turned my back on everything I was and everything that constituted my superficial way of living, then. I'm yours, Joscelin, if you want me."

"I want you for ever," he answered.

"Then that is good enough for me," she said, and went into the house.

* * *

They worked all night, every one of them, every servant, every child, master and stable boy side by side, until by dawn the task was done. Every valuable that could be carried with ease had been stowed in their baggage, the rest, including the red rose portrait of Arabella Attwood, put into a cart for Meraud to take away.

"As for the other stuff," said Joscelin, looking round sadly, "Black Tom can take his pick."

"But what of the servants, my Lord?" asked the major domo apprehensively.

"You must all stay on here. You'll not be harmed by whoever comes, in fact they'll probably be only too glad to have you. The Lady Meraud will pay your wages until a new master stakes his claim. Now get everyone into the great hall, Jenks. I must bid them farewell."

It was like a scene from a film, Nichola thought; the weeping retainers gathered together to bid farewell to their master and mistress, caught in the cruel toils of war. Proceeding slowly, Joscelin shook each and every one of them by the hand, giving thanks for their service to his family. And finally, at the end of the line, he came to Emmet.

"But you're going with us surely."

She flushed uncomfortably. "May I speak to the Mistress alone, my Lord?"

"Of course you can," Nichola answered, and with that she took the girl by the arm and led her up to what had once been the master bedroom, now stripped of its elaborate finery.

"You want to stay, don't you?" Nichola asked, coming straight to the point.

Emmet looked wretched. "Not here exactly. The Lady Meraud has a place for me in Dartmouth, her having so many children now. And besides . . ."

"Will would like you to remain near to him?"

All the girl's old sparkle shone from her face. "Well, he hasn't said I shouldn't. And he still thinks I've got funny eyes."

"Then that settles it, stay you must." She took Emmet's hands in hers. "But I shall miss you, so very much. You've been a kind and loyal friend and companion. And, besides, you were the first person I ever saw, do you know that?'

"What do you mean?" asked Emmet, bewildered.

"After I came here. After Miranda was born."

Emmet put on an expression of great severity. "Now don't you start," she said, and bustled off to finish the packing.

At dawn, they picked their way to Dartmouth, following the track in the faint early light. The air was sharp with cold and the first few flakes of fresh snow floated down softly as they proceeded through the trees. A mile or two below Kingswear Hall, where the Dart was at its narrowest, the party of four adults and two children, for Meraud and Emmet were accompanying them, dismounted and crossed the frozen river on solid ice, leading their horses to lighten the load. Then with the sun coming up in an angry crimson ball and the snow starting to sting their faces, the group proceeded carefully and cautiously to the harbour where Job Atkin, his son Will alongside, already awaited them.

"They're terrible conditions for setting forth, my Lord," Job said, gazing at the ferocity of the increasing blizzard.

"They're not as bad as the ones I'll be in if I'm caught," Joscelin answered. "Though I don't want to put anyone else at risk, I might add."

"Why don't we get away from Dartmouth then moor up until the storm passes?" Will suggested.

"We must," said Nichola firmly. "It's the only way."

She turned, taking first Meraud then Emmet into her arms, tears suddenly running down her icy cheeks.

"I can't bear to leave either of you," she said. "You've both been such wonderful friends."

"God bless you, dear Arabella," her sister-in-law answered chokingly.

"Take care, my Lady," said Emmet, kissing her. "I'll never forget all the years we've had together."

Nichola turned, one foot already on the bobbing fishing boat. "Did I improve as I got older?"

"You improved so much," Emmet answered with a smile, "that

had I not known otherwise, I could have sometimes believed you were two different people."

And then she turned away so that no one should see her weep as the boat containing the people she loved most in the world slipped out of the harbour through the thickening snow and put out towards the open sea.

Chapter Thirty-four

The extent and quality of the communications network in the seventeenth century, an age devoid of telephones, television and mass circulation newspapers, had never ceased to astound Nichola, and now she was amazed afresh. Almost as soon as they had sailed from Dartmouth and eased their way gingerly round the coast, sheltering in coves and bays when the weather was fiercest, they had heard news of the town being stormed by Fairfax's troops. Then, as they proceeded round that rough and rugged route, word had come that Black Tom was moving on to Torrington where he hoped to engage Sir Ralph Hopton, now called out of retirement by the Prince of Wales to replace Lord George Goring, who, pleading poor health, had left the country to seek the pleasures of France.

"We had better make our way there if there is to be a fight," Joscelin had said determinedly.

In this matter, however, his resolve had not been as great as that of Nichola who had pointed out, very sensibly, that his guardians would move the Prince on from Tavistock the moment danger threatened and that it would be much better to await him at Truro. So they had sailed on, rounding the great sweep of Cornwall's curving leg, finally entering Falmouth Bay and steering into the intricate maze of tidal rivers and creeks that led to the quays of Truro, a lively port despite the fact that it lay over ten miles away from the sea.

Because of the inclement conditions which forced them to lie at mooring for several days, the trip had taken longer than anticipated and it wasn't until the end of January that

Nichola and Joscelin finally went ashore and took rooms at The Merman, whose very name excited her, speaking of old legends and strange occurrences as it did.

But there was to be no peace, no browsing round the old harbour, no investigation of the merman story, for Joscelin was full of a restless nervous energy, constantly worried that Hopton would need help, that the Prince would feel betrayed. It was then that Nichola lost her patience with him for the first time ever.

"Go then," she had said. "Go and join one or other of them – or both! Leave me behind as you always do while you make sure that everyone else is being attended to."

Instead of reacting sharply as he was quite capable of doing, Joscelin had pulled her on to his knee. "Listen to me, Nichola, and listen well. I told you once that I had shared the King's salt. Well, I also swore a coronation oath to be his liege man. Yet I too gave my word that I would not leave you alone again. So now think, if you will, of my dilemma. I vowed to you that I would stay by your side. Yet, equally, I feel beholden to lead the Prince of Wales out of danger into safety. I am a man of my century, not yours alas. So can you understand how I am torn?"

"I suppose so," she had answered unwillingly. "But we are together as a family at last and now you want to ruin everything by charging off. We have got this far. Why do you have to spoil it?"

Joscelin had said very gravely, "I cannot give an answer that would satisfy you. I love you and I love my children, you know that, but while I sit inactive and others face the gravest danger, I can enjoy no peace of mind."

"You promised me," Nichola had replied, aware of how peevish she sounded.

"I know. And because of that I will stay here. My final loyalty, when all is said and done, must be to you."

He had looked at her with those great golden eyes of his

and, just for a moment, she had cherished the victory, then given in. As is the way of the world in the face of capitulation, she had back tracked. "I wouldn't like you to feel guilty."

"I'm afraid I cannot help that, sweetheart."

"Oh, Joscelin, now you're making me ashamed."

"Please don't. You are quite right, my darling. I have left you unprotected far too long."

"But I'm not in any danger here, not as I have been in the past."

"I suppose that is true," he had answered, and looked away.

"If you did go to rescue the Prince, how long would it take?"

"Dressed roughly and going across country I could reach Tavistock within a day, two at the most."

She had smiled and shaken her head, thinking that Nichola Hall would never have allowed herself to be manipulated in such a way. And then she had stopped worrying about manoeuvres and games and briefly put herself in the Prince's place, cut off from both parents, aware that the enemy was closing in hard, and wondering where and when Fairfax would appear next.

"Go to him," she said suddenly.

He had looked at her in amazement. "But you said that just now and were angry."

"Well, I'm not any more. For all the fact he's a brave brash lad, poor Charles must be very frightened. Go and get him, Joscelin. Play your part in history and bring him to Truro from where he can sail away to the destiny that lies ahead of him."

"How beautifully put. Do you mean it?"

"I mean it," she said, and did.

He left early the next morning, St Valentine's Day, 1646. Nichola had watched Joscelin ride away with such incredibly mixed emotions that she could hardly bring herself to think about them. For here was she, once so selfish and self-centred, placing the fears and feelings of a young Prince above her own, and because of them letting her husband go into danger once more.

After Joscelin had disappeared from sight and she was alone again, Nichola had taken the two children and wandered down to the quays where once the vast fleet of great ships taking Cornish tin to all the countries of the known world had been moored. Trade had diminished since the start of the war, but vessels with gleaming hulls and tall arrogant masts still lay on the tidal waters. Staring at them, Nichola saw herself as just such a ship, floating on the sea of time, and knew then in a piercing moment of truth that despite any differences caused by the centuries which lay between them, she had, in finding Joscelin, finally sailed into peaceful harbour.

Word of the ultimate agonies of the Cavaliers had soon reached Truro. According to rumour, Hopton had made a stand at Torrington on 16 February and after a short spell of fighting in the streets, Fairfax had put the remainder of the Royalist army to flight. After that there could be no hope left of recruiting another such body and now there was nothing but for the Prince to obey his father's orders and escape the country.

Hoping daily that he and Joscelin would soon return, Nichola had been woken from her sleep one rosy dawning by the clattering hooves of a troop of horses and a few rather pathetic cheers. Rushing to the window, she had looked out – and there they were. Riding at the head of his retinue, flanked on one side by Sir Edward Hyde and on the other by Lord Culpeper, formally Sir John, both of whom had accompanied the Prince when he had gone to Bristol and had remained as his guardians ever since, was young Charles himself, emulating his cousin Rupert by being brilliantly dressed for the occasion. Behind him, with the rest of the loyal retainers, rode Joscelin.

"Thank God," Nichola had said, and had called out a greeting, blowing kisses at the royal party.

And then had come the rushing to get dressed and the hurrying downstairs to greet them, a pretty woman amongst so many admiring men, loving every minute of their warm-hearted flattery.

They dined late that day, since there was much to do about the wharves, organising a ship to take the party to the Scilly Isles. But when they finally sat down, almost two dozen people, it was an occasion never to be forgotten. Two long tables covered with white cloths had been set out in the inn's dining room, and there, beneath the oaken beams, all the company took their places on tapestried stools, only the Prince having a chair with arms.

The food was humble but good; a leg of mutton, a plate of pullets and larks, a great tart, and all the finest fruits the sea could offer, this last being both baked and stewed. There were side dishes of anchovies and another of prawns and cheese, both put on the tables with the main courses. Before any of this had been touched, the party had stood ceremoniously and the King's health been drunk amidst a great huzzah of cheers. After that the wine had circulated freely and there had been a great display of the kind of high spirits common to those who have lost but are determined to go out with a good showing. Finally, Joscelin had risen to his feet.

"Madam, gentlemen, pray rise and drink with me a loyal toast to His Royal Highness, the Prince of Wales."

They stood and raised their glasses, then the Prince had spoken.

"Gentlemen, I thank you, not just for your loyalty but for the support you have given me during these last terrible months. I salute you all. Yet there is one person present whom I would like to single out for a special word, and that is Arabella, Lady Attwood. She entered my life as a stranger but ended my friend. Arabella, thank you for coming among us."

And his voice was echoed by that of Joscelin, who added softly, "To Nichola, my wife. A woman of her times and of mine, who was with me on the greatest adventure of them all."

That night, after she had gone quietly to bed, the dream came, clearer and more sharply defined than ever before. Though she had believed, particularly after the birth of her son, that she would never again experience its strange and disturbing imagery, still it had come out of the darkness to haunt her once more. It began, as it sometimes did, in a hospital corridor down which she felt compelled to go, carried along like a leaf on a brook, unable to control her actions. As ever, this eddying flow ceased before a room, the door of which swung open to receive her.

The body lay inside the room, the body that over the passing years she had seen so many times before. Yet on this occasion it was different, in its natural state, all the tubes that had been attached to it in order to help it live, removed. It lay like the Sleeping Beauty, awaiting the kiss that would awake it, the kiss that now would never come.

There were people in the room, parents, friends, and Nichola saw to her surprise that some of them were weeping. Two doctors were present, one of whom turned down the dials on the ventilator.

"Will she go peacefully?" said a woman's voice, breaking with emotion.

"Oh yes," the doctor answered quietly. "Now she'll just drift away."

And then he raised his hand and switched off the life-saving machine.

The dreamer shuddered as, for a second more, she hovered by the shell of what had once been a human being, then she turned and ran, on and on down the never ending corridor, on and on and into darkness. Then Nichola sat bolt upright in bed, breathing deeply to calm herself, slowly realising that she was finally safe and that none of it could ever harm her again.

Yet tonight there seemed a special need to think about everything that had taken place. So it was that Nichola got slowly out of bed and went downstairs to the inn's little parlour, where a fire still burned low in the grate. And there, sitting in the shadows, gazing into the flames, completely and utterly alone, Nichola Hall remembered.

EPILOGUE

Though they had never particularly liked one another, while greatly respecting each other's professional ability, now they sat huddled close, friends in adversity.

"For Christ's sake get me a drink," said Glynda, the cyclamen slash that was her mouth trembling so violently that it drooped a little in one corner.

Lewis looked at her, the famous eyes brimming. "Brandy?"

"Yes, a double."

He brought her a glass and drained his own. "I wish I hadn't gone to that. I only did it to please the parents."

"Same here," Glynda answered, downing her drink and holding the glass out for a refill.

Lewis took it automatically but did not go to the bar straight away. "She died so quickly once that bloody machine was off. I would never have believed it."

"What I can't understand," said Glynda, blowing her nose, "is why she went downhill like that. I mean, at first there were signs of life. She seemed to respond sometimes, didn't she?"

"There's no doubt about it. I was visiting once and saw her body twitching, while her eyes were rolling under her lids. I told her to come back, tried hypnotic techniques, I did truly, but nothing happened." The actor spread his hands helplessly.

"It's almost as if she didn't want to, after a time. Apparently, the initial tests were quite positive, yet later ones showed that her cerebral function had deteriorated."

"But why should Nichola not want to get better? She had everything to live for."

"I suppose so," Glynda answered slowly. "And yet..."

"And yet what?"

"Get me a drink and I'll tell you." She took the glass he handed her, sipping more slowly this time. "Thanks. Didn't you notice something just before she died?"

"No," answered Lewis shakily, "I don't think I did. What was it?"

She turned to look at him and he thought that he had never seen the great actress so serious, so utterly devoid of any kind of pretension.

"She smiled," said Glynda. "I'd swear to God she smiled."

"What are you saying?" asked Lewis fiercely. "Just what are you saying?"

"That perhaps, in the words of John Donne, Nichola roamed giddily in her dreams and was everywhere but at home. And finally such freedom did a banishment become."

HISTORICAL NOTE

The period known as the First Civil War is obviously well documented though, surprisingly, there are still minor discrepancies between the various accounts. However, for the sake of clarity, I have simplified some of the more complicated details of the conflict and have told the story only as Nichola would have known it, making little reference to what was taking place in London and amongst the forces of Parliament. I hope historians will forgive me for this.

The sequel to the Roundheads' ultimate victory is well known, but I thought I might go over the pattern of those events once more in order to tie up the book's loose ends.

When the Prince of Wales and his retinue sailed from Truro to the Scilly Isles and thence to Jersey on 2 March 1646, they left behind a critical situation. The King was in Oxford with the Princes Rupert and Maurice, and his son James, Duke of York. All Charles had left by now was the beleaguered city itself, menaced by Fairfax's soldiers, the garrison at Newark, and three thousand men in Worcestershire under Lord Astley, formerly Sir Jacob, tutor to Prince Rupert. When this troop were trapped at Stow-on-the-Wold on 21 March, Charles knew that the end was in sight. He left Oxford on 27 April, disguised as a servant, and headed north, preferring rather to surrender to the Scots than Parliament. On 6 May he clattered into the courtyard of the Saracen's Head in Southwell, a small town lying between Newark and Nottingham, and there he gave himself up.

In true Judas fashion, the Scots demanded £1.8 million for his return, but eventually settled for £400,000 to be paid in two instalments. Fairfax came to meet the King at Nottingham and kissed the royal hand before conducting His Majesty to Holdenby House in Northamptonshire, there to place him in 'safe custody'.

Charles and Cromwell finally came face to face in a house at Childerley, near Cambridge. When taken in to see the prisoner, Cromwell and his son-in-law, Henry Ireton, felt unable to pay him respect, though Black Tom again kissed the King's proffered hand. But for all that, Cromwell wept when three of the royal children, James, Henry and Elizabeth, were brought to dine with Charles at the Greyhound Inn, Maidenhead, and he witnessed that good father's obvious joy in being reunited with his family.

Eventually, the King was placed under house arrest at Hampton Court, living in great ease and comfort. He entertained, listened to music, played billiards and also tennis, wearing "a new tennis suit of wrought coloured satin lined with taffeta". Nonetheless, he escaped from this comfortable confinement on 11 November 1647, and in company with two associates fled to the Isle of Wight where he put himself in the hands of the island's Governor, Colonel Robert Hammond. However, after welcoming his royal guest Hammond became suspicious of the King's continued negotiations with the Scots and treated Charles as a prisoner.

By the end of that year the series of uprisings known as the Second Civil War had erupted. The Prince of Wales moved to Calais to watch events and Henrietta Maria mobilised exiled Cavalier officers, many of whom mustered at Edinburgh. Violence broke out in the counties of Kent and Norfolk but it must be remembered that this was not so much a show of Royalist fervour as a protest against the Army and Parliament. In Norwich, the apprentices went on the rampage, demanding of the Puritan city fathers that they be allowed to celebrate the traditional festivals of old. After this, national violence ensued and it took Parliament a year to quell the trouble. There was, as in the previous Civil War, grievous bloodshed and loss of life.

In November 1648, Fairfax issued orders for the King to be moved from Carisbrooke Castle on the Isle of Wight and taken to Hurst Castle, a gloomy fortress built on a strand of shingle by the Solent. From there he was brought to London to stand trial for his life. The prisoner at the bar was only forty-eight years old and yet his hair was completely grey, his eyes and cheeks sunken. While the charge was read out, Charles stared round Westminster Hall, where the proceedings were being held, and once laughed bitterly when he heard himself described as a "tyrant, traitor and murderer". Fairfax, in disgust that his sovereign should be so treated, absented himself from the trial but when the King was urged to remember that his accusers were the people of England, a woman stood up in the public seats and yelled, "Not a quarter of them! Oliver Cromwell is a traitor!" Soldiers were ordered to fire into the box in which the protestor sat, but found that it was Black Tom's wife, Lady Fairfax herself, who was causing the commotion. She was forcibly removed in order to avoid further disturbance.

As everyone knows, the ultimate price was demanded of the King, and Charles, resigned to his fate, bade farewell to two of his children, Henry and Elizabeth. Yet he was torn to shreds emotionally by their hopeless sobbing and shook violently, the only time his prodigious courage failed him. At ten o'clock on the morning of 30 January 1649, he walked across the park to the Banqueting House in Whitehall. Then, after an agonising and cruel wait, strode out beneath Rubens's magnificent ceiling to the scaffold erected at first floor level. There he bravely met his end. His head was severed with a single blow, the cavalry thundered from round the scaffold in order to clear the streets, and with that a strange and unnerving quiet fell over London.

And what of the others? Prince Charles, who had fled to France from Jersey on the very day of the fall of Oxford, came back to play his part in the Second Civil War but eventually retired to The Hague. On the day of his father's execution, the Prince, now aged eighteen, was recognised as King and in 1651 led an army into England to reclaim his birthright. He was defeated at the Battle of Worcester and made a daring escape, first hiding in an oak tree on the Boscobel estate in Shropshire then, disguised as a peasant, his black curly hair cut close to his head and crammed beneath a filthy hat, took a circuitous route to the Sussex coast. After six weeks on the run he sailed from Brighton, then called Brighthelmstone, and was put ashore at Fécamp in Normandy. His Wanted poster read "a malicious and dangerous Traitor, Charles Stuart, son of the late Tyrant, a tall black man over two yards high". He was restored to the throne on 29 May 1660, amidst great public rejoicing. It was his thirtieth birthday and he had spent seventeen years in exile.

Charles I's second son James, Duke of York, was taken prisoner when Oxford fell and sent into house arrest at St James's Palace with his brother and sisters. However, he escaped to Holland shortly before his father's execution, disguised as a girl and sometimes forced to sleep rough during the journey. At the time of the Restoration he returned to England and was appointed Lord High Admiral. He married, first Anne, Edward Hyde's ugly daughter, then Mary of Modena. He ascended the throne as James II when his elder brother, the sire of so very many royal bastards, was unable to produce a legitimate heir. However, James was deposed in 1688 because of his Catholic beliefs and his daughter by Anne Hyde, Mary, succeeded with her husband, William of Orange. James's son by Mary of Modena became Jamie the Rover, the Old Pretender, and James's grandson was the Young Pretender, Bonny Prince Charlie.

On their father's death, Prince Henry and Princess Elizabeth were sent first to Penshurst Place then to Carisbrooke Castle, where Elizabeth died a year later. Henry survived, however, and was allowed to leave the country in 1652. On the Restoration of his brother he came back to England but died of smallpox at the age of twenty-one.

Charles's youngest child, Henrietta Anne, known to history as Minette, was taken prisoner by Fairfax and sent to London to join Henry and Elizabeth under house arrest. However, she was released shortly afterwards and went to France to join her mother. They were together when news came through of the King's execution. Minette was married to the bisexual Duc d'Orleans when she was sixteen, then had a brief affair with his brother, Louis XIV. She later became the mistress of the Comte de Guiche and died in 1670 at the age of twenty-six. It was rumoured by some that she had been poisoned.

The two other people who played such a large part in the King's life, his Queen, Henrietta Maria, and his dashing nephew Rupert, also survived him. The Queen, who had fled to France almost within days of Minette's birth, lived as an impoverished widow until her fortunes improved following the marriage of her daughter and the Restoration of her son. But though she frequently visited England she did not return to live there, preferring to remain in France where she died at her château in 1669, not yet sixty years old.

Rupert was in Oxford when the city fell and was taken prisoner. Shortly afterwards, he was sent into exile. He immediately went back into active service abroad and led the English troops in the French army. In 1649 the Prince was given command of a fleet of eight vessels and was sent to relieve the Royalists in Ireland. Having been driven off by the Parliamentary fleet he was pursued to the Mediterranean where, with his usual reckless courage, he took up piracy, plaguing the merchant ships of the new Commonwealth, as England now called itself. Refitted, his fleet finally sailed to the Azores and a year later reached the West Indies. In 1652, several of Rupert's ships were lost in storms and his beloved brother Maurice, who had been in Oxford at the surrender and had left the country with him, was tragically drowned. The Prince returned to England at the Restoration and was appointed Vice-Admiral. Later, he was made Constable of Windsor Castle and at last settled down, deciding to live there. Rupert spent his latter years involved in chemical and mechanical researches. An ingenious inventor and excellent engraver, he was responsible for the introduction of mezzotint engraving. Strangely, for such an extremely attractive man, Rupert of the Rhine never married, thus giving credence to my idea that he had possibly given his love to one unobtainable woman. Instead, the Prince kept a string of comely mistresses who continued to visit him up to the end of his life. He died in London at his house in Spring Garden in 1682.

Oliver Cromwell, whom the Earl of Essex had condemned as 'an Incendiary', signed the King's death warrant and became Lord Protector of England, ruling the country for several years but refusing to take the crown. Yet for all that he reached heights of power never achieved before or since by an English commoner. When he lay dying there appears to have been a hurricane; trees, including mighty oaks, were uprooted, roofs, steeples and walls went crashing down and ships were sunk. The superstitious believed it to be a sign of disaster – and they were right! The Protector's son, Richard, known as Tumbledown Dick, was a hopeless successor. He was finally dismissed from the country and, once his debts had been settled, sailed for Paris. He lived there for some time under the name of Clarke before returning to England and dwelling in obscurity in Hertfordshire. Fairfax came out of retirement to support General Monck in his bid to end the lawlessness which ensued. The Long Parliament, the 'Rump' of which had been forcibly ejected by Cromwell's soldiers, was recalled. In accordance with its wishes and those of the people of England, King Charles II was invited to return to his realm.

Black Tom Fairfax, who became Baron Fairfax in 1648 when he succeeded to his father's title, retired to Yorkshire after the King's execution, busying himself with various hobbies. His relationship with Cromwell, whom he disliked, grew ever more strained but, having seen the monarchy restored, Lord Fairfax retired once more, preferring to live a quiet country life. His lively wife died in 1665 and he followed her six years later.

A few words about some of the other people mentioned in the story. Old Lord Astley, Rupert's tutor, was imprisoned in Warwick Castle after his defeat at Stow-on-the-Wold, but was finally allowed to return to his home in Kent on bail. Sir Arthur Aston, the hated Governor of Oxford, "kervetting on horseback in Bullingdon Green before certain ladies, his horse flung him and broke his legge: so that it being cut off and he rendered useless for employment." Aston went on to serve in Ireland, where he was hacked to bits at Drogheda when the garrison was massacred. His brains were smashed from his skull by his own wooden leg. Baron Byron, formerly Sir John, was the eldest of seven brave brothers, all of whom fought for the King. After the surrender of Chester, he held Carnarvon Castle but was eventually forced into exile where he became Superintendent General of the Duke of York's household. He died abroad in 1652 and the title passed to his brother Richard, Governor of Newark from 1643–1645 and ancestor of the poet. The aged Earl of Forth, who had pretended to be even deafer at Council meetings than he actually was in order to avoid arguing with Rupert, was superseded by the younger man as Commander-in-Chief in 1644. Despite being "much decayed in his parts, and, with the long-continued custom of immoderate drinking, dozed in his understanding", Forth sailed with the Prince of Wales into exile. He returned to Scotland in 1650 and died at Dundee the following year. Sir Bernard de Gomme, who designed the Oxford fortifications, came back to England at the Restoration and was appointed Quartermaster-General. He married an Englishwoman and remained in this country, dying in 1685. George, Lord Goring, having fled from the West Country, sailed for the Continent without permission, obtained a military command in the Spanish Army of Flanders, took a similar command in Spain, and died in Madrid, lonely, ill and destitute. Ralph, Lord Hopton, who had been so grievously blinded and burned at Roundway Down and was called out of retirement by the desperate Prince of Wales, was wounded again at Torrington, then forced to surrender Truro. He finally sailed to the Scilly Isles to join the Prince and died in exile in 1652. Edward Hyde, who also embarked with the Prince, was confirmed in the office of Lord Chancellor after the Restoration but became a victim of court intrigue and was impeached. He went abroad and died at Rouen in 1674. His daughter, Anne, became Duchess of York, having been seduced by Prince James. Henry Ireton, Cromwell's son-in-law, who also signed the King's death warrant, was appointed Cromwell's deputy in Ireland, where he ruled with much severity. He died of a fever at the age of forty. Henry Jermyn, Earl of St Albans, remained in exile with Henrietta Maria but came back to England at the Restoration and was granted large areas of land north of Pall Mall. The streets leading off Jermyn Street were subsequently named either after himself or members of the royal family and household. The Earl's residence was in St James's Square and he died there in 1684, enjoying gambling and high living to the last. Colonel William Legge, who succeeded the hated Aston as Governor of Oxford, shared Rupert's disgrace after the surrender of Bristol. However, he was restored in the King's affections and managed to patch up the quarrel between Charles and his nephew. Legge was accused of high treason in 1649 and imprisoned both in Exeter Castle and the Tower. At the Restoration he was created Lieutenant-General of the Ordnance. James Stuart, Duke of Richmond, friend and supporter of the King, died as he had lived, "with the good liking of all and without the hate of any". Finally, we come to Henry, Lord Wilmot, who, it will be remembered, believed that a negotiated peace was the only way to end the senseless war and for his temerity was arrested by Charles, a fact that almost caused a mutiny, and sent into exile. There he became a close companion of the Prince of Wales. He returned with him, as Charles II, to Scotland and thence to England. He fought at the Battle of Worcester, escaped, and went on the run with the young King, enduring the same six weeks of great danger. After this life-threatening experience, Henry drew even closer to Charles and became his trusted secret agent. He was created Earl of Rochester in 1652 and died at Sluys six years later.

A sad postscript to the Civil Wars can be added in the words of the Earl of Berkshire, who took up arms for his King. When the conflict was over, when thousands had lain down their lives, when the countryside had run with the blood of both men and beasts, the Earl remarked bitterly, "Nobody can tell what we have fought about all this while."

And, indeed, when it is remembered that the horse Charles II rode to his coronation was a personal gift from Lord Fairfax, the dam of which had been the chestnut mare Black Tom had ridden at Naseby, it seems that the principals involved could no longer tell either.

Bibliography

Elizabeth, the Winter Queen, Jessica Gorst-Williams.
Cavaliers and Roundheads, Christopher Hibbert.
The Civil Wars of England, John Kenyon.
The English House-Wife, Gervase Markham.
The Winter Queen, Joan Rees.
English Society 1580–1680, Keith Wrightson.